Kisses After Dark

The McCarthys of Gansett Island Book 12

Marie Force

Kisses After Dark
McCarthys of Gansett Island Series, Book 12
By: Marie Force

Published by HTJB, Inc.

Cover by Kristina Brinton
Interior Layout by Isabel Sullivan
ISBN: 978-0991418275

www.marieforce.com

The McCarthys of Gansett Island Series

McCarthys of Gansett Island Boxed Set

Book 1: Maid for Love

Book 2: Fool for Love

Book 3: Ready for Love

Book 4: Falling for Love

Book 5: Hoping for Love

Book 6: Season for Love

Book 7: Longing for Love

Book 8: Waiting for Love

Book 9: Time for Love

Book 10: Meant for Love

Book 10.5: Chance for Love,

A Gansett Island Novella

Book 11: Gansett After Dark

Book 12: Kisses After Dark

Author's Note

Welcome to *Kisses After Dark*! I've been looking forward to writing Shane and Katie's story, especially since their memorable encounter in *Gansett After Dark.* Bringing together Laura's brother and Owen's sister was something I've had planned for quite some time.

I've had to laugh at some of the questions I've gotten about whether their relationship is "legal" since they are now "family." It doesn't seem odd at all to me because my mother's brother and sister married a brother and sister, giving me nine "double" cousins. To make things even more complicated, both the "brides" had the same first name, so they basically traded last names. Are you scratching your head yet? It takes new members of our family quite some time, as well as diagrams, to fully understand how we're all related! Twenty-two years in, my husband still jokes that he doesn't get it. I also know two sisters who married a pair of brothers. I think it happens more often than we think. But yes, it's perfectly legal as Shane and Katie are not actually "family" to each other.

It's always so much fun for me to go back to Gansett Island for another visit with the McCarthys and their crew. I want to thank the faithful readers of this series who turn up book after book to show their love and support for my characters and my fictional island. If you're not yet a member of the McCarthy Reader Group on Facebook, come join the nearly 9,000 other fans of the series to chat about which couple is your favorite or whose story you most want to read in an upcoming book. Find the group at Facebook.com/groups/McCarthySeries.

When you're done reading *Kisses After Dark*, join the reader group to dish about Shane and Katie's story and to speculate about what's ahead for our favorite fictional family and their friends: Facebook.com/groups/KissesAfterDark/. If you're not yet on my mailing list, please consider joining at marieforce.com to be kept updated on new books and possible appearances in your area. If you're on the mailing list and not receiving regular emails from me, check your spam filter to make sure you've allowed my messages to get through to you.

Profound thanks to my amazing behind-the-scenes team: Julie Cupp, Lisa Cafferty, Holly Sullivan, Isabel Sullivan, Nikki Colquhoun and Cheryl Serra. Thank you to my editorial team, Linda Ingmanson and Joyce Lamb, as well as my beta readers Anne Woodall, Ronlyn Howe and Kara Conrad. Special thank you to labor and delivery nurse Brenna Hessler and Sarah Spate Morrison, family nurse practitioner, for keeping me straight on the medical details.

On the home front, thank you to Dan, Emily and Jake, who are great supporters of my writing career and put up with all the time I spend with my fictional people.

One of my most frequently asked questions is whether there will be more Gansett Island books. I always say that as long as the readers seem to be enjoying the series, I'll keep writing it. If you love the book (or even if you don't), consider leaving a review on the retail platform of your choice and/or Goodreads. I read every one of them, and they help to keep me engaged in the series and planning more books. In addition, your reviews help to draw new readers to the series, so thank you in advance for leaving a review. I hope to write Paul Martinez's book next, so watch for more from Gansett Island in 2015.

Thanks again for all your support of the McCarthys of Gansett Island Series. Happy reading!

xoxo

Marie

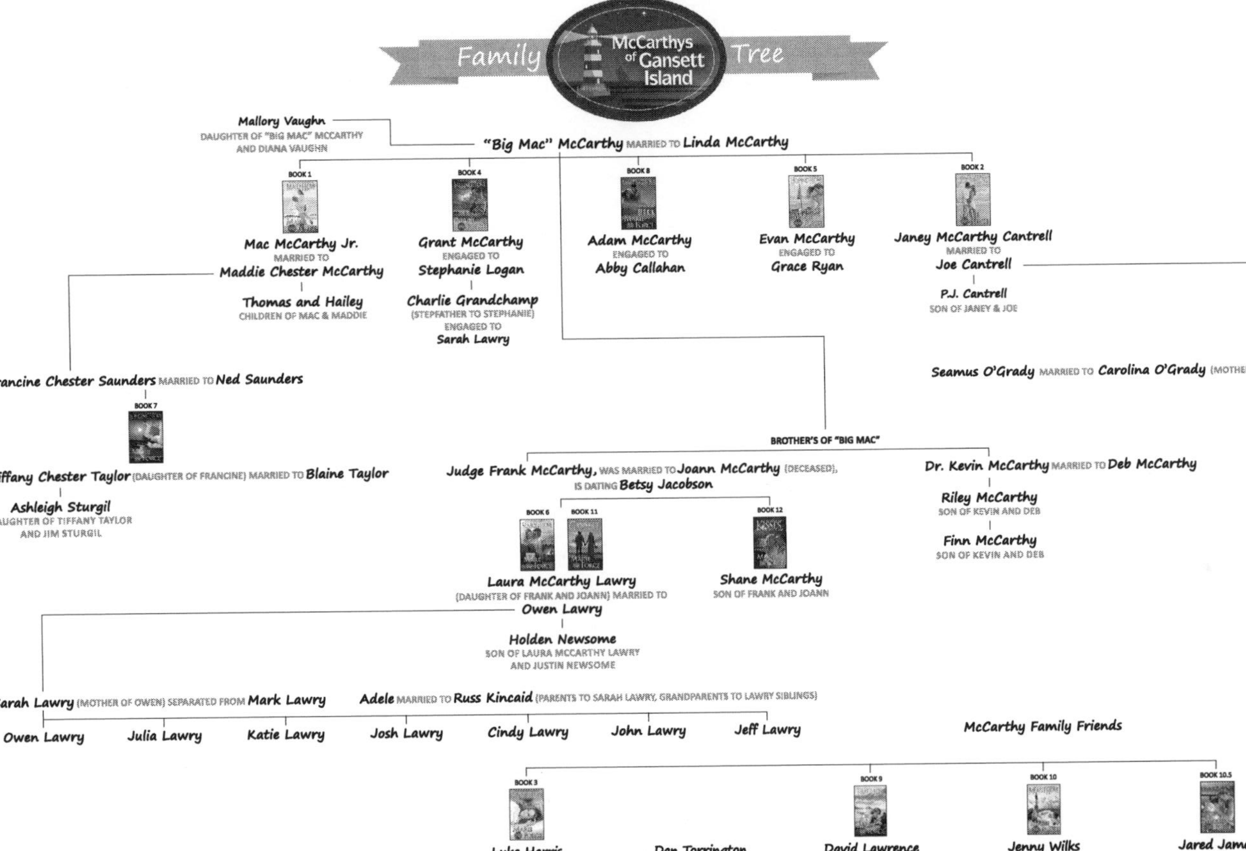
Family Tree
McCarthys of Gansett Island
Mallory Vaughn
DAUGHTER OF "BIG MAC" MCCARTHY AND DIANA VAUGHN
"Big Mac" McCarthy MARRIED TO Linda McCarthy
BOOK 1
Mac McCarthy Jr.
MARRIED TO
Maddie Chester McCarthy
Thomas and Hailey
CHILDREN OF MAC & MADDIE
BOOK 4
Grant McCarthy
ENGAGED TO
Stephanie Logan
Charlie Grandchamp
(STEPFATHER TO STEPHANIE)
ENGAGED TO
Sarah Lawry
BOOK 8
Adam McCarthy
ENGAGED TO
Abby Callahan
BOOK 5
Evan McCarthy
ENGAGED TO
Grace Ryan
BOOK 2
Janey McCarthy Cantrell
MARRIED TO
Joe Cantrell
P.J. Cantrell
SON OF JANEY & JOE
Seamus O'Grady MARRIED TO Carolina O'Grady (MOTHER TO JOE)
Francine Chester Saunders MARRIED TO Ned Saunders
BOOK 7
Tiffany Chester Taylor (DAUGHTER OF FRANCINE) MARRIED TO Blaine Taylor
Ashleigh Sturgil
DAUGHTER OF TIFFANY TAYLOR AND JIM STURGIL
BROTHER'S OF "BIG MAC"
Judge Frank McCarthy, WAS MARRIED TO Joann McCarthy (DECEASED), IS DATING Betsy Jacobson
BOOK 6
BOOK 11
Laura McCarthy Lawry
(DAUGHTER OF FRANK AND JOANN) MARRIED TO
Owen Lawry
Holden Newsome
SON OF LAURA MCCARTHY LAWRY AND JUSTIN NEWSOME
BOOK 12
Shane McCarthy
SON OF FRANK AND JOANN
Dr. Kevin McCarthy MARRIED TO Deb McCarthy
Riley McCarthy
SON OF KEVIN AND DEB
Finn McCarthy
SON OF KEVIN AND DEB
Sarah Lawry (MOTHER OF OWEN) SEPARATED FROM Mark Lawry
Adele MARRIED TO Russ Kincaid (PARENTS TO SARAH LAWRY, GRANDPARENTS TO LAWRY SIBLINGS)
Owen Lawry
Julia Lawry
Katie Lawry
Josh Lawry
Cindy Lawry
John Lawry
Jeff Lawry
McCarthy Family Friends
BOOK 3
Luke Harris AND Sydney Donovan
Dan Torrington AND Kara Ballard
BOOK 9
David Lawrence AND Daisy Babson
BOOK 10
Jenny Wilks AND Alex Martinez
BOOK 10.5
Jared James AND Elisabeth "Lizzie" Sutter
UPDATED AFTER BOOK 11

CHAPTER 1

His first thought at the start of every day was always the same.

He's home in the cozy apartment he shared with his wife. It's winter, and they're snuggled under the down comforter they'd gotten as a wedding gift from his sister. His wife is warm and naked, her body soft as she sleeps in his arms. The scent of her shampoo, the expensive stuff he bought for her at the salon she loves, surrounds him. He would recognize that scent anywhere, the scent of his woman.

His body responds predictably to her nearness. Any time he's awake and naked with her, he's hard and ready to claim her. He moves his hand from her flat belly, up to cup a full breast, toying with the nipple that awakens instantly to his touch.

Wanting to see her and watch her reactions, he opens his eyes and is punched in the face by reality.

Every damned morning.

He's not in bed with his wife. He's alone in the room he calls home now at the Sand & Surf Hotel on Gansett Island. The wife he'd loved beyond reason, to the point of blindness to the faults that ended them, is long gone. She divorced him after ruining him in just about every way a man can be ruined, leaving behind memories that torture him.

Shane McCarthy stared up at the ceiling he'd painted white the winter before when the Surf had undergone extensive renovations overseen by his sister, Laura, and her now-husband, Owen Lawry. The call from Laura, pleading with him to come help them get the hotel ready for the summer season, had finally drawn him out of the dark hole he'd been in for nearly two years, mourning the loss of his marriage—and a big chunk of his sanity.

He needed to get up, grab a shower before his nephew Holden woke up and get them both to the brunch Owen's grandparents were hosting to celebrate the newlyweds. Shane was thrilled to celebrate his sister's happiness with a man he liked and respected, but the minute he got up, he would lose Courtney for another day.

The beginning of every new day was the only time he gave her anymore. If he had his druthers, she wouldn't even get that. But he was unable to control the places his mind went in that ambiguous space between dreams and wakefulness. So he gave her those minutes and nothing else. He took the time, upon waking each morning, to mourn what'd been lost, to grieve for what would never be again and to wallow, however briefly, in the past.

He'd experienced the highest of highs and the lowest of lows with Courtney, extremes so jarring it was a wonder he could function in the aftermath of the wreckage she'd left behind. But he was functioning. He was working on an affordable-housing project with his cousin Mac and making a worthwhile contribution to the Gansett Island community.

He was involved on a daily basis with his sister, his father, his nephew, his new brother-in-law and the large extended family that lived close by on the island they all called home. The hotel that had initially served as a refuge had begun to feel like home. The dark apartment in Providence that had been ground zero for the end of his marriage was a distant memory now that Laura and her hotel had forced him back into the land of the living.

If only he could do something about these early morning visitations with the past. He needed an exorcism or something equally dramatic to remove Courtney from his DNA. She'd worked her way all the way in during the years they'd spent together, and removing her was turning out to be one hell of a difficult challenge.

Too bad you couldn't flip a switch in your brain and stop thinking about something or someone who made you sad and angry and regretful and horribly, miserably lonely. Shouldn't there be a way to *make that stop*? At this point, Shane would pay good money to find that switch in his own brain, because it was high time for this shit to *stop*. It needed to stop.

Courtney was nothing to him anymore, except for his ex-wife. He'd practically bankrupted himself to put her through rehab after discovering her addiction to prescription pain meds that predated their marriage. Her way of thanking him for everything he'd done for her was to serve him with divorce papers the minute she was sober again.

Talk about a wake-up call. He sure as hell hadn't seen that coming as he'd counted down the ninety days she'd spent in rehab, living for the day when they could get their lives back on track. While he'd been blindsided by the drug problem, the divorce had left him demolished. The worst part was he still didn't know why she'd done that. Had she met someone else in rehab? Had she suddenly decided he didn't look as good to her when she was no longer hopped up on pills?

The *why* of it tortured him almost as much as the reality of living without the woman he'd expected to spend forever with. Even after all this time, he still didn't understand *why*. He'd been served with papers on the day he'd expected to pick her up from the clinic and start over again. He hadn't even gotten the courtesy of a conversation. She'd disappeared from his life as quickly and as dramatically as she'd entered it his senior year of college.

Running his hands over his face, filled with frustration and anger at himself for dwelling on things that shouldn't matter so much after all this time, he thought about yesterday, about his sister's wedding and the palpable joy between her and Owen. It had been a truly perfect day, a rare gem in the mess his life had been for quite some time now.

And then he remembered the incident that had nearly marred that rare gem of a day. Hell, it had nearly ruined a lot more than his sister's wedding. He'd been swimming at the beach in front of the hotel when a distressed cry from another swimmer had put him in rescue mode. Upon reaching the woman, she'd latched on to him in a panic and dragged them both under. For a brief moment, he'd thought she was going to kill them both. Then he'd begun to fight, freeing himself from her tight grip after an epic struggle.

He'd managed to eventually get them both to the beach, but not before she lost her bikini top. When he'd brushed back the blond hair from her face, he'd realized she was Katie Lawry, Owen's sister. Though their families were now connected by marriage and despite the fact that Katie was Owen's sister, Shane couldn't stop thinking about the most perfect set of breasts he'd seen since his divorce.

Hell, they were the only *breasts* he'd seen since his divorce, which was probably why he couldn't seem to scrub the memory of them from his brain. Again, that off-switch would come in handy as he was about to see her at the after-wedding brunch, and he needed to be able to look at her without thinking *breasts* at the first sight of her.

Christ, he needed to get laid if he got so worked up over a pair of bare breasts. It was sad to realize he couldn't remember the last time he'd had sex or even wanted to. Well before Courtney went to rehab, which was… Shit, almost two years ago.

How pathetic was it that the sight of Katie Lawry's breasts triggered the first pang of desire he'd felt since then? Was he the same guy who'd had sex with his wife nearly every day—sometimes two or three times a day—before it went to shit? He couldn't remember what it had been like to be that guy. That guy was so far removed from his current reality, it was like he was someone else altogether.

Pathetic was definitely the word of this day, and it wasn't even seven o'clock yet. Weekends provided hours upon hours of time that needed to be filled. This weekend had been better than most with all the wedding festivities to help keep his attention on the present where it belonged. He was better off on days when he could lose himself in work and stay so busy he had no time for dwelling.

A tiny squeak from the room next door wiped away all unpleasant thoughts and gave Shane a genuine reason to smile. His nephew, Holden, the brightest light in Shane's life, was awake and in need of the uncle who'd stayed with him so his parents could enjoy their wedding night.

Shane got up, hit the bathroom and went into Holden's room, where the baby was sucking on his own toes, a relatively new addition to his arsenal of adorable tricks. Then again, Shane thought everything Holden did was adorable. "Hey, bud. Did you sleep well? I don't know what your mama is talking about with all these middle-of-the-night stories."

Holden rewarded him with a big spitty smile that showed off his two new bottom teeth and reached up with his arms and legs.

Shane laughed and scooped him up, hugging him close for a full minute before transferring him to the changing table to dispose of the heavy overnight diaper.

"Dude, that's a lot of pee. How many beers did you have at the wedding anyway?"

Holden squeaked and squealed and giggled, his infectious joy a balm on the wounds Shane carried with him. Holden gave him hope, an emotion he'd been sorely lacking until his nephew came along to remind him that life goes on even when you think it can't possibly.

"Mammammamma."

"Mama is across the street with Daddy, and trust me, bud, you don't want to know what they're up to."

His comment was received with more squeals and lots of wrestling to get the new diaper on. Owen had warned him to feed Holden his cereal before he tried to get him dressed, so they moved to the apartment's tiny galley kitchen, where he plopped Holden into his high chair and mixed up the cereal while the baby enjoyed some Cheerios scattered on the tray.

Shane had expected to have a couple of kids of his own by now. That'd been the plan anyway, before he discovered his wife had been hiding a raging addiction to pain meds. What if she'd gotten pregnant while she was still addicted? He shuddered thinking now about the bullet he'd dodged.

Pushing those thoughts aside, he gave his full attention to his nephew. As long as he stayed focused on the present, the past couldn't catch up to him. At least that was what he told himself as he moved through every day, still trying to outrun the relentless pain.

*

She'd dreamed about drowning. The reality Katie Lawry was still processing, hours after she'd nearly drowned on her brother's wedding day, was how quiet it had been under the water. It had drawn her in a like a lover, stealing over her with its awesome might, pulling her down, down, down into endless darkness.

A small part of her had welcomed the quiet darkness, not that she'd ever admit that to anyone. She'd seen the harshness, lived with it for much of her life, thus the slight temptation to let go and surrender. She'd struggled, she realized now, because of Owen. Because she couldn't do that to him, especially not on a day on which he would finally get the happiness he deserved more than just about anyone she knew.

He'd always been there for her, and she'd fought like a tomcat to be there for him, nearly killing Laura's brother in the throes of battle. In the shower afterward, she'd trembled so violently she'd been afraid it wouldn't stop in time for her to attend the wedding.

She trembled just as violently as she relived the entire episode and allowed herself to imagine what could've happened if Shane hadn't been there to save her. She trembled to think about what it would've meant to her mother, brother, siblings and grandparents to lose her so suddenly, especially after all they'd been through lately with her father's trial.

The Lawry family finally had a reason to celebrate. Mark Lawry was going to prison—for years—after having abused his wife and children for decades. Katie would never forget the feeling she'd experienced upon hearing the news that her father had pleaded guilty to the charges rather than allow an old family friend to testify about the years of abuse he'd inflicted upon his family. General Lawry would rather plead guilty than allow his family's dirty laundry to be aired out by the wife of one of his former subordinates.

Thank God for his arrogance. Thank God for his hubris. Thank God it was over for all of them, although she'd often had reason to wonder if it would ever really be over. Owen was the first of the seven Lawry siblings to find love and get married. The rest of them had chosen to remain stubbornly single rather than chance the kind of relationship their mother had found herself in after marrying their father.

Katie admired Owen more than just about anyone she knew. He'd taken many a fist on behalf of her, her twin sister, Julia, their sister Cindy and their brothers John, Josh and Jeff. Owen had looked out for all of them, had sacrificed his own dreams to stay close to them after their father kicked him out of their home.

And now he'd taken the huge step of committing himself to Laura and their children for the rest of his life. That took guts when you came from what they did. Katie wished she had the guts to take that kind of risk, to let someone in, to allow herself to have feelings for a man.

She wouldn't know what that was like because she'd never even been on a date. Sure, she'd been asked plenty of times, but she always said no. How was she to know if that perfectly nice drug rep who'd come to the doctor's office where she worked would turn into an abusive monster the minute he had her under his thumb?

It was easier to say no than it was to take that kind of gamble. Except... Last night, watching Owen dance with Laura, seeing the love they had for each other, knowing what they'd been through to get to this day, realizing he hadn't let fear rule him... Katie had begun to wonder if the fortress she'd erected around herself was keeping the heartache out or trapping it inside.

She suspected the latter. As long as she kept the doors and windows locked, nothing could get in, but nothing could get out either. And now that her father was gone from their lives forever, now that he would be locked away and made to pay for what he'd done, perhaps now...

"No," she said emphatically. "Absolutely not. Just because he's out of the picture doesn't mean his kind aren't still out there looking for their next victim." She said the words out loud, hoping they'd permeate the unreasonable longing her brother's wedding had generated in her. She wanted what he and Laura had. Anyone would, especially a thirty-two-year-old woman who'd never been kissed.

Her thoughts wandered back to Laura's ridiculously handsome brother who had saved her life and stared at her breasts like a hungry man who'd just found a thick, juicy steak. The memory of his hands on her, bringing her back to life after the near miss, carrying her up the stairs when her legs had been too unsteady to hold her… She trembled, with embarrassment now, as she recalled the heat in Shane's eyes when he'd stared at her bare breasts as if he'd never seen breasts before.

And then later, in the white shirt he'd worn to the wedding that had offset his deep tan and the blond sun streaks in his hair. The way he'd looked at her, as if trying to forget he'd seen parts of her that no man had ever seen, not that he could possibly know that.

Her nipples tightened under the lightweight T-shirt she'd slept in, making her squirm in her bed, trying to get comfortable. A needy ache between her legs took her by surprise, reminding her that while she might've sworn off men forever, she was still a young, healthy woman who had no control over her body's decision to rebel.

She tamped down those urges the way she always had, determined to steer clear of men and all the trouble that came with them. Her brother's wedding had shown her what she might be missing, but it hadn't made her forget the many reasons she'd taken this path to begin with.

Katie would never forget her upbringing at the mercy of a violent, unpredictable man and couldn't risk letting that nightmare back into her life—even if it meant spending the rest of that life alone.

CHAPTER 2

Waking as a married man for the first time, Owen Lawry experienced a feeling of pure contentment and relief. The contentment came from having his new wife sleeping naked in his arms. The relief was because he could now finally admit he'd been waiting for something to go wrong.

He'd worried about his father's trial somehow derailing their plans. He'd worried Laura would wise up and realize she could do better. He'd worried about… well, everything. But none of the things he'd worried about had come to fruition, and now he was married to the only woman he'd ever loved, with twins on the way and her son, Holden, in Owen's life to stay.

Speaking of Holden, they needed to get up and get going to relieve Uncle Shane, who'd been good enough to spend the night with the baby so they could have their wedding night to themselves.

Owen began kissing Laura's back, starting at her shoulder and working his way down.

"Mmm, is that my husband trying to wake me up?"

"Who else would it be?"

Her soft, sleepy laughter was an immediate turn-on, although everything about her turned him on, from her blonde hair to her blue eyes to her gorgeous breasts and the belly that was just starting to protrude with pregnancy. He adored every perfect inch of her.

"What time is it?"

"Just after nine."

She jolted. "Holden."

"Is with Shane, who would've called if he couldn't handle the morning routine."

Laura relaxed, but only slightly. "We should get going."

"We have an hour until brunch."

"A whole hour?"

"Sixty minutes to do whatever we want before we have to rejoin our lives already in progress."

"Whatever shall we do?"

He nudged at her from behind. "I have a few ideas."

Laughing, she said, "You always have that idea."

"Never more so than right now. I'm so happy you're finally my wife, and I get to keep you forever."

She curled her hand around his, which was nestled right beneath her breast. "You got to keep me forever before vows were spoken. Yesterday was just a formality."

"Still…"

Laura turned onto her back and looked up at him, propped on his hand as he gazed down at her. "Were you worried something would go wrong?"

He thought about dodging the question, but there was no dodging the honesty or the love he felt coming from her every time she looked at him. "A little."

"Why?"

Owen felt stupid for letting his insecurities invade their first morning as a married couple. "Doesn't matter now."

"Yes, it does. Tell me."

He blew out a deep breath and looked down at her, so perfectly beautiful and all his for the rest of his life. "I guess I still wonder how I got so lucky to find you, first of all, and then… That you fell in love with me. Still boggles my mind, Princess, even after all this time."

She reached for him, and he went willingly into her loving embrace. "You know when I fell in love with you?"

"When?" He already knew, of course, but he loved to hear her tell him anyway.

"The first time you picked me up off the bathroom floor when I was so sick with Holden. There I was, pregnant with another man's child, and you took care of me like the baby was yours, like I was yours."

"You were already mine. Both of you were. You just didn't know it yet."

"And you were already mine. I love you as much as you love me, and I want you to have faith in that—always."

"I do."

"So you said yesterday."

He laughed at the witty comment that was so in keeping with who she was. She made him laugh every day. She made him think. She made him want like he'd never wanted anything or anyone.

"Please don't worry about something going wrong between us. You're stuck with me forever."

"Never been happier to be stuck with anyone."

Her lips lifted into the sexy, sultry smile he loved so much. "Is that right?"

"You know it."

"How about you prove it."

"Haven't I already proven it multiple times?"

"I'm not yet fully convinced."

"In that case…" He began at her neck, kissing her until she squirmed under him, aroused as always by any attention he paid to that area. Moving down, he focused next on her breasts with gentle strokes of his tongue to her nipples that had her moaning and arching her hips. "So sensitive when you're pregnant. I love it."

"I honestly think I could come from that alone."

"Want to try?"

"Not this time, but maybe next time."

"Ah, something to look forward to."

Her fingers combed through his hair, always trying to bring order to shaggy locks that refused to be tamed.

Owen kissed the small bump protruding from her belly. Their babies were in there, getting bigger and stronger every day, and he was counting down the days until they got to meet them. He settled between her legs, propping them on his shoulders and ensuring her comfort before he opened her to his tongue.

Her sharp gasp of pleasure was nearly his undoing. She was always so responsive to him, so willing, so loving. And she wondered why he felt incredibly lucky to have earned her love. How could he not feel lucky to be married to such an amazing woman who was beautiful inside and out, not to mention strong, resilient and incredibly joyful? Her infectious joy had filled his life with the kind of happiness that had eluded him before her.

He stroked her with his tongue and slid his fingers into her, aided by the flood of moisture between her legs.

"Owen," she said, panting, "come up here. I want you."

"Not yet." He redoubled his efforts, not letting up until she came with the sharp cry of pleasure he lived for. Then he moved up, kissing her as he went.

She wrapped her arms around his neck and drew him into a deep, passionate kiss. He never broke the kiss when he took himself in hand and began to push into her, moving slowly to give her time to accommodate him. Going slow when she was hot and wet and tight around him was the purest, sweetest form of torture he'd ever experienced.

Laura broke the kiss and drew in a deep breath. "So much more than your share."

"There it is! Every time."

She smiled up at him. "It's tradition now."

Owen hooked his arm under her leg and bent it toward her chest, mindful of the babies who rested between them. The new position opened her and eased his entry. "Ah, God, Laura… So good. Always so good."

"Owen…"

"What, honey?"

"I need you to move."

"Are you sure? Are you sore from last night?"

"A little. Doesn't hurt, though." She cupped his ass and pulled him deeper into her, a move that made him see stars.

"Christ," he whispered. "You almost finished me off with that maneuver."

She giggled softly, and he melted on the inside. He loved the way they laughed all the time, even when making love. "Give me what I want. I'm your wife, and you have to obey me."

"Oh damn, what've I signed on for?"

"A lifetime as my sex slave."

"I can live with that." He picked up the pace but kept a tight rein on the desire pounding through him as he lived in mortal fear of ever hurting her. He'd rather die than do anything to cause her pain of any kind.

"*Yes.*" She moaned and arched into him. "Like that."

She brought him right to the brink with the way she moved and the way she sighed and moaned and gripped him from the inside. This was going to be fast, and he wanted to make sure she was with him, so he reached down to where they were joined, pressed his fingers to her clit and watched her ignite under him. That was all it took to finish him off, too.

Because he was so much bigger than she was, he didn't dare flop down on top of her. Rather, he used the last of his strength to turn them so she was sprawled on top of him, still impaled on him, still quivering from the force of her orgasm. Her hair was all over him, her hand resting on his heart and her legs tangled with his.

This, right here, was all he needed to be happy for the rest of his life. As long as he had her, he could get through anything that came his way. "I love you more than life itself, Laura Lawry."

"Love you just as much, Owen. I always will."

*

Sarah came awake slowly, uncertain at first where she was or why she was naked. And then the memories of the night before came flooding back to remind her that she was in Charlie's bed, where they'd made love for the first time. And the second time… Which was why her body ached in a few places where it hadn't ached in longer than she cared to remember.

Her skin flushed and tingled with heat as she recalled the passion she'd experienced in Charlie's arms. Sarah's quiet, sweet fiancé had shown her a side of himself she hadn't known existed until he got her in his bed.

Thinking about the discoveries she'd made not only about him but also about herself had her blushing from head to toe, her eyes squeezed tightly closed in embarrassment. How would she ever face him in the bright light of day after the way she'd behaved?

The brush of his lips over her forehead let her know she was no longer alone with her salacious thoughts.

"Good morning."

"Mmm, morning." She couldn't bring herself to look at him, so she kept her eyes tightly closed.

"I come bearing gifts."

"Is that coffee I smell?"

"It is indeed, but you have to actually look at me before you can have it."

"I can't look at you. I might never be able to look at you again."

His bark of laughter rang through the room.

Sarah raised the covers up and over her head.

"Now you're just begging me to come in there to find you." His hand sneaked under the covers, and naturally, the first thing he encountered was her bare breast.

Sarah gasped from the painful pleasure when he rolled her sore nipple between his fingers, sparking a throb between her legs. How was it possible that she could want more already? "Charlie…"

"Hmm?"

"I can't..."

"Yes, you can."

"No, I really can't."

"Have I ever told you how much I love a challenge?"

Before she could begin to formulate a reply to that, he was under the covers with her, drawing her nipple into the heat of his mouth with gentle tugs and soft strokes of his tongue.

Sarah wrapped her arms around his head, holding him to her chest even when she knew she ought to be pushing him away. Her body couldn't take any more of his brand of passion. But even as she had the thought, her legs were wrapping around his narrow hips as he pressed his erection against her aching core.

As the mother of seven, she'd certainly had her share of sex. But there was no comparison whatsoever to what she'd done with her ex-husband and what she was apparently about to do again with Charlie.

"I won't be able to walk for a week," she said in a protest that sounded less than convincing even to her.

"Yes, you will. I'll go easy."

"You don't know how to go easy."

"It's you... You make me crazy."

"How do I make you crazy?"

"The way you look at me and the things you say to me and the way you want to take care of me. And then you get naked with me, and I can't help that I want to devour you."

Sarah finally opened her eyes and looked up at him in amazement. "Did you really ask me to marry you last night?"

"I really did, and you said yes, so you can't take it back now."

"I would never take it back."

As he rocked his pelvis against hers, he cradled her head in his big hands and kissed her softly. "Your lips are swollen."

"Gee, I wonder why?"

His face lifted into a grin full of male satisfaction.

"Don't look so smug. You nearly broke me in half."

He laughed again at the grimace she directed his way, but that didn't stop him from pressing ever so gently into her. "I showed you hard and fast last night. Let me show you slow and sweet this morning."

"I'm never going to survive you. Don't you know I'm an old lady with seven grown children? I can't be carrying on this way."

"Yes," he said with a low chuckle, "you can. And there's nothing old about you. You're beautiful and all mine."

Sarah was mortified all over again when her eyes flooded with tears. Her emotions were hovering close to the surface after her son's beautiful wedding and the life-changing night she'd spent with Charlie.

At the sight of her tears, Charlie froze. "Does it hurt, honey?"

"No. Well, sort of, but in a good way. Don't stop."

He kissed away the tear that rolled down her cheek. "Why the tears?"

"I'm so happy, Charlie. I had no idea that something like this, like you, even existed."

"Aw, baby, hearing you're happy is all I need." He continued to move slowly and carefully as he made love to her.

Sarah reached up for him and brought him down for another kiss. She'd waited a long time to kiss him, and now she was addicted to his kisses. Her fingers dug into the taut muscles on his back.

"That's it," he whispered gruffly against her lips. "Scratch my back like you did last night. I love that."

"God, you turned me into a madwoman."

"I love that, too."

"You're out to embarrass me to death, aren't you?"

"No way. I'm out to love you until death do us part, starting right now."

He picked up the pace, stealing the words from her lips, the thoughts from her brain and the breath from her lungs.

*

As an innkeeper for most of her adult life, Adele Kincaid was an early riser. Even years after she and her husband had retired to Florida, she was still, as Russ would say, "up with the roosters" every day.

Being here, back at the Sand & Surf Hotel she and Russ had owned for more than five decades, felt like being home. She'd forgotten how much she loved the old hotel, which had been brought lovingly back to life by Laura and Owen over the last year. Adele was so proud of what the two of them had accomplished here, and deeply thrilled to see the boy she'd loved so much all his life settled with a woman who not only loved him passionately but also suited him perfectly.

If anyone deserved that kind of love more than Owen, she'd be hard-pressed to name him or her. Well, except maybe for his mother, Sarah. Her daughter was happily in love with a wonderful man after living through a nightmare with her abusive ex-husband who was now going to jail, where he belonged.

When Adele thought about what Mark Lawry had put his family through... She was a peaceful woman, but left alone in a room with that monster, she might be tempted to commit murder. Each of the seven Lawry kids bore scars from their upbringing. Owen was the only one of them to find love and settle down. Adele hoped he would be the first of them to take a chance on love, not the last.

Sitting on the hotel's back deck with a cup of coffee, looking out over the wide expanse of water, she watched for the first ferry from the mainland that was due to arrive in South Harbor in twenty minutes. The routine of island life was one that had suited her for many years, and she'd missed it during their time in Florida. They'd moved there when their grandson Jeff had needed them after his suicide attempt. There they'd been able to get him the medical attention he needed, the kind of help that wasn't available on a small island like Gansett.

It had been the right thing to do at the time, but she was tiring of the incessant sun and the heat. She missed the New England seasons and the variety of weather that came with them. Perhaps it was time to speak to Russ about moving home.

She glanced at the cream vellum envelope sitting on a table next to her and smiled from the anticipation of presenting their wedding gift to Owen and Laura. They were going to do it at brunch, and Adele was excited to see how they reacted. She and Russ had talked it over and agreed it was the perfect gift for the happy couple.

Sipping her coffee, Adele breathed in the fragrant sea air and let the sun shine warm upon her face. The back deck of the Sand & Surf Hotel was, without a doubt in her mind, the most beautiful spot on the face of the earth.

On the beach below, Adele noticed her granddaughter Katie walking along the shoreline and was forced to relive the horror she'd witnessed the day before when Katie had nearly drowned after being caught in a riptide. Adele had seen the whole thing unfold from her perch on the deck. Before she could move to call for help, Shane had been there to save the day.

Watching both young people go down together had been one of the most heart-stopping moments of her life. Again, they'd rallied while she'd remained frozen with fear and panic—a reaction she wasn't proud of with hindsight. The thought of that kind of tragedy befalling Owen and Laura on their wedding day, not to mention the rest of their family, reduced Adele to tears all over again.

Watching Katie walk on the beach, her blonde hair billowing in the summer breeze, Adele recalled the way Shane had carried her onto the beach, breathed life into her lungs and then held her while she sobbed in the aftermath of the frightening incident.

Adele didn't know Shane all that well, but Laura had shared some of what he'd been through with his ex-wife. She'd watched him during the wedding and had been impressed with his obvious devotion to Laura and his nephew, Holden, who'd spent most of the wedding snuggled up to his Uncle Shane.

He was quiet and reserved compared to his far more boisterous McCarthy cousins. Shane sat back and took it all in, participating, but not leading the charge. Although, in that animated group, it was a challenge to get a word in edgewise. He was handsome as could be with sun-streaked hair and a dark tan from working outside during the summer.

Adele had also tuned in to the way he watched Katie during the wedding. He'd probably be surprised that anyone had noticed, as he'd been so subtle about it. But every time she looked at him, he was looking at Katie. As far as she knew, Katie had never had a boyfriend. According to her twin, Julia, Katie had never been on a date. Adele didn't need a PhD in psychology to deduce it was because of her violent upbringing. At some point, Katie must've decided it was easier to avoid men altogether than to encounter someone like her father.

Although Adele wasn't one to meddle in the lives of her precious grandchildren, seeing Owen happy and settled with Laura had her wanting that for the others, too. While Shane certainly had his own scars on his soul, perhaps the two of them would be good for each other. Adele tapped her finger against her lip as she contemplated the possibility of them as a couple.

In light of what he'd been through with his wife, Adele wasn't entirely convinced he'd be good for her Katie. But she planned to keep an eye on them for what remained of the weekend, and she also planned to talk to Russ about the possibility of moving home. It was time.

CHAPTER 3

Katie walked along the shoreline with her feet in the water, trying to ignore the panic that tugged at her when she thought about being nearly swept out to sea. She'd always loved this beach and swimming in the surf and couldn't imagine never doing it again.

When she and her siblings had been kids, they'd spent their summers here with their grandparents, which had been the only respite they'd gotten from their violent, unpredictable father. The thought of being afraid of this beach was inconceivable to Katie. It was her happy place. It was the place she'd gone to in her mind any time the violence erupted at home, which was often. Thinking of this beach and the endless blue ocean would take her away from it all.

She'd have to go back in the water at some point. Maybe not today, but someday soon. Today she had another challenge to confront—telling her sister she wouldn't be returning home to Texas with her. Not wanting to spoil the wedding festivities, she hadn't told anyone, even her twin and closest confidant, that she had quit her job before coming to the wedding.

The doctor she worked with, a family practitioner, had been coming on to her for years. It had started with teasing comments about her clothes, her hair and her smile and had progressed to more pointed remarks in recent months. On Thursday, she'd had the rare misfortune of being the last one in the office, which left her alone with him—something she went out of her way to avoid.

The office manager had to leave early to pick up her son at camp, which had left Katie alone with the randy doctor. While he'd often been inappropriate with her, he'd never scared her until that night after their last patient had left, and he'd blocked the doorway to keep her from leaving the office.

It'd been years since Katie had experienced that kind of fear, and it had taken her right back to the darkness of her childhood.

"You've been teasing me for a long time now," Dr. Marcus Gould had said as he advanced toward her, forcing Katie to back away from him until she encountered her desk.

With nowhere to run and no way out, she'd begun to tremble violently. "I… I haven't teased you." She rarely talked to him except when she absolutely had to. How did that translate into teasing?

"We both know better." Other women found him attractive. Katie knew that from the way her coworkers and even some of the patients speculated endlessly about his personal life. Katie had never participated in those conversations because he made her sick with his lecherous looks and inappropriate comments.

Carmen, the office manager, told Katie she was "lucky" he liked her so much and that she was jealous of the attention the doctor paid to Katie. For her part, Katie wished he'd leave her alone and let her do her job in peace.

"What're we to do about this attraction between us?" he asked as he advanced even closer to her.

"What attraction?" If he touched her, Katie was quite certain she would throw up all over him.

"I love how you play hard to get. It's a huge turn-on."

"I'm not playing anything." She hated how her voice wavered. "I'm here to work, and that's it."

"Katie," he said in the condescending tone she hated. "We both know better. When are you going to quit fighting the inevitable?"

Inevitable? That was when she knew she had to get out of there or risk being molested—or worse—by this pig of a man. The things she'd learned in the self-defense classes Owen had insisted his sisters take when they were in junior high school came rushing back to her.

Choose your moment carefully.

Though it pained her to remain passive while the doctor continued to close in on her, Katie remembered the instructor's advice to wait until she had a clear shot. Swallowing the bile that collected in her throat and willing her limbs to cooperate, she waited until he was inches from her before she acted, jamming the heel of her hand into his nose and her knee into his groin. He went down like a felled oak tree, landing in a screaming, bleeding mess on the floor.

Katie grabbed her purse and stepped over him.

"You fucking bitch! I'll have you charged for assault!"

"Do it, and I'll ruin you with years of recorded come-ons and innuendos. Oh, you didn't think I was smart enough to build a case for when this day finally arrived? Think again. Have me charged, and I'll sue your ass off for harassment. And by the way, I quit, you miserable son of a bitch."

She'd shaken for hours after the confrontation, sitting at home waiting for the police to show up and arrest her. Fortunately, Julia had been out for most of the night, so she didn't have to explain her odd behavior to her sister. She'd been awake all night, but the police never came. Apparently, he'd believed her when she said she had proof of his harassment, which she did not.

After a long and sleepless night, she realized she'd called his bluff, and in the process, had quit a job she needed. It was for the best, though. God only knew what might've happened in the office that night if she hadn't known how to defend herself. She couldn't even think about it without feeling sick to her stomach.

"Katie?"

Jarred out of her thoughts, Katie discovered she'd walked quite a ways down the beach and was staring out at the ocean.

Shane McCarthy, with Holden on his shoulders, eyed her inquisitively. "Are you okay?"

Katie shook off the unpleasant memories of her now ex-colleague and forced a smile for Shane. "I'm fine, thank you. How are you guys this morning?" Shane wore plaid shorts and a white T-shirt that made him look extra tan. His feet were bare as he walked along the water's edge. She caught a whiff of sporty cologne or maybe it was shampoo. His hair was still damp from an earlier shower, but he hadn't shaved, and his whiskers were golden in the early morning sunlight. All in all, he was incredibly handsome, not that it mattered. He was Laura's *brother,* for crying out loud.

"We're great. Just out for a stroll on the beach before brunch."

"How did Holden do last night?"

"Slept through the night. I've decided his mother is making up all this middle-of-the-night business."

Holden let out a happy-sounding squeal that made Shane and Katie laugh.

"Be careful telling her that, or she'll want you to stay with him every night." As she spoke to him, Katie tried to forget that his hands had been all over her, that he'd seen her naked breasts and blown air into her mouth. It was mortifying to remember the way she'd clung to him in her panic and nearly managed to drown them both. Not to mention afterward, when he'd held her while she sobbed.

"I'd happily stay with him every night. He's the best thing… well, ever."

"He sure is cute."

"You want to hold him?"

"Um, sure."

"Go see Auntie Katie, buddy," Shane said as he handed Holden to her.

She took the baby into her arms, noting how solid and sturdy he was at just over six months old. He had soft dark hair and eyes that looked up at her curiously as if to determine who this stranger was holding him. "He must look just like his father."

"He does," Shane said, his smile fading. "Don't get me started on that guy."

"I never heard what happened between him and Laura, not that it's any of my business. Whatever it was brought her to Owen, which is where she belongs."

"It sure is. Her ex never quit dating after they got married. She found out when he made a date with one of her bridesmaids who'd seen his profile online and set him up."

"Oh my God. Seriously? When he had someone like Laura at home?"

"My thoughts exactly. It was all I could do not to kill him."

"I bet."

With Katie still holding the baby, they started back toward the Sand & Surf, where the post-wedding brunch would begin shortly.

"Is he too heavy for you?" Shane asked after a few minutes of silence.

"Not at all. He's adorable."

"No arguments here. I think he's the cutest baby in the history of the world."

"It's really nice of you to stay with him so Laura and Owen could have a night alone."

"I love being with him."

"He smells so good. I love that baby smell."

"We took a shower together, and I discovered he's like a slippery eel when he's wet. It was all I could do to hold on to him. We ended up sitting in the tub." He laughed and shook his head. "It was a disaster, but he loved it."

The image of Shane McCarthy, naked and wet in the shower, had Katie swallowing hard. That he was obviously smitten with his nephew only made him more attractive. What was wrong with her that she could go from reliving the horror of the near attack by the doctor she worked with to thinking Shane was attractive?

So he was good-looking as well as kind and attentive toward his nephew. That didn't mean he was always that way. People often had two sides to them, as she knew all too well. Keeping her focus on the baby, she walked with Shane beside her.

"How long are you here?" he asked.

"I'm not sure." Now that there was nothing to go home to in Texas, she'd thought about staying awhile, if Laura and Owen didn't mind having her around. She'd wanted to get past the wedding before she brought that up with them. "Do you live here, or are you just here for the wedding?"

"It seems I live here now."

"It seems?"

"I hadn't planned to move here, but Laura asked me to come help with the hotel renovations. Then our cousin Mac asked me to stay through the summer to work on a project of his. Next thing you know, I've been here eight months with no end in sight to the work."

"Where do you normally live?"

"I used to live in Providence."

"Do you like it here?"

"I love it. I came here as a kid to visit my cousins in the summer. Those were the best times. With Laura here and now our dad out here year-round, too, it's begun to feel like home."

"We used to come in the summers to visit our grandparents. I loved it then, and it's hardly changed at all since the last time I was here."

"I wonder if we were ever here at the same time when we were kids."

"The last time I was here in the summer was when I was seventeen. So fifteen years ago."

"You're thirty-two?" he asked, sounding surprised.

"Yeah, so?"

"You don't look it. I would've guessed twenty-three or -four."

"Oh come on! No way."

"Yes, way! I'm not kidding. I never would've guessed you're older than me."

She glanced at him out of the side of her eye. "By how much?"

"Only two years. Don't worry."

"That's a relief," she said teasingly.

"Speaking of relief, let me take him." He reached for Holden. "He gets heavy after a while."

While Katie had enjoyed holding the baby, her arms tingled as blood flowed through them after she was relieved of his weight.

Holden squealed when Shane plopped him back on his shoulders, keeping a firm grip on the baby's tiny body. He grasped a tight handful of Shane's hair, making his uncle wince.

"Easy, buddy. You'll give me a bald spot." He extricated his hair from Holden's grip without losing a beat in their walk. "I think we might've been here at the same time. Maybe we met way back then."

"Maybe."

"So what do you do down there in Texas?"

"I'm a nurse practitioner."

"Oh, really? That's cool. In a hospital?"

She shook her head. "For a doctor. Until recently anyway." The words popped out before she remembered no one knew she'd quit her job. "I'll be job hunting eventually, but do me a favor and don't mention that to my family. I haven't told them I quit my job."

"I won't say anything."

"Thanks."

"So why'd you leave your job?"

Katie was astounded to realize she wanted to tell him. He was so nice and easy to talk to. It would be such a relief to unburden herself, but she couldn't do that. Not when she hadn't even told Julia. "It's a long story." As they were close to the stairs that led up to the hotel, the generic response was an easy out.

"Some other time, then."

"Sure."

He stopped walking and turned to her. "I was wondering…"

"About?"

"Since you're going to be here awhile, could I take you to dinner some night? Maybe tonight?"

After a lifetime of avoiding men, brushing off their unwelcome attention and generally dodging situations like this one, she had no idea how to respond to him.

She'd become adept at blowing off the advances of men who didn't matter to her. But this situation called for an unusual amount of finesse.

"Katie?"

"I… It's very nice of you to ask, Shane, but I can't. I'm sorry."

"Oh. Okay. Sorry if I was out of line by asking."

"You weren't." God, could this be any more awkward? Because their siblings were married, she needed to keep things friendly with him. Their families were tied to each other forever now, and their paths would cross frequently. "Not at all."

He gestured for her to go up the stairs ahead of him.

As she went, she figured her heart was racing from the exertion of climbing the stairs. It couldn't be because a handsome, sexy, seemingly nice guy had asked her out. It wasn't that at all.

Chapter Four

Following Katie up the stairs, Shane couldn't figure out what had possessed him to ask Owen's sister to dinner the way he had. He hadn't asked a woman to have so much as a cup of coffee with him in two years. So why now? Why her?

He couldn't say exactly, except there was something so sweet and peaceful about her, and he couldn't deny he was drawn to those qualities. But obviously the attraction was one-sided. At least the spontaneous gesture had proven he wasn't totally dead inside, which was progress.

Asking her out was a big deal for him, not that she could possibly know that. It was probably just as well she'd declined. With their siblings now married and babies on the way who'd be their shared nieces or nephews, it was better not to let things get weird or complicated with Katie. They'd see each other at family events, and the last thing either of them needed was that kind of awkwardness every time they got together.

At the top of the stairs, the family gathered at a big, long table for brunch. Shane carried Holden toward the table, where Adele and Russ were holding court. Katie was surrounded by her siblings, several of them blond and athletic-looking, like her and Owen. Her twin, Julia, and two of their brothers had darker hair.

Katie smiled and laughed as she interacted with her brothers and sisters, each of whom hugged their mother, Sarah, when she and Charlie joined the party.

When Shane's dad, Frank, came in with his girlfriend, Betsy, Shane walked over to say hello to them. Holden let out a happy squeal at the sight of his grandfather, who took him from Shane.

"Hey, guys." Frank peppered the baby's chubby cheeks with noisy kisses that made him laugh. "How was boys' night?"

"Perfectly uneventful."

"Your sister won't be happy to hear that."

"I'm told I shouldn't tell her or run the risk of getting 'stuck' with him every night, which I wouldn't mind." If nothing else kept him on the island after the latest job he was doing for Mac ended, remaining close to his nephew would be a major incentive to figuring out a way to stay on Gansett.

That his father and sister were here, too, was also great, but Holden… He was more than enough on his own to have his Uncle Shane thinking about putting down some roots. Shane didn't want to miss a thing with Holden or the babies his sister was expecting. If he wasn't destined to have a family of his own, at least he'd have Laura's kids to love and spoil.

It was probably time to talk to Mac about a permanent job on the island, if his cousin was amenable to keeping Shane on the payroll.

"Your sister is lucky to have such a hands-on brother to help out with the baby," Betsy said as Holden wrapped his pudgy hand around her index finger.

At first it had been odd to see his dad with another woman. He'd been single for more than twenty years, since his wife—and Shane's mother—died of cancer when Shane was seven and Laura nine. Betsy was the first woman Frank had been serious about since then, and Shane couldn't be happier for them.

"I love him," Shane said in response to her comment. "It's certainly no hardship to help out with him."

"You're going to be a wonderful father someday," Betsy said.

The comment, which he knew Betsy meant as a compliment, hit him like a spike to the heart. He should've had kids of his own by now and would have if his wife hadn't lied to him about everything. They'd wanted to be young parents so they could enjoy raising their kids and then fully enjoy the years they'd have to themselves afterward.

But none of that had happened, and now, as he approached his thirtieth birthday, it seemed like it never would. Fortunately, Laura and Owen's arrival saved Shane from having to reply to Betsy's well-meaning statement.

Holden let out a shriek at the sight of his mother, who lit up with joy as she scooped her son out of his grandfather's arms and swung him around.

"There's my big boy! How was your night with Uncle Shane?" She rained kisses down on the baby's face, making him chortle with baby laughter. "Did you keep him up all night?"

Shane smiled at his sister. "Um, no, not exactly…"

"If you tell me he slept through the night, I'll… I don't know what I'll do, but it won't be pretty."

"All right then, I won't tell you that."

"Are you *kidding* me?" She stared into Holden's big brown eyes. "Are *you* kidding me?"

"Are we kidding her, buddy?" Shane asked his nephew, who replied with a big gummy grin. "He got a little wasted on champagne at the wedding. That might explain it."

"Explain what?" Owen asked as he joined them, putting his arm around Laura and leaning in to kiss Holden.

"How our son managed to sleep through the night, for the first time, when we were elsewhere."

"*What*?" Owen said. "No way."

"Way," Shane said with a smile for his brother-in-law.

"I say we go away more often," Laura said to her husband.

"You got that right."

"Without sharing details that'll scar me for life," Frank said, "did you have a nice evening?"

"It was all right," Laura said with a shrug. "Nothing special."

Owen poked her gently in the ribs, making her laugh. "Nothing special, my ass."

Frank put his hands over his ears. "Don't say one more word, or I'll have you arrested."

"She's my wife."

Frank scowled at his new son-in-law. "She's *my* little girl."

"He's got you there, Owen," Betsy said, patting Frank on the back.

"Now, boys," Laura said, "there's plenty of me to go around." She placed a hand over her growing baby bump. "And getting more plentiful all the time."

Adele touched a knife to a crystal goblet and summoned them all to brunch. The table had been set with the festive china that Shane recognized from a hutch in the hotel's sitting room where he'd hung out with Laura, Owen, Holden, Sarah and Charlie on many a winter night.

"I thought the whole crew was coming to brunch," Frank said.

"I bet they're all hung over," Owen replied with a droll smile. "Which is indication of a successful wedding."

"Indeed," Laura said proudly.

Shane found his name on a card next to a plate and took a seat as the others did the same. He glanced at the plate to his right and saw Katie's name on the card. He hoped it wouldn't be awkward to sit her after he'd asked her out and been turned down.

She took her seat a minute later and offered him a shy smile. "We meet again."

"So it seems. I'm Shane. Laura's brother." He extended his hand, hoping she'd get that he was going for a clean slate.

Eyeing him curiously, she shook his hand. "Katie. Owen's sister."

"Nice to meet you, Katie."

"You, too." She laughed at the little game they were playing, as if the uncomfortable exchange on the beach had never happened.

Julia sat across from them with their brothers Jeff, the youngest of the seven Lawrys, and Josh as well as their sister Cindy. If Katie was quiet and somewhat reserved, Julia was bubbly and chatty. The fraternal twins bore a slight resemblance to each other. Katie had blue eyes while Julia's were grayer, and her hair was darker than Katie's. Their smiles were similar, but Julia was much freer with hers than Katie was.

"What's up with Mom?" Julia asked the others. "She's all glowy looking."

"Um, that would be called happiness," Jeff said. "Something we've never seen on her before."

"What do we know about this guy?" Josh asked. "We should get John to check him out for us." John was a cop in Tennessee and had been unable to get away from work to attend the wedding.

"He's a great guy," Shane said of Charlie Grandchamp.

Julia eyed him skeptically. "Oh yeah? Do tell."

Shane decided Charlie's story was one that Charlie should tell Sarah's children himself, if he chose to. It wasn't Shane's place to tell them that Charlie had spent fourteen years in prison for a crime he hadn't committed, or that his stepdaughter, Stephanie, had devoted herself to getting him released. "He's first class. I'll let you figure out the rest for yourselves."

"So there's more," Julia said with a sigh. "Isn't there always more?"

"It's not always bad," Shane said, even though in his experience it often was. For some reason, he wanted Sarah's kids to give Charlie a chance. "Trust me when I tell you that you have nothing at all to worry about where he's concerned."

"You'll have to excuse us if we're a little cynical," Cindy said in a soft Southern accent that was in sharp contrast to the steel behind her words.

"I understand." How could he not understand when he'd lived with Owen and Sarah as they prepared for the trial? He knew far more than he wanted to about the way the Lawry children had been raised and empathized with their desire to protect their mother from any more harm.

A waitress came to take drink orders, and since he was off baby duty, Shane ordered a Bloody Mary.

"That sounds good," Katie said. "Make it two."

Charlie's stepdaughter, Stephanie Logan, came out to welcome them all to Stephanie's Bistro and to hug and kiss the newlyweds. She'd been one of Laura's bridesmaids and would marry Shane's cousin Grant on Labor Day.

She listed the brunch specials for them and then left the party to her capable waitstaff.

"Does everyone know about us?" Katie asked him softly as he perused the menu and tried to decide between eggs Benedict and the French toast special.

"Excuse me?"

"Does everyone on the island know about our family? About our father and what he did?"

"I wouldn't say *everyone* knows, but some people do."

"Do you know?"

"Some of it," he said tentatively. Both Laura and Owen had talked to him about the trial, the charges and the horror of Owen's upbringing, but Shane didn't see the need to tell Katie that, not when she seemed ashamed that people knew.

Katie gazed over the heads of her siblings to the ocean that stretched endlessly before them.

"Hey," he whispered. When she looked over at him, he said, "It's no reflection on you—any of you. You didn't do anything wrong."

"Intellectually, we know that. Emotionally… That's a whole other can of worms."

What could he say to that? He'd been born into a loving home with two parents who'd worshiped each other and their children. He had no way at all to relate to what she'd been through. Except Laura had been raised the same way and had found a way to relate to what Owen had endured at the hands of his father.

Still, he felt he should say something, so he went with the most innocuous thing he could think of. "Everybody's got something, you know?"

"Even you?"

His laugh was sharper than he intended. "Ah, yeah, you could say that."

"Something bad?"

"Yeah, it was pretty bad, and people know about it, which is tough. So I understand better than you might think."

"I'm sorry you had to go through something bad."

"Me, too. I mean, I'm sorry you did, too."

Baskets of muffins and croissants and delicate pastries were brought to the table, which gave them something else to focus on other than the increasingly intense—and intimate—conversation.

The more he talked to her, the more he wanted to talk to her. And then he remembered she'd rejected his offer of dinner and told himself to keep the desire to talk to her in check. She wasn't interested in him, and he had no business being interested in her or anyone when he was still so messed up over Courtney.

When the waitress came to take his order, he went with the eggs Benedict and then smiled when Katie ordered the same thing.

"Copycat," he said in the same soft tone they'd been using.

She laughed, which caused a curious feeling to unfurl inside him as he watched the way laughter lit up her face and eyes. It totally transformed her.

"Eggs Benedict are my favorite," she said, "but I never order them because they're so fattening. Special occasion. So I'm *not* a copycat."

"Whatever you say."

After everyone had ordered, Adele stood at the head of the table and held up a glass of champagne. "I'd like to propose a toast to the newlyweds, Laura and Owen. On this first day of your married life, we wish you a lifetime of happiness and joy and love. To Owen and Laura."

Everyone toasted the newlyweds and drank champagne, except for Laura who settled for ice water.

"Now I believe our friend Charlie has something he wishes to say. Charlie?"

Looking extremely nervous, Charlie Grandchamp stood, holding a glass of champagne in his hand. "This day—and this weekend—belongs entirely to Laura and Owen, but since many of you are heading home this afternoon, Sarah and I wanted to take this opportunity to share some news with you. Yesterday, I spoke with Russ and received his blessing to ask for his daughter's hand in marriage. Last night," he said, looking down at Sarah with a warm smile on his face, "Sarah agreed to be my wife. We're very happy, and we hope all of you will be happy for us, too. I'm really looking forward to getting to know the children Sarah speaks of so often. I want you all to know that your mother will never know another minute of unhappiness or unrest or fear or anything other than the love and respect she deserves. That's all I wanted to say, and well, to Sarah."

"To Sarah," the others said.

The Lawrys seemed shell-shocked by the news of their mother's engagement, but each of them got up to hug and kiss her.

When Katie returned to her seat, she glanced over at Shane. "Wow. Didn't see that coming."

"They seem really happy."

"I've never seen my mother look happier than she does today. I thought it was because of the wedding. I guess we're going to get to know Charlie better after all."

"I know him quite well, and I can assure you he'll take very good care of your mom."

"That's good to hear."

She said the right thing, but he could see and *feel* the hesitancy coming from her anyway. This was a woman who didn't trust men. Even though she had good reason to feel that way, it was a daunting realization.

"While I have your attention," Adele said when the Lawrys had returned to their seats, "Owen, your grandfather and I thought long and hard about what to give you and your lovely bride for a gift, and we kept coming back to the same thing time and again. We hope you'll accept this gift in the spirit in which it's given and know that you have brought us so much pleasure with what you both have done here." She handed over a cream-colored envelope to Owen. He glanced at Laura, who shrugged.

Owen opened the envelope, pulled out the paper inside, shared it with Laura, and they gasped in stereo. "No way," he said.

"Oh my God." Laura raised a hand to her mouth as her eyes filled with tears. "You can't do this, Adele!"

"It's already done, my love." To everyone else, she said, "Meet the new owners of the Sand & Surf Hotel!"

A collective gasp preceded cheers and congratulations for Owen and Laura, who were visibly stunned by the extravagant gift from his grandparents.

"I want all my other grandchildren to know you'll receive a gift of equal value on the day you marry."

"What if we never get married?" Julia asked.

Adele shrugged. "Then you'll have to wait for us to kick the bucket, which we don't plan to do for a long, long, *long* time. So it would be easier and quicker to fall madly in love and get married."

"That's right," her husband, Russ, said. "We're going to live to be really old and really crotchety, so you're better off getting married than you are waiting us out."

"You're already crotchety, my darling," Adele said to laughter from her husband and the others. "While I have you all, I have one more thing I'd like to say. Something happened yesterday that I feel you should know about. There's a hero among us, and we owe him a tremendous debt of gratitude."

Shane felt his stomach drop as Katie sucked in a sharp, deep breath next to him. Without thinking, he reached for her hand under the table.

She held on to him almost as tightly as she had the day before when he'd saved her from drowning.

"While everyone was getting ready for the wedding, our beautiful Katie took a swim and was pulled into a rip current that took her quite a ways from the shore."

"Oh my God," Sarah said, her gaze shifting to Katie.

"Fortunately," Adele continued, "Shane was also on the beach, realized she was in trouble and swam out to rescue her. I saw the whole thing from up here on the deck. You saved her life, Shane, and we'll always be grateful to you."

Seeming stunned by the news, Laura looked at him with tears in her eyes.

Everyone began talking at once, asking Katie if she was all right and telling Shane how thankful they were for what he'd done. All the while, Katie clung to his hand like a lifeline.

"Why didn't you say anything?" Owen asked them.

Shane cleared his throat. "We didn't want to put a damper on your special day."

"God," Owen said, unable to take his eyes off his sister, "I can't even imagine..."

"Neither can I," Julia said tearfully, reaching across the table to grasp her twin's free hand. "Thank goodness you're all right."

"I'm fine," Katie assured them. "Thanks to Shane."

"Proud of you, son," Frank said gruffly. "And I'm glad you're both okay."

"We're fine," Shane said for both of them as he squeezed Katie's hand under the table.

"I'm sorry." Laura handed Holden to Owen and got up to come to where Shane was sitting. "But I really need a hug right now."

Shane had no choice but to release Katie's hand to get up and hug his sister.

"Thank you so much," Laura said for his ears only. "Owen never would've gotten over losing her."

"It was no big deal." He was grateful that Adele had left out the part about Katie panicking and nearly taking him down with her.

"It's a huge big deal, and we're so thankful you're both all right."

"Couldn't let anything ruin your big day," Shane said.

"That would've ruined a lot more than our wedding."

She released her brother and hugged Katie, too. And then Laura wiped up her tears and went back to her seat. "I'm better now."

Shane sat and was stunned when Katie reached for his hand, smiling as she gave him a squeeze that caused his heart to contract. Before he could begin to contemplate the meaning of her sweet gesture, she released his hand to accept the breadbasket from Julia.

For the rest of the meal, Shane was acutely aware of Katie next to him, her leg occasionally brushing against his, the flowery scent of her hair blowing in the morning breeze, her quiet laughter and her easy rapport with her siblings. More than once he found himself leaning closer so he wouldn't miss a word of what she said.

Over the course of brunch at the Surf, Shane felt like he was waking up from a long slumber, his senses suddenly more alert than they'd been in years and all of them focused on the woman sitting next to him. Since she'd already turned him down, he knew it was stupid to be so fixated on her. But knowing that didn't stop him from wanting to try again. Soon.

Chapter Five

After brunch, Katie went with Julia to their room on the third floor. As her sister began tossing clothes into the suitcase she'd never bothered to completely unpack, Katie sat on her bed and thought about holding hands with Shane McCarthy. She'd never done anything quite so forward as reaching for his hand under the table. She could tell she'd caught him by surprise, and she'd liked that.

She'd liked the way he looked at her and listened to her and paid attention to her. She liked *him*. She couldn't deny that as much as she wanted to. Knowing Owen thought highly of Shane mattered greatly to Katie. Owen had been much more than an older brother to his siblings. He'd been a surrogate father, a protector and a friend to them all their lives. If he liked and trusted Shane, maybe she could, too.

"Why aren't you packing?" Julia asked. "The ferry leaves in an hour, and we can't miss it if we're going to make the flight."

Here was the moment Katie had been dreading all weekend, telling her sister she wasn't going back to Texas. Not right away anyway. "Um, so I'm not going back."

Julia stopped what she was doing to stare at Katie. "What?"

"I quit my job."

"*When*? Why didn't you say anything?"

"It happened Thursday, and I didn't say anything because of the wedding."

Julia plopped down on the bed next to her. "Did something happen with Doctor Strangelove?"

Katie loved her sister's nickname for the lecherous doctor. "You could say that."

Julia stared at her. "He didn't…"

Katie shook her head. "I didn't let him, but I think he would have. Owen's self-defense classes got me out of a jam, but I can't go back there. Not when I told him I had evidence of his harassment and I'd be going to the police if he dared to press charges against me."

"Why would *he* press charges against *you*?"

"I might've left him bleeding from his nose and clutching his boy parts."

Julia howled with laughter as she hugged her sister. "Good for you. He's had that coming for years now."

"He scared me, Jule," she said softly. "I think he would've raped me if I hadn't put a stop to it."

"You should report him. He can't get away with that."

"The thing is, he never actually touched me. I assaulted him, so I can just imagine how he would spin it." Katie shuddered at the idea of having to face that creep in court, or anywhere else, for that matter. "I never want to see him again or hear his name."

"You could sue him. He's been bothering you for years."

"And I never bothered to report it in all that time. No, I'm not going to sue him or have him charged. I'm satisfied with the way I left him bloody and moaning on the floor. That's more than enough for me."

"What're you going to do now?"

"I don't know, but I'm hoping to stay here for a while and try to figure it out. I've got money saved I can use to help with the rent, so don't worry."

"I don't care about that." They both made good money and could easily handle the rent on their own, if need be. "I'm far more worried about you. First Doctor Strangelove attacks you and then you nearly drown."

"Not the best week of my life, although seeing Owen happy yesterday—and today—makes it all better."

"And how about Mom? She's positively glowing with happiness. We've never seen her like that before."

"I know. Shane says Charlie is a great guy."

Julia raised a brow in inquiry. "Shane says, huh?"

"Uh-huh."

"You two were awfully cozy at brunch."

"We were just talking."

"From all reports, he's a nice guy, too."

"I guess," Katie said, shrugging. "He asked me out, but I said no."

"You said no. Of course you said no." Julia got up from the bed and began moving around the room again, gathering belongings that were strewn all over the place in typical Julia style. She exploded into every room she occupied.

"Why does that make you so mad?"

"Because! You're thirty-two and have never had so much as a date! How long are you going keep this up? You've got a perfectly nice guy who our brother thinks the world of asking you out, and you *still* can't bend your rigid rules? Even for him?"

"It's not that simple, and you know it."

"I do know. I grew up exactly the same way you did, but I haven't chosen to seal myself off from the world in a protective bubble where nothing bad can ever find me. Newsflash, bad stuff happens. Two bad things happened to you *this week*, and you lived to tell. Do you honestly think Laura's brother is going to take Owen's sister out and treat her badly? Do you *really* think that?"

"No, I don't, but still… You never know."

"No, you don't. But one thing I do know is you're wasting your entire life because of someone who doesn't deserve that level of sacrifice."

"I'm not doing it for him," Katie said distastefully. The idea that Julia could think Katie's life was still run by Mark Lawry was disgusting to her.

"You're letting him win, Kate. Every time a nice guy asks you out and you say no, the general scores another point."

"That's not true!"

"It's exactly true. Look at Mom. Who has more reason to hide out from men than she does, and she's found a great guy who loves and respects her and wants nothing more than to make her happy."

"So he says now. How does she know that won't change after he puts a ring on her finger?"

Julia shook her head. "You're hopeless. I give up. Do what you want, but I'm sticking to my story. When you say no to a guy like Shane McCarthy, *the general wins*. He wants you terrorized and afraid, and you're playing right into his hand."

"No, I'm not! He's going to jail. He's out of our lives forever."

"Is he? Is he really? If that's the case, then go out with Shane."

"I… I can't."

"You can! You just won't. There's a huge difference."

She and Julia had had this fight many times before, but Julia had never framed the argument in such stark terms. The general wins. The thought of that made Katie feel sicker than the idea of actually going on a date with a man did. "Fine. I'll go out with him. Will that make you happy?"

"I don't believe you'll actually do it."

She was closer to Julia than anyone in the world, but no one could make her madder than Julia could. Glaring at her sister, Katie got up from the bed, opened the door and went across the hall to bang on Shane's door.

He opened it, looking surprised to see her and curious about the racket.

Katie forced herself to look him in the eye and say the words, knowing Julia was watching and listening. "What you asked me earlier… Do you still want to do that?"

"Um, yeah?"

"Tonight at seven?"

"Is good."

"All right." Katie turned and went back into her room, slamming the door behind her. "Satisfied?"

"Extremely satisfied." Julia smiled victoriously. "And if you play your cards right, you will be, too."

*

Leaving Julia gloating in their room, Katie went to find her mother, who was still on the porch with her parents and Charlie as well as Laura and Owen, who held a sleeping Holden. Before she allowed the ferry to leave without her, Katie needed to make sure it was okay with them if she stayed for a while.

"Hey, honey," Sarah said when she saw Katie approach them. "Are you all packed?"

"About that... Could I talk to you for a minute?"

"Of course." To the others, Sarah said, "I'll be right back."

Charlie, who'd been holding Sarah's hand, kissed the back of it before he released her.

The warm smile her mother gave him sparked a pang of yearning inside Katie. What would it be like, she wondered, to share that sort of connection with a man? The question had her thinking of Shane, as if it were normal for her to yearn or to think about a man when neither of those things was in any way normal for her.

Sarah hooked her arm through Katie's and escorted her through the lobby to the rockers on the front porch. "Why do you look troubled?"

"Do I?"

"You do indeed. What's wrong, honey?"

Though it was her way to keep her troubles to herself, she rarely had a moment alone with her mother and found herself spilling the story of Doctor Strangelove's near attack and how she'd quit her job in Texas.

"Good Lord, Katie! The man should be in jail!"

"Which is where he'll end up if he doesn't change his ways, but I'm not putting him there. After everything with the general, I don't have it in me to go after him.

I just don't." The Lawry children had long ago stopped referring to Mark Lawry as anything other than "the general" or "the sperm donor."

"I understand. Better than you might think. When I arrived here last fall, beaten to within an inch of my life, I just wanted it all to go away. The last thing I wanted was to prosecute him."

"What made you change your mind?"

"The doctor who saw to me is a mandatory reporter, meaning he had to report my injuries to the police. David, the doctor, and Blaine, the police chief, along with Owen and Laura, convinced me to go forward with charges this time. I'm glad now that I did. I don't think I would've been able to move forward with my life if I hadn't done it."

"It's different in my case. He never actually touched me, and truth be told, he's probably got a bigger case against me after what I did to him. I quit my job, so he's out of my life."

"True."

"The reason I really wanted to talk to you, though, is I'm thinking about staying here for a while—until I figure out my next move. I thought I'd take advantage of the time off to take a vacation, if it's okay with you and Laura, of course."

"I know I speak for Laura when I tell you my room is all yours for as long as you need it."

"Where will you go?"

Before her eyes, Sarah Lawry blushed like a schoolgirl.

Katie laughed. "Oh, stupid question. You'll be with Charlie."

"He's asked me to move in with him, and I'm going to do it."

"I'm happy for you, Mom. We all are. But are you sure it's not moving too fast?"

She didn't expect her mother to laugh at her question. "Charlie would tell you it's moved slower than molasses. It took me almost a year to kiss the poor guy. Nothing about this has been fast, honey."

"I guess it's old habit to worry about you."

"And I'm sorry you had to for so long, but I promise you there's nothing at all to worry about where Charlie is concerned. He treats me like a queen."

"You certainly deserve that." Katie stared out at the ferry landing where the boats came and went just about every hour all day long in the summer. "Where do you get the moxie to take a chance on another guy after what you went through?"

"It's not so much taking a chance on just any guy. It's about taking a chance with *Charlie.* He showed me night after night, week after week, month after month that I had nothing to fear from him. And for all that time he didn't know why I flinched every time he moved too quickly or why I shied away from the most innocent of touches. He never asked, and I never told him, yet he kept coming back."

Katie found herself riveted by her mother's words as well as the strength and determination she heard behind them.

"He proved himself to me one minute at a time, Katie. He showed me who he was over those months of friendship and companionship. Our relationship didn't become romantic until right before your father's trial, when I had no choice but to tell him where I was going and why."

"What did he say?"

"All the right things and other things I never expected to hear—like how much he loves me and how badly he wants a future with me. I sure as heck didn't see that coming, although with hindsight I should have. I realized I'd been in love with him for quite some time at that point."

Katie realized she was crying when her mother reached over to wipe the tears off her cheek. "That's such a lovely story."

"Yes, it is, and if I hadn't lived it myself, I wouldn't believe such things were possible after having endured life with your father."

"I hate him for what he put you through. What he put all of us through."

"Don't hate him. Don't give him that much of your energy. He doesn't deserve it. Take all those negative emotions and turn them into something positive. I wish I'd left him years ago and spared all of you from having to grow up the way you did. I wasn't strong enough then. I was never as strong as you've always been."

Katie shook her head, laughing bitterly at the irony as tears fell in earnest now. "I'm not strong. I'm weak and frightened of everything and pathetic in so many ways."

"Why in the world would you say such awful things? You, all of you... I admire my children more than anyone. That you survived and thrived in spite of the nightmare you lived through... I give you tremendous credit for that."

"I've survived, but I haven't thrived. I've avoided men like the plague and erected a fortress around myself to keep them at arm's length."

"How long has this been going on?"

Katie wiped away her tears, hating how weak they made her feel. "Always," she said softly.

"Katie... Sweetheart, that's no way to live."

"You sound like Julia."

"You know I never take sides with my children, but I have to agree with her."

Katie looked over at her mother. "Shane asked me to go to dinner with him."

Sarah's eyes widened with pleasure that stretched across her face in a wide smile. "Did he now?"

Katie nodded.

"Are you going?"

"Only after Julia shamed me into it."

Sarah hooted with laughter. "Good for her."

"My first date at age thirty-two. How ridiculous is that?"

"I think it's lovely that you waited for one of the nicest, sweetest, kindest men I've ever had the good fortune to meet."

"Really?" Hearing her mother's ringing endorsement of Shane, Katie felt her heart begin to beat faster with excitement and anticipation.

"He's wonderful. He's quiet, so it takes awhile to get to know him, but he's so sweet and devoted to Laura and the baby. He'd do anything for me and for Owen. We're all quite fond of him around here—and not just because he's Laura's brother.

And now, after hearing what he did for you yesterday, he's earned a permanent place in my heart."

"That's nice to hear."

"You have nothing—and I do mean *nothing*—to fear from him, Katie."

"I keep telling myself that, because I want to change. I want to be more courageous and take some chances."

"Then that's exactly what you should do." Sarah paused, seeming to choose her words carefully. "You should know... He hasn't had it easy either."

"What do you mean?"

Sarah shook her head. "That's for him to tell you—if or when he decides he wants to. Until then, take my word for it. He's a good guy, and you should go out with him tonight and enjoy yourself and relax about all the things that have held you back in the past. Think of this as a fresh start, a whole new you."

A whole new me... Was that what she wanted? Yes, she decided right then and there. She desperately needed a change, and going out to dinner with Shane would signal the start of a new phase in her life, one in which she wouldn't spend so much time being afraid.

Everyone who mattered to her had endorsed him as a good guy, and he'd shown her that himself with the way he'd come to her rescue the day before, not to mention the tender way he treated his nephew. It mattered greatly that her mother and Owen thought highly of him. Somehow that had to be enough. There'd never been a more ideal circumstance for wading into the dating pool than a night out with Shane McCarthy.

Sarah took hold of Katie's hand. "I'm so glad you'll be staying awhile. I've missed you so much."

For the first time in a long time, Katie felt excited about something. "Me, too."

CHAPTER 6

Shortly after the astonishing exchange with Katie, Shane took a call from his cousin Mac, who invited him to join other family members on a fishing trip for the afternoon.

"I've got something I have to do at seven," Shane told Mac. "Will we be back in time?" No way was he going to be late for his date with Katie, not when it had taken all his courage to ask her and seemingly all of hers to accept.

"Oh yeah, we'll be back long before seven."

"Sounds good, then."

"Come on over to the marina as soon as you can."

"I'll be there in ten." Shane changed into swim trunks and a T-shirt, and tossed sunscreen and a bucket hat into a backpack. On the way downstairs, he met up with Laura and Owen, who were on their way up with Holden asleep on Owen's shoulder.

"Where're you off to?" Laura asked.

"Going fishing with Mac and some other guys." To Owen, he said, "Want to come?"

"Not this time." Owen glanced at Laura. "But thanks for the invite."

"He's on his honeymoon," Laura added. "It's the stay-cation kind of honeymoon."

"Spare me the details," Shane said with a grimace. "I'll see you later."

"Have fun," Laura called after him.

"Thanks!" Shane went out through the kitchen to the parking lot behind the hotel where he kept the motorcycle he'd bought from an elderly island resident who couldn't use it anymore. The bike was perfect for getting around the island in the summer, but he planned to invest in a truck before winter set in.

He strapped on the helmet his father had made him promise to wear every time he used the bike. Frank McCarthy, who'd been both father and mother to him and Laura since their mother died, was still overprotective.

Shane would never admit to his father that he barely remembered his mother. Losing her was something he didn't like to think about too much. His memories of her were tied up in photographs more than reality. He remembered her being sick for a long time before she died. He remembered the fear of knowing something bad was happening and watching the adults in his life carefully for signs of trouble.

His Aunt Linda and Uncle Mac had come to Providence from their home on Gansett frequently during the winter his mother died, and the following summer, Shane and Laura had come to stay with them on the island, which was something Shane vividly remembered. The time with his cousins, aunt and uncle had been therapeutic for him and for Laura, who'd taken the loss of their mother even harder than he had.

Shane remembered being numb for a long time after his mother died, sort of the same way he'd felt after his marriage imploded. Today, when Katie had come to his door—her eyes crackling with emotion that might've been anger at her sister who had obviously been goading her—Shane had felt anything but numb. He'd felt *alive* for the first time in two years.

It wasn't wise, he knew, to get too excited about one date, but that one date was a major step forward for him after having been stuck on pause for two long years. Maybe nothing would come of it other than an enjoyable evening with a woman who interested him.

That was fine, or so he told himself as he drove the bike from South Harbor to the McCarthy's Gansett Island Marina in North Harbor, dodging traffic of all sorts on the way—cars, trucks, mopeds, pedestrians, bicycles and even baby strollers filled the island roadways on summer weekends when the population swelled dramatically.

At the marina, he found a big crowd of family members surrounding his uncle "Big Mac" McCarthy, one of Shane's favorite people in the world. His uncle was all about family and fun and laughter, and Shane loved being around him. In addition to Mac Junior, Big Mac's other sons, Grant, Evan and Adam, were there, as were Shane's Uncle Kevin and his sons, Riley and Finn, who'd come for the wedding. The group also included Big Mac's son-in-law, Joe Cantrell, who was married to Shane's cousin Janey, along with Luke Harris, who'd worked at the marina since he was fourteen, and Big Mac's best friend, Ned Saunders.

"Shane!" Big Mac's bellow welcomed him as he parked the bike and stowed his helmet. "Get over here."

"I'm coming," Shane said, amused as always by his larger-than-life uncle. "Where's Dad?"

"On his way," Kevin said.

"Oh good." Frank would never miss a gathering of McCarthy men, especially when there was fishing, beer and good times to be had.

"Meet my friend Buster," Big Mac said of the stocky man standing next to him. "That's his boat over there." Big Mac pointed to what had to be a fifty-foot powerboat with huge towers and serious fishing equipment built in. "When he heard my whole family was in town for a wedding, he offered to take us out for a few hours today."

Shane noticed his cousin Grant eyeing the boat with trepidation and wondered if he or his brothers had been on a boat since the catastrophic sailboat accident they'd been in last spring. Killed in that accident had been the captain, Steve Jacobson. Shane's dad, Frank, was now dating Steve's mother, Betsy, who'd come to the island after the accident to find out more about what'd happened to her son.

Seeing his dad and Betsy together, both of them nursing deep hurts, had given Shane a glimmer of hope that it was possible to move on after a terrible loss.

Granted, his loss couldn't be compared to what his dad or Betsy had endured, but it had been every bit as catastrophic to him. That Courtney had chosen to leave him was almost worse than losing her to death. Or so he suspected. He couldn't imagine anything more painful than his wife choosing to leave him when he was still completely in love with her, despite the mess she'd made of their lives.

"You okay, man?" his cousin Riley asked Shane. Younger than him by five and six years respectively, Riley and his brother, Finn, closely resembled their cousins Mac and Adam with their dark hair and McCarthy blue eyes.

"Yeah, I'm good." Better than he'd been in a while, Shane realized all at once.

"Haven't seen you in a long time, but I hope you know..."

Shane saved his cousin the trouble of finishing the sentence by squeezing Riley's shoulder. "I know. Thanks."

Frank arrived, full of apologies for holding them up, and Big Mac ushered everyone onto the boat that he'd already outfitted with coolers full of food and drinks. His uncle did spontaneous fun better than anyone, and a day on the water with all his favorite guys made what was already shaping up to be a rather awesome weekend even better.

*

Shane caught the biggest fish of the day—an eighty-pound bluefin tuna that put up one hell of a fight. It took Shane and four of his cousins working together to land the beast. Victorious and euphoric, Shane accepted slaps on the back and congratulations from the others even as his arms shook with fatigue.

"That's my boy," Frank said proudly, embarrassing the hell out of Shane with his effusiveness.

"We'll cook it up tonight," Big Mac declared. "Tuna for everyone at the marina."

Shane didn't mention he had other plans and wouldn't be joining them.

"Do ya even know how ta cook a tuna?" Ned asked his buddy.

"Nope, but I bet Linda does. She knows everything."

"How long are you married before you admit that?" Mac asked his father.

"If you're a smart man like me, you figure it out *before* you get married."

"Oh, *puleeze*." Grant rolled his eyes at his brothers and cousins, who made barfing noises that had the older men laughing.

Big Mac dismissed their ridicule with the sweep of his hand. "Boys, listen to me when I tell you… The two most essential words required for a happy marriage are 'yes' and 'dear.'"

"Would it be okay if we mentioned this advice you shared with us to Mom?" Adam asked.

"It might be better if you didn't," Big Mac said to much laughter. "You know that saying, 'what happens in Vegas stays in Vegas'? Well, the same can be said for when you're at sea."

"You are so full of shit it's not even funny," Kevin said.

"Now that just hurts my feelings," Big Mac said to his younger brother.

"Sure it does," Frank said. He handed out cans of beer to everyone on board as they headed back to the marina after a fantastic afternoon on the water.

With the others heading up to the bridge for the ride, Shane found himself alone with his father on the back deck.

Frank raised his can in tribute to his son. "That was one hell of a battle."

"My arms hurt like a mo-fo."

Frank laughed. "You won't be able to move tomorrow."

"So much for thinking I'm in pretty good shape."

"You're in great shape, and unless my eyes deceive me, getting better all the time. Am I right?"

Shane knew his father meant more than physical shape. "I'm better." He was tired of mourning for what he'd lost. Almost against his will, his broken heart had begun to heal. Life had gone on, whether he'd wanted it to or not.

"I can't tell you how happy I am to hear that. I've spent a lot of time worrying about you the last couple of years and wondering if you'd ever be the same again."

"Sorry to have worried you."

"Not your fault. What happened to you… Well, suffice to say, it still boggles my mind."

"Mine, too."

"You got dealt a shitty hand, son. One you didn't deserve. It pains me to think of you spending the rest of your life alone because you think all women are like her. They're not."

"I know." Shane glanced at his dad, who'd been the most important person in his life until the day he married Courtney. Since she left him, his father and sister had propped him up in every way they could. "I'm going out with Katie tonight."

A smile stretched across Frank's face. "Are you now?"

"Don't make a big thing of it—and don't tell Uncle Mac." Big Mac would definitely make a big thing of it. Everything was a big deal where he was concerned, which was one reason his nickname suited him so well.

Frank laughed. "Don't worry. I won't. I gotta say, though, hearing about what happened with you two yesterday about stopped my heart."

"Adele didn't tell the whole story."

"What do you mean?"

"I saw Katie was in trouble, and I swam after her, but she panicked and dragged us both down. For a minute there…"

"Oh my God, son." Frank rested his hand on his heart, his face slack with shock.

"I had to fight her off so I could save us both. It was pretty hairy."

"You truly are a hero. I'm so proud of you."

Shane shrugged off the praise. "I did what anyone would've done."

"Regardless, I'm still proud—and incredibly thankful you're all right. And just think, if something comes of this thing with Katie, you'll have a hell of a story to tell the grandchildren."

Shane laughed. "*Jeez,* Dad! We're going out for the first time tonight, and you've already got us married with grandchildren?"

"I was watching you two during brunch. Call me crazy, but I see a spark there."

Shane couldn't deny he'd felt the spark his father had seen, but he didn't dare encourage him. "She's really nice and sweet."

"And beautiful."

"Is she?" Shane said, teasing. "I hadn't noticed."

"Sure you haven't."

"Do me a favor? Don't say anything about me going out with her. She's… hesitant. I wouldn't want the McCarthy mob scene to scare her off before I get the chance to know her."

"She's hesitant, no doubt, because of the monster who raised her."

"Which would make anyone hesitant."

"I want to say something here, but I don't want you to take it the wrong way..."

His father's unusual hesitancy made Shane curious. "What?"

"After everything you've already been through, I'd hate to see you get hurt again. I know more than I probably should about how Mark Lawry treated his wife and children. Their scars run deep."

"We're just going to dinner, Dad. You're the one who has us married with grandchildren."

"Touché," Frank said with a laugh. "Just please be careful. I never again want to see you flattened the way you were after everything with Courtney."

"Believe me, I have no desire whatsoever to go through anything like that again."

"Moving forward… It's a risk, but one worth taking."

"Are we talking about me now or you?"

"Both, I suppose."

"Things are good with Betsy?"

"Things are great. We're taking it slowly, but it gets better all the time."

"I'm glad for you. You were alone for a long time."

"I was never alone. I had you and your sister and this great big family around me. I was okay."

"But this is better, right?"

"Yeah," Frank said with a small smile. "This is much better."

CHAPTER 7

When they returned to port around three o'clock, Frank left the marina with promises to be back later for tuna and headed straight for Betsy's cottage. They had plans to get together that night, but after the conversation with his son on the boat, he wanted to see her now. Her car was in the driveway, so he knocked on the door and waited for her to answer.

She smiled at the sight of him standing on her doorstep, sunburned and salty after a day on the water. "This is a nice surprise."

"I hope I'm not interrupting your work." Since moving to the island for the summer, she'd been exploring her interests in painting and photography. Judging by the paint-splattered smock she wore, today was a painting day. Her dark curls were tied up in a messy bun that he found adorable.

"I was about to take a break. Come in."

Frank followed her into the tiny but cozy cottage she had rented from Ned Saunders. She hadn't made any decisions about whether she planned to stay for the winter, and Frank was trying not to pressure her. She knew he wanted her to stay, and she'd promised to think about it. For now, they were enjoying the time they got to spend together.

"How was the fishing?"

"Fantastic. Shane bagged an eighty-pound tuna."

Betsy retrieved a pitcher of lemonade from the fridge and poured two glasses over ice. "Wow, good for him."

"He had a great time. Nice to see him smiling and happy."

"I'm sure it is."

Frank wanted to shoot himself for being so insensitive. "I'm sorry. That was thoughtless of me."

"What was?"

"Talking about my happy, smiling son."

"Frank, please don't worry about that. Of course you're happy that your son, who's been through such an awful ordeal, seems to be doing better. I don't want you to feel you can't talk about your kids just because I lost mine. That wasn't your fault. It wasn't anyone's fault. It was a tragic accident, and I miss him terribly. But being around your family and your kids makes me feel better."

"I'm glad." Needing to be closer to her, he moved across the kitchen until he was standing right in front of her. "Being around you makes me feel better, too. In fact, you make me feel better than I have in more than twenty years."

"Is that right?" she asked with the warm smile he'd come to adore, especially when it was directed at him.

"Yep." He put down his glass and placed his hands on the counter on either side of her hips. "You've got paint on your cheek."

"I do? Where?"

He ran his finger over the spot where a dot of navy blue paint had landed. "Here."

She leaned into his touch, her eyes closing and her lips parting.

Frank couldn't resist the powerful need to kiss her, and her enthusiastic response made him groan with desire for more of her. He'd kissed her for the first time after their friends Seamus and Carolina's wedding, and their physical relationship had been confined to kissing thus far. But he couldn't deny he wanted much more of her. "Betsy…"

"Hmm?"

"I really like kissing you."

"I really like when you kiss me."

He shifted to her neck, breathing in the earthy, feminine scent of her. Taking a chance, he moved his hands from the counter to her hips, bringing her in closer to him. There'd been other women, here and there, since his wife died, but never anything serious. Until now. Until her. And this was starting to feel awfully serious to him.

When her arms encircled his neck and her body molded to his, there was no hiding his reaction to her.

He found her mouth again in another kiss, his tongue tangling with hers as her fingers combed through his hair. "It's been," he said between kisses, "a very long time since I've wanted a woman the way I want you."

"How do you want me?"

The question as well as the sexy tone in which it was asked only added to his desire for her. "Naked in a bed, under me."

"Well…" Her nervous laugh had him wondering if he'd been too blunt. "Tell me how you really feel."

"I think I just did." He kissed her again, softly this time, but that packed no less of a wallop than their earlier, frantic kisses had. "I'm sorry if that's too much too soon."

"It's not. It feels like just enough at the perfect time."

Frank raised his head to meet her gaze. "It does? Really?"

She nodded and then shocked him when she took hold of his hand to lead him into her bedroom.

"Where are you taking me?"

"Where you said you wanted to go."

"Is it what you want, too?"

"It's what I've wanted for a while now."

"You might've clued me in," he said with a chuckle.

"You figured it out—eventually."

He put his arms around her and drew her into his embrace, gazing down into her beautiful, smiling face.

"What're you thinking?" she asked.

"That it's been such a long time since I felt this way."

"How do you feel?"

"Happy, content, excited about the future, intrigued, curious, eager..."

"Eager for what?" she asked with a coy smile.

"To hold you and make love to you."

She kissed him. "Mmm, I'm eager for that, too."

"I should take a shower. I've been out in the sun all day."

"I could use a shower, too."

"How about we conserve on water and take one together?"

"I'm all for conservation." She gestured for him to follow her to the bathroom across the hall from her bedroom. After she started the water, she turned to him, her smile suddenly shy and uncertain.

"What is it?" he asked.

"I'm not twenty anymore. I hope you aren't disappointed."

Frank couldn't believe she would say such a thing. Disappointed? In her? Never. "Betsy, honey, I think you're gorgeous and vivacious and amazing. And speaking of not being twenty anymore, how do you think I feel? I'm fourteen years older than you—an official senior citizen cavorting with a youngster."

"Cavorting? Is that what we're doing?"

"Call it what you will."

She pulled the smock up and over her head, revealing a black lace bra that barely contained her full breasts.

Frank knew it wasn't polite to stare, but damn, she was sexy.

She tugged at his polo shirt. "Your turn."

Frank whipped it up and over his head, hoping she liked what she saw as much as he did. He'd taken care of himself over the years, spending a lot of his free time in the gym, and if her heated gaze was any indication, those hours had paid off. "Your turn."

She unbuttoned and unzipped her shorts, letting them drop to the floor, leaving her wearing only the bra and a matching pair of barely there panties.

"Why do I feel like you knew this was going to happen when I had no clue?"

Betsy laughed at his distress. "I like nice underwear. I always have."

"I like your nice underwear, too, but I think it would look better on the floor."

"Your turn."

Holding her challenging gaze, Frank removed his shorts and kicked them out of his way. Standing before her wearing only a pair of boxers that didn't do much to hide what her striptease had done to him, he reached for her. "I'd be happy to help with the next phase."

"By all means."

He reached around her to unfasten her bra, pushed the straps off her shoulders and sighed with pleasure as her lush breasts sprang free into his waiting hands. "Beautiful," he whispered as he kissed her.

"We're wasting water," she reminded him as she very casually divested him of his boxers and then allowed him to remove her panties.

Frank expected to feel awkward or self-conscious, but all he felt was desire beating through him in a steady thrum that heated his blood as it zipped through his veins. And then she turned toward the shower, showing him her gorgeous ass, and it was all he could do not to drool. How had he managed to attract such an amazing woman?

This was no time for such questions, he told himself as he followed her into the shower. This was the time to show her what she'd come to mean to him, and he planned to fully enjoy every second of what was about to happen. He'd waited a long, lonely time to feel this way again, and as he wrapped his arms around her from behind, he was grateful for this second chance with her.

"You feel so good," he whispered as the warm water beat down upon them.

"So do you." She reached for a bottle of shampoo and handed it to him. "Would you like to do the honors?"

"I'd love to."

Betsy turned to face him, wetting her hair under the spray.

Frank took advantage of the opportunity to kiss her before he got to work shampooing her long dark hair.

She laid her hands flat against his chest as she leaned forward, giving him access to her hair.

He took his time, massaging her scalp and spreading the shampoo liberally through the strands.

"Feels so good," she said. When he was finished, she rinsed the suds and added conditioner. "My turn."

"Am I going to smell all fruity and girly after this?"

"Possibly."

"I'm cool with that."

Her laughter took his desire to a whole new level as he bent his head so she could reach his hair. When his hair was washed and rinsed, he found a bottle of citrus-scented body wash and filled his hands and took great pleasure in spreading it all over her soft, warm skin. He gave extra special attention to her breasts, sliding his soapy hands over the nipples that tightened against his palms.

"Frank..."

"Hmm?"

"You're making me crazy."

"Am I?"

"You know you are!"

She grabbed the bottle of body wash and returned the favor, her hands sliding from his shoulders to his chest and then down to his stomach. As her soapy hand encircled his erection, he had to remind himself he wasn't a boy doing this for the first time. But, damn, she made him feel like an unseasoned virgin.

"Christ, Betsy," he said through gritted teeth.

"Something wrong?"

"No. For once, everything is just right."

She smiled up at him, her eyes aglow with pleasure and anticipation and desire.

Ready to move things along, Frank reached behind her and killed the water. They dried each other with the same towel, their movements hasty and jerky. "Bed," he said, biting down on her shoulder and making her gasp. "Now."

He followed her across the hall and into her bed, where she reached for him, wrapping him in her arms as their legs intertwined and their lips came together in a combustible kiss. With her soft, fragrant, welcoming body pressed against his, Frank needed to be inside her.

"Do we need protection?" he asked as he kissed her neck.

"I don't. Do you?"

He shook his head. "I'm clean, and I can prove it."

"So am I."

"And no chance of later-in-life offspring?" he asked teasingly but seriously, too.

"No. I had a procedure to stop my horrible periods that also ended any chance of more babies."

Looking down at her, he kissed her softly as he began to enter her, slowly, giving her time to adjust. "God, you feel so good."

"You do, too. You don't have to go slow."

"I do unless you want this to be over before it starts."

She laughed at his distress, which caused her muscles to clamp down on him, nearly triggering his release.

"You're out to wreck me, aren't you?"

"Nah. I like you exactly the way you are." She drew him down for a kiss that started softly and escalated quickly to tongues and teeth and moans of pleasure.

He broke the kiss and bent his head to give her nipple some attention, sucking and teasing it with his teeth while she squirmed under him. Though he'd planned to take his time, his plans were shot straight to hell by the incredible pleasure he found in her arms, and he couldn't hold off.

Determined to take her with him, he reached down to where they were joined to coax her and was gratified by her sharp cries of pleasure. He gave up on trying to hold off and picked up the pace, hammering into her until his release was upon him, intense and consuming.

He came down from the incredible high to find her blissed out and smiling, her eyes closed and her arms around him. That little smile made his heart ache with emotions he hadn't experienced in so long he'd forgotten what they felt like. "Am I crushing you?"

"Not at all." She wrapped her legs around his hips, encouraging him to stay where he was, which was more than fine with him.

"That was…"

"Mmm," she said, her eyes still closed. "For me, too."

"We might have to do that again. Soon."

"I could be convinced."

Frank dropped his head to her shoulder, thankful to have found her and to have all the time in the world to spend getting to know her better.

CHAPTER 8

After seeing off her siblings on the noon ferry, Katie moved her things into the room that had been her mother's, three doors down the hall from Shane's room.

"You don't have to do that, Mom."

"I don't mind," Sarah said as she hung Katie's clothes in the closet. "What're you planning to wear tonight?"

"I hadn't thought about that."

"This one's nice." Sarah held up a lightweight orange dress.

"Is it too dressy for a casual night out?"

"I don't think so. It'll look great with your tan."

"Am I tan?"

"You're more tan after one day at the beach than I'll be at the end of the summer."

"If you say so."

"I say so, and I'm the mom, so you have to believe me." She came over to hug Katie. "I'm so glad you're staying for a while and we get to spend some time together. I know I've already said it, but I've missed you so much."

"I've missed you, too, and I can't tell you how happy it makes me to see you glowing with happiness."

"That's nice to hear. I hoped you kids would be happy for me."

"How could we not be?"

Sarah's smile faded, and she looked down at the floor. "I wondered if you'd think I was selfish."

"*Selfish*? Why in the world would we think that?"

"Because I stayed with your father for so long when all of you were begging me to leave him, and then while most of you stay stubbornly single because of the way you were raised, I go off and fall in love with someone new."

Katie led her mother to the double bed that took up most of the space in the room. They sat next to each other. "Mom, please don't think that. All we've ever wanted was to see you safe and happy. If Charlie makes you feel safe and happy, we're all for it."

"He does," Sarah said softly. "He's incredible."

"No one deserves that more than you do."

"You do, too."

"What I went through was nothing compared to what you endured."

"It wasn't nothing. It was a nightmare, and it was my fault that it went on for as long as it did. If I could turn back time—"

"Don't do that. Don't beat yourself up over things that are so far in the past they don't matter anymore."

"They do matter, Katie. You said yourself that you've never even been on a date with a man because you're afraid of finding one like your father. That's on me as much as it's on him."

"No way is that true. I blame him—and *only* him—for what happened in our home. None of us blame you, Mom. You were as powerless in that situation as we were."

"Not quite."

"You think that now that you've had some time and space away from the situation, but when you were in it, you certainly didn't feel powerful."

"No, I didn't," Sarah said with a sigh. "I just wish I'd been stronger then."

"What matters is you're stronger *now*—strong enough to see something you want and to reach for it. That takes tremendous courage after everything you went through with what's his name."

"I want you to know the truth about Charlie before you hear it from someone else and jump to the wrong conclusions."

"What truth?"

"He was in prison for fourteen years—"

"Mom!"

"—for a crime he did not commit. He was accused of kidnapping and beating Stephanie, his stepdaughter, when in fact he rescued her from her mother, who surely would've beaten her to death if he hadn't intervened. Stephanie spent just about every minute of those fourteen years trying to get him out of jail."

"Wow," Katie said on a long exhale. "I'm sorry if I overreacted."

"Don't be. I understand why you did. I did, too, when I first heard about it."

"How long has he been out?"

"Almost a year. He came here to be close to Steph and to figure out his next move. He did some work here at the hotel during the renovations, which is how we met. He told me the truth right away and gave me the chance to decide if it was too much for me to take on."

"I've got to give him credit for coming clean at the outset."

"I did, too. When you get to know him, and I hope you will while you're here, you'll soon realize he couldn't harm a flea, let alone Stephanie, who he loves beyond reason."

"That's quite a story."

Sarah ran a hand over Katie's hair, brushing it back over her shoulder. "Will you do something for me?"

"Anything."

"Will you allow yourself to take a real, honest chance with Shane?"

"We're just going to dinner, not planning a wedding."

Sarah smiled. "I simply want you to put aside all the concerns that have kept you away from men in the past and give one very nice man a chance to show you what you've been missing. There's nothing quite like spending time with a man who knows how to treat a woman."

"And you think Shane knows how to treat a woman?"

"I'm sure he does. If you could see the way his cousins treat their women, you wouldn't have a doubt. He was raised by the same kind of man they were. Frank is wonderful, and so is Shane."

"I'll give him an honest chance, but I'm not making any promises beyond tonight."

"That's fair enough." Sarah kissed Katie's cheek and gave her a one-armed hug. "I hope you have a wonderful time, and I'll want to hear all about it."

"Could I ask you something else?"

"Of course."

"How do you feel about Gram and Pop giving the hotel to Laura and Owen?"

"I think it's a brilliant idea, and I was all for it."

"So they talked to you about it before they did it?"

Sarah nodded. "They wanted to ensure that I wasn't interested in the place—and I'm not. I've seen how hard Laura and Owen work here, and I'm more than happy to defer to them. Besides, apparently I'm not going to need the income."

"What do you mean?"

"It's not public information yet, so keep it between us, but Charlie is getting a seven-million-dollar settlement from the state—half a million for every year he spent in prison. He's already told me I can pick out any house I want on the island and decorate it any way I see fit."

"That's amazing, Mom. Congratulations to both of you."

"My only wish now is to see all my children as happy as I am and as happy as Owen is."

"It may take some time, but I think we'll get there."

"I sure hope so." Sarah stood. "I've got to get going, but I'll be by tomorrow to see how your evening went."

Katie got up to walk her mother to the door. "I'll look forward to that."

Sarah hugged her. "Have the best time tonight. Let go of the past and embrace the present. I promise you won't be sorry you did."

"Love you, Mom."

"Love you, too, sweetheart. See you later."

Katie closed the door and went to stretch out on the bed, thinking about everything her mother had told her about Charlie's story and the risk Sarah had taken to open her heart to him. Her thoughts turned to Shane and how adorable he'd looked earlier as he tried to figure out what had possessed her to change her mind about his invitation.

She giggled softly to herself as she pictured the look on his face as he dealt with a crazy woman on his doorstep. Maybe she was fifteen years overdue for her first date, but she was glad she'd waited for him. All at once, she couldn't wait to see him again and spend more time with him.

*

Shane felt ridiculous for being so nervous about a date. It was just dinner, so how had he managed to build it into such a big deal in his mind? The answer, he knew, was because it was his first date since his divorce, which made it a bigger deal than it normally would've been. He'd done plenty of dating before he met Courtney and even had a couple of girlfriends. But no one date had ever felt so important, not even his first date with the woman who'd become his wife.

As he stepped out of the shower and reached for a towel, he pushed those thoughts right out of his mind. The last thing he wanted to think about right now was *her*. She was firmly in the past, where she belonged, and tonight he had something to look forward to with another woman who interested and intrigued him.

He dressed in a pair of khaki shorts and a yellow linen button-down shirt that he'd actually ironed for the occasion. Returning to the bathroom, he combed his hair and dabbed on some of the cologne Laura had bought him for Christmas. At the time he'd asked her where she expected him to wear it, and she'd replied, "You never know when it might come in handy."

As usual, his sister was right. When someone knocked on his door, he went to answer it, wondering if it might be Katie. But it was Laura with Holden in her arms. The baby let out a happy squeak at the sight of his uncle.

"Hey, there." He took the baby from Laura and swung him around, making him squeal with laughter.

"Careful." Laura closed the door behind her. "He just ate, and you look nice."

"You wouldn't puke on me, would you?" Shane asked his nephew, who replied with the gummy, drooly smile Shane adored. "I didn't think so. What're you guys up to?"

"Just coming to check on you." Laura sniffed the air. "You used the cologne I gave you. Told you it might come in handy someday."

"I was just thinking about that when I put it on, and you don't need to be so smug about it. You were right, as always."

"Could you tell Owen that? He's still fighting the 'Laura's always right' program."

"You're on your own there," he said with a chuckle. "How's married life treating you?"

"So far so sublime."

"Don't say another word."

"What? You asked."

"Holden, tell your mommy she shouldn't talk dirty in front of you."

"He's on my side. He loves Daddy, too." Laura's happy smile faded ever so slightly. "Speaking of daddy, Justin wants to come over in the next week or so to see Holden."

"Yeah? Is that a problem?"

"No, it's fine. It's just always weird to see him after everything that happened, but he has a right to see his son."

"If you say so."

"What's that about?"

"I just think you could've gotten full custody if you'd pushed for it."

"Maybe, but that wouldn't have been in Holden's best interest. And besides, he doesn't get out here that often, so I sort of do have full custody, and he'll grow up with Owen as his everyday dad. It's the best possible arrangement under the circumstances."

"I guess."

"I know you're still mad at him for what he did, but I've made my peace with it and moved on. If he hadn't screwed up so royally, I never would've met Owen, and what a tragedy that would've been."

"Indeed."

"I hope that someday you might feel the same way about what happened with Courtney—that all the pain and sorrow led you to where you were meant to end up."

"It would be nice to have it make sense."

"Someday it will. Maybe not today or tomorrow, but someday."

Shane glanced at the clock on his bedside table. Five minutes to seven. "I need to get going."

"Katie moved down the hall earlier to Sarah's old room."

"Oh, okay. Good to know. Where did Sarah go?"

"To Charlie's."

"Ahh, not wasting any time, huh?"

"Nope. I'm so happy for them. What a great couple they are."

"I agree."

"Did you hear he's getting a huge settlement from the state for the time he spent in prison? Seven million bucks!"

"Wow. That'll set them up for life."

"No kidding. That's what Owen said, too."

"Nice to know some people get a happy ending," Shane said.

"I have a good feeling where you're concerned. You're going to get yours, too."

He rolled his eyes at her. "On that note, oh wise one, I gotta go. Go on back to your new husband. He'll be wondering where you are."

"He knew I was coming to check on you before your date."

"Does he know who I'm going out with?"

"Um, he might?"

"Laura!"

"What? He asked me, so I told him."

"I should've told him myself or asked if he minded or something."

Laura laughed at his distress. "Why would he mind, Shane? She's thirty-two years old, and he knows you're a good guy."

"Still… I should've said something to him."

"He thinks it's great, and he hopes you guys have a good time."

"He said that? Really?"

"Yes! Now go, will you?"

"Before I do, I just want to say… Thanks, you know, for everything. For dragging me out here and giving me a reason to get up in the morning again. And for Holden, who is quite simply the best thing since ice cream and beer."

Laura laughed again, which made Holden giggle in response to his mother. "Yes, he is, and I should be thanking *you* for showing up just when we needed you most. We say all the time that we never would've been ready for the season without you."

He gave Holden a kiss and bent to kiss Laura's cheek as he handed the baby back to her. "I'll see you guys in the morning, and thanks for coming to check on me."

"Have fun tonight, Shane. Let loose and whoop it up."

"*Right…*"

"I mean it." Carrying the baby, Laura followed him out the door. "You're still young with a lot of life left to live. I want to see you enjoy every minute."

"That would certainly beat the alternative. See you later."

In the hallway, she went left toward the apartment she shared with Owen and Holden while he took a right toward what used to be Sarah's room and was now Katie's. He glanced down the hallway to make sure his sister wasn't spying on him as he knocked on Katie's door. When the door flew open, he was surprised to find her still in a robe with her hair wrapped in a towel.

"Did I get the time wrong?"

CHAPTER 9

"No, not at all," Katie said. "I fell asleep and just woke up fifteen minutes ago. I'm so sorry I'm not ready."

"No worries. Should I come back?"

"No, come in. Have a seat. I'll be just a few more minutes."

"Okay." He followed her into the room where the only place to sit was the bed that was still rumpled from her nap. The air in the room was humid and fragrant from her shower. In the bathroom, the hair dryer went on. With a few minutes to kill, he went to the window to look out at the water, where the sun was inching closer to the horizon. It was going to be an amazing sunset.

The encroaching sunset reminded him of the spectacular sunsets he and Courtney had seen on their honeymoon in the Bahamas. And here, once again, that off-switch would come in handy. Why was she creeping into his mind—*again*—when he had far better things to think about tonight? "Just leave me alone," he whispered.

"Did you say something?"

He turned to find Katie, her hair dry, wearing a sexy orange dress as she affixed the back of an earring. "Talking to myself. A bad habit that comes from working alone most days."

"Ahh, so I won't cart you off to the loony bin just yet, then."

Shane laughed. "Thanks for the second chance."

"So sorry again for not being ready. I had all day and then ended up running late."

"Not to worry. Our reservation isn't for a while yet."

"You made a reservation?"

"Only so we don't have to wait two hours to eat. Sunday nights in the summer are busy around here."

"Is it just me or do the crowds seem bigger than ever these days?"

"It's not just you. This place is a madhouse from June through September." He cleared his throat. "You, um, you look really nice."

"Oh, thanks. I'm a little thrown together."

"If that's the case, I'd love to see what you're capable of when you have more time."

She smiled at his feeble attempt at charm.

"I'm just realizing that I should've borrowed my sister's car."

"Why's that?"

"Because I have a motorcycle, and you're wearing a dress."

"A motorcycle, huh? You don't seem the biker type."

"Because I don't have tattoos and wear leather chaps?"

"Among other reasons," she said, hiding a giggle behind her hand.

"I'm thoroughly insulted." He lightened his words with a smile to let her know he was kidding. "The bike is easy when parking is tight, and it gets me where I need to go. We can take a cab over to Domenic's if you'd like."

"I don't mind the bike if you have an extra helmet."

"I have two."

"Okay, then."

"You're sure?"

"Uh-huh."

The thought of Katie Lawry wrapped around him on the bike had him trying to think of something else—anything else—to avoid a predictable reaction. "So, um, are you hungry?"

"Starving! I haven't eaten since brunch."

"I had lunch, and I'm still starving." He held the door and gestured for her to go out ahead of him in a cloud of perfume and female fragrance that had him leaning in for a closer sniff. "I went fishing with my dad, uncles and cousins this afternoon."

"How was it?"

"Great. I bagged an eighty-pound bluefin tuna."

"Wow. Was that fun?"

"I don't know that 'fun' is the word I'd use. It was one hell of a battle. My arms will be useless tomorrow."

"You let a little ol' fish put that much of a hurt on you?"

Shane's ringing laughter echoed through the empty hallway as they headed for the stairs. "That 'little ol' fish' was a monster. Took five of us to land him."

"Did you throw him back after you caught him?"

"Nope. My aunt and uncle are serving him for dinner at the marina tonight. The whole family is going."

"You didn't want to go?"

"I'd rather go out with you. I can see them anytime."

"But you can't eat your eighty-pound badass tuna anytime."

"It's all right. I honestly don't mind missing it."

"I'd be fine with doing that, if you want to."

"That's really nice of you, but I'm not sure you're ready for full immersion into the madness known as the McCarthy family." They cut through the lobby and into the kitchen, which led to the parking lot behind the Surf. Since Stephanie's Bistro was closed on Sunday nights, the kitchen was quiet and spotless.

"I met them all this weekend. They were super nice."

"They were on best behavior for the wedding."

"It doesn't seem fair that you caught the fish but don't get to enjoy the fruits of your labor. I honestly don't mind going if you want to."

Shane hesitated. How to explain to her the way news and gossip flew with lightning speed through the Gansett Island pipeline?

"If you don't want them to know we're going out together, that's fine, too," she said.

"That is definitely not it. I'm thrilled to be going out with you. In fact, you have no idea how thrilled I am. But if we show up over there—together—the whole island will be talking about us long before we're ready for that."

"Oh."

"Yeah, so… Still want to go?" He watched her intently, looking for a hint as to what she was thinking.

"Yes, I think I do want to go. It would be very nice getting to know your family a little better, since they're now also my brother's family."

"If that's what you want, I'll cancel the reservation. We can go to Domenic's another time—that is, if you want to go out with me again after being exposed to my family."

"I'm sure I'll want to go out with you again even after being exposed to your family."

Shane held the screen door for her, delighted they were already talking about a second date when the first one had just begun.

*

Katie absolutely loved the McCarthys. She couldn't recall a more enjoyable evening than the one she spent with Shane and his family. He was an attentive date, making sure she had plenty to eat and drink and was surrounded by fun people.

Walking into the party already in progress had been a bit daunting, but she'd been given a warm welcome by Shane's uncle, whom everyone called Big Mac. He was one of those people who immediately felt like a friend, and he told her the full story of how Shane had managed to catch the biggest fish of the day.

"This impromptu party is all his doing," Big Mac told her.

"And you *hate* impromptu parties," Shane said sarcastically, earning a huge smile from his uncle.

"Wonder where your dad and Betsy are," Big Mac said. "I left him a message earlier but haven't heard from him."

"I'm sure he'll be here at some point. He knew you were cooking up the tuna."

"Actually, Stephanie is doing the cooking," Big Mac said sheepishly. "Turns out, Aunt Linda had no clue how to cook it. Fortunately, Stephanie and her chef from the Bistro know what to do."

"So you've got them spending their night off working."

"They were happy to do it."

"Only because you were the one asking."

"I have no idea what you're talking about." He winked and scooted off to welcome his son Adam and his fiancée, Abby.

"He's full of beans, huh?" Katie asked, amused by Big Mac.

"That he is, but he's also the best guy you'll ever know. Well, second only to my own dad."

"You're so lucky to have them in your life," Katie said wistfully. How might she have been different if she'd been born to a man like Mac or Frank McCarthy rather than the beast who'd fathered her?

"I know I'm lucky. I never take them for granted."

His Aunt Linda came over to hug and kiss him and to welcome Katie. "So nice to have Owen's sister joining the group. He's one of our favorites."

"I'm rather partial to him myself."

"Are he and Evan playing tonight?" Shane asked.

"Of course they are. Wouldn't be a party without them. Excuse me. I've got to help Stephanie in the kitchen."

Linda ran off toward the kitchen, leaving Shane and Katie to the mayhem of a McCarthy family party. They'd taken over the entire marina restaurant as well as the picnic tables outside.

"A lot of business gets tended to at those tables," Shane said of the picnic tables.

"What kind of business?"

"The solving of world problems and overall bullshitting every morning over coffee and doughnuts with my Uncle Mac presiding and my dad in attendance since he retired. The morning meeting is one of his favorite things about living here."

"That's so funny. I can picture it from the way you describe it. How long ago did your dad move here?"

"Earlier this summer. He retired after a long career as a superior court judge. My sister and I worried he'd be bored because his work was such a big part of his life, but he's loving retirement. He and Big Mac take off at least once a week to go fishing, and they're always coming up with some other adventure. They're like two little boys back together again."

"That's very sweet."

"Their younger brother, my Uncle Kevin, is here for the weddings."

"Plural?"

"My cousin Grant and Stephanie on Labor Day."

"Oh, that's right."

"Anyway, they've had poor Kevin hopping since he got here. He'll need to go home to get a break from his vacation."

"They sound like really fun guys."

"They are. I hope to be just like them when I'm their age."

"It's good to know there are men and fathers like them in this world. It gives me hope."

"I have to believe there are far more like them than there are like yours. I hope it's okay to say that. I don't mean any offense."

"None taken, and I'd like to think you're right about that."

"The men in my family worship the women they love, Katie. We don't know any other way to be after being raised by them. Look at my cousin Mac." He gestured to a table on the far side of the room where Mac was supervising two young children while his wife sat back and relaxed. "The boy, Thomas… He's Maddie's son from a previous relationship, but Mac adopted him and gave him our name, and as far as he's concerned, he's the boy's father—the only father he'll ever have."

"That's lovely."

"Mac is crazy about that kid. Their daughter, Hailey, was born—at home—during Tropical Storm Hailey. I wasn't here then, but I heard about how wild it was. They're expecting their third child now. You met my cousin Grant, right? He's Stephanie's fiancé. When he met her, Charlie, who's her stepfather, was still in prison." He paused and looked stricken. "Oh crap, you know about that, right?"

Smiling, she nodded. "My mother told me today. It's an amazing story."

"It really is. Grant called his friend, Dan Torrington—"

"The lawyer? I've heard of him."

"That's him right there." He pointed to Dan, who was sitting with a pretty woman with red highlights in her long brown hair. "With his fiancée, Kara. Anyway, Dan made a few phone calls, threw his weight around, and next thing we knew, Charlie was sprung from prison. Then Dan came here to write a book about his innocence project and met Kara. They're getting married next year."

"What is it about this place and people finding their soul mates?"

"Mac says there's something in the water."

Katie laughed. "I'll take a glass!"

"Coming right up." After he fetched her a glass of Gansett Island water and a bottle of the light beer she'd requested, he returned to his seat next to her. "Want to hear more about my cousins?"

"Absolutely."

"That's Evan over there. He's sitting with his fiancée, Grace Ryan. They're getting married in January. He was playing a gig right here at the marina with Owen last summer when he noticed Grace crying at one of the tables. He took the time to find out what was wrong and learned her date had left her stranded on the island after she refused to have sex with him."

"*Whoa.*"

"I know, right? So Evan took her home to his parents' house for the evening and paid her way home to Connecticut. She came back a few weeks later to reimburse him, and from all accounts, they've been together ever since. Now she owns Ryan's Pharmacy in town."

"I love that. What a great story."

"Now, my cousin Adam is engaged to Abby, who was with Grant for ten years."

"That sounds dicey."

"It might've been if Grant hadn't been happily in love with Stephanie. They worked it out, and everyone is happy for Adam and Abby. They're great together."

"Another amazing story."

"I'm beginning to think that bringing you here was the best thing I could've done."

"Why's that?"

"After hearing all about my cousins and their smooth moves, you might be tempted to go out with me again."

Before she could form a reply to that audacious statement, Adam and Abby took seats at their table, followed soon after by Shane's cousin Janey and her husband, Joe, who carried their son, P.J.

"What a cute baby," Katie said of the tiny blond boy who watched the world go by with big blue eyes.

"We're quite fond of him," Joe said, gazing down at his son.

"You McCarthys make cute babies," Katie said. "Holden is adorable, and so are Mac's kids." She caught Shane watching her with a guarded expression and wondered if she'd said the wrong thing.

"Holden is super cute," Janey agreed. "He's going to be tall, dark and handsome when he grows up."

"Could Auntie Abby take a turn with P.J.?" Abby asked.

"Absolutely." Joe handed the baby over to Abby, who melted before their eyes.

Adam watched her intently as she snuggled the baby, and then whispered something in her ear that had her smiling softly at him.

Apparently eighty pounds of tuna fed a lot of people, because they kept arriving. First Owen and Laura with baby Holden, and then Ned and his wife, Francine. Katie was introduced to Joe's mom, Carolina, and her new husband, Seamus.

"Wow," Katie whispered to Shane. "Good for her."

He chuckled at her comment. "Apparently, their age difference was quite the scandal when they first started dating. Now it's no big deal."

Surrounded by happy couples, all of whom had risked their hearts to find true love and happiness, had Katie thinking about the rules that had governed her life and whether it might be time to say to hell with the rules. She leaned back against Shane and forced herself to remain calm when he casually put his arm around her, announcing to anyone who might be looking that they were together.

And people were most definitely looking.

"Is this okay?" he asked, his lips brushing against her temple.

She nodded and tried to get her rigid muscles to relax and enjoy the moment. Here she was with a nice, handsome, sexy man who seemed interested in her. They were surrounded by a big, boisterous, loving family that wanted only the best for him—and probably her, too, due to her relationship to Owen.

It was okay to relax and enjoy herself. It was okay to let him touch her. It was okay to talk about second dates and things she'd never allowed before. "Shane?"

"Yes?"

"I have to tell you something."

"I'm listening."

The others were engaged in their own conversations, which gave Katie the opportunity to speak privately to him. "I… I want you to know…"

"What do you want me to know?"

At that moment she was glad she couldn't see his face. Rather, she watched his father come into the restaurant holding Betsy's hand, which he released only to hug his brothers before reclaiming his woman. The two of them were smiling and fairly glowing with happiness that only bolstered her courage.

"Katie? What do you want me to know?"

"This is the first date I've ever been on."

CHAPTER 10

Shane's entire body seemed to go still behind her as he absorbed what she'd said. "Like, ever?"

"Like, ever."

"*Why*?"

"Because..."

"Because of your dad, right?"

"Partially."

He spoke softly to her, ensuring their conversation couldn't be overheard. "I would never, *could* never, *ever*, raise a hand to you to cause you anything other than pleasure." As he spoke, he ran his fingertip down her bare arm, setting off a series of reactions that had her squirming in her chair. "Do you believe me?"

"I want to."

"Katie..."

Encouraged by his kind response to her confession, she turned so she could see his face, which was tight with tension.

"We'll talk more later," he said. "When we're alone."

His low, intimate tone as well as the thought of being alone with him later set off another set of tremors inside her, all of them seeming to land in a tight knot of need between her legs. He continued to stroke her arm, and Katie wanted to purr from the sweet pleasure of such a simple caress. It had her wondering what else might be possible with him.

Being around his family, hearing the stories of how his cousins had fallen in love as well as his heartfelt pledge had Katie relaxing in a way she never would've expected she could with a man.

And then Stephanie announced dinner was served, and the little bubble around them burst as everyone began getting up to head for the buffet Stephanie and her chef had set out at the counter where customers placed their orders during regular hours.

"This is amazing, Steph!" Maddie proclaimed as she checked out the spread that included the grilled tuna along with two kinds of potatoes, several types of vegetables, a huge Caesar salad and rolls.

"Don't be too impressed," Stephanie replied. "A lot of it is left over from the wedding last night."

"I'm very impressed," Maddie said, "mostly because it looks fantastic, and I didn't have to cook it."

"Hear, hear," Grace said.

With Shane behind her, Katie filled her plate and returned to their table. She didn't want to confess that she'd never had tuna, except for the kind that came in a can, so she wasn't sure she'd like it. Before Shane joined her, she took a quick bite to try it and was pleasantly surprised by how good it tasted.

"How is it?" he asked when he had taken the seat next to her.

"Excellent. I've never had it before, but I really like it."

"You might find that to be true of a lot of things," he said with a playful smile and the suggestive waggle of his brows.

Katie stared at him, incredulous and amused at the same time. "Did you really just say that?"

"I really did, and I really mean it."

Katie found it difficult to swallow her food with him sitting so close to her and obviously thinking about other things he wanted to introduce her to. How did she feel about being introduced to those things by him?

"Stop thinking so much," he whispered. "Nothing will happen between us unless you want it to."

Buoyed by his reassurances, she said, "You don't think I'm weird because I've never been on a date before?"

"No, Katie. I don't think you're weird at all, because you had a good reason to keep your distance from men. I think you're sweet and beautiful and kind, and I want to get to know you better."

"Fancy meeting you here," Laura said from behind them, where she stood with Holden in her arms.

"Oh, hey," Shane said to his sister, as casual as could be, as if he hadn't just tipped Katie's world upside down with what he'd said to her. "What's up?"

"I could ask you the same. Didn't expect to see you at a family thing tonight."

"Katie wanted to meet my tuna."

She held up a forkful of the succulent fish. "He's delicious."

"I wish I could have some," Laura said wistfully.

"Why can't you?" Shane asked.

"Tuna has a lot of mercury, which isn't good for the babies."

"That's a bummer. I would've caught something else for you if I'd known that."

"But I see there are potatoes," Laura said, her eyes widening.

"One of her cravings," Owen explained.

Shane reached for the baby. "Let me take him while you guys eat."

"Are you sure?" Laura asked. "You're still eating."

"I'm positive. Come see Uncle Shane, buddy."

Holden's arms and legs went wild as he tried to get to his uncle, making his mother and Katie laugh.

"It's so not fair," Laura said. "You're sick as a dog while you carry a baby for nine months, and then he picks your brother over you every time—*and* sleeps through the night for him when he won't do it for you!"

"What can I say?" Shane kissed the baby's chubby cheek. "We're buddies."

"Not fair," Laura said again before she went off to see about some dinner.

"You're so good with him," Katie said.

"I'm crazy about him."

Watching him snuggle the sleepy baby made Katie's heart melt. Right then she decided she wanted to get to know Shane better. For the first time in her life, she wanted to take a chance on a man and let him show her what she'd been missing for all the years she'd kept her distance from such things.

*

Shane was grateful for the distraction Holden provided as he tried to process what Katie had told him. This was her first date. Ever. Which meant she hadn't done anything else with any guy. Ever. He had to force air into his lungs as he absorbed the implications of her confession.

Suddenly, this evening out with her was about much more than his first date after a crushing divorce. This date was much more important to her than it could ever be to him. Imagine living thirty-two years without ever going on a date. Shane had been dating since he was sixteen with a newly issued driver's license in hand. His father had lectured him endlessly about safe sex, even going so far as to buy him his first box of condoms.

Shane would never forget the mortification of that conversation, but he'd been damned grateful to have them six months later when he had sex for the first time with his high school girlfriend.

Katie had skipped that entire phase of her life, preferring to be alone rather than risk being treated the way her father had treated her mother. She hadn't needed to draw him a map for him to understand the why of it. He knew just enough about the Lawry family to get the picture.

But was he the right guy for her to take this monumental step with? He wasn't sure about that, and before things went any further between them, he needed to tell her about Courtney and what he'd been through so she could decide if she wanted to continue seeing him. The thought of talking about all that garbage with Katie turned his stomach and ruined what was left of his appetite.

He pushed his plate away and focused all his attention on Holden, rubbing his back. Shane loved the way the baby snuggled into the space between his head and shoulder, making himself comfortable in his uncle's arms. And then he noticed that Holden had wrapped his hand tightly around Katie's index finger. He shared a smile with her.

"He's so perfect," she whispered.

"I know. Being an uncle is the best thing ever."

"It looks good on you."

"Thanks."

"Do you want kids of your own?"

"Someday." He didn't mention that he'd expected to have a couple of them by now. But he'd tell her that later, when they were alone. "What about you?"

"When I was little, I wanted a big horde of kids like my mother had. But I haven't thought about that in ages."

Sitting on the picnic tables outside the restaurant, Owen and Evan began playing their guitars as their friends and family sang along to "Brown-Eyed Girl."

Katie watched her brother with a look of love and pride on her face. "He's so good. Always has been."

"I love listening to him play. He kept us entertained all winter. He and Laura and the baby, Sarah and Charlie and me… We spent many an evening in the sitting room at the hotel with a fire burning and Owen's guitar for entertainment."

"That sounds really cozy."

"It was. From the time he was born, Holden has been mesmerized by Owen and the guitar."

"He was probably already used to hearing it while he was in utero."

"Really?"

"Uh-huh. Babies can hear all sorts of things before they're born, especially music and their parents' voices."

"That's so cool."

The island's police chief, Blaine Taylor, and his wife, Tiffany, came into the restaurant. "Did you guys eat all the tuna?" he asked.

"There's plenty left," Big Mac said. "Help yourselves."

The party continued to grow when Alex Martinez and his fiancée, Jenny, arrived with Alex's brother, Paul, along with Dr. David Lawrence and his girlfriend, Daisy Babson, as well as Jared and Lizzie James. Shane introduced Katie to all the late arrivals when they came by their table to say hello.

"Do you guys do this sort of thing often?" Katie asked him.

"There's always some sort of gathering going on. It's a really fun group of people."

"I can see that."

And he could see her desire to be part of it. He wondered if she knew her expression gave her away as she took in the happy people gathered around them.

Laura returned to claim her sleeping baby.

"Do I have to give him back?" Shane asked.

"Afraid so. Hand him over."

"If you insist." As Shane transferred the baby to his mother's waiting arms, the baby never stirred. "He's out cold. My work here is finished."

"We're going to listen to Daddy play," Laura said.

"We're heading out shortly," Shane said. "I'll see you tomorrow."

Laura flashed a saucy, suggestive smile. "Have fun, you kids."

"Go away, Laura."

"What?"

"*Go*!"

"He's not usually so rude, Katie. I apologize for him."

Katie laughed at the scowl Shane directed at his sister.

"You're going away now, Laura."

"Fine. Be that way."

"Sheesh," Shane said when his sister took off with the baby. "What a pain she is."

"You love her."

"Unfortunately, I do, and she knows it."

"You guys are tight."

"Always have been. Our mom died when she was nine and I was seven. We've been through a lot together."

"I'm sorry about your mom. That's awful."

"It was pretty bad for a while, but we got through it." He wanted to tell her what else he'd been through and give her an out if she wanted it. "What do you say we hit the road?"

"Sure. Whatever you want to do."

He got up and held out a hand to help her and hung on to her hand even after she was standing. They went around to say their good-byes to his family, all of whom made a big deal out of the fact that he'd caught dinner for the whole clan. "I do what I can for the family," Shane said to laughter from his dad and uncles.

"Have a good night, son," Frank said. "Nice to see you again, Katie."

"You, too, Mr. McCarthy."

"Please, honey. Call me Frank."

"Thank you, I will."

Shane put his arm around her as they walked to where he'd parked the motorcycle. He helped her put on the helmet and waited until she was settled on the back before he donned his own helmet and climbed on. "Hang on extra tight."

Katie laughed at his flirtatious comment.

He loved the way her arms felt around him as he drove out of the marina and headed for town. With his entire family at the marina, they'd have the hotel sitting room to themselves. It was the perfect place for the conversation they needed to have before this went any further.

*

When they pulled into the parking lot at the Surf, Katie was disappointed that they'd come home so early. He'd seemed to be enjoying himself, but maybe she'd read that wrong. How would she know anyway?

Would it be awkward when they said good night? What if he tried to kiss her? Would she let him? Right… When he hadn't even wanted to stay out past ten o'clock, he wasn't likely to try to kiss her.

He took the helmet from her and gestured for her to go on ahead of him into the hotel.

"Thanks for a nice time," she said when they stepped into the lobby. With the restaurant closed for the evening, no one was around. "Your family is amazing."

"Yes, they are, but our date isn't over. Unless you want it to be."

"Oh. I thought…"

"You thought I was bringing you home and calling it a night."

"Yes," she said, feeling foolish now.

"I was hoping we could find a quiet place to talk, if that's okay."

Katie couldn't believe how relieved she was to learn their date wasn't over. "I'd like that."

"Come on in here." He led her into the sitting room, where he stashed the helmets on the floor next to the hutch that housed her grandmother's favorite china. Then he joined her on the sofa, sitting with one leg curled up so he could face her. "I wanted to say that I appreciate you trusting me enough to tell me what you did earlier."

"It's sort of embarrassing."

"Don't be embarrassed. There's no need to be."

"That's nice of you to say, but honestly... How many thirty-two-year-old women do you know who've never been on a date or... well, anything else?"

"I'm so honored to be your first date, Katie." He took hold of her hand and brought it to his lips, running them over her knuckles. That simple contact was all it took to set off a fever inside her.

"It wasn't that I didn't want to date. When I was younger and everyone was doing the group-dating thing, my dad wouldn't let me go. He didn't approve of the boys I was friends with, and I knew better than to argue with him. And then later, when I got to college, they were all such *players*, you know? I was surrounded by immature jerks who were *awful* to my friends. I wanted nothing to do with any of them. Before I knew it, I'd created a pattern of avoidance that became an unintentional lifestyle."

"I can see how that would happen, and I understand it. I want you to know some things about me that might make you reconsider whether you want me to be the first guy you date."

Katie couldn't imagine any scenario that would make her not want to spend more time with him. "Okay..."

"I was married for a couple of years, but I'm divorced now."

"Oh."

"My wife, Courtney, was a drug addict. She was addicted to pain meds, and I didn't find out until we'd been married for quite some time."

"Oh God, Shane. I'm so sorry."

"Yeah, it was a rough time. And I was literally blinded by love. It never occurred to me that she was an addict. She hid it incredibly well."

"How'd you find out?"

"It all came to a head when I started getting calls from bill collectors. She took care of the bills, so I didn't know where the money was going. When I dug a little deeper, I found out she'd basically bankrupted us with her habit." He released a deep breath and ran his fingers through his hair repeatedly, as if it was excruciating to talk about this. "After an ugly, horrible confrontation, I got her into rehab. I borrowed money from my dad to pay for it."

"She was so lucky to have you."

"So lucky she divorced me the second she got out of rehab. I haven't seen her since the day I dropped her off there."

Katie had no idea what to say to that. His pain was so palpable, even after what had to be some considerable time if he was already divorced. "I'm sorry she treated you that way. No one deserves that."

"I really loved her. She was the real deal for me. To find out it wasn't for her was… Well, it took me a really long time to get past it. Sometimes I wonder if I'm actually past it, and I thought you should know, since our date was a big deal for you, too. This is the first time I've been out with anyone since everything happened with her."

"Oh, wow," she said on a long exhale. "We're quite a pair, huh?"

He smiled, but the sadness lingered around his eyes. "Yeah, I guess we are. I'd understand if my crap is too heavy for you, Katie. You've had enough of your own, and it wouldn't hurt my feelings if you told me it's too much for you."

Katie thought about what she should say. "You're completely divorced, right?"

"For about eighteen months now."

"Then I don't see any reason why we can't spend some time together and see what happens."

"Really?"

He was so cute and so eager. She wondered if he had any idea how adorable he was. The thought of his ex-wife treating him so callously made her furious on his behalf. "Yes, really."

"You want to go for a walk on the beach?"

"I'd love to."

CHAPTER 11

With everyone fed and happy, Stephanie filled a plate and went to sit next to Grant, who was sharing a table with Dan, Kara, Evan and Grace.

"Everything was amazing, as always," Grace said to Stephanie.

"Thank you. Glad you enjoyed it."

Grant put his arm around her and kissed her cheek. "Great job, babe. Only you could prepare a quick dinner for forty and not freak out."

"What else can I do when my adorable future father-in-law calls me for help?"

"This was way above and beyond with everything you've got going on," Evan said.

"It was fun," Stephanie said.

"How are the wedding plans coming along?" Kara asked. "I can't believe you're putting together a wedding as quickly as you are. I have almost a year, and I'll be lucky to get it all done in time."

"We're going very simple," Stephanie said, smiling at Grant. "That makes it easier."

"That's what we should've done," Kara said, sighing.

"I offered to elope to Vegas," Dan replied with a cheeky grin for his fiancée.

"There's simple and then there's cheesy," Kara said as the others laughed. "Two very different things."

"I think she might be insulting me," Dan said.

Grant rolled his eyes at his close friend. "You're lucky you found someone willing to marry you. If I were you, I'd do anything she wanted me to do."

"This is true," Dan said gravely.

Kara smiled at him. "He's taking me to LA to meet my future in-laws after the season."

"And she's taking me to Bar Harbor to meet the rest of mine."

"That sounds like fun," Stephanie said. "When are you leaving?"

"Right after Columbus Day," Kara said. "I'll shut down the launches for the winter, and off we go."

"Wait till you see his place in Malibu," Grant said. "Very swank."

"I can't wait," Kara said. "I've always wanted to live in a beach house."

"Now you'll have your very own any time we get out to the West Coast," Dan said.

"Where do you guys plan to live after you're married?" Grace asked.

"Here," Kara said. "We both love it here."

"Oh good," Grace said. "I was worried for a minute that we'd be losing you after the wedding."

"No way," Dan said. "We're here to stay. I'll have to get out to LA once in a while for work, but I can do most of it from here and tend to my accidental practice on the island at the same time."

"I like that," Grant said with a chuckle. "'Accidental practice.'"

"That's what it is. I never had any intention of practicing here, but one thing led to another…"

"And Jim Sturgil lost his mind," Evan added.

"That didn't hurt," Dan conceded.

"What's the latest with him anyway?" Stephanie asked.

"He's been charged with felony assault for the stunt he pulled at our engagement party." Dan ran a finger over the healing scar on his hand where Jim had slashed him with a knife. "I haven't heard anything more than that."

"Damn," Evan said. "If he's convicted—and how could he not be with so many witnesses—he'll be disbarred."

"I don't feel sorry for him at all," Kara said indignantly. "He brought it all on himself by being an asshole to Tiffany and then by trying to blame Dan for his practice going belly-up. It's no one's fault but his."

"Listen to my little hellcat." Dan put his arm around Kara. "Don't get her started on Jim Sturgil."

"He could've killed you with that knife. You'll have to pardon me if I don't find that one bit funny."

"Wow," Grant said. "She really does love you."

"I know, right?" Dan said. "It's just as shocking to me."

"Shut up," Kara said, laughing at the amazement on Dan's face. "Before I forget why I love you so much."

"Please don't do that."

Sitting with Grant and their friends, her stepfather across the room with his new fiancée, Sarah, Stephanie wanted to pinch herself to believe this was actually her life now. After spending fourteen years totally on her own while trying to free Charlie from prison and having no luck until Grant and Dan had entered her life, she would be forever grateful to them. Grant had called Dan to tell him about Charlie, and Dan had taken it from there.

They would never know the full measure of her relief and gratitude for what they'd done for her—and, more important, what they'd done for Charlie.

"Whatcha thinking about, babe?" Grant asked, his lips close to her ear as he spoke to her.

"Everything that's happened in the last year and how it's still amazing to me how different my life is now. And Charlie's life, too. We owe it all to you."

"All I did was make a phone call."

"That's what you always say." He never took any credit for what he'd done to help them, and now was no different.

"It's true. Dan did the rest."

"But there would've been no Dan without you."

"I hope you know by now," he said, his lips brushing her ear, "that there's absolutely nothing I wouldn't do for you."

His love surrounded her like a warm blanket, filling her with the kind of security she'd never had before she fell in love with him during Tropical Storm Hailey. Despite all the many ways she'd tried to sabotage their relationship since then, he'd remained steadfast in his devotion to her.

"I could use your help with something in the kitchen," she said. The others had begun to migrate out to the picnic tables in the parking lot, where Big Mac had started a fire in a portable fire pit he produced from somewhere, and Evan and Owen had everyone singing along with them to "Margaritaville."

"Sure. Lead the way."

Stephanie took his hand and led him around the counter to the kitchen. "Actually, where I need your help is down this hallway here." With a quick glance to make sure no one had seen them slip away, she took him into the windowless room that had been hers when they first started seeing each other. Big Mac and Linda had hired her to run the marina restaurant that summer.

She ducked into the room with him in tow and then turned to shut the door behind them. Since she was still overseeing the marina restaurant while she ran the Bistro in town, the manager's room was not in use this summer.

"What're you up to, my love?" Grant asked with an amused glimmer in his gorgeous eyes. She never, ever got tired of looking at him.

"A little trip down memory lane."

"Ahh, yes." He put his arms around her and drew her in tight against him. "As I recall, we had some good times in here under the watchful eye of Winnie the Pooh."

"Poor Pooh was traumatized by our behavior."

"And yet he still sits on our bed watching everything we do."

"I can't be without Pooh. I've had him since I was three."

"Did you bring me in here to talk about Pooh, or did you plan to ravish me?"

"The plan was to ravish."

"Don't let me stop you."

"I just want you to know…"

"What, baby?" He kissed her neck and made her shiver. "What do you want me to know?"

"Sitting out there now, surrounded by our family and friends… I feel so incredibly grateful for our life. You'll never know how much it means to me to have Charlie here with me, and you and your family to call my own. You'll just never know…" Her voice broke, and he kissed her softly.

"I do know. And as grateful as you are to have us, we're equally grateful to have you. I mean, who would've cooked Shane's tuna if you weren't around?"

Stephanie laughed and brushed away tears as he kissed her again.

"In two weeks, I get to marry you and keep you forever," he said between kisses. "How cool is that?"

"It's the coolest thing ever."

"Now, about that ravishing…"

He reached around her to lock the door and then worked quickly to remove all their clothes. They fell onto the twin-size bed in a tangle of arms and legs, kissing and touching and moaning in response to each other.

"God, Steph… What you do to me."

"I feel the same way." She arched into him, her legs entangled with his. She took him in hand, trying to direct him to where she wanted him most. "We have to hurry before someone notices we're gone."

Grant groaned and surged into her in one swift stroke. "You want fast, baby? I can do fast."

"Mmm. Just like that only faster."

His laughter caused him to falter, but only for a second. He took hold of her hands, raised them over her head and gave her exactly what she'd asked for.

Stephanie loved him like this—a little wild and a whole lot out of control. She loved that she could do that to him—that they did it to each other, every time.

"Babe," he said, "I can't wait."

"Right there with you."

He thrust into her one more time, which was all it took for both of them.

She pulled her hands free and wrapped her arms around him as they clung to each other.

"I love you," he whispered after a long moment of contented silence.

"I love you, too."

"I can't wait to marry you."

For a long time, Stephanie had doubted whether she could be everything he wanted in a wife, but those doubts were long gone now. "I can't wait either."

*

"Looks like it's going to rain," Shane said as they walked barefoot along the water's edge. He'd taken hold of her hand to help her down the stairs and had never bothered to let go, which was fine with Katie. Her first official date had been better than anything she could've hoped for, all because of him.

He was easy to be with, caring but not suffocating. He was affectionate without being overwhelming. In short, he was everything she'd never expected to find in a man, and he made her feel hopeful about what might be possible for them.

"I hope it's not a thunderstorm," she said.

"How come?"

"They scare me. I remember so many of them when we came here for the summer and the way the lightning would light up the room. I used to run into my grandparents' room and sleep with them. I wasn't allowed to do that at home." She hadn't meant to say that last part. That she'd said it indicated how comfortable she was with him.

"How come?"

"My father didn't believe in sharing his bed with his children—for any reason."

"Even when you were scared?"

"Especially then. He would tell us to toughen up and stop acting like a bunch of babies. I'd crawl in bed with Julia, and we'd hide under the pillows until it was over."

"How old were you then?"

"I don't know. Four, maybe?"

"You were just a baby." He dropped her hand and put his arm around her.

Katie's heart skipped an erratic beat at the feel of his arm around her, drawing her in close to the heat of his body. Did he expect her to put her arm around him, too? She wished she knew what people did at moments like these. "The Lawry kids were never babies. We were expected to be tough as soldiers from the second we were born."

"I'm glad you're not tough. I like you the way you are, afraid of thunderstorms and everything."

"I'm afraid of the water now, too." She eyed the waves that rolled gently to the shore. "And I hate being afraid of that."

"You'll have to ease your way back in gradually."

"I don't know if I can do that after what happened."

"If it's something you enjoy, you have to try."

"I suppose you're right."

"I'll help you."

"You will?"

"Of course I will. It sort of scared me, too, so you'd be helping me."

"Right," she said with a laugh. "You're just saying that so I'll feel better about being scared."

"That's not true. I've heard about rip currents all my life, but I've never seen one do what yours did to you. It scared me. Don't think it didn't."

"If you say so."

"I say so." He smiled down at her, and the sweetness of his words along with that adorable smile did funny things to her insides. She felt like she was on a zero-gravity ride, like the ones they had at the big amusement parks in Texas, only she was nowhere near an amusement park.

They walked for a long time with only a half moon to light their way. She was about to thank him for the lovely evening when a sharp pain sliced through her foot, stealing the breath from her lungs.

"What?" he asked, stopping to face her.

"I think I cut my foot."

"Oh shit." He withdrew his cell phone from his pocket and turned on the flashlight. "Let me see."

Katie placed her hand on his shoulder for balance and raised her right foot, which was already covered in blood. As a nurse, the sight of blood never bothered her—except, apparently, when it was hers. She felt immediately queasy when she realized the cut was deep and would probably require stitches.

"Don't put it down in the sand," Shane said as he used the flashlight to identify a broken bottle sticking up out of the sand. "There's your culprit." He pulled the piece of glass free and tucked the neck into his back pocket. "I'll throw it away when we get back." He lifted Katie into his arms.

"You can't carry me all the way back!"

"You don't think so?"

"I'm too heavy."

"You're light as a feather."

"No, I'm not."

"Hey," he said, compelling her to look at him. "You're not heavy, and I've got you, unless me carrying you makes you uncomfortable. If it does, I'll put you down and call the rescue."

"I don't want to cause trouble for anyone."

"You're no trouble." He started walking back the way they'd come. "Should you keep it elevated?"

"Yeah, probably."

He adjusted the way he held her to make it easier for her to extend her injured foot.

"I've got to be too heavy for you, especially with your arms worn out from battling tuna."

"I already told you you're not too heavy, and I'm fine. I promise. Try to relax and let me enjoy holding you."

"You really are shameless, aren't you?"

"What can I say? I'm a McCarthy. Shamelessness runs through my genes."

Katie smiled as she rested her head on his shoulder, the sharp pain in her foot the only thing keeping her from being as happy as she could ever recall being.

He got them back to the hotel faster than she would've thought possible and headed up the stairs effortlessly, as if carrying her was no big deal. His obvious strength was another thing to like about him.

"I've already been carried more by you than by anyone else ever, and I've only known you for three days."

"I like carrying you."

"I'm not usually such a damsel in distress. I hope you know that."

"I do know. I bet in your real life as a nurse practitioner, you're endlessly capable and always solving problems for other people. Am I close?"

"Pretty darned close," Katie said, astounded by his insight.

"Thought so."

He deposited her gently in a chair on the hotel's porch. "I'll be right back with something to clean that up. After we get a better look, we can decide if we need to call Doctor David."

Katie hated the idea of calling in the doctor to see to her silly injury. She hoped it was something they could tend to at home.

Shane returned with a first aid kit and turned on the porch light so he could see the sole of her foot. He was gentle as he cleaned the wound and wrapped it in gauze. "It's pretty deep."

"I was afraid you were going to say that."

"I'm going to call David, okay?"

Katie bit her lip and nodded, trying not to cry over something so silly. So she'd cut her foot. Big deal. It was just that the cut foot had ruined her first date, and she'd been having a marvelous time.

Still in a squat before her, he leaned forward to kiss her forehead. "It's going to be fine, so don't worry. I'll be right back."

CHAPTER 12

Shane went inside to look up David's number, leaving Katie to gaze out over the moonbeams on the water and wish she hadn't managed to find the one piece of broken glass on the beach. Shane was back a minute later. "He's meeting us at the clinic."

"How are we getting there?"

"I've got the keys to Owen's van." Once again, Shane lifted her as if she weighed next to nothing and carried her to the parking lot, where he loaded her into the front seat of Owen's vintage yellow Volkswagen Vanagon.

"My brother's pride and joy."

"I know. He loves it, but I think he's going to get rid of it when the twins arrive. They'll need something a little more family friendly."

"I can't believe he's going to have three children before the end of the year."

"I don't think he can believe it either." He glanced over at her. "You okay?"

"Yes, I'm fine and sorry for ruining our evening."

Shane took hold of her hand. "You didn't. We'll get you stitched up, and we'll pick up where we left off, minus the sharp thing."

"You're a good sport. Thank you."

"Spending time with you has been my pleasure." He only let go of her hand to shift gears and then took hold of it again.

David was waiting for them when Shane carried her into the clinic. The doctor shook Katie's hand and re-introduced her to his girlfriend, Daisy. "We were still at the marina when Shane called," he said, "so it was quicker to come here than to take Daisy home."

"Sorry to mess up your evening," Katie said.

"You didn't," Daisy said. "Happens all the time. I'm used to it by now."

David kissed Daisy. "I'll see you in a few, honey." To Katie, he said, "She waits for me in my office."

"I've even got my own stash of magazines in there now."

"I'll try not to be too injured so he can get out of here."

Daisy squeezed Katie's arm before she left them. "Take your time."

David gestured for Shane to take Katie into a room where he deposited her on the exam table. "Let's take a look, Katie." He unwrapped the gauze Shane had applied, which had soaked through during the short ride to the clinic. David examined the wound while Shane kept an arm around her shoulders, holding her tighter when she winced from the pain of David's exam.

"We're definitely looking at some stitches here. Do you know what you stepped on?"

"A broken bottle."

"What's the status of your tetanus shot?"

"I'm due for one this fall."

"I'd recommend we do it now." He moved around the exam room, gathering the items he needed to stitch her foot. "I'm going to have you lie back on the table." David produced a pillow and helped her to get comfortable. "Shane, here's a stool for you so you can sit with Katie."

"Thanks."

"So, you're Owen's sister," David said.

"Yes, one of his three sisters."

"The wedding was incredible. They got such a perfect night for it."

"They really did."

"Just a couple of pinches while we numb you up," David said.

She turned her head, looking for reassurance from Shane.

He gripped her hand and held her gaze as the needle burned the sole of her foot, taking her breath away. Damn, that hurt!

"You doing okay?" David asked.

"Uh-huh."

"Two more and we should be good."

The second one hurt as much as the first one had, bringing tears to her eyes. By the third one, the first two had begun to take effect and the pain was greatly diminished. She blew out a couple of breaths, trying to calm her racing heart.

David moved quickly and efficiently to clean and suture the wound. "So, what do you do back in Texas?"

"I'm a nurse practitioner, although you'd never know it from how much of a baby I'm being right now."

"Are you kidding?" David said. "I was just thinking you're a stud. Three shots to the bottom of your foot and not so much as a whimper."

Shane smiled and made her feel better with the reassuring way he looked at her.

Fifteen minutes later, she'd received ten stitches that were now covered with gauze and tape, as well as a tetanus shot that had stung like hell, a prescription for an antibiotic and a stiff orthopedic shoe.

"You know the drill—keep it dry and clean for the next week and in the morning make an appointment to have the stitches removed."

"Thank you so much for coming in when you were off duty," Katie said.

"I'm never off duty," David said with a laugh. "But I love my job, and I'm happy to do it. Give me one second, and I'll find a pair of crutches for you."

When they were alone, Shane put his arm around her. "Are you all right?"

"I'm fine."

"Next time we'll wear shoes on the beach."

She smiled up at him. "What fun will that be?" Before she had a second to gauge his intentions, he was kissing her—just the soft press of his lips against hers, but a kiss nonetheless. And then he pulled back, seeming stunned by what he'd done.

"I'm sorry to just do that, but you were so adorable and sweet, and I couldn't resist."

"I'm glad you didn't resist."

He stared at her, but the moment was interrupted when David returned with the crutches.

"Could she deal with them tomorrow?" Shane asked.

"Of course," David said. "I'll carry them out for you."

"Ready?" Shane asked Katie.

"You're going to be in here tomorrow with your back thrown out."

"Nah."

When he lifted her off the table, she put her arms around his neck. He carried her to the van, where they said good-bye and thank you again to David. Back at the hotel, Shane carried her inside, up to her room on the third floor, and set her on the bed. Then he went back for her crutches and returned with them and some pain pills, too.

"Is there anything else I can get for you?" Shane asked.

"I think I'm good, but..."

He sat on the edge of her bed, propping his arm over her legs. "But what?"

"You said our date wouldn't be over when we got back. And if you don't mind staying for a while..."

He smiled. "I don't mind."

She patted the other side of the bed, which was the only other place in the small room to sit.

He got up and went around the bed. "I didn't see our first date ending in bed," he said with a teasing grin.

"Neither did I."

"And yet here we are."

"Here we are."

A rumble of thunder and a flash of lightning drew a gasp from her. "Now you really can't leave."

"I wouldn't dream of leaving when you're scared."

"Other than the needle portion of the program, I had a really fun time tonight."

"Me too. Best time I've had in years, in fact."

"Really?"

"Really."

Katie looked at him for a long time, trying to find the courage to ask for what she wanted. "What you did before, at the clinic... Would you do it again?"

"Hold your hand?"

She shook her head, amused by his teasing.

"Put my arm around you?"

"Not that either, but I did like when you did that."

"Oh, wait, I know." He scooted closer to her, cupped her face in his work-roughened hand and leaned in to brush his lips over hers. "That?"

"Yes," she said breathlessly. "That."

"You liked that, huh?"

She nodded as her heart pounded.

"I liked it, too."

"Did you like it enough to do it again?"

"Let me think about that."

A gurgle of laughter escaped from her lips, which had been pressed tightly together.

He leaned in so his lips were a heartbeat away from touching hers. "I'm done thinking." And then he kissed her again, and Katie couldn't seem to breathe or move or do anything other than wait to see what he would do next.

A slash of lightning followed by a crack of thunder made Katie startle and pull back from him. "Sorry," she muttered.

He smiled and brushed her hair back from her face. "Don't be sorry."

"I feel like such a fool for still being scared of thunder and lightning at my age."

"Is there an age limit on being afraid of something?"

"No, but… I still feel silly about it."

"No need to feel silly on my account."

She turned on her side to face him, wincing when her skin pulled against the cut on her foot. "Are you really this nice, or is this just your first-date-impress-the-girl-with-your-awesomeness act?"

He was even more adorable, she discovered, when he laughed. Falling onto the pillow on his side of the bed, he covered his eyes with his forearm as he continued to laugh. "You're too much, you know that?"

"I've heard that a time or two."

He lifted his arm off his face and looked at her. "My father always told us to be ourselves because it was too much work to be ourselves and someone else, too. So I hate to tell you that what you see is what you get. I have no reason to be anything other than nice to you, Katie. Do you want to know why?"

She nodded.

"Because I really, really want to go out with you again." He checked his watch. "Tonight. And maybe tomorrow night, too. And the night after."

"Do you have to work tomorrow?"

"Today, you mean?" he asked, reminding her it was after midnight already. "Yes, I'm working."

"You're going to be tired."

"Nah, I'll be fine."

"You really don't have to stay. I've survived many a thunderstorm on my own. You should see the epic storms we get in Texas."

"I don't mind staying awhile. There's no need for you to survive this one alone." He somehow managed to arrange them so his arms were around her and her head was resting on his chest.

The subtle scents of soap and sporty deodorant and laundry detergent filled her senses and calmed her racing mind. She was lying in bed with a man for the first time in her life. Shouldn't she be freaking out or telling him to go or something?

"I can almost *hear* you thinking," Shane said as he casually ran his hand up and down her arm, setting off a flood of sensation that seemed to gather between her legs.

"You can't hear someone think."

"No, but I can feel your tension and your hesitancy and your internal debate about whether it's worse to be in a bed with me or to live through the storm on your own."

Since she couldn't deny that she'd been having those very thoughts, she didn't bother to try.

He pressed his lips to her forehead. "It's okay to relax, Katie. I promise you're safe with me."

Little by little, her muscles gave way to the drowsiness that tugged her under. She shifted her legs, trying to find some relief from the dull throb between them. The sensation was new to her and one she looked forward to exploring more in-depth. She choked back a giggle at the direction her thoughts had taken.

"What're you thinking about now?" he asked.

"I can't tell you."

"Oh come on! Now you have to tell me."

She dissolved into laughter. "I really can't."

"Yes, you can! Do I need to tickle it out of you?"

"Don't you dare."

He raised his hand in a menacing claw that hung above her, making her forget all about the storm raging outside or all the reasons she'd stayed away from men for so long.

"Shane?"

He dropped his arm and put it around her. "Yeah?"

"I'm really glad I waited to have my first date with you."

Leaning in, he kept his eyes open when he kissed her. "So am I, honey."

CHAPTER 13

The sharp pain in her injured foot woke Katie the next morning. Shane was long gone, but he'd left a note on the pillow next to her.

Morning! Hope your foot doesn't hurt too much. I have to work until about five today, but I'll come by after I get home and grab a shower. What do you think of Italian food? I had a great time last night. Shane

Katie sighed with happiness as she reread the note. He was so sweet and had been incredibly kind and accommodating last night—not only when she injured her foot, but after she told him theirs was her first-ever date. He'd made her feel special, and she was eager to see him again later.

She got up, reached for her crutches and hobbled to the bathroom. Figuring out the stairs and getting around the hotel ought to be fun, she thought after she'd brushed her teeth and hair and struggled into a tank top and a pair of shorts, nearly losing her balance several times in the process.

A knock on her door had her hobbling to answer it.

"I was hoping I wasn't too early," her grandmother said before stopping to stare at the crutches. "What happened, honey?"

"Stepped on something sharp on the beach last night."

"Oh my goodness! Are you all right? Did you see the doctor?"

Katie nodded and went to sit on the edge of her bed. Adele came in after her, shutting the door. "I was with Shane, and he took me to the clinic where Doctor David stitched me up."

"I'm so sorry you got hurt. You could've come to get me. I hope you know that. I almost came up to check on you during the storm."

Katie swallowed hard and tried not to laugh at the thought of her grandmother finding Shane offering comfort during the storm.

"I remember how much you hate them."

"I was fine, but thanks for thinking of me."

"I was hoping I could talk you into some shopping and maybe lunch today, but I can see we'll need to do something much more relaxing, such as lounge on the deck all day and let people wait on us hand and *foot*."

Katie laughed at her grandmother's irreverence. The time she and her siblings had spent here with Adele and Russ had saved their childhood from being utterly miserable, and her grandparents had stayed faithfully devoted to their grandchildren even after they'd become adults. "I'd love to do that."

"Let's figure out how to get you downstairs."

Adele carried one of the crutches while Katie went down a stair at a time, using the rail and the other crutch as she made her way. Shane's method the night before had been far more efficient—and enjoyable. Thinking about him made her feel giddy and excited as she anticipated spending more time with him.

Her grandmother helped her get settled at a table on the deck and asked that coffee be delivered to Katie.

"I do love how you get stuff done, Gram."

Adele took the seat across from Katie. "I may be retired, but I still know how to make things happen."

Katie gazed out at the sparkling blue water. "This is still the best view in the whole world."

"Even after what happened the other day?"

"I'm trying not to let that ruin one of my favorite places."

"I'm glad to hear that. You've always loved the beach and swimming."

"I'll get back to it. As soon as I'm allowed to get my foot wet."

"So you were walking along on the beach and sliced it open?"

As their coffee was delivered, Katie nodded. "We'd come back from the dinner at Shane's uncle's marina where they cooked the huge tuna Shane caught yesterday. He suggested a walk on the beach, and we were having a really nice time when I cut my foot. He was great about it. He even carried me back to the hotel and took me to the clinic after he called Dr. David."

"I'm not surprised. He seems like a very fine young man."

"He is."

Adele raised her brow in question. "And we already know this for sure?"

"Everyone has sung his praises—Owen, Laura, Mom. He's... Well, he's easy to talk to and fun to be with. I don't feel worried about all the things I always worry about when I'm with him. I'm not constantly waiting for him to turn into someone else, because people I trust have assured me he won't. That goes a long way with me."

"I'm so happy to see you taking this step, my darling. I can't tell you how much I've worried about you and the others." She shook her head. "The worry has been overwhelming at times."

"I speak for all of us when I tell you we don't want you to worry about us. We're all doing well and coping in our own ways. It's going to be better now that the legal stuff is over and with Mom getting engaged. What do you think of that news?"

"I'm delighted for her. Charlie is a wonderful guy and treats her so lovingly. No one deserves that more than she does."

"You're so right. I love to see her so happy. I realized yesterday that I've never seen her look like that before—happy, content, relaxed. She was always on edge, waiting for the next explosion." Katie shook her head to rid her mind of those unhappy memories.

"It is indeed nice to see—not just on her, but on you, too."

The waitress returned to their table to see if they were interested in ordering breakfast.

"Nothing for me," Adele said. "I ate hours ago, but my granddaughter is probably hungry."

"I am," Katie said. "The egg white omelet would be great."

"Coming right up."

She enjoyed more coffee, the omelet and a lively conversation with her always-entertaining grandmother. It was such a relief to not have to dread going back to work to deal with Doctor Strangelove.

Speaking of doctors, Katie was surprised to see David Lawrence coming across the deck to their table.

"Hi there," David said.

"Gram, this is Doctor David Lawrence. David, my grandmother, Adele Kincaid."

"Yes, we met at the wedding," Adele said as she shook his hand. "Nice to see you again. I understand we owe you a debt of thanks for coming in last night to tend to Katie."

"I was happy to do it. How is it today?"

"Sore."

"It will be for a day or two. A couple of ibuprofen will take the edge off."

"I'll take some now that I've eaten."

"Do you mind if I join you for a few minutes?" he asked.

"Of course not. Please, grab a chair."

While he did that, Katie exchanged quizzical glances with her grandmother.

"Sorry to barge in on your breakfast," he said when he was settled in a chair.

"It's fine," Katie said. "We were done and just chatting."

"After we met last night, I was thinking about how you mentioned you're a nurse practitioner at home. We're desperately in need of more help at the clinic, and I wondered if you'd have any interest in relocating."

Katie stared at him as her grandmother beamed with pleasure. "What a lovely offer," Adele said. "What do you think, Katie?"

"I, um, I don't know what to think."

"I'm sorry to drop it on you this way, but we've been overwhelmed for quite some time now, and our uptick in patient load has made it possible to consider hiring another full-time nurse practitioner. We already have Victoria Stevens, our nurse practitioner-midwife, but the two of us are utterly swamped. When you said you were a nurse practitioner in a family practice, my wheels began to spin."

Katie's wheels were spinning right along with his.

"What's your situation at home?" he asked.

"Funny you should ask. I recently quit my job in that family practice."

David placed his hand over his heart. "Don't play with me."

Katie laughed at his boyish grin. "I really did quit right before I came here and was going to look for a job when I got back to Texas after some time here with my family."

"Would you consider relocating to our lovely island?"

Katie thought about the momentous few days she'd already had on Gansett and how much she'd enjoyed spending time with her mother, grandparents, Owen, Laura, Holden—and Shane, not to mention the rest of the McCarthy family. What would it be like to be here all the time, surrounded by her family and new friends like Shane and his family?

"Katie?" Adele said. "What do you think?"

"I'd love to hear more about the job."

"Fair enough." David withdrew a business card from his wallet and handed it to her. "My cell number is on there. Feel free to give me a call when you're getting around better, and we'll set up a time for you to come in. Or just stop by, and I'll fit you in between patients."

"Thank you so much for thinking of me for the job."

"No problem. I hope you'll give it some thought and remember the word 'desperate' as you do your thinking."

Katie laughed at the pleading face he made to go with the word desperate. "I'll definitely be in touch."

"I'll look forward to hearing from you. Adele, it was a pleasure seeing you again."

"Likewise."

"Back to the salt mines," he said, leaving them with a wave.

"Well, how about that?" Adele said when they were alone again.

"Rather unexpected."

"A very interesting offer, to say the least, and allow me to sweeten the pot by telling you that Pop and I are talking about moving back to the island in the spring."

"You are? Really?"

"Uh-huh. We've had enough of the Florida sun. We'll be looking for a little place on the island before we go home later this month."

"No one moves from south to north, you know. It's just not done."

Adele laughed. "Especially at our age, when we're considered 'snow birds.' We'll probably keep our place down there to run away to when the Gansett winter gets too cold, but we want to be here. It was our home for a long time, and we miss it."

Katie reached across the table for her grandmother's hand. "None of us will ever forget what you guys did for Jeff when he needed you."

"That was the very least we could do. After we found out the truth of what'd been going on for all those years… I think I could've actually committed murder if I'd gotten your father alone in a room."

"You'd have to get in a very long line."

"I don't want to spend one more second of my life—or yours—thinking or talking about him. I'd much rather talk about your evening with the oh-so-handsome Shane McCarthy."

Katie was well aware of the fact that her face was turning bright red, because she could feel the heat stealing into her cheeks.

Adele never missed a thing, especially a good blush. "Oh. *My.* So I take it you had a good time?"

"A very nice time, except for the trip to the clinic and the stitches portion of the evening. But even then, he was terrific." She leaned in closer to her grandmother. "And he stayed with me during the storm."

"Did he now?"

"Uh-huh. He was very nice about everything."

"I'm so glad you agreed to go out with him, honey. You can't do better than that handsome young man. He's all dark and broody until his little nephew is around, and then he lights up. It's good to know he has that kind of joy in him."

Katie absorbed her grandmother's astute assessment like a hungry sponge. "The reason he's dark and broody is because he had a miserable experience with his ex-wife, who hid a serious addiction to pain meds from him the whole time they were married. He paid for her to go to rehab, and she thanked him with a divorce."

"Oh dear," Adele said. "No wonder why he seems so quiet and withdrawn much of the time."

"He's really sweet and easy to talk to and everything, but I wonder..." She looked up to find her grandmother watching her intently. "We both bring such heavy crap to the table. Do you think it's too much? Not that I'm planning to marry him or anything. But if we're going to spend time together, I just... I wonder. That's all."

Adele propped her chin on her upturned fist. "You've waited a long time to take a chance with any man, so it's understandable that you have concerns. Let me tell you what I know to be true—everyone has crap. You don't get to be thirty years old without accumulating crap—some of it good, some of it not so good. If you're looking for someone with no crap, you'll be hard-pressed to find him."

"That's true. And it's not like I don't have my own bag of crap dragging along behind me."

"Listen to me, Katie. That bag of crap isn't yours. It's your father's. The worst thing you can do is let one man's insanity influence and color the whole rest of your life. Look at our wonderful Owen and how happy he is with Laura. Those kids fought long and hard for their happily ever after, and there's no reason you can't have yours, too. It's a choice, my darling, to not allow the past to ruin the future. It's a conscious choice you have to make to be happy."

"I want to be happy. I really do."

"Then go for it. Maybe you'll make something lasting of this connection with Shane, or perhaps it'll just be a fun late-summer romance. No way to tell how it'll all work out. But I promise if you don't try, honestly *try*, you'll regret it."

"I know. I've already had that thought myself."

"There're no guarantees in this life, and when we risk our hearts, there's always a chance of getting hurt. Speaking only for myself now, I'd much prefer taking a chance on being hurt over never knowing real, true love. I look at your grandpa after fifty-five years of marriage and I still think, 'There he is. There's my guy.' I want you to have that, too, my sweet girl."

Katie laughed as she dealt with a sudden onslaught of tears. "You've made me all sloppy over here."

Adele smiled widely. "Then I've done my job."

"You know... Last night was his first date since the divorce."

"That sort of puts you on somewhat equal footing, then."

"Um, not really, since he's done everything, and I've done nothing."

"Oh, but imagine the *fun* you're going to have doing *everything* with that gorgeous hunk of man."

Scandalized, Katie stared across the table at her irascible grandmother. "Did you really just say that?"

"You know I did."

"I love you so much, Gram. I hope you and Pop know you have to live forever, because we'll never be able to survive without you."

"Duh, of course we know that. Living forever is the plan."

"Good," Katie said with tremendous relief that went far beyond her grandmother's plan for eternal life. She felt like Adele had just given her permission to fully enjoy her burgeoning relationship with Shane, and she was ready to find out what happened next with him.

CHAPTER 14

As he prepared a kitchen for the arrival of appliances, Shane thought about the evening he spent with Katie. For the first time in recent memory, his first thoughts of the day hadn't been about Courtney. Rather, they'd been about Katie, about the deeply personal things they'd shared about their lives, the laughs they'd had and the way she'd rolled with her injury like a trouper.

He thought about how sweet she'd looked sleeping next to him when he left her room before dawn, her hair fanned out on the pillow, one arm tossed over her head and her lips pursed as if she were dreaming of kissing him. Hey, a guy could hope, right?

A racket outside caught his attention, and he stopped what he was doing to go investigate. Lisa Chandler and her sons, Kyle and Jackson, had pulled into the driveway. Like always, the boys were out of the car before Lisa had even turned off the engine and were bounding up the stairs to the front porch Shane had completed last week. At five and six years old, the boys were full of energy.

The single mom and her two boys would be the recipients of the latest house that he and his cousin Mac were building on land left to the town by the late Mrs. Chesterfield.

"Hey, guys." Shane held the door for the rambunctious boys and the mixed-breed puppy that followed them. They stopped by at least once a week to check on the progress. Shane had a feeling they'd come by every day if their mother would allow it.

She brought up the rear, looking tired and worn, the way she always did. Today she was also coughing. Tall and extremely thin, Lisa had long dark hair, a pale face and big brown eyes with deep, dark circles under them. She worked in three different restaurants in town to support her children, and Shane always felt sorry for the obvious strain she was under.

"Hi, Shane," she said when the coughing let up. "Sorry. I can't seem to shake this darned cough."

"Have you seen Dr. Lawrence about it?"

"Not yet, but it's on my to-do list one of these days." Another fit of coughing interrupted them.

Shane got a bottle of water out of the cooler he'd brought to work and gave it to her.

"Thank you. Sorry to interrupt your work. The boys were dying to come by."

"It's no problem. You know I'm always happy to see you guys."

"Wow." She studied the kitchen that was all but finished except for the appliances that would arrive on the ferry tomorrow. "It's almost done."

"We're getting closer. Another week, maybe two, and we should be ready for your carpet and paint choices. Do you still have the samples Mac gave you?"

"That's also on the to-do list." She was besieged by another coughing spell.

"You should run over to the clinic and get that checked, Lisa. The boys can stay here with me until you get back. I'll put them to work."

"It's nice of you to offer, but I can't afford it, unfortunately."

"Lisa…"

"I'll pick up some cough medicine at the pharmacy. Do you mind if I check out the master bedroom again? I'm worried about my bed fitting in there."

"Sure, go ahead."

She made it halfway up the stairs before she was coughing again.

Mac came in right as the boys came pounding down the stairs. “Hey, it’s the monkeys who’re going to live here!”

“We’re not monkeys!” Kyle said.

“You look like monkeys to me. What do you think, Shane?”

“Definitely monkeys.”

The boys loved Mac, and he always took a few minutes to wrestle with them. Shane and Mac weren’t exactly sure what the deal was with the boys’ father. Lisa had said only that he wasn’t in the picture. He must’ve been blond, however, because both boys had white-blond hair and their mother’s brown eyes.

“Go outside and play in traffic,” Mac said after a heated wrestling match.

“We’re not allowed to play in traffic,” Jackson, the older of the two, said disdainfully.

“Oh, really?” Mac said. “We used to love playing in traffic, didn’t we, Shane?”

“Our favorite thing to do when we were kids. Our parents were always sending us to play in traffic.”

“You’re lying,” Kyle said.

“Yeah,” Mac said, “we are. If you don’t go near the street, you can run around in the backyard, but stay where we can see you.”

They pushed and shoved their way through the door, screaming like banshees as they went, the dog hot on their heels.

“I’d give anything to have even half their energy,” Mac said.

“You and me both.”

Upstairs, Lisa was hacking again.

“Whoa,” Mac said. “That doesn’t sound good.”

Lowering his voice, Shane said, “She said she can’t afford to go to the doctor.”

“Ah, damn. I’m heading to the clinic from here for Maddie’s appointment. I’ll mention it to David. Maybe he can swing by and see her.”

“That’d be great.”

“So let’s go over everything we’ve got coming in on the boat tomorrow. Are you still good to make the pickup?”

Shane nodded. "No problem."

The most difficult part of building houses on the island was getting materials sent over from the mainland. Fortunately, Mac had figured out the ins and outs of that and had it down to a science. It didn't hurt that his brother-in-law, Joe Cantrell, owned the ferry company and saw to it that they got everything they needed.

While keeping an eye on the boys, who were running around the big backyard that would soon be theirs, Mac went down the list of materials and appliances Shane would be picking up the next day at the ferry landing.

"If you have any questions or if anything doesn't show up, check with Seamus."

"Got it, will do. Seamus has been great to work with."

"He does an excellent job managing the ferries. Joe always says he doesn't know how he ever survived without him."

"And now Seamus is married to Joe's mom, too."

"Life is funny, that's for sure."

"While I have you, I was wondering if I could ask you about the plans for fall and beyond."

"Why? You aren't thinking about checking out on me, are you?"

"I've been hoping I'm not wearing out my welcome."

"So you think I've been manufacturing work to keep you busy, when in fact you've been saving my ass for months now?"

"When you say it like that, I feel sort of stupid for asking," Shane said with a laugh.

"We've got two more of these houses to build, and I get calls every day for everything from new construction to renovation to repairs. And we've got to deal with the marina all summer, too. Make no mistake—I need you—desperately, but if you've got somewhere else to be, I'd understand. You didn't sign on for a full-time gig."

"No, but I think I'd like to if you're offering."

"Done."

Shane laughed. "That was easy."

"I've been wanting to talk to you about it for a while now, but I was so worried you'd tell me you were going back to Providence after the season that I chickened out. Luke's been after me to talk to you about your plans."

"There's nothing for me in Providence anymore. Everything—and everyone—I care about is here."

"That's what I wanted to hear. The rest of the family will be equally thrilled to hear you're staying. I've talked to Riley and Finn about sticking around for the off-season, too, and they're thinking about it."

"That's great." Their younger cousins worked in construction and would be excellent additions to their team on the island.

Mac checked the time on his phone. "I gotta go. Maddie and I have an appointment with Victoria at the clinic. I can't be late for that."

"Good luck."

"Thanks. You know what one of my buddies in Miami said when I told him I was having a third kid?"

"What's that?"

"'When you go from two to three,' he said, 'you go from a man-to-man defense to a zone.'"

Shane laughed at the basketball analogy. "I can't imagine three kids under age five, so better you than me."

"The thought of it gives me hives, but don't tell Maddie," Mac said with his trademark grin. "She'll tell you it's all my fault for knocking her up in the first place."

"Which I'm sure was *such* a sacrifice for you." His cousin was wild about his wife and made no effort to hide it.

"You know it. The things I do for that woman."

"Get out of here before you make me barf," Shane said, laughing.

The sound of more serious coughing from upstairs sobered them.

"Don't forget to talk to David," Shane said.

"I won't. I'll let you know what he says."

"Thanks again, Mac. For everything."

"Same to you. Later."

*

Mac drove away from the job site, thinking about Lisa and her boys and the other families they'd helped through the affordable-housing project. He gave Maddie full credit for the idea that had kept his construction company busy for the last year. Lisa's family would be the third to move into one of the houses, and he took tremendous satisfaction in knowing he'd had a hand in making those families' dreams of home ownership come true.

Life on Gansett Island could be difficult for people who worked in the service industry, as Maddie had before they met. The tourist season was short, and the winter long and cold and quiet. Maddie had helped him to see how challenging it was for people whose livelihoods dried up in the off-season. She'd even suggested they offer a community Thanksgiving dinner at the marina to help out those in need. It had been a huge hit last year, and they were looking forward to doing it again this year.

On the way to the clinic, he thought about how lucky he'd been to step off a curb more than two years ago and collide with the love of his life. If he could rewrite their story, the only thing he would change was the fact that she'd been badly injured in the fall from her bike. Other than that, every minute they'd spent together had been pure bliss.

Well, except for the night she delivered their adorable daughter, Hailey, at home during a tropical storm with the island's only doctor off-island at the time. Mac could've done without that drama. He shuddered now, even after all this time, thinking about what could've happened if David Lawrence hadn't been home visiting his family.

The baby they were expecting now had been an "accident," if you could call the miracle of a new life an accident. It was the happiest kind of accident. Thinking back to the night that Maddie had gotten drunk on champagne and ordered him to "do her" could still make Mac laugh out loud more than two months later. He'd been powerless to resist her, so powerless that he'd forgotten all about the protection they'd been using while she continued to nurse Hailey. That had also been the night their son, Thomas, had caught them in the act. A memorable evening all the way around.

He pulled up to the clinic a few minutes later to find Maddie sitting in the black SUV he'd bought when they first started dating so he could drive her and her son, Thomas, around on the island. Now Thomas was his son, too, and they'd added a second car seat when Hailey was born. Soon enough, a third seat would join the other two in the back, and he was excited to meet their new son or daughter. Either was fine with him as long as the baby and his beautiful Maddie were healthy.

This time he was leaving nothing to chance. They were moving to the mainland six weeks before her due date. He'd already secured the use of his brother-in-law Joe's house and had a doctor lined up to see to Maddie's needs in the final trimester. He hadn't mentioned his plans to her quite yet, but he had a feeling she wouldn't protest too vociferously. Hailey's delivery had scared the hell out of both of them, and only because of David's quick action had their daughter even survived the birth.

No way was anything like that happening again. Not on Mac's watch.

Maddie was ending a phone call and waved, smiling brightly at him.

He got out of his truck and went to her, as powerfully drawn to her today as he'd been the day he met her. More so, he decided, after everything they'd already been through together. She made him feel things that no other woman ever had or ever could, and she was the center of his entire world.

She got out of the car and started to say something, stopping short when she took a closer look at him. "What?"

He put his arms around her and backed her up against the warm black paint on her SUV.

"Mac?"

"I just need this for one minute. We've got one minute, don't we?"

"Yes," she said, relaxing into his embrace. "We've got one minute, but not much more."

"Okay."

He loved the way her body felt pressed against his. The overly abundant breasts she hated so much, the still-flat belly where their baby resided, the heat between her legs and the sweet smell of summer flowers in her hair... He was filled with gratitude to be able to hold her and touch her any time he wanted or needed to, which was pretty much all the time.

"Are you all right?"

"I'm fine. I just wanted to hold my wife for a minute."

"I'm glad you did, but we need to get going. Victoria is always on a tight schedule."

He brought his hands up to cup her face. "One kiss and then we can go in." He stared at her precious face for a long moment before he brought his lips down on hers, keeping his eyes open and focused on her.

"What's gotten into you today?"

"Nothing that's not in me every other day." He slung his arm around her as they headed for the main doors to the clinic.

"Mac?"

"Hmm?"

"Love you."

"And now my day is made."

She laughed and nudged his ribs with her elbow. "You already knew I love you."

"Hearing it is the best part of my day."

"You're so easy."

"So you tell me."

They checked in at the main desk and were told to take a seat and that Victoria would be out for them in a few minutes.

"So tell me what kind of traumas I can expect to experience at this appointment."

"What kind of traumas *you* will experience? Are you the one half-naked with your feet in stirrups getting probed in front of your husband, whom you hope will still want to have sex with you after what he's about to see?"

He swallowed hard. "Um, no, I'm not the one in the stirrups, and newsflash, babe, your husband will *always* want to have sex with you."

"Good to know. Vic said she's going to do an ultrasound at this appointment, even though I'm only at eight weeks. The usual routine is to wait awhile, but because we're on an island, they like to do it earlier in case there's anything to be concerned about."

A pang of fear stabbed his belly at the thought of anything wrong with her or the baby. "I don't like the sound of that."

"It's perfectly routine, and if there's anything going on, wouldn't you like to find out now so you can whisk me to the mainland and boss people around at the hospital?"

"I can't even think about anything going on."

"Don't worry, Mac. When you worry, you stress me out."

"Sorry. I'm trying, but Hailey's birth is still fresh on my mind and then P.J. ..." He shuddered over how close his sister had come to bleeding to death when her son was born. Once again, David Lawrence to the rescue. Thanks to his heroics in both cases, Mac had all but forgiven the guy for cheating on Janey.

"Stop. You're spinning. Breathe."

He panted in an imitation of Lamaze breathing, which made her laugh as she patted his leg.

"Very good."

Chapter 15

Victoria called them back a few minutes later. The dark-haired nurse practitioner-midwife greeted Maddie with a hug. "You look great!"

"I'm being more careful about what I eat this time around," Maddie said with a frown. "I was way too indulgent with Hailey and paid for it after."

"You were gorgeous when you were pregnant with Hailey," Mac said.

"Gorgeous and fat."

"Not that I ever saw."

"You have to say that. You did this to me."

"Oh no. Not this time. This one is *all* on you."

Victoria laughed at their banter. "I'm not even going to ask…"

"Suffice to say there was champagne involved," Maddie said with a laugh.

After Maddie was weighed and provided a urine sample, Victoria handed her a gown. "You know the drill. Everything off from the waist down."

"Oh joy," Maddie said.

"Victoria," Mac said, "before I forget. Do you know Lisa Chandler?"

"Sure, she comes in with her kids to see David. Haven't seen her in a while, come to think of it. The boys must be healthy."

"They are, but she's got an awful cough. She told my cousin Shane she can't afford to come to the clinic."

"Ugh," Victoria said. "I'll tell David. He'll stop by to check on her."

"Thanks," Mac said, relieved to know Lisa would get some help.

"I'll be right back," Victoria said.

"I'd be happy to help you out of your clothes," Mac said to Maddie when they were alone.

"Stay over there. This is a no-hanky-panky zone."

"You're no fun." Deciding to make his own fun, he started opening drawers in the exam room, checking things out. Some of the items were positively draconian and made him cringe as he imagined what they might be used for. "Holy shit, they've got a gross of condoms in here. Wish I'd known that when I was sending Janey out to buy them for me. Could've saved me a ton of grief."

"*Mac*! Knock it off. Close that drawer and don't touch anything."

"What? I'm just looking."

"You're stressing me out worrying that she's going to come in here and catch you."

"What'll she do? Kick me out?"

"Mac." She pointed to the spot right next to the exam table.

Because she was adorable and he loved her, he moved to the appointed spot. "Happy now?"

"Stay. Behave."

"Yes, ma'am. Am I allowed to put my arms around you?"

"That and nothing else."

"I love when you're stern with me. It turns me on."

"Mac! Shut *up*."

He was still laughing when Victoria knocked on the door and came into the room.

"Sorry for the delay. Things are crazy as usual here today." Always efficient, Victoria got right down to business, moving Maddie to the edge of the exam table and settling her feet in the stirrups.

"Do not look down there," Maddie said to him. "You're allowed to look right here and nowhere else." She pointed to her eyes.

"Yes, dear."

While Maddie grimaced her way through the internal exam, Mac did as he was told, even though he'd much rather be watching the goings-on below. But he knew his wife well enough by now to know when she was being dead serious.

"Don't you know most guys don't want to see what goes on down there when their wives are being probed?" Maddie asked.

"Very true," Victoria said. "Most of them require smelling salts after their wives have a routine pelvic exam."

"I'm not most men."

Maddie grunted out a laugh. "No, you're not. You're a freak show."

"Thanks, love."

Maddie rolled her eyes at him.

The snap of latex gloves indicated the end of the invasive part of the program.

While Victoria washed her hands, she said, "As I mentioned last time, we do a quick ultrasound at eight weeks to make sure everything's going according to plan. If we see anything that needs further examination, we send our moms to an OB on the mainland. It's all perfectly routine, okay?"

"Yep," Maddie replied, reaching for Mac's hand.

Victoria covered Maddie's lap with a sheet and raised her gown over her belly. Next came some gel stuff followed by the ultrasound wand.

Even though he'd seen this done before with Hailey, Mac was fascinated by the view that appeared on the screen. Not much more than a blob, but that blob was his kid. Mac's heart melted at the first sight of their baby.

Victoria ran the wand around on Maddie's belly, watching the screen intently. "Hmm," she said.

"What?" Maddie asked.

"I'm going to have you turn onto your left side for me, if you will."

With Mac's assistance, Maddie shifted into the requested position.

"What's wrong, Vic?" Maddie asked.

"Just give me a minute." She moved the wand around while continuing to watch the screen, almost without blinking.

A tingle of anxiety went down Mac's spine.

"Let's try it vaginally." They moved her to her back for the more invasive procedure that ended when Victoria removed the wand.

"Hang on just a second, Maddie," Victoria said before she left the room.

"What's going on?" Mac asked.

"I don't know."

She sounded scared, and Maddie never sounded scared. While they waited for Victoria to return, Maddie gripped his hand tightly.

After about five very long minutes, Victoria returned. When Mac saw that David was with her, his heart sank. That couldn't be good.

"Hey, guys," David said, his tone friendly and relaxed.

"What's wrong?" Mac asked the man who would've been his brother-in-law.

David glanced at Victoria, who took a deep breath before she spoke. "I wasn't able to find the baby's heartbeat."

"Oh God," Maddie said, her eyes filling. "No."

Victoria rested her hand on Maddie's shoulder. "David is going to give it a try before we jump to any conclusions."

David went through the same ritual with the gel and the wand, but the room remained stubbornly silent.

In all his life, Mac had never heard a louder silence. *God, please. Please don't let this happen.*

After a thorough exam with lots of clicking on the computer screen, David removed the device from Maddie's belly and used a paper towel to wipe up the gel.

Mac felt like he was going to be sick or pass out or something equally unpleasant while he waited to hear what David had to say. The small room was suddenly closing in on him. Since flaking out on Maddie, who was crying silently, wasn't an option, he forced air into his lungs and swallowed frantically to keep from puking.

"We'd like to do a blood test to get some more information," David said.

"Am I… Did the baby…" Maddie fumbled over her words as she continued to sob.

"We don't know anything for certain yet." David rested his hand on Maddie's shoulder. "The blood work will tell us more."

Mac had only felt this helpless one other time—the night Hailey was born during the storm.

"I'll get that going right away," Victoria said, scurrying from the room.

"David, please…" Mac cleared his throat. "Be straight with us. What do you think is happening?"

"I'd hate to say before we have all the information."

"Please," Maddie said, hiccupping. "Just tell me."

David sighed. "I'm so sorry to say that we could be looking at a miscarriage, but we won't know anything for certain until we run the blood work."

Mac's chest ached as he tried to comfort Maddie from an awkward angle. Her heartbroken sobs destroyed him.

Victoria returned and made quick work of drawing the blood.

"We'll be as quick as we can," David said before he and Victoria left the room.

When they were alone, Mac said, "Let me hold you, sweetheart."

Maddie let him help her up so he could sit behind her, his arms around her.

"It's m-my f-fault," she said.

"Why in the world would you say such a thing? It's not your fault. You're a wonderful mother."

"I-I didn't want to be p-pregnant again. How many t-times did I say that?"

"Maddie, honey, of course you didn't want to be pregnant again so soon after Hailey was born. But just because we didn't plan this baby doesn't mean we didn't want him or her."

"I wanted him. He's a b-boy. I know he is. I wanted him."

"I know, honey. I did, too." Mac wanted to weep and wail, but more than that, he wanted to comfort her. "No matter what happens, sweetheart, it'll be okay. I promise." He would make it okay for her or die trying. "We have each other and our two beautiful kids." With the back of his hand, he brushed away his own tears, determined to stay strong for her.

David and Victoria returned, and their grim expressions told the story.

"I'm so sorry," Victoria said, "but we believe the fetus is no longer viable."

"Why, Vic? What did I do wrong?" Maddie asked.

"Nothing at all," Victoria assured her. "Early-term miscarriage is far more common than you realize. And there's hardly ever a satisfying reason. It just happens."

"Here's the deal," David said. "We can give you some meds and send you home. You'll have what would seem like a particularly painful and heavy period over the next few days and then it would be over. The other option is we send you to the mainland for a routine surgical procedure."

"What would you do?" Mac asked, trying to remain calm for Maddie's sake.

"Because of where we are, I'm concerned about the remote possibility of complications—"

"We'll go to Providence then," Mac said. The possibility of complications—even a remote possibility—made the decision easier. To Maddie, he said, "Is that okay?"

She nodded.

"I'll make the call to get you a referral," David said. "How soon can you get there?"

"We'll go tonight." Mac's mind began to spin with details and things that needed to happen. He'd call Joe to get the truck on the next ferry. His parents could stay with Thomas and Hailey. He needed to let Maddie's mom and sister know what was going on. They'd need clothes… The details gave him something to focus on besides the overwhelming, awful pain in the vicinity of his heart.

He helped Maddie up and got her dressed, going so far as to slide flip-flops onto her feet. "Can you walk, honey?"

She nodded, but he didn't take any chances as he pocketed the referral paperwork that David handed him and put his arm around Maddie.

"If we can do anything, please call," Victoria said tearfully as she hugged them both.

"Thank you," Mac said. Every nerve in his body was on fire as he walked Maddie out of the clinic, her face turned into his chest so no one could see her. Thankfully, he didn't see anyone he knew in the waiting room as they left. He got her into the SUV and fastened her seat belt. They'd come back to the clinic to get his truck later and take it to the mainland. His parents would need the SUV with the car seats in the back.

While Maddie cried softly and quietly, Mac made his calls.

"What's wrong?" Joe asked after Mac told him he needed a spot for the truck on a boat later in the day.

Mac couldn't bring himself to say the words out loud, especially with Maddie sitting right next to him. "I'll, um, I'll tell you later."

"I'll get you on the six o'clock boat."

Grateful that Joe hadn't pressed for more information, Mac said, "Thanks."

Next, Mac called his mother. "Can you meet me at my house?"

"Why?" she asked. "What's up?"

"Could you just come? Please?"

"Mac… You're frightening me. The kids—"

"Are fine. I'll meet you there, okay?"

"Of course. I'll be right there."

"Bring Dad."

"Okay…"

Mac ended the call before she tried to pump him for information he was incapable of giving. He would call Tiffany and Francine later, when Maddie was out of earshot.

"The kids," Maddie said. "We need to get them from my mom."

"I'll take care of everything, sweetheart. Don't worry about a thing."

"Don't want them to see me upset."

"They won't." He grasped her hand and held on tight, giving as much as taking comfort. He would get her through this, and then he'd fall apart.

*

With her mother's assistance, Katie was able to take a shower without getting her injured foot wet. The entire thing required an inelegant balancing act that had her constantly on the verge of falling. Somehow she managed to wash her hair and condition it, which was critical to controlling her propensity for frizz near the ocean.

While Katie sat on a chair with her foot propped on a footstool, Sarah blow-dried her hair. "I feel very pampered," Katie said.

"I haven't done your hair in ages. It's fun."

"Remember when Cindy was eleven and decided she was going to cosmetology school? She 'practiced' on us?"

"I recall several unfortunate haircuts before I had to take away her scissors."

"Oh my God! I thought Julia was going to kill her."

"The pageboy," Sarah said, cringing. "Not a good look on Julia."

"That's not a good look on ninety-nine percent of all women."

"As Cindy soon discovered." Sarah brushed Katie's hair until it was soft and shiny. "I'm glad to know that not all your memories of growing up are awful."

"They're not. Of course they're not." She grinned at her mother in the mirror. "We had deployments."

Laughing, Sarah rested her hands on Katie's shoulders and met her gaze in the mirror. "That we did."

"So how's it going over at Charlie's?"

"Good, but…" She shook her head when she seemed to think better of whatever she had planned to say.

"But what?"

"Your father is being bullheaded about the divorce."

"Naturally."

"Charlie says it doesn't matter, that we can live in sin for the rest of our lives if we have to."

"What does your lawyer say?"

"Dan Torrington handled everything for me, and he's on it. But he can't make your father sign the papers, and he's holding out because I get half of his pension. He's so bitter about that."

"What right does he have to be bitter about anything when you did the real work of raising seven children, often on your own and frequently with his rages to contend with?"

"Part of me wants to tell Dan to forget about the pension because I don't really need it now that I'm going to be with Charlie, but the other part of me thinks…" She met Katie's gaze. "I earned that money. I *earned* it."

"You're damned right you did, and I know everything is great with Charlie, but what if, down the road, you change your mind? You should have your own resources to fall back on."

"I don't think anything will go wrong with Charlie or that I'll change my mind about him, but you're absolutely right about having my own money."

"The whole thing makes me furious. Why doesn't the general just set you free once and for all?"

"I didn't tell you this to upset you, honey."

"I know you didn't, but still… Where does he get off stonewalling you when he's put you through hell for more than thirty years already?"

"He doesn't think he put me through hell. In his mind, he was keeping a tight rein on the little woman."

"I'm so glad you're free of him, Mom. Even if he doesn't ever give you the divorce, you never have to spend another second in his presence."

"And for that I'll be eternally grateful."

"I'm so happy for you and Charlie. From what everyone says, he's a really nice guy."

"He's amazing, and one of these evenings, I'd like to have you over for dinner so you can get to know him better. Bring Shane with you, if you'd like to."

Katie felt her face heat at the thought of inviting Shane to dinner at her mother's new home to spend time with her mother's new fiancé. Four days on Gansett and her life bore no resemblance whatsoever to what it had looked like a week ago. "That would be fun. We'll do that sometime soon."

"You look beautiful, honey. Go have a nice time with a wonderful young man and let your hair down a little."

"My hair is down."

"Don't be obtuse with me, Katherine. You know exactly what I mean." Sarah leaned in closer. "Go a little crazy. It's high time, wouldn't you say?"

"What's with you and Gram today? Who are you and what have you done with my mother who'd never allow me to talk to a boy, let alone go wild with one?"

"Your mother wants to see you happy. I want to sit back and watch you fall madly in love with an incredible guy and have him love you back the way you deserve to be loved."

"Mom! It's our second date. You're going to jinx me."

"I never said you had to fall madly in love with Shane, but if you do... Well, I'd be thrilled to be that lovely man's mother-in-law."

"Mother!"

Sarah laughed heartily, and even though Katie was a little horrified by the assumptions her mother was leaping to where Shane was concerned, the sound of her mother's unfettered laughter was music to Katie's ears.

A knock on the door interrupted the revelry.

"Oh, let me get that." Sarah moved to the door before Katie could stop her. "Hello there, Shane. Don't you look so handsome!" He did look really nice in a light-blue dress shirt rolled up over his tanned forearms and khaki shorts. The shirt did crazy things for his blue eyes. The word "dreamy" came to mind, which made Katie feel like a simpering teenager.

"Thank you, Sarah. You're looking quite lovely yourself this evening."

"You don't have to suck up to my mom," Katie said. "She's already in love with you."

Shane laughed at Katie's saucy comment. "What does Charlie think of that?"

Sarah patted his chest. "He approves wholeheartedly."

"*Mother…*"

"My beautiful daughter is ready to go. What do you have planned for the evening?"

Before Katie could intervene and tell him he didn't need to tell her, Shane said, "Dinner to start with, and then we'll see."

Katie felt a shiver of anticipation go through her at the thought of what "and then we'll see" might entail.

"Well, don't let me keep you," Sarah said. "I was just saying to Katie that Charlie and I would like to have you two over for dinner. Maybe tomorrow night?"

"We'd love that. Wouldn't we, Katie?"

When had her mother become so brazen? "Sure," Katie said. "That'd be nice."

"Great!" Sarah clapped her hands gleefully. She came over to kiss Katie and then kissed Shane on the way out. "You kids have a great evening, and we'll see you tomorrow. Is six thirty good for you?"

"Fine by me," Shane said.

"Wonderful! I'll see you then."

CHAPTER 16

With Shane still standing in the doorway, Katie shook her head at her mother's audacity. "Okay, that was mortifying."

"What was?"

"She's already pinned you down for a third date, and we haven't even left on the second one yet."

"You don't see me complaining, do you?"

The way he looked at her, as if he were taking in every detail and liking what he saw, made her skin tingle and burn with awareness.

"I love your mom and Charlie, too. They've become good friends since I've lived here. It's never a hardship to spend time with them." He closed the door and stepped closer to where she stood, riveted by the intense way he looked at her. "And it's never a hardship to spend time with you either."

Say something. Be normal. Be witty. She cleared her throat and said the first thing that came to mind. "Except for that time I almost drowned you."

He threw his head back and howled with laughter. It was the first time she'd seen him laugh like that, and she couldn't believe the way it transformed his normally serious demeanor. "You're funny, Katie Lawry." He tugged on a lock of her hair as he said that, which sent tingles through her scalp. Was her scalp directly linked to her nipples? They stood up to take notice of his nearness, and she hoped he didn't notice.

"Yes, I love to joke about near drownings and other such topics."

"All's well that ends well on the drowning thing, and besides, it gives us a good story of how we met."

"We actually met the night before," she reminded him.

"We can leave that part out. Me saving your life is so much more dramatic than saying we met at a dinner when my sister married your brother. That's boring." His fingers moved over her face in a light caress that made her want to beg him to touch her everywhere. "Did you think about me today?"

"For a minute. Or two."

He smiled. "I gave you five whole minutes."

Her mouth fell open with surprise. She quickly closed it again when he stepped even closer, his hands landing on her hips and his gaze sweeping over her face.

"I'm lying." His lips hovered over hers, close enough to make her entire system go haywire with anticipation.

"Oh." She licked lips that had gone dry. "You are?"

Nodding, he said, "I thought about you all day."

"You did?"

"Uh-huh. Want to know what I thought about?"

"Um… *yeah.*"

"This." He touched his lips to hers so lightly she barely had time to enjoy it before he pulled back. "I thought about that a lot."

"Could you please refresh my memory on that one? It's all fuzzy." The moment the words left her lips, Katie was appalled at how forward she'd been. But if his bright smile was any indication, he was more than happy to oblige her request.

His lips met hers again. His hands cupped her face, tilting her to improve the angle.

Katie was utterly captivated by the gentle way he held her face and moved his lips over hers in an undemanding caress that made her entire body go hot with feelings she'd never experienced before.

"Katie," he whispered as he pulled back ever so slightly, making her want to beg him to keep kissing her. "You're so sweet. I love kissing you."

"Me, too. I mean… I love kissing you, too."

His smile made his eyes glow as he bent his head and came back for more. This time his lips were parted, which had her straining to get closer to him. She had no idea how to tell him what she wanted or where to put her hands.

"Shane…"

"Hmm?" He kissed a path from her mouth to her ear. She gasped when he bit down on her earlobe, which seemed to be directly connected to the place between her legs that she'd always thought of more in a clinical sense as a nurse. As it came alive with a startling throb of sheer pleasure, she could think of it only as a woman awakening to desire for the first time in her life.

"I… I want…"

"What do you want, Katie? Tell me."

"I want… more." She couldn't think of any other word to convey the restless energy pulsing through her body, which had been electrified by his touch.

"How much more?" He continued to kiss her neck and throat. "I know this is all new to you, and I don't want to do anything to scare you off."

"I… I haven't avoided… *this*… because I was scared. It was for other reasons."

"I know, but that doesn't answer my question. You have to tell me what you want, Katie, so I'll know."

Like a wildfire sparked by lightning, a flashpoint of heat traveled through her, making her feel lightheaded and needy. "I want to do everything."

He raised his head to look down at her, as if to gauge her meaning.

She swallowed. "Eventually."

"You're killing me right now. I hope you know that."

"I'm so sorry. I have no idea what I'm doing. I'm like a bull in a china shop when it comes to this."

"I didn't mean you were killing me in a bad way." He dropped his hands from her face and moved them to her hips, drawing her in closer to him, until their lower bodies were pressed together and she could feel what their chaste kisses had done to him.

"Oh." She wiggled against him, needing to get closer.

His head fell back and his eyes closed. "*Katie…*"

"Help me. Show me what to do."

He captured her lips again, and this kiss was nothing at all like the earlier ones. This one was all need and desire and heat, blistering heat. His tongue slid over her lips before dipping inside her mouth in little dabs that made her want to beg him to stop teasing her.

She wasn't sure what he expected her to do, so she let instinct take over, rubbing her tongue against his, which made him groan into her mouth.

His hands moved from her waist, up over her ribs, coming to a halt just under her breasts.

She wanted his hands on her there more than she wanted her next breath, so she squirmed against him, trying to tell him what she wanted. But his hands stayed stubbornly still. Breaking the kiss, she said, "Please, Shane… Touch me." Hearing the neediness in her tone as she all but begged him should've been humiliating. However, knowing she could ask him for whatever she wanted and he'd give it to her was incredibly liberating.

He went slowly, probably because he still feared frightening her.

As she clung to his shoulders, he moved his hands up and over her breasts, running his thumbs over the tight points of her nipples. Katie wanted to sob from the pleasure that coursed through her, pleasure unlike anything she'd ever known.

"Is that good?" he asked, his voice rough and gravelly.

"So good."

"Is your foot hurting?"

"Not when I stand on my toes."

He tugged on the button that held the front of her dress in place. "Yes?"

"Yes. *Please.*" Tomorrow, she would regret the way she'd all but begged him, but right now, in this moment, she couldn't take the time to worry about her future regrets. She was too busy processing each new sensation and committing them to memory.

Her dress fell open, and Shane slid the straps off her shoulders until she stood before him, bare from the waist up with only a black satin bra covering her. He touched her everywhere—her arms, her shoulders, the valley between her breasts. And then he dipped his head to kiss all the same places, making her legs go weak beneath her.

He seemed to realize that so he guided her backward until she was sitting on the bed, her dress pooled at her hips. "Still okay?"

She bit her bottom lip and nodded.

"Lie back and try to relax."

The thought of relaxing in this situation was so preposterous she nearly laughed.

"The other day," he said, starting all over again with more kisses to her neck, along her collarbone and down to the upper slopes of her breasts, "after what happened at the beach, all I could think about was your amazingly gorgeous breasts."

She buried her fingers in his hair, needing to hold on to something. "You said you didn't look."

"I lied. I looked, and I loved the view." He nuzzled her nipple through her bra, making her nearly levitate off the bed. "I'd really love to see them again to make sure my memories are accurate."

Katie wouldn't have expected to laugh just then, but how could she not? "It was only a couple of days ago."

"Feels like a lifetime." He pulled lightly on the front clasp, obviously waiting for a sign from her that it was okay to proceed.

Part of her was appalled at her behavior, and she had a fleeting thought that she ought to regain control of this situation before it was lost for good. But the other part of her, the part that was feeling alive for the first time in her life, told her to nod, to give him permission to be the first man to touch her intimately.

The bra sprang loose, and he pushed the cups aside. "Mmm, just as I recall. Beautiful." He met her gaze. "Why me, Katie? Why now?"

"I really like you, and I'm incredibly attracted to you."

"There must've been others who appealed to you."

"A few," she said with a shrug. "Everyone who matters to me adores you. And..."

"Tell me," he said as he left a trail of kisses along her jawline. "I want to know."

"You know what it's like to hurt."

"Yeah, I do."

"That makes me feel less alone with my hurts."

"You're not alone." He put his arms around her and brought his lips down on hers in a deep, devouring kiss.

Katie clung to him, wanting to get as close as she could to him. In the span of a few minutes, a lifetime's worth of inhibitions had melted away. Now, all that remained was overwhelming desire.

He broke the kiss and gazed into her eyes. "Tell me if anything is too much, okay?"

Robbed of speech and the ability to breathe, she nodded.

He touched her first, cupping and caressing, before he bent over her to add subtle touches of his lips everywhere but where she wanted him most.

She arched her back, hoping he'd get the message, but he kept up with his plan to drive her completely crazy. Until he latched on to her left nipple, rolling it between his teeth and then sucking it into the heat of his mouth. As if she'd been electrocuted, because this was how she'd imagined it to feel, she went perfectly still under him.

He used his tongue, his teeth and the gentle suction of his mouth to set her on fire with needs she hadn't known she had before this, before him. Then he moved to the other side and did it all over again, changing her forever one kiss at a time. She spread her legs, looking for some relief from the throbbing heartbeat of desire between them.

Seeming to understand what she needed, he pressed the hard column of his erection against her there, making her see stars, especially when he sucked on her nipple at the same time. Her entire world was reduced to the two places where he touched her.

"Katie," he whispered, his breath warm against her wet nipple. "We should stop before we can't."

"Don't stop. Please don't stop."

"Are you sure?"

She wasn't sure of anything other than that stopping was not an option.

"I don't want to mess this up," he said. "I like you so much, and I love touching you and kissing you. I don't want you to be sorry."

"I've waited thirty-two years already. I won't be sorry."

"Do you promise?"

He looked so genuinely concerned that she reached up to caress his freshly shaven face. "I promise."

"I'll hold you to it." He left her then, standing to remove first his shirt, revealing a tan, muscular chest covered in golden-blond hair, and then his shorts. As he undressed, he never took his eyes off her, eating her up with his gaze. Still wearing a pair of well-tented boxer shorts, he reached for her dress, which was bunched under her. "Lift up."

When she did as he asked, he swept it away, leaving her wearing only the black panties that matched her bra.

He shocked the hell out of her when he dropped to his knees by the bed and pulled her toward him, easing her legs apart with his hands on her inner thighs.

Katie stared up at the ceiling, concentrating on drawing air into her lungs while she waited to see what he would do next.

"I want to kiss you here." He nuzzled her core, leaving no doubt about *where* he wanted to kiss her.

A wave of heat flashed through her at the thought of what it might feel like to be kissed there. God, she was so far out of her comfort zone it wasn't even funny.

"Katie? Is that too much?"

"No," she said, squirming on the bed. "I want…"

"Say it." His lips were warm and soft and insanely erotic against her inner thigh.

"Everything."

He let out a low groan as he continued to kiss her thigh. And then he was tugging at her panties and removing them, leaving her bare before him.

Katie resisted the overpowering urge to cover herself, to turn away from him, to escape before she did something that couldn't be undone.

"Katie."

The single word cut through her panic, forcing her to look at him. His gaze was intently focused on her face, gauging her reaction.

"Do you want to stop?" As he said the words, he ran his hands over her legs, leaving goose bumps behind.

"No, don't stop." If she knew anything for certain right then, it was that if she stopped him now, she might never work up the courage to try again.

"Are you sure?"

"Yes… Yes, I'm sure."

"Close your eyes," he said. "Are they closed?"

She nodded.

"Now breathe."

Katie forced air into her lungs in an effort to relax.

"That's it. Do it again."

She kept her eyes closed and focused on breathing while he continued to kiss and caress her legs.

"Ready for more?"

"Uh-huh." She'd read her share of romance novels and knew what he intended to do. However, reading about it and experiencing it firsthand were two very different things.

He used his fingers to open her to his tongue, and Katie gasped from the charge of heat that ripped through her body at the first touch of his tongue against her most sensitive flesh. She curled her fingers around the comforter and bit her lip to keep from crying out.

The hotel was old, and the walls were thin. No sense broadcasting to the family members nearby that Katie Lawry was finally getting lucky. And, oh, how lucky she felt to be in bed with a man like Shane, who was handsome, sexy and sensitive.

She was just becoming accustomed—or as accustomed as one ever gets—to the feel of his tongue when he slid two fingers into her and changed the game completely. He touched something inside her that triggered a tsunami of new feelings that she hadn't begun to process before there were even more.

He gave her no choice but to let go and give in to the release that seemed to build upon itself like a wave crashing toward the shore. Her entire body heated as if she had a fever until the need became nearly unbearable, bursting forth in a blast of pleasure unlike anything she'd ever experienced. It left her panting, sweating and gasping.

"Damn, that was amazing," Shane said as he kissed his way to her belly while keeping his fingers buried deep inside her.

Aftershocks rippled through her body, making her tingle from the soles of her feet to her scalp and everywhere in between.

"Are you okay?"

"Mmm, yeah, very okay."

His smile lit up his face and made him seem lighter somehow, less burdened.

She brushed the hair back from his forehead. "I'm making this all about me, when it's a rather big deal for you to be doing this, too."

His brows furrowed ever so slightly at the reminder that he was having sex for the first time since his divorce.

Katie immediately regretted the statement. "Sorry. I didn't mean to dredge up the past."

He looked up at her, the furrow gone as fast as it appeared. "You didn't. It's a big deal for both of us. No sense pretending otherwise."

"You want to know what I think?"

"Absolutely."

Katie smiled at his firm reply. "I think we ought to get the first time over with and out of the way so it stops being such a big deal."

"Is that what you think?" His smile was a thing of beauty and made her realize how solemn his countenance usually was.

Nodding, she said, "What do you think?"

"I agree wholeheartedly." As he said the words, however, he began to withdraw from her.

"Where're you going?"

"Just right here." He picked up his shorts from the floor and pulled his wallet from the back pocket. In the same compartment where he kept his cash, he had stashed a strip of condoms.

Katie was stunned to realize she'd never given birth control a single thought before then. "Good thing one of us is thinking with more than their hormones."

"I've had Frank McCarthy's voice in my head on these matters since I was a teenager. Some things never change." He removed his boxers and took care of business, keeping his back to her.

Katie wanted to ask him to turn around so she could watch, but there was always next time. Or so she hoped.

"Are you still sure?" he asked as he leaned over her and she caught the first glimpse of his erection.

She swallowed hard at the realization of what was about to happen. "What if..."

"What if what?"

"It doesn't fit?"

He dropped his head to her stomach, his shoulders shaking.

"You'd better not be laughing at me."

"I wouldn't dare."

"I think you would," she said indignantly.

"It'll fit, sweetheart."

"It's kind of..."

"Oh, please, for the love of God, *please* finish that thought."

"Big," she said, swallowing hard.

"I thought you didn't have anything to compare it to?"

"Don't forget, I'm a nurse. It's not like it's the first one I've ever seen, so quit laughing!"

"I can't help it. You're so damned cute."

"Cute... whatever. It's absolutely insane that I'm doing this for the first time at my age, so quit laughing at me and just do it, will you?" She watched, aghast, as he seemed to get bigger before her eyes.

"Have I mentioned that I dig bossy women? Especially in bed?"

"N-no, I don't think you mentioned that."

"Relax, honey," he said on a low chuckle. "There's no way in this world I'd hurt you after being given the most amazing honor of sharing your first time."

Katie sighed. Could he be any sweeter?

"There, that's better. Just relax and keep breathing."

Sure, she thought, *keep breathing as he presses that great big penis against my untouched flesh. No problem...*

True to his word, he went slowly, pressing in and retreating, over and over, going a little farther each time. She waited for the expected stab of pain that never materialized.

"So hot and so tight," he whispered against her ear, setting off new goose bumps that miraculously merged into more tingles between her legs. "Feel good?"

"Yeah," she somehow managed to say. "Good" wasn't the right word for how it felt. Amazing, incredible, overwhelming... Those were better words, but she'd have to wait until later, until she could speak again, to tell him that.

"Katie..." He sounded tortured as he quickly withdrew from her.

"What's wrong?"

With his forehead on her chest, he took a series of deep breaths. "Been awhile for me. I don't want it to be over before it begins."

When she realized he was fighting to maintain control, she experienced a feeling of profound pleasure at knowing she was having the same effect on him that he was having on her. The pleasure was followed immediately by a swell of tenderness toward him. That he was willing to sacrifice his own needs to make her first time special told her she'd chosen the right man to share this moment with.

He refocused his attention on her breasts, tugging first one nipple and then the other into the heat of his mouth.

Combing her fingers through his hair, she kept him anchored to her chest even as she wanted to beg him to continue what he'd started. But she forced herself to be patient, to wait until he was ready to keep going even if he was driving her mad with what he was doing to her nipples.

"Shane…"

"Hmm?"

"Please…" She lifted her hips, hoping he'd get the hint.

He did, pushing into her almost completely this time, before stopping again. "God, Katie… I'm trying to go slow, but you're so wet and hot."

"Don't go slow. It feels so good." She dug her fingertips into the muscles of his back, which seemed to trigger something in him as he picked up the pace.

His lips came down on hers in a fierce, desperate kiss that was unlike any of their earlier kisses. This one was all tongue and teeth and passion.

She was surrounded by him, overwhelmed by him—his scent, his chest hair brushing against her nipples, the tight pressure of him inside her. The sensations built on top of each other until she was at the point of exploding once again. Then he added his fingers between her legs and set her off as he surged into her, taking his own pleasure at the same time.

"Whoa," he said, his breathing choppy as he continued to pulse inside her. Without losing their connection, he rolled onto his side, taking her with him, raising her leg up and over his hip. His finger traced her smile. "Is it safe to assume that was okay for you?"

"Oh yeah. Much better than okay. Incredible." She opened her eyes and met his intense gaze.

Shane cupped her cheek, caressing her with his thumb and making her feel adored as well as satisfied. "I'm really glad you waited for me."

"So am I."

CHAPTER 17

Shane kissed her again, softly this time, the perfect kiss at the perfect moment that was only interrupted by the loud, sustained growl of his stomach. They broke apart, laughing. "Sorry about that."

"You have to be starving. You worked all day."

"I could eat, but this, right here, is way better than food." He made his point by running his hand down her back to cup her bottom, pulling her in tighter against him.

"No reason you can't have both."

"So if I were to order us a pizza and go pick it up, you'd stay right here, nice and naked, waiting for me to get back?"

"Would the pizza have pepperoni on it?"

"That could most definitely be arranged."

"In that case, I could be convinced to stay here nice and naked until you get back."

"Excellent." He kissed her and withdrew carefully, making sure to take the condom with him. "Be right back." After a quick trip to the bathroom during which the water ran and the toilet flushed, he emerged, giving Katie a full, unobstructed view of the front of him. He had muscles on top of muscles and was tanned everywhere except from his waist to his mid-thighs.

He produced a warm washcloth that he pressed between her legs, as if that was the most natural thing in the world for him to do.

Katie wanted to die of mortification. "Wait. You don't have to—"

"You're going to be sore." His tone was matter-of-fact as he closed her legs around the warm compress. "This'll help."

"Oh. Well. Okay." As she took a greedy look at him, he hardened before her eyes.

"Knock it off," he said teasingly as he pulled on his clothes.

"What? I'm just looking."

"That's not all you're doing."

"What else am I doing?"

"You're getting me all fired up again."

"How is that my fault?"

He leaned over the bed and kissed her, looking fierce and amused and hot as hell. "I'll tell you how it's your fault when I get back."

"Don't take too long. I might get bored here all by myself." Katie wondered who this woman was who'd lost her virginity and become a flirt all in the same ten-minute period. Whoever she was, Katie liked her, and judging from his sexy grin, Shane liked her, too.

"I'll be back before you have time to get bored."

"We'll see."

He was still grinning as he went out the door.

Katie knew a moment of unease when she thought about which member of her family might see him leaving her room looking happy and satisfied. Oh well, she thought, if they were going to carry on a fling right there in the Sand & Surf, it wouldn't take long for others to catch wind of it.

A *fling*... The word made her giggle softly to herself. She was having a *fling*. She'd always found that word to be somewhat tawdry.

Lying flat on her back, looking up at the ceiling, her body still tingling and throbbing from her first time, Katie decided there was a lot to be said for tawdry.

*

Shane headed for the stairs, dialing the number for Mario's as he went. After he'd ordered a large pepperoni pizza and a house salad, he kept the phone in his hand. Consumed with thoughts of Katie and what they'd just done, he nearly smacked into his sister in the lobby.

"Where're you off to in such a hurry?" Laura asked. "And I thought you were going out with Katie again tonight."

For a second, his mind went totally blank as he realized he should've planned for what he'd say if he ran into her. "We decided to stay in and watch a movie. I'm going to get a pizza."

"Oh." She took a closer look at him. "*Oh*!"

"What're you oh-ing about?"

She took him by the arm and all but dragged him into the sitting room. "*Did you sleep with her*?"

"None of your business." Shane tried to wrench his arm free from her freakishly strong grip.

"It is too my business! She's Owen's *sister*!"

"Um, I know?"

"So how can you say it's none of my business?"

"Because it is, in fact, none of your business. We're both adults. We can do what we want."

"So you *did* do it with her."

"I never said that."

She looked at him with those shrewd blue eyes that had seen right through him since they were little kids. He never had been able to lie to her. "Your lips are swollen and you look all…" She waved her hand in front of his face. "Pleased with yourself. The signs are all there."

Shane laughed at her annoyed expression. "Aren't you supposed to be on your honeymoon or something? Go find your husband and butt into *his* business and stay out of mine."

"My husband who happens to be her *brother*? Is that who you mean?"

"Laura, come on. Don't do this. We're hanging out and having fun. Don't blow it up into a bigger deal than it is."

"She means the world to him," Laura said softly. "If you hurt her, it'll hurt him—and me."

"I have no plans to hurt her. I like her—a lot. I thought you'd be thrilled to see me going out with someone else after everything." He didn't need to spell out what "everything" meant in this case. She certainly knew.

"I am thrilled."

"You don't look thrilled."

"I worry about Owen. He's been through so much with his family, and he's finally getting some peace now that we're married, his dad is going to jail and his mom is happy with Charlie. I'd hate to see anything happen to mess with that."

"I'd hate that, too. He's not just my brother-in-law, Laura. He's also my friend. Do you honestly think I'm going to do anything to harm his sister? I saved her life, for crying out loud."

Shane's phone dinged with a text. He took a quick look and saw it was from Mac.

Going to the mainland for a few days. Hold down the fort for me. Will be in touch.

"That's odd."

"What is?"

"Mac. He's going to the mainland for a few days. I was just with him earlier, and he didn't say anything about leaving." Shane returned the text. *Got it. Everything okay?*

No, but I'll tell you about it when we get back.

"Shit." Shane shared the exchange with Laura. "What do you suppose that means?"

"I don't know, but it doesn't sound good."

"He was headed to Maddie's appointment at the clinic when he left me earlier."

"Oh God..." Laura took the phone out of his hand and began dialing.

"Who're you calling?"

"Janey. She'll know what's up." She paused before she said, "It's not Shane. It's Laura, and I'm with Shane. He just got a cryptic text from Mac. Do you know what's going on?"

Laura held the phone so Shane could hear their cousin as she said, "At Maddie's appointment today, they couldn't find the baby's heartbeat." Janey sounded like she'd been crying.

Laura deflated before Shane's eyes. "Oh no."

Shane put his arm around his sister, and she leaned into him, her hand curving naturally over her abdomen.

"They're going to the mainland because David didn't want to take any chances on complications here," Janey said. "They're staying at your dad's house in Providence tonight, and she's having a procedure in the morning."

"God, poor Maddie," Laura said, sniffling. "And Mac. They must be so upset."

"My mom said they were in pretty bad shape. She and my dad are staying at the house with the kids."

"Tell your mom to let me know if I can do anything to help. Anything at all."

"I will, thanks."

"I'll check in with you tomorrow." After ending the call, Laura handed the phone back to Shane and then hugged him. "Sorry to sob all over you."

"Any time," he said, rubbing her back.

That's where Owen found them when he came downstairs, wearing only a pair of gym shorts and carrying the handheld baby monitor. "There you are. I was wondering why you didn't come back up." He took a second look. "Are you crying? What's wrong?"

Shane handed his sister over to her husband.

"You tell him," Laura said.

Shane passed along the news they'd gotten about Mac and Maddie.

"Oh God," Owen said, putting his arms around Laura.

"Sorry to be so emotional. It just hit me hard."

"Of course it did," Owen said soothingly.

"It must've been so shocking for them," Shane said. "Mac was excited about the baby when I saw him earlier."

Their conversation was interrupted when several hotel guests came in through the main door, forcing Laura to wipe away her tears and be cheerful for her guests, who had questions.

"I thought you were out with Katie tonight," Owen said to Shane.

"I am. I was on my way to get a pizza for us when I ran into Laura."

"So you're not going *out.*"

Shane called upon every ounce of self-control he possessed not to squirm under Owen's intense glare. "We decided to hang here and watch a movie." He was saved from further questioning when Laura rejoined them.

She took hold of her husband's hand. "I want to go to bed."

"That's my cue to get the heck out of your honeymoon," Shane said. "See you both in the morning." He headed out the main door, feeling as if he'd made a narrow escape. Hopefully, Laura wouldn't share her suspicions with Owen. Not that he was worried about what Owen might say. But he and Katie had a right to a modicum of privacy, despite where they were currently living.

Maybe it was time to talk to Ned Saunders about a rental. Now that he knew Mac was counting on him to stay past the summer, Shane felt confident about putting down some roots on the island. The one thing stopping him from jumping on an immediate rental was the thought of moving away from Holden. Though they'd still live on the same small island, Shane liked having his nephew a few doors down the hallway from him.

At Mario's, his pizza wasn't quite ready, so he took a seat at the bar and ordered a beer. He couldn't stop thinking about Mac and Maddie and what they must be going through and how horribly devastated they must be. And then he thought of

Katie, waiting naked in her bed for him to return. Fearful of embarrassing himself in public, he refrained from reliving every second of their earlier encounter. He'd have plenty of time to think about that later.

Someone slid onto the stool next to him, and Shane realized it was Ned. "Speak of the devil. I was just thinking about you."

"Oh yeah? Whatcha thinkin' 'bout?"

"A possible rental."

"Stickin' around, are ya?"

"Starting to look that way."

Ned glanced at him with watery eyes. "Ya talk ta Mac tonight?"

"Yeah," Shane said with a sigh. "A short time ago. I feel awful for them."

"'Tis a terrible thing indeed. They were so excited 'bout that little one."

"Francine must be upset, too."

"Poor gal's been cryin' all afternoon. I offered ta pick up dinner." He shrugged and sighed. "Feels bad ta not be able ta do nothing fer them."

"We can rally around them when they get home," Shane said.

"True."

One of the restaurant staff appeared with Shane's pizza and salad. He tossed a twenty on the bar and gestured for the bartender to include Ned's beer, too.

Ned raised his bottle to Shane. "Thanks."

"Any time."

"Give me a call when yer ready. I'll set ya up with a good place not too far from that baby ya dote on."

Shane smiled at the older man. "You really are a mind reader, aren't you?"

"Nope. I just pay attention."

He squeezed Ned's shoulder. "I'll call you."

"Have a good night."

"You, too. Tell Francine we're all thinking about her and Maddie."

"I'll do that."

Pizza in hand, Shane walked the short distance back to the hotel, his mind spinning with thoughts of Mac and Maddie, of Katie and of Ned and the possibility of a rental close enough to town that he could still see Holden any time he wanted to. While his heart ached for Mac and Maddie, the rest of Shane's life was looking more promising than it had in a long time.

He had a job he enjoyed, working for a cousin he considered a close friend, and he had his sister and her family nearby. His dad was living on the island, and now there was the start of something promising with Katie. After years of slogging through the nightmare of Courtney's addiction and their subsequent divorce, Shane felt like the sun was finally emerging from behind the clouds.

Back at the hotel, he took the stairs two at a time, eager to get back to Katie. Would she still be naked in bed, or would she have gotten up and put on some clothes? He hoped she was still naked. The third-floor hallway was blessedly deserted as he made his way to her room, entering without knocking to find her exactly where he'd left her.

She was propped up on one elbow. "I thought you forgot about me."

"No chance of that. I ran into Laura downstairs and was subjected to the third degree. Then I got an odd text from my cousin Mac about an unexpected trip to the mainland, which Laura naturally had to investigate further."

"Did you find out what's up?"

"Yeah." Shane sighed as he put the pizza on the bedside table and sat on the edge of the bed. "It seems his wife is miscarrying, so they've gone to deal with that at a medical facility more equipped for it."

"That's so sad. I'm sorry to hear it."

He caressed her arm and bent to kiss her cheek. "I can't stop thinking about how excited he was earlier when he was on the way to meet her at the appointment."

She held out her arms to him, and Shane went willingly into her embrace, breathing in the clean, sweet scent of her shampoo. "So Laura gave you the third degree, huh?"

"I was hoping you'd missed that part of the story."

"No such luck."

"She *tried* to give me the third degree. I wouldn't tell her anything."

"Which, of course, tells her everything."

"I suppose we were naïve to think we could get away with anything surrounded as we are by family here."

"It's okay. I don't care if they know we're seeing each other or whatever it is we're doing. If you don't."

He tugged at the sheet she hugged to her breasts. "We're definitely *seeing* each other," he said when her breasts were fully revealed to him.

Her husky laughter had him forgetting all about the pizza or how hungry he was. As she drew him back into bed, he decided the pizza could wait.

CHAPTER 18

After the clinic closed for the day, David Lawrence spent an hour on charts and other paperwork, barely making a dent in the never-ending stack on his desk. He sent Daisy a text to let her know he'd be a little later and then locked up the clinic. Days like today made him question his choice of profession.

Having to tell Mac and Maddie that their baby was no longer viable had broken his heart—and Victoria's. He'd found her sobbing in the break room after they left. In a small-town practice like theirs, you became personally invested in your patients and their families. Their sadness became your sadness.

Though Mac and Maddie were still young and could have other children if they chose to, that didn't take the sting out of having to deliver such devastating news to people he'd known all his life.

Victoria had passed along Mac's message about Lisa Chandler, which was why he was on his way to her house now, hoping she'd allow him to assess her condition and not let pride stop her from accepting his help. Their island community was a mishmash of extremely affluent families, extremely poor families and everything in between.

Lisa and her sons fell on the lower end of the scale. David had checked her chart before he left the clinic and realized she hadn't been seen in more than three years. Her children, however, had regular checkups and their vaccinations were up-to-date. That didn't surprise him. He often saw low-income parents go without to ensure their children had what they needed.

As he approached Lisa's house, he saw her neighbor, Seamus O'Grady, by the side of the road, getting his mail. David slowed to say hello to Seamus.

"Evening, Doc," Seamus said in his thick Irish brogue. "What brings you out to our neck of the island?"

"Stopping by to see Lisa and the kids," David replied vaguely.

"The boys aren't sick, are they? I just saw them yesterday. They're around all the time. We sure are going to miss them out here when they move into town."

"They're fine."

Seamus glanced at the driveway next to his. "I know you can't talk about their private business, but if they need anything—anything at all—come to me. Caro and I get a kick out of those kids."

"I'll keep that in mind. You have a nice evening, Seamus."

"You, too, Doc."

David took the left-hand turn into the dirt driveway that led to a small house, thinking about what Seamus had said and how much he appreciated living on an island where neighbors looked out for each other. He wasn't at all surprised to learn that Seamus and Carolina knew the boys and were fond of them. People reached out here. He wasn't sure if it was the isolation or the quiet or what, but the island's residents were far more engaged with each other than people seemed to be elsewhere these days.

Predictably, the boys were running around the yard with their dog chasing after them. As they dashed over to greet him, David noticed they were dirty from a long day of play and both their noses were red from the sun.

"Doctor David!" the older boy, Kyle, said as David emerged from his car. "What're you doing here? Do we hafta have shots?"

David laughed at the predictable question. Everywhere he went in town, children shied away from him as if they thought he carried hypodermic needles in his back pocket. "No shots today, boys."

"Oh, good," Jackson said, his lips puckering adorably. "I hate shots."

"Believe it or not, I hate giving shots. Is your mom around?"

"She's inside," Kyle said. "Come on. I'll take you."

"Hang on one second." David retrieved his medical bag from the trunk of the car and then followed the boys to their mother. Inside the cluttered house, he was surprised to find her asleep on the sofa. David knew her well enough to know it wasn't like her to leave her young boys unsupervised. "Has she been asleep for long?" he asked the boys, trying to keep his tone casual. At first glance, he could see that Lisa had lost a tremendous amount of weight she hadn't had to lose.

"A little while," Kyle said.

"Have you guys had dinner?" David asked.

"Not yet," Jackson said. "We're gonna make PBJs tonight."

"We know how to do it ourselfs," Kyle said proudly.

David's heart sank at the realization that the boys were apparently fending for themselves quite frequently. "Will you do me a favor and see if you can wake up your mom for me? Be gentle so you don't scare her."

They kissed her until her eyes fluttered open. She did a double-take when she saw David.

"What's going on?" she asked before a coughing fit overtook her.

That did not sound good.

"I heard you were feeling poorly and thought I'd stop by to check on you," he said.

She sat up slowly, as if her entire body ached. "You didn't have to do that." More coughing. "Sorry."

"How long have you had the cough?"

"I don't know. Awhile."

"All summer," Kyle said. His brother nodded in agreement.

Jesus, David thought.

"Not that long," Lisa said.

"Yes, suh," Jackson said.

A knock on the door had the boys and the dog scurrying from the living room to see who was there.

David heard Seamus's distinctive voice as he told them Carolina had made lasagna for dinner and did they want to come have some.

"Let me ask my mom," Kyle said.

The boys came running back into the living room, both speaking at once as they conveyed the invitation.

Lisa looked up at Seamus, who stood in the doorway to the living room. "Are you sure you don't mind?"

"Of course not. We love when they come ta visit."

"They're filthy after playing outside all day."

"We'll wash our hands," Jackson said gravely, making all the adults laugh.

"In that case, sure," Lisa said with a grateful smile for Seamus. "Thank you."

"No problem. We'll send some back for you."

"That's very nice of you."

"Let's go, boys." Seamus herded them toward the door. "You haven't lived until you've had my Caro's lasagna."

When David returned his attention to Lisa, he was shocked to see tears rolling down her face.

"Everyone is so nice," she said softly.

"That's Gansett for you."

"I think I'm really sick." She looked down at the blanket that covered her lap. "As in really, really sick."

"Why haven't you come to see me before now?"

Her small smile didn't reach her eyes as she met his gaze. "I've been in denial. I kept thinking I'd shake it off the way I always do."

"Do you mind if I take a listen?"

When she gestured for him to go ahead, he withdrew his stethoscope from his bag, and with just a quick check, he could detect abnormal breath sounds. He continued to listen carefully in multiple locations until she let loose with another coughing fit that had him seriously concerned.

"What've you been taking for it?"

She pointed to a bottle of over-the-counter cough medicine on the coffee table. There was also a bag of lemon-flavored cough drops. Neither was strong enough to put a dent in the cough.

"I'd like to get you in for a chest X-ray in the morning," David said, hoping that would be soon enough. He was alarmed by her fragile condition.

"I can't afford to pay for it."

He'd pay for it himself if he had to, not that he shared that thought with her. "We'll take care of it."

New tears slipped down her cheeks. "I'm scared for my kids."

"Is there anyone you can call to come out to help you?"

She shook her head. "It's just us."

David tried to imagine what it would be like to be so alone in the world. He immediately thought of Daisy, who was estranged from her family. He'd been blessed to be born into a great family that had stood by him during his fight with lymphoma. They not only helped him to recover from his illness but also to put his life back together after the mess he'd made of it.

"How about I ask Seamus and Carolina if the boys can stay there tonight? That way, you can get a good night's sleep and then come see me in the morning."

She shook her head. "That's too much to ask of them."

"I saw Seamus on the way over here. He didn't ask why I was coming, but he told me if there was anything at all they could do for you and the kids to let him know. He said they're extremely fond of the kids."

"He said that? Really? I'm always afraid they're bothering them when they go over there. They're newlyweds after all."

David smiled and hoped his plan would be okay with Seamus and Carolina. "They don't seem to mind. So what do you say? Should we pack a bag so they can stay there tonight, and we'll see what's what in the morning?"

She nodded. "Thank you."

"No problem."

Lisa used the last of her energy, or so it seemed to him, to pack an overnight bag for her sons.

"Is there anything I can get for you before I go?"

She shook her head.

He handed her his business card, the one that had his cell phone number on it. "If it gets worse overnight or if you have any trouble breathing, I want you to call me. Don't hesitate to call."

She took the card from him. "Thank you so much."

"We'll get to the bottom of this tomorrow."

Nodding, she said, "Will you tell the boys to call me before they go to bed and will you please thank Seamus and Carolina for me?"

"Of course." David put his medical bag in the trunk but left his car parked in Lisa's driveway. He followed the well-worn path that led through a thicket of trees into Seamus and Carolina's backyard. The scent of baked lasagna wafted through the screen door on the back porch, making David's mouth water.

"Come on in," Seamus called when he knocked.

David stepped into the cozy house, where the foursome was eating dinner at the kitchen table. "How's the lasagna, guys?" Both boys sported freshly washed faces and hands.

"So good!" Kyle said as he shoveled in a huge mouthful.

Carolina smiled at his enthusiasm.

"Told ya," Seamus said.

"So your mom said if it's okay with Seamus and Carolina, you guys can have a sleepover tonight. What do you think of that?"

"Is she okay?" Kyle asked, his brows knitting adorably.

"She's not feeling so great. A good night's sleep is just what the doctor ordered." He kept his tone light, but he could see the concern on the faces of Seamus and Carolina.

"Is it okay with you guys?" Jackson asked his hosts.

"Absolutely," Seamus said. "We can make popcorn and watch a movie. It'll be fun."

"He talks funny," Jackson said, giggling.

Seamus stuck his tongue out at the boy, setting off him and his brother into gales of laughter.

David sent Seamus a grateful smile. He'd made a lot of assumptions in putting together this plan. "Lisa is coming to see me in the morning, so if you could hang on to these guys until she gets back, that'd be a big help."

"We'd be happy to." Carolina got up from the table and returned with a plastic container that was soon full of lasagna. "Take this home to Daisy," she said as she covered it and handed it to David.

"You don't have to do that."

"We'll never eat it all. Happy to share."

"That's so nice of you. Thanks. For everything."

"Our pleasure," Seamus said.

David drove home feeling worse than he had before, if that was possible. He didn't like the looks of what was going on with Lisa—at all. The chest X-ray would tell him more. He wished she hadn't waited so long to get medical help. As a seasonal worker in several of the island's restaurants, she didn't work enough hours at any one job to qualify for insurance coverage.

The system was still imperfect, despite recent reforms, and providers were forced to do the best they could within the existing parameters. It was frustrating as all hell in cases like Lisa's when someone needed urgent care but didn't seek it out because they couldn't afford to.

He arrived home feeling exhausted and out of sorts but excited to see Daisy after a long day apart. David was so damned thankful to have her to come home to every night. She made everything better just by being there. As he parked next to his landlord Jared's Porsche, Jared and his wife, Lizzie, came out of their house, dressed up for a night out.

"Hi there," he said to his friends as he emerged from his car, carrying the container Carolina had given him. "Where are you off to?"

"A fundraiser at the Chesterfield," Jared said, referring to the estate they'd bought earlier in the year and turned into an event venue.

"What's this one for?"

"Open space," Lizzie said.

"How about you do one for single parents who can't afford basic medical care?" David said with more of an edge to his voice than he'd intended.

"Talk to me," Jared said sincerely. He'd made his fortune on Wall Street and was now "retired" from the financial rat race.

"Sorry." David rolled his shoulders to shake off the stress. "Just a long day."

"Do you know someone who needs help?"

"Yeah, I actually do. I've got a young mom with two young boys who might be seriously ill. The boys are five and six."

"What can we do?" Lizzie asked.

"Can I get back to you about that tomorrow when I know more about what we're dealing with?"

"Absolutely," Jared said. "Anything she needs, you let me know."

"I was having a horrendously shitty day until about five minutes ago. Thanks, you guys."

Lizzie walked over to David and hugged him. The gesture didn't surprise him. He'd come to know her quite well since she married Jared, and she was easily affectionate with him and all their friends. David could see why Jared adored her. "Whenever you encounter something like this, you come to us, okay? We have everything we could ever want or need, and it's my pleasure to spend Jared's money on worthwhile causes and people in need."

Jared snorted with laughter. "She's quite good at it, too."

"I don't believe in doing anything if I can't do it well," Lizzie said, returning to her husband's side.

He put his arm around her and kissed her forehead. "And that's why I love you so much."

"You two have a great evening," David said, amused by them, as always.

"We'll expect to hear from you tomorrow," Lizzie said.

"You got it. Thanks again." He waved them off as they left in the Porsche and then took the stairs to the garage apartment he shared with Daisy.

She was curled up in a ball on the sofa, sound asleep.

David smiled at the sight of her. She worked so hard at the hotel this time of year that she was worn out at the end of every long day. But she loved the job managing the housekeeping staff at McCarthy's Gansett Island Hotel, and since she was the best thing to ever happen to him, he loved that she was happy.

Because he couldn't be in the same room with her and not want to touch her, he put the container of lasagna in the kitchen, pulled off his tie, released the top three buttons on his shirt and went to join her on the sofa.

"Mmm," she said, her voice sleepy and sweet. "There you are. Long day."

"That just got three thousand percent better."

"Only three thousand?"

"Make that three billion."

She smiled without opening her eyes. "That's a good number."

David put his arms around her, and she snuggled up to him. "Now my awful day is perfect."

"I heard about Maddie and Mac. Are you okay?"

Since Maddie was one of her closest friends, he was touched that she thought to ask if *he* was okay. "It was horrible. Devastating."

"I'm so sad for them."

"Did you get to talk to Maddie?"

She shook her head. "I tried to call her, but it went right to voice mail. I left a message for her and one for Linda offering to help with the kids if need be."

"I'm sure Maddie knows we're all thinking about her and Mac tonight."

"I hope so." She took a deep breath and perked right up. "What do I smell?"

"Carolina Cantrell's lasagna. Or I guess I should say Carolina *O'Grady's* lasagna."

"My mouth is watering. Does this mean we don't have to cook or go anywhere?"

"That's exactly what it means."

"What do you think of dinner in bed?"

"Other than deciding to love me, that's the very best idea you've ever had."

As she laughed, he kissed her and felt the troubles of his day melt away when she kissed him back with all the love and enthusiasm he'd come to expect from her.

Chapter 19

Mac tucked Maddie into bed in the guest room at his uncle's house and sat with her in the dark until she'd cried herself to sleep. She hadn't said a single word since they left the island, and Mac had respected her need for quiet even as he was dying inside.

Under no circumstances had he imagined this day ending here, at his uncle's house in the city. The house had been stuffy and hot from being closed up all summer but had been made available to them within minutes of his Uncle Frank hearing the news from Mac's father.

His parents had come running and had done their best to hide their own heartbreak as they helped Mac gather what they needed for a few days away while they stayed with Thomas and Hailey. Now that he was certain Maddie was asleep, for the moment anyway, he went downstairs to call home to check on them.

"Hey, Mom."

"Hi, honey. You got there all right?"

"Yeah. Maddie's sleeping. How are the kids?"

"They're both fine, but Thomas has a lot of questions."

"Is he still awake?"

"Dad's up with him. Let me check." She was quiet as she went up the stairs, which told Mac that Hailey was already asleep. He pictured her in her crib, her bum in the air as she slept, thumb in her mouth. His eyes filled as he thought about her and Thomas. He'd once thought he'd never get around to having kids of his own, and now they and their mother were his whole world.

He wiped away tears that rolled unchecked down his face.

"Dada! Where you go?"

Thomas still called him the name he'd given him when Mac first came into his life. Someday he'd probably drop that second a, but Mac hoped it didn't happen too soon. "Mama and I had something we had to do in Providence. But we'll be home soon, okay?"

"Okay."

"Are you being a good boy for Grandma and Papa?"

"Papa is reading books, but he keeps falling asleep!" In the background, Mac heard his father making snoring noises and Thomas's accompanying belly laugh.

"He's silly," Mac said even as he continued to wipe away tears.

"He's *so* silly. Are you sad, Dada?"

Knowing his son could hear the anguish in his voice made Mac ache. "Maybe a little, but I'll be all right. You need to get to sleep now, okay?"

"Can Papa read me one more story?"

"One more." Right then he'd give his son anything he asked for. "And then it's time for night-night."

"Okay, Dada. Can I talk to Mama?"

"She's asleep, buddy. She'll call you tomorrow. I love you and so does Mama."

"Love you, too."

After some rustling in the background, the phone was returned to his mother. "How's Maddie?" Linda asked.

"Quiet."

"She will be for a while."

Mac sat on the sofa, elbows on knees, head bent.

"But she'll bounce back. In time."

"You're sure of that?" Maddie's unusual silence had given him an uneasy feeling over the last few hours.

"I'm positive." After a pause, Linda said, "I've been where she is."

"What? You have?"

"About a year before you… I was twelve weeks along."

"I… I had no idea."

"That's because we didn't talk about it. Still hurts, all these years later. The initial shock passes, but you never forget."

"I don't want to forget," Mac said, his voice breaking.

"You won't, honey."

"I don't know what to do for her. She's…"

"She's traumatized and heartbroken, but she'll be all right. She just needs a little time to get her head around it. As do you."

"She feels like she caused it because she said so many times she didn't want to be pregnant again yet." His throat closed, and tears streamed down his face. "We didn't plan this one. We said it was an accident."

"Sweetheart, everyone says that when they end up pregnant with a baby they didn't set out to have right then and there. Neither of you said anything that anyone else wouldn't say in the same situation."

"Still," he said. "We feel guilty about having said that stuff."

"You were joking and coping with the idea of three kids under the age of five, Mac. Was there any doubt that you would love this new baby as much as you do Thomas and Hailey? Not in my mind. And you're both still young and healthy. There's no reason at all you can't have another baby when you feel ready to try again."

"I can't fathom that after going through this."

"Good thing for you that I was able to move past it when it happened to me, huh?"

Mac chuckled despite the grim conversation. "True."

"This isn't the time for big decisions or sweeping statements you might come to regret later."

"What do I do for her, Mom? I feel so helpless."

"Just be there. That's all you can do."

"She doesn't seem to want my comfort."

"That might be the case tonight and maybe tomorrow night, but she'll turn to you when she's ready to. You'll be the first one she wants."

Mac drew in a shuddering deep breath. He hoped his mother was right. He couldn't bear the thought of distance between him and Maddie.

"Take an extra night or two to yourselves. Francine and I will take care of the kids. You come back when you feel ready to."

"Thanks, Mom, for coming when I called you, and for everything else."

"I'm always here for you, honey. We love you both. Let us know how you are tomorrow. When you can."

"I will. Talk to you then. Love you, too." After he put down his phone, he sat for a long time in his uncle's living room, trying to get his own emotions under control so he could be there for Maddie if she needed him during the night.

As he scanned the array of family pictures Frank kept on a table, Mac thought about the many blessings he and Maddie had experienced in their lives so far as well as the challenges they'd endured. They'd gotten through it all—the good and the bad—by turning to each other, and Mac planned to be ready when she turned to him this time.

Using the hem of his shirt, he wiped his face and then went around checking the locks before he went upstairs to take a shower. A short time later, he got into bed with Maddie, moving carefully so he wouldn't disturb her. Without waking, she snuggled up to him the way she often did at home, and he brought her into his embrace, comforted by the fact that she'd reached for him in her sleep.

Hopefully, she'd keep doing that in the days ahead.

*

With sleep proving elusive, Seamus O'Grady found himself staring at the darkness at two o'clock in the morning as he thought of the two little boys sleeping soundly in the spare bedroom. He'd encountered them often in the last few weeks, always together, always dirty and usually hungry. After providing them with snacks and drinks, he'd had a few less-than-charitable thoughts about a mother who let her little kids run wild when there were all sorts of hazards they could get into.

Now that he knew their mother might be quite ill, he was riddled with guilt. Instead of judging, he should've looked into their situation, and he should've done it a lot sooner. Rather, he'd become absorbed in his busy season at work and his new wife at home while those two kids suffered.

Back home in Ireland, such a thing would be unheard of in their village, where everyone paid far too much attention to their neighbors. Minding other people's business was a way of life he'd abandoned after almost twenty years in the States.

He was ashamed of himself. It was that simple.

Carolina turned over and wrapped an arm around his waist.

As he tugged her close to him, her silky hair brushed against his face.

"Why're you awake?" she asked in a low murmur.

"Just thinking."

"What about?"

"Those boys and their mother." He sighed. "I thought she was negligent, but she's sick. I never bothered to check why they were running wild. I just made assumptions."

"For what it's worth, I made the same assumptions. More than once I've thought they were awfully young to be left to their own devices so often. Joe says I didn't let him out of my sight until he was thirty."

Leave it to his Caro to make him laugh when he felt like shit. "I believe him."

"He's not that far off," she conceded.

"I want to help them, but I don't know how."

"Tomorrow, we'll talk to Lisa, and we'll ask what we can do."

"Do you think she'll let us help?"

"If she's sick and alone with two kids, she may not have any choice but to accept whatever help is offered."

"They're cute little buggers. I'll give them that."

"They are indeed." She kissed his cheek and then his lips when he turned toward her. "You feel better?"

"I always feel better when you're talking sense into me."

"Someone's gotta do it."

With a low growl, he said, "I've got much better uses for that fresh mouth of yours if you're interested in using it for something other than giving me a hard time."

Her hand drifted from his chest down to find him fully erect. "A hard time, you say?"

He gasped when she stroked him, making him even harder, if that was possible. "A very hard time."

*

For the first time in her life, Katie Lawry woke the next morning to a man in her bed. And not just any man. No, this one was incredibly sexy and handsome and thoughtful and adorable in his sleep. Overnight, he'd sprouted whiskers on his jaw that only added to his sexiness.

Katie checked the bedside clock to make sure he wasn't oversleeping. It was only seven, so he had time. He'd said he liked to be at work by nine.

As she watched him, she wondered what he'd do if she touched him. Would he wake up? Would he sleep through it? Would he want to have sex again? They'd done everything short of actual sex before falling asleep long after midnight. He'd said he was worried about her being sore if they did it a second time.

While she'd appreciated his concern, she'd wished he'd been a little less concerned.

Before he woke up, Katie decided to get up to use the bathroom and brush her teeth. She moved slowly so she wouldn't disturb him. As she stood on her injured foot, two dull stabs of pain greeted her—one on the bottom of her foot and the other between her legs.

Maybe he'd been on to something with his worries about her being sore. She hobbled to the bathroom, where she discovered just how sore she really was and was thankful for Shane's foresight. She brushed her teeth and limped back to bed, wincing as she sat on the edge of the mattress.

"How bad is it?"

The rough morning scratch of his voice sent a tingle down her spine as she turned to face him. "Not too bad."

"Are you lying to me, Katie Lawry?"

She pinched her fingers together. "Just a little."

"Come here."

Katie moved carefully to comply with his request, scooting across the mattress until she was pressed up against him.

He kissed her forehead and then her lips. "Morning."

"Morning."

"Sorry you're sore."

"I'm not."

"Oh no?"

She shook her head. "Best night of my life. Hands down."

"Really. Well… That's quite nice to hear."

It was okay if he didn't feel the same way. He'd been married after all, and by all accounts had been crazy in love with his wife. Of course he'd had better nights than the one he'd shared with her.

"I know what you're thinking," he said, startling her.

"How do you know?"

"Your eyebrows become a straight line when you're overthinking something." He traced his finger over them to make his point.

"They do?" No one had ever told her that before, but then again she'd never let anyone get close enough to notice such quirks.

"Uh-huh."

"So what wisdom are you gaining from my eyebrows?"

"You're thinking that I was married, so naturally this was just another night for me, but it wasn't. It was really important—and special—for me, too. For many reasons, but primarily because I got to spend it with you."

"And that was the most perfect thing you could've said."

He smiled. "I thought you might like that." After another kiss, he said, "I really do mean it. I've been stuck in a bad place for a long time now, and it's so nice to feel good again. The time that we've spent together has made me feel very good, which is a huge improvement in a short time, so thanks for that."

"Happy to be of assistance."

Shane checked his watch. "I've got some time before I need to be anywhere. How about some breakfast on the porch?"

"That sounds delightful."

As he helped her to shower while keeping her foot dry, she was astounded by how quickly she'd adjusted to being naked with him. What should've been awkward and embarrassing simply wasn't. It was like an extension of the night before when he'd gone out of his way to ensure her comfort.

She became extremely uncomfortable—in a good way—when he filled his hands with liquid soap that he ran all over her body, making her tingle from head to toe.

"So sensitive," he said softly, kissing her neck as he cupped her breasts.

Katie's legs began to tremble as he worked his way down to her belly and below.

"Nice and easy," he said as he let his fingers slip between her legs.

Katie gasped from the soreness as much as the exquisite knot of desire that overrode the pain.

"I can't wait to taste you again," he said. "Tonight, after dinner at your mom's, I'm going to taste you again."

"You can't say that and mention my mother in the same sentence," she said with a nervous laugh.

"Why not?"

"Because!"

His low chuckle echoed off the walls of the shower stall.

When he withdrew his hand from between her legs, she nearly toppled over. His arm came around her waist to hold her steady.

"I want to wash you."

"Hold on to me." He rearranged them so he was in front of her, keeping her injured foot outside the shower.

She ran her hands over his bulging biceps. "That was very smooth."

"We can't get that foot wet for another couple of days. Wait till you see what we can do then."

"I can't wait." She held out her hand. "Soap, please."

He filled the palm of her hand with liquid soap that she took great pleasure in spreading all over his muscular body, working her way down slowly until he was nearly panting from waiting for her to get to the erection that hung hard and heavy between his legs.

"I need more soap to finish the job," she said, giggling at the tortured grimace on his face.

He gave her a refill and then propped a hand on the wall.

Katie loved that he seemed to be bracing himself for her touch, so she decided to make it well worth it. She started again at his shoulders, smoothing her hands over his nipples and rippling abs before she grasped his erection and began to stroke him.

"Shit," he whispered.

"Is this good?" she asked, fascinated by the velvety soft skin that covered his hard length.

"Harder." A muscle in his cheek pulsed as he covered her hand with his own and showed her how he liked it.

"That doesn't hurt?"

"Hurts in the best possible way. Don't stop."

Even when the shower in the old hotel began to go cold, Katie didn't stop. Emboldened by his heavy breathing and the hand he curled around her neck, she used her free hand to cup his balls.

"God… Katie…"

She watched, fascinated, as he came hard. Then he wrapped his arms around her and held her for a long time, until they both began to shiver under the increasingly cold water.

"Best cold shower ever," he whispered against her ear, making her laugh.

CHAPTER 20

After they were dressed and Katie had put her wet hair into a ponytail, Shane walked slowly by her side as she hobbled down the stairs.

"I wish you'd let me carry you."

"Not happening. It's bad enough you had to carry me the other night."

"So being held in my arms was *bad*. That's what you're saying."

"I did not say that," she said, laughing, "so don't twist my words."

"Are you two kids already bickering?" Laura asked from her post at the reception desk. "Shouldn't you still be in the rose-colored glasses stage?"

"Who's in the rose-colored glasses stage?" Abby asked as she came out of the gift shop. "*Oh,*" she said, when she saw Shane and Katie. "I know who. Come down and tell us everything."

"While that's a lovely offer," Shane said sarcastically, "we'll pass."

"I'll get it out of him and fill you in later," Laura said to Abby.

"No, you won't," Shane said firmly.

Though she was horrified by the idea of Laura "getting it out of him," Katie laughed at their banter. They reminded her of the way she spoke to her siblings now that they were older and out from under the black cloud they'd lived under as children.

Shane handed Katie her other crutch. "We're going to breakfast. Leave us alone."

"Do I have to?" Laura asked, chin propped on her upturned hand.

"Yes," her brother said, "you have to."

"He has no idea how things work around here, does he?" Abby asked.

"None at all," Laura replied. "By the way, Katie, we're getting up a girls' night out for tomorrow. We'd love to have you join us."

"She's busy," Shane said before Katie could reply.

"I am?" Katie asked him.

"Very, *very* busy."

"Doing what?"

"Come with me, and I'll tell you."

Katie smiled at Laura. "Thanks for the invite, but it seems I have other plans."

"If you change your mind, you know where to find me."

"She's not going to change her mind."

Katie knew he was joking around with his sister, but something about the way he said that gave her pause. "Wait."

"What?" Shane asked.

Katie looked over at Laura. "I'd love to go tomorrow night. Thanks for asking me. Let me know what time."

"Oh," Laura said. "Okay."

Keeping her head down, Katie moved slowly and painstakingly into the restaurant, uncertain if Shane was following her or not. Her heart beat fast from the exertion as much as the fear of what he might have to say to her. She wasn't actually "afraid" of him or anything like that, but where she came from, being assertive and overruling a man led to trouble.

"Table for two, please," Shane said from behind her as Katie reached the hostess stand.

They were led to the same table Katie had shared with her grandmother the day before. As she settled into her chair, Shane took the crutches from her and leaned them against the porch rail.

Maybe it was less than courageous of her, but while he took a seat, she took an interest in the menu.

"Katie."

She glanced at him, hoping he couldn't somehow tell that her heart was racing and her hands were trembling ever so slightly. This, right here, was why she'd avoided men all her life.

"I'm sorry. I shouldn't have done that. I was doing what I do with Laura. I shouldn't have answered for you. If you want to go out with her and the others, that's exactly what you should do." He smiled. "I'll find a way to get by on my own for the evening."

His adorably heartfelt apology and innate understanding of what had upset her went a long way toward calming her rattled nerves. "Thank you for apologizing. That scenario…" She gestured toward the lobby. "Sort of a hot-button issue for me."

"I understand. It won't happen again."

She stared across the table at him.

"What?"

"I… I didn't expect that to be so easy."

"Why not? I was way out of line and realized it about two seconds after I said what I did. You don't think I'm going to fix that ASAP?"

"How in the world did your wife ever let you get away?"

The stricken expression that overtook his face made Katie instantly sorry for asking the question. She shook her head. "I shouldn't have said that. My turn to apologize."

"It's okay. It's a question I've asked myself lots of times. I mean, don't get me wrong. I'm as far from perfect as it gets, but I was always good to her. I put her first, which turned out to be a huge mistake."

"It might've been a mistake with her, but that doesn't mean it's a mistake with everyone. If you're with the right person, they're putting you first, too, or at least that's how it seems it should work."

"You're absolutely right, and as much as I loved Courtney—and I did love her—she never put me first. Our marriage was all about her, which is something I've come to see with some rather painful hindsight."

"That makes me sad for you. I've only known you a short time, but I already know you deserve better than that."

"Yes, I do, but it took me a long, *long* time to come to that conclusion."

Katie sat back in her chair, feeling relaxed and at peace, which was a rare state of being for her. She'd been intimate with a man, and the world hadn't ended. It was, she realized, a relief to have finally taken that step. Everything seemed brighter today—the sparkle of the sunshine on the water, the clean fresh air, the mouthwatering scents coming from the plates of nearby diners. Even the coffee they were served tasted more robust. She felt more *alive* than she ever had before.

Despite the lingering ache between her legs, she had no regrets. She'd chosen the right man to take this important step with. No matter what happened between them—or what didn't—she'd never forget how sweet and tender he'd been. Shane had given her another important gift last night—hope, which had been in short supply in her life.

Maybe last night would be the start of something lasting with him, though she had no way to know if that was what he wanted, and she wasn't about to ask him. Not now anyway. There would be time for that conversation much later. For now, she planned to enjoy the peaceful atmosphere, the company of a smart, sexy, sweet man and the rare tingle of hope that made everything seem fresh and new on this glorious morning.

*

Sitting alone in the surgical waiting room, Mac stared at a poster on the wall and tried to think about anything other than what was happening to Maddie. The picture of the meadow filled with wildflowers reminded him of their backyard. He'd much rather be sitting on his own deck looking at the real thing than forced to exist in this cold, sterile room, looking at pictures that were intended to provide fake serenity.

The table next to him was stacked with magazines, and a nearby coffee station was well stocked. Mac didn't partake of either. He couldn't work up the interest in anything other than his wife. At times like this and the night Hailey was born, his mind traveled to worst-case scenarios that made him crazy.

The thought of life without Maddie was so unbearable it could bring him to his knees. He couldn't stand to be without her for even a single day. Hell, the two hours they'd told him it would take to perform the procedure and see her through recovery seemed endless to him.

He scrubbed his hands over his unshaven face, and when he dropped them, his father's big frame filled the doorway. Mac blinked repeatedly, certain he was seeing things. "What the… What're you doing here?"

Wearing his summer uniform of a faded logo T-shirt, khaki shorts, deck shoes and sunglasses propped on his thick gray hair, Big Mac dropped into the seat next to Mac's. "I thought you might like some company."

Mac had managed to hold it together all morning for Maddie's sake, but his father's kind words broke his composure.

Big Mac's heavy arm came around Mac's shoulders, offering comfort the way he had all of Mac's life, from skinned knees to broken hearts and everything in between.

"I can't believe you're here." Mac wiped his face.

"Joe got me and the truck on the eight o'clock boat. It was no big deal."

"It's a huge big deal. Thank you."

"You don't have to thank me. I've been where you are right now, son. It's a bitch. No way around it."

Mac couldn't have said it better himself. "Yes, it is."

"How's Maddie?"

"She's… She's quiet. Very, very quiet."

"She's processing it in her own way."

"I want us to process it together, but she's... It's like she's somewhere else."

"As hard as it is, you've got to follow her lead. She's going to think she did something wrong to cause this."

"She already does. That was her first question to Victoria. And I told Shane yesterday, right before the appointment, that the thought of having three kids gave me hives. I didn't mean that. I was excited to meet our new little person."

"Course you didn't mean it. It's not her fault and it's not yours for saying what any dad expecting his third kid would say." He glanced at Mac out of the corner of his eye. "I heard Mom told you what happened to us."

"She did, and I'm sorry. I had no idea."

"Wasn't talked about so much in those days. It happened, and you went on with your lives. Took your mother a long time to understand it wasn't her fault, but she got there eventually. Was one of the more difficult stretches in our life together."

"So I should prepare for a long siege?"

"Possibly."

The idea of distance between him and Maddie depressed him profoundly.

"Just remember... You'll get past this. It might take awhile, but you guys are solid, and you'll bounce back. Maybe you'll even have another baby someday."

"Maybe." Mac wondered if either of them would be willing to try again. "I'm sorry it happened to you."

"I'm sorry it happened to *you*."

"Do you still... You know... Think about the one you lost?"

"All the time. I figure he had to be a boy because we had four boys before we got our girl. He'd be thirty-eight now." Big Mac shook his head at that realization. "But then if we'd had him, we might not've gotten you when we did, because it would've been too soon after him. And I simply can't imagine this world without you in it. So things work out the way they're meant to, you know? Even shitty things like this."

"Yeah, I guess so."

"I'm going to tell Mallory this isn't a good weekend to come out to the island."

"Damn, I forgot she was coming." They'd recently discovered that Big Mac had fathered a daughter before he was married. Mallory had come to the island to find her father after her mother's death.

"She'll understand."

"Don't cancel on our account. You wanted to get together with her again before Grant's wedding, and that's coming up soon. Keep the plans. We might not be there, but the rest of you can carry on without us."

"Are you sure?"

"I'm positive."

After a long, companionable silence, Big Mac said, "How long did they say it would take?"

"Couple hours."

Big Mac nodded.

"Hey, Dad?"

"Yeah?"

"Means the world to me that you came."

"Had a feeling it might help to have some company."

"It does. More than you'll ever know."

*

After breakfast with Katie, Shane headed for the marina, hoping he could borrow his uncle's truck, since Mac had taken his to the mainland. However, when he arrived, he found his dad and Ned sitting with Luke Harris at the picnic table where Big Mac usually held court in the morning.

"Hey, guys," Shane said when he joined them.

"Hey, son," Frank said with a big smile for Shane. "What brings you to the meeting of the minds this lovely morning?"

"I was actually looking for Uncle Mac."

"He's gone over to keep Mac company," Frank said.

Of course that was where he was, Shane thought, knowing his own father would've done the same thing, because that's how they rolled. "I assume he took his truck?"

"Since he wouldn't be caught dead in Linda's yellow bug, you assume correctly," Frank said as Ned grunted with laughter.

"I'm kind of in a bind," Shane said. "I've got a ton of stuff to pick up at the ferry today and no truck." It was time to look into getting one of his own.

"Take mine," Luke said, producing the keys.

"Are you sure?"

"Positive. With both Macs off-island, I'm here for the day."

"Thanks a million."

"You need help with the delivery?" Frank asked.

"I wouldn't say no to some help if you feel up to it."

Frank flexed his biceps. "I'm up to it."

"Shit..." Ned muttered. "Don't hurt yerself."

Shane took the time to have a coffee and a couple of doughnuts before he and his father left to meet the ferry. On the way there, Shane glanced over at his dad in the passenger seat. "So I talked to Mac the other day about the off-season, and I've decided to stay."

"That's great news, son."

"He says there's plenty of work to keep me busy, so no sense leaving when everything and everyone I care about is here."

"Good thinking."

"It's that baby's fault. He's got me totally hooked. I can't imagine not seeing him every day."

"Babies do that to the best of us. I've got a bad case over him myself, and two more coming soon. Lots to look forward to."

"Yeah, there is. For the first time in a long time, that's very true."

"So just a few babies keeping you here?" Frank asked, trying to affect a casual tone that Shane saw right through.

"Why don't you say what you really mean?"

"Which is?"

Shane laughed. "Same tricks, different decade. You're still trying to pry personal info out of me."

"That's my job."

"Am I staying because of Katie? Is that what you're asking?"

"I'm wondering if she factored into the decision."

After last night, she definitely factored into the decision, but he kept that thought to himself. "She's part of it. I haven't known her long, but we're having fun together. But it's more than that. I feel at home here. You're here, Laura's here, the rest of the family… It's a good fit."

"I'm glad you feel that way. I do, too."

"What about Betsy? Is she staying for the off-season?"

"She hasn't decided anything yet. I hope she'll stay."

"Are you going to be okay if she doesn't?"

"Sure I will. I've been through worse. But I'll sure as hell miss her if she goes."

"Are you doing everything you can to get her to stay?"

"Um…"

"Does she know you love her?"

"Oh, well," Frank said, sputtering, "I don't think it's come to that."

"Hasn't it?"

Frank was quiet for a long moment. "Yeah, it has."

"Then tell her."

"I'm not sure she's ready to hear it."

"Don't let her get away, Dad. I'd hate to see you have regrets later. Put your cards on the table."

"What if she doesn't feel the same way?"

"Then at least you'll know, but I don't think she's going to be unhappy to hear it. She seems really into you for some strange reason."

"Ha-ha, very funny. I could say the same about Katie."

"Don't try to turn this around on me. We're talking about *you*."

"Now we're talking about *you*."

"I walked right into that, didn't I?" Shane asked, amused by his dad.

"She's a nice girl."

"She's a nice *woman*."

"That, too."

"I nearly screwed it up this morning."

"This morning, huh?"

"Pay attention, Dad."

"Oh, I am. What'd you do?"

"I got a little bossy with her, which was totally Laura's fault, but Katie didn't like it and let me know that. It's a touchy issue for her after everything with her dad."

"That family's been through the wringer. I know Owen has his demons where his father is concerned. It's only natural that Katie would, too. Owen, Katie and her twin, Julia, are the oldest. They witnessed the worst of it."

"Despite everything, she's very sweet and sincere. She's cautious but willing to take some risks, too. I like her. A lot."

"Thrills me to hear you say that. For a long time, I feared you'd never date again, let alone anything else."

"Who says 'anything else' is going on?"

"A father knows these things."

"Oh Jesus..." As skeptical as he sounded, Shane was all too familiar with how tuned in to both his kids Frank was. It had driven them nuts as teenagers, and now was no different. "Do me a favor and keep the speculating to yourself. She's special, and I'm trying not to screw it up before it even starts."

"My lips are sealed." After a long pause, Frank said, "Just one more thing, and then I'll shut up."

"Promise?"

Laughing, Frank said, "Yeah, I promise. I only wanted to say that I hope you won't let what happened with what's her name keep you from going all in again with someone else, maybe even Katie."

Shane thought about that. "A few months ago, I would've said no way to going all in again. It's just not worth the aggravation. But now… I might be open to changing my mind on that."

"Which is the best news I've heard in weeks."

"I don't want you to worry about me. I have absolutely no desire to ever again be where I was when she left me. I'm being careful."

"Good. I never want to see you in that place again. Ever."

"You won't. Don't worry."

"Of course I'll worry. That's my job."

CHAPTER 21

Shane and Frank arrived at the cargo area at the ferry landing, which was bustling with forklifts moving freight around with a precision that made sense only to them. Emerging from the truck, Shane waved to Seamus, who was directing traffic with a clipboard in one hand and a cup of coffee in the other.

"Big load for you today, Shane." Seamus tucked the clipboard under his arm to shake hands with Shane and Frank. "You need some help? I might be able to spare a couple of guys for an hour or two."

"I'll take you up on that."

"Hey," Frank said. "You've got me."

Shane pointed to the huge refrigerator box.

"On second thought," Frank said, "we'll gladly take you up on that."

Seamus laughed. "Thought you might." He whistled to a couple of young guys who were chasing after one of the forklifts. "Help Mr. McCarthy load up his truck and then go with him to offload. Get your asses back here, pronto." He handed over keys to the taller of the two young men. "Take my truck, too, so you can do it in one run."

"Yes, sir." They ran off to get Seamus's truck.

"Thanks so much," Shane said. "That's a huge help."

"No problem. I heard what's going on with Mac and Maddie. Happy to help him out where I can."

"I'll let him know that. I'm sure he'll appreciate it."

As they loaded the freight into a couple of borrowed trucks with the borrowed guys helping them, Shane thought about the sense of community on Gansett Island. Everyone was willing to lend a hand to whomever needed help. He liked being part of that. From the house he was building for Lisa and her kids and the satisfaction he got from meaningful work to his adorable nephew to the burgeoning relationship with Katie, Shane had a lot to be thankful for these days.

After everything he'd been through, he'd never take any sort of happiness for granted ever again.

*

Between the four men, they managed to get the appliances into the house and in position in the kitchen before the ferry workers left to go back to work.

"Thank goodness Seamus offered them up," Frank said, wiping a bead of sweat from his face.

"No kidding. We never could've done this on our own. I should've planned it better, but I thought Mac would be here to help."

Frank rubbed his throbbing biceps. "All's well that ends well."

"Take some painkillers at bedtime."

"I believe I will. If I was looking for a reminder that I'm not as young as I used to be…"

"Happy to be of assistance."

Frank took a good look around at the house his son had been working on all summer. "This place looks great. You've gotten a lot done since I was here last."

"We're almost there."

"Who's getting this one?"

"A woman named Lisa Chandler and her sons, Kyle and Jackson."

"Incredible thing you guys are doing for them and others here. I'm proud of you and Mac for taking this on."

"I give him and Maddie all the credit. It was their idea."

"And your hard work. You deserve part of the credit."

"It's been fun. The boys are so excited about their new house. They were here yesterday." Shane's brows furrowed as he seemed to remember something unpleasant. "Lisa hasn't been feeling so good lately. She's got an awful cough. I asked if she'd been to the clinic, and she said she couldn't afford it. Mac was going to ask David to stop by to see her. I wonder if he got around to that with everything else that happened yesterday. I'll have to check on them later. Anyway… Let me give you a ride back to the marina so I can grab my bike."

"I hope you're being careful on that contraption."

"I love that contraption."

"I hate it."

"You should take Betsy for a ride on it. Chicks dig guys with bikes."

"They also dig guys with all their limbs intact, so I think I'll pass."

"Chickenshit."

"Yep."

Fortified by the quality time with his son, Frank parted company with him, promising to talk soon. He loved seeing Shane doing so much better and moving on with his life. If he ever ran into his ex-daughter-in-law, he'd have a few choice words for her after the way she'd treated Shane. Same could be said for the ex-son-in-law. Laura had gotten it right the second time around, and Frank could only hope the same would be true for Shane.

He liked him with Katie, who was a total sweetheart. Anyone could see that after a few minutes in her presence. Despite everything she'd been through with her father, there was an aura of serenity about her that Frank respected. Anyone who could grow up the way she had and come out of it serene was a winner in his book.

Leaving the marina, he thought about what Shane had said regarding Betsy. Once again he found himself heading for her house rather than his own. That had been happening more and more often lately, and she never seemed to mind his visits.

Today he found her outside in the garden doing some weeding. Her face was flushed from the heat, and she wore a huge floppy hat that made her look about twelve. She was incredibly lovely no matter what she wore.

She greeted him with a big smile as she got up and brushed dirt off her hands. "Hey."

"Hey yourself." Without hesitation, he went right up to her and kissed her. Her arms encircled his neck and kept him there for a second kiss. "Nice to see you, too."

She smiled up at him, and all of a sudden he could no longer hold back the things he wanted to tell her.

"What is it?" she asked, taking a closer look at him.

"I need to tell you something."

"Bad news?"

"No, sweetheart, the best kind of news. At least I think it is. I hope you will, too."

"Okay…"

"It seems that at some point over this amazing summer we've spent together I've fallen hopelessly in love with you, and my son told me I ought to tell you that so you know."

"He said that, huh?"

Frank nodded and then kissed her again. "I'm hoping that might make a difference when you're thinking about whether to spend the winter here. And perhaps the spring, too. And maybe next summer as well."

Betsy laughed. "Are you making some plans, Your Honor?"

"I don't know. Am I?"

"Sounds that way to me."

"Is that okay?"

She took hold of his hand and led him inside, shedding the hat as she went. In the kitchen, she turned to him and put her arms around him at his waist. "It seems," she said as she kissed him, "that I've fallen rather hopelessly in love, too, which was the last thing I expected to happen when I came here looking for answers about Steve's accident."

Frank experienced a profound sense of relief at hearing she shared his feelings. "And does this development make you happy?"

"Very happy. Happier than I've been in a long time, which also makes me feel guilty in some ways."

"Because of Steve."

She nodded. "Like, what right do I have to be falling in love when his life is over?"

"Would he want you to feel that way?"

"Oh God, no. He was the ultimate optimist. 'Everything will work out,' he'd say, no matter the situation."

"Then perhaps it might be okay for you to follow his lead and allow yourself to be happy if that's what he would've wanted for you."

"It is. He was always after me to start dating since he was grown and out of the house." She looked up at him with the soft brown eyes that had slain him from the first time he saw her. "He'd like you."

"Would he? That's nice to hear."

She nodded. "He liked honorable men who did the right thing as a matter of course and not just when it suited them."

"That's a very nice thing to say."

"It's true."

"So…"

"So…"

"Where do we go from here?" he asked.

"How does bed sound?"

Frank hadn't expected her to say that and laughed at her audaciousness. "It sounds like an exceptional idea. Except… I was working with Shane all morning. Once again, I could use a shower."

"I'm kind of dirty myself after gardening."

She took off toward the bathroom, and Frank followed her, feeling like a teenager caught in the throes of first love.

*

Katie hitched a ride to the clinic with her mother, who'd spent the morning working with Laura in the hotel office and was on her way to the hair salon. "I'll pick you up after my appointment," Sarah said when she pulled up to the main doors of the Gansett Island Clinic.

"Take your time. I have no idea if David will be able to see me today."

"I'll text you when I'm leaving the salon."

Katie smothered a laugh.

"What's so funny?"

"You and your texting. We all think it's funny."

"Why? You can teach an old dog new tricks. I'm proof of that."

"Yes, but we had to tell you that LOL means 'laugh out loud' not 'lots of love.'"

"Why can't it be both?"

Katie leaned over to kiss her mother's cheek. "I suppose it can be."

"Do you need help with the crutches?"

"Nope. I got it. See you in a while." As Katie hobbled inside, she thought about her mom and the texting. Her father had refused to allow Sarah to have a phone of her own when they were together. So when the seven Lawry kids received a text message with their mother's new cell phone number, it had been cause for celebration, despite the teasing.

When Katie thought about how far her mother had come in one short year, it was nothing short of miraculous. "And look how far you've come in one short week," she said to herself, suppressing a laugh as she moved slowly toward the reception desk.

"May I help you?" the older woman working the desk asked.

"I wondered if Dr. Lawrence has a few minutes."

"Your name, please?"

"Katie Lawry."

She eyed Katie's crutches. "Do you have an appointment?"

"No, I don't. He asked me to stop by, though."

"I'll check with him. Have a seat."

"Thank you." Katie hobbled to the row of chairs and had just sat down when David emerged through double doors, escorting a patient to the reception desk. The woman was young but frail-looking, and he spoke softly to her.

She nodded, thanked him and walked out the main door.

David watched her go with a look of trepidation on his face.

Katie wondered what that was about.

Then David saw her, and his expression totally transformed as he walked over to her. "Tell me you're here to solve all my problems."

Katie laughed. "I'm not sure I can solve *all* of them, but I'm here to talk."

"Come in." He waited for her to get up and held the crutches for her.

"Thank you."

"How's the foot?"

"Better than yesterday."

"That's the goal. I'll take a quick look while you're here." He escorted her into his office and told the medical tech working the floor that he'd be a few minutes. "Another day, another bout of insanity," he said as he dropped into the chair behind his cluttered desk. It was only ten o'clock, and he already looked exhausted. "Tough case this morning. Thirty-one-year-old single mother of two. I suspect late-stage lung cancer."

"Oh my God. That's awful. Was that her who just left?"

He nodded and then grimaced. "She put off coming in because she couldn't afford it."

"I hate hearing that."

"You and me both. Anyway…" He seemed to make an effort to shift gears. "Let's talk about you and your plans."

"I don't really have any plans at the moment, which is a first. I'm enjoying some unexpected time off."

"You said you worked for a family practice in Texas."

"Yes, for nearly seven years. I did two years in an emergency room before that."

"How do you feel about a small-town practice? No two days are ever the same."

"It sounds… challenging."

"It is, but it's also very rewarding in its own way. You get to know your patients and their families really well, and with medical services so limited here, you feel like you're making a big contribution to the community."

"I like the sound of that."

"What I really need is someone to see to the routine appointments while I handle patients who are actually ill or injured." He talked about salary and benefits and schedules for a few minutes. "If you're interested, I'll put it all in writing."

"How soon are you looking to fill the position?"

"Yesterday?" he said with a grin that faltered when he glanced at his computer screen after a chime sounded. "*Shit*… I'd hoped I was wrong." He turned the screen to show her the images that showed huge tumors on both lungs.

"Oh wow." Katie's heart broke for the young mother and her children. "I have some hospice training, too, if that would help."

"Please say you'll take the job," he said quietly.

"I'll take the job with one condition."

"Name it."

"You'll understand if I decide later that island life isn't for me."

"Give me six months. You'll get a taste for winter here in that time, so you'll know what you're in for."

"Done."

"Really? You don't need to think about it?"

"I've thought a lot about it since we first talked about it, and it's time for something new. This feels like the right move at the right time."

"I can't tell you how much I appreciate it. We'll pay for you to get your license in Rhode Island, and I just need to check some references. A formality, of course."

Katie swallowed hard. "Um, about that... I left my job with the family practice under less-than-ideal circumstances."

"How do you mean?"

Katie did not want to talk about this, but what choice did she have if she wanted the new job? "He... The doctor... He came on to me, and I, well... I think I broke his nose, among other things."

To his credit, David showed no reaction other than a raised eyebrow. "Other things?"

"Testicles," she said with a grimace.

"Ouch. Sounds like he had it coming, though."

"He'd had it coming for years by the time it actually happened."

"Are there, perhaps, other people or doctors in the practice who could attest to your qualifications?"

"I can give you a couple of names."

"Excellent."

"So the fact that I basically assaulted my former employer isn't a problem?"

"Not for me. Probably was for him, though."

Katie laughed. "I sure hope so."

A knock sounded at the door. "Come in," David called.

A dark-haired woman stuck her head in. "I need you."

"Come here for one second."

She came into the office.

"Victoria Stevens, nurse practitioner-midwife, meet Katie Lawry, nurse practitioner, who'll be joining our team..."

"The Tuesday after Labor Day." Katie decided she deserved some more time off after what she'd put up with from Doctor Strangelove.

"You're not screwing with me, are you?" Victoria asked David, who laughed.

"Definitely not screwing with you."

"You'll understand my need to hug you, right?" Victoria said to Katie as she proceeded to do just that while Katie laughed.

"Thank you, *Jesus*," Victoria said.

"You can call me Katie."

"I like her," Victoria said to David, who laughed. "I like her so much."

Katie decided she liked Victoria, too, and she was looking forward to her new job.

Chapter 22

Katie was leaving the downstairs kitchen with a tall glass of lemonade and a new magazine she'd bought at Abby's store when Shane came in from work. She took one look at him—handsome, tanned and dirty from working all day—and she wanted him.

Judging by the heated gaze he directed her way, he felt the same.

"What happened to the crutches?" he asked.

"I've discovered if I walk on my toes, I can get around without irritating the cut. And the crutches were killing my arms." She looked up at him, drinking in the sight of his handsome face. "I have some big news."

"Do tell."

"I got a job at the clinic, starting next Tuesday."

His eyes went wide. "So you're staying?"

"Looks that way."

"That's fantastic news. I'm staying, too. Mac told me the other day he wants me here for the winter."

"So we're both going to be here all winter."

"And here I thought I was going to be so bored."

Katie smiled up at him. "You look hot and thirsty." She offered him the glass of lemonade and watched him guzzle most of it down.

"That was good. Thank you. I'll get you a fresh glass."

"I'll come with you." Katie followed him into the kitchen, where he washed his hands before he poured her another glass of lemonade and one for himself. "Hard day?"

"We brought in appliances today. Those suckers are heavy."

"You had help, I hope."

"My dad and a couple of guys Seamus loaned us from the ferries. They saved the day, but I'm sore."

"You should go for a swim and cool off."

"That's a great idea. Come with me?"

"I can't get my foot wet."

"We can work around that." He went rifling through some drawers until he found a plastic bag and a roll of duct tape. "What do you say?"

Katie eyed the supplies with trepidation. "Not sure I'm ready to go back in the water after what happened the other day."

"I'd be right there with you, and I'd keep you perfectly safe."

She stared at the plastic bag, trying to work up the courage she'd need to confront her fears. "I don't want to be afraid of the water, but I am."

"We'll take baby steps. Up to your knees this time."

"You won't let go?"

"I won't let go. I promise."

"Okay." She took a sip of the lemonade, the drink cool against her suddenly parched throat.

"Want a lift upstairs?"

"You just said you're sore and tired."

"From carrying a refrigerator. You'd be like lifting a feather after that."

"As flattering as it is to be compared to a feather and a refrigerator, I can walk. But thanks for the offer."

"Damn. I was hoping to get my hands on you again, and that was the only way I could think of."

Flattered for real now, she smiled up at him. "That's the *only* way you could think of? Are you suffering from a lack of imagination?"

He moved toward her, placing his hands on the counter on either side of her hips. "Nothing wrong with my imagination. In fact, it was working overtime today."

"Was it?"

"Uh-huh."

"You could come a little closer if you wanted to."

"I really want to, but I'm filthy, and you look gorgeous."

"I do?" Her hair was caught up in a messy bun, and she wore an old tunic with a pair of denim shorts that had seen better days.

"You do." He leaned in to kiss her, and she discovered that the rough scrape of his late-day whiskers on her cheek was an instant turn-on. "Why did your eyes just light up like that?"

And he paid attention. Katie wished she could fan her face. It was getting warm in here. "I like the way your whiskers feel against my cheek."

He stared at her, effectively stealing the breath from her lungs. "Swimming," he said after a long silence. "We were going swimming."

"Right. I need to change."

"So do I."

They went up the stairs together. Halfway up, he surprised her by cupping her bottom and squeezing. "Making sure my imagination is still working properly."

Katie laughed even as her entire body reacted to his brazen gesture. "You sure you want to go swimming?"

"Why? What else is there to do?"

"Nothing I can think of."

"And you say *I* suffer from a lack of imagination…" He patted her bottom again as he left her at her door. "See you in a minute."

Katie watched him walk away, paying particular attention to the flex of muscles in his legs and backside. As she went into her room to change, she tried to find the right word to describe the way she felt after being with Shane.

The symptoms were varied—racing heart, dry mouth, warm face, a dull ache between her legs and an increased awareness of her body as a whole. She stopped in the middle of tying her top behind her neck. It was lust. She was lusting after him.

Katie giggled at the realization that she was normal after all. She'd had reason to wonder, especially with her sister telling her all the time that living like a nun, when she wasn't actually a nun, was ridiculous. Julia would barely recognize the new Katie.

The new Katie… She liked the sound of that as she embarked on a whole new life in a new place with a new job and a new man. Speaking of her new man…

She grabbed her beach bag, a towel, and slid her good foot into a flip-flop and the other foot into the ugly medical shoe David had given her, wincing when the cut rubbed against the shoe. Katie opened her door to find Shane about to knock. At the sight of his raised fist, she took an instinctive step back and then instantly regretted it.

"I was about to knock."

"I know. Sorry. Natural reaction."

He straightened his fingers and rested his palm against her face, moving slowly so as not to startle her further. "I will never, ever, *ever* hit you, Katie," he said softly. "There's nothing you could say or do that would lead to that. I swear to you."

She swallowed hard, caught off guard by the emotional wallop that accompanied his sweet words. Did he know what it meant to her to hear him make such a promise? Yes, of course he did. He got it without her having to explain it to him, because he was close to Owen and had known her story before he ever met her.

"Do you believe me?"

Katie forced herself to hold his intense blue-eyed gaze. "I believe you." And she did. He was one of the good guys, as Julia would say when she tried to convince Katie that not all men were monsters.

He kissed her forehead and took her bag. "Ready?"

"Ready." She was ready for a lot of things, she thought, as she took the hand he offered and went with him to the beach.

He walked patiently at her slow pace, and as they reached the bottom of the last set of stairs that led to the beach, he presented her with his back. "Hop on."

"I can walk."

"This will keep the sand out of the cut, and it will give me a chance to get my hands on you."

"I see how it is."

"I'm using my imagination." Over his shoulder, he grinned at her. "Let's go."

He was so cute and so sincere and always thinking of her comfort. A girl could get awfully attached to such a thoughtful guy, Katie thought as she took him up on his offer. He carried her effortlessly, the way he had several times before, putting her down when they reached the wet sand by the water.

"Hang on to my shoulder."

Katie did as he instructed while he spread an old sheet on the sand and helped her to sit. All of this was done without any sand touching her injured foot. "I'm impressed."

"That's the goal."

She liked that he still flirted with her even after they'd had sex. She took that as a good sign that he was interested in more than that. During her years of abstinence, she'd wondered how women could tell when a guy was genuinely interested in them or just wanted to have sex with them.

Now that she had one who seemed genuinely interested in her, she discovered it was quite easy to tell the difference.

Shane sat beside her on the sheet and went to work on her foot, encasing it in plastic and then securing it with a band of duct tape that he wrapped around her leg. "Is that too tight?"

"No, it feels fine."

"It might not keep all the water out, but it should keep your foot fairly dry."

"It's very ingenious. I'm impressed again."

"You're easy to please."

"Am I?"

"Very." He put his arm around her and leaned in for a kiss.

Katie raised her hand to his face, needing to touch him, to get closer to him.

His tortured groan ended the all-too-brief kiss. "Damn, you are so sweet. I can't get enough of you." He looked down at her, seeming as stunned as she felt by the desire that one kiss roused in her. "Where did you come from, Katie Lawry?"

"Um, Texas?"

He smiled and kissed her nose and then her lips. "Let's swim."

At that, Katie's good mood burst like a soap bubble hitting cactus.

Shane tuned right in to her hesitation. "We'll stay close to the shore."

She took his outstretched hand and let him help her up. When she was standing, he linked their fingers and squeezed, his reassurance and presence giving her the courage to limp toward the water even as everything in her protested.

"Breathe, Katie. I'm right here. I won't let anything happen to you." His softly spoken words were all she could hear as a wave broke close to the shore, sending cool water flooding around their feet. "Feels good, right?"

She bit her bottom lip and nodded, focusing on his voice and the tight press of his hand around hers.

"The water is nice and calm tonight," he continued. "Nothing to worry about."

They waded in to their knees, the sand soft beneath their feet, the water cool and refreshing. In a blaze of red and orange, the sun headed for the horizon, casting a warm glow upon the water and the island.

"Pretty this time of day," Katie said.

"Sure is."

"The sun is already setting earlier, though. I remember being here as a kid and feeling sad when the days started to get shorter. It meant it was almost time to go home."

"You know what I remember from late-summer visits to my cousins?"

"What?"

"How rude the restaurant workers were by this point in the season after months of dealing with tourists. It always cracked us up."

Katie laughed in agreement. "My grandmother used to remind the hotel staff that the late-season visitors paid the same price and deserved the same service. She used to stress out when the college kids would leave in mid-August for school. She'd put us to work cleaning rooms and doing laundry."

"That sounds like fun."

"It was," Katie said wistfully. "We'd do anything she asked of us. She was—and is—our hero. She got us out of hell for two months every year. She could've asked us to walk barefoot over fire, and we would've done it for her."

"Why didn't any of you ever tell her what was going on at home?" Shane asked.

"Because he told us to keep our mouths shut or else. 'What goes on in our home is our business and no one else's,' he would say." Katie shrugged. "We were terrified of him."

"I hate that you had to live like that for so long. No one should have to grow up that way."

"I hate it, too, but it wasn't all bad. He deployed a lot, so we got breaks from the insanity. And we had each other, so no one felt completely alone with it. Except for maybe Owen. Thank God for him. He ran interference for all of us at great personal expense." She looked up at him. "Did you know he received an appointment to West Point?"

"No," Shane said, seeming astounded to hear that. "I can't picture him in the military, though."

"Well, my dad could. He pushed him so hard."

"So why didn't he go?"

"He refused to leave the rest of us, which led to a huge fight between them. For once, Owen prevailed and knocked the general out cold."

"Wow."

She could almost see Shane wondering what it would be like to punch his father unconscious.

"That must've been vindicating."

"It was until my father had him charged with assault."

"*Seriously*?"

"Yep. He pressed charges and saw to it that Owen spent a few nights in jail to 'teach him a lesson about respecting his elders.' At first they charged him with felony assault, but that didn't stick. He ended up with a misdemeanor on his record, but the incident was enough to make West Point change its mind. That only further infuriated my father, and of course it was all Owen's fault." Katie shook her head, sickened by the memories of those dark days.

"Owen is such an amazing guy," Shane said. "To have been through all that and still be so kind and loving toward Laura and Holden."

"It took a really long time for him to get to a place where the relationship he has with Laura was possible. But no one, except for maybe my mom, deserves to be happy more than he does. We're all so thankful he has Laura and that she makes him so happy."

"You deserve to be happy, too, you know."

"Not like he does."

"Sure you do. You lived through hell and survived just like he did. Maybe he fought more of the battles, but judging from how often he speaks of you and Julia, in particular, you propped him up through it all."

"He talks about us?"

"All the time—all of you, but you two in particular."

"That's nice to hear. We love him unreasonably."

"I'd venture to guess he loves you just as much."

"Sometimes it feels like our childhood was so long ago it didn't really happen, like it was a bad movie we saw once or something. And other times it feels like it happened five minutes ago, and any second he's going to reappear out of the woodwork like the bogeyman."

"That's not going to happen. You know that, don't you?"

"I'm working on convincing myself." She realized all at once that while they talked they'd walked out to waist-deep water. "Well, aren't you the clever one, getting me to talk about my painful past as you lured me into the deep."

"You make me sound so devious."

"Are you?"

"Not usually." Without releasing her hand, he dropped into the water, letting it wash over his head. He stayed under long enough that Katie worried about him.

She tugged on his hand, and he squeezed hers. Then she felt him between her legs and let out a squeak of surprise when he lifted her onto his shoulders. Katie fisted handfuls of his hair as she tried to keep from falling off. "*That* was devious!"

He spun her around, making her laugh hysterically.

"Stop! I'm going to puke."

"We can't have that." He dropped suddenly again, taking her down with him this time.

She resurfaced, sputtering from the mouthful of water she'd swallowed. Before she could express her displeasure, he'd lifted her again, this time into his arms as he remained largely under the water. "That was mean."

"You have brothers. How does that count as mean?"

"You make a good point. I've been the victim of dirtier tricks."

"And you're not stressing out about being in the water."

Which had been his goal, she realized as she returned his smile. "Also true. Thank you for that."

He tightened his hold on her. "Very much my pleasure. Speaking of my pleasure, you could kiss me if you wanted to."

Katie wanted to. She really, really wanted to. So she linked her arms around his neck and pressed her lips to his. At first, she wondered if he was going to respond, but then she got that he was waiting to see what she would do. So she started by stroking his bottom lip with her tongue before withdrawing it and then doing it again.

Only the tight squeeze of his hands on her arm and leg indicated that her efforts were yielding results, so she did it again and again, until his mouth opened and he groaned in response.

Feeling victorious, Katie smiled against his lips.

"You're quite pleased with yourself, aren't you?"

"Not bad, since I hadn't kissed anyone until recently."

"Not bad at all. How about you do it again? They say practice makes perfect."

"I need lots and lots of practice."

"I'm more than happy to help you catch up."

Katie laughed as she kissed him—until he shifted her so she straddled his lap. Her laughter turned into a moan as he pressed his erection between her legs and cupped her breasts under the water. Remembering where they were and that anyone could see them, she turned away from the kiss.

"What's wrong?"

"Not out here."

"We're just kissing."

"Someone might see."

"So?"

"I'm not ready for that yet."

"Yet. Does that imply that someday you might be?"

She gauged the teasing glint in his eye. "You'll have to wait and see."

"Is underwater touching allowed?"

"I suppose that's okay."

"Mmm," he said as he nuzzled her neck and cupped her breasts, running his thumbs over her tight nipples.

"Hey! You untied my top!"

"You said touching was allowed."

"I didn't say *naked* touching was allowed."

"An important distinction. It's not my fault I wasn't given all the information."

"You really are a scoundrel, aren't you?"

"No one has ever called me that before," he said with a chuckle. He put his arms around her, bringing her breasts in tight against his chest.

As they floated in the water, waves rolled gently toward the shore and the sun dipped closer to the horizon. Far off in the distance, she noticed what looked like lights strung across the water. "What is that?"

Shane turned to see what she meant. "The Newport Bridge."

"Oh, I couldn't tell."

"Have you been there? To Newport?"

"Nope."

"All the times you came here, you never went there?"

"My grandparents had seven kids underfoot. It was a big deal to go out for ice cream. They bought a ten-passenger van just so they could drive us around when we were here. We didn't make it to Newport."

"I'll take you if you want to go."

"I'd love to go."

"Tomorrow?"

"Don't you have to work?"

"I can take a day off."

"You really want to go to Newport tomorrow?"

"What I really want is to spend a full day with you, so yes, I really want to go to Newport tomorrow."

She smiled at his sweetness. "Okay. That sounds like fun."

"It's a lot of walking, though. Do you feel up for that with your foot?"

"It's a lot better than it was. I'll be okay. But the more pressing question is will I be back for girls' night out?"

"I can make that happen. But now we have to go clean up for dinner with your mom and Charlie."

Katie tightened her legs around his hips. "I'm sort of wishing now that we hadn't made those plans."

"Why's that?"

She rubbed against him suggestively. "No reason."

Laughing, he moved his hands down to cup her bottom. "You know what the best news of all is?"

"What?"

He pressed his erection against her. "He comes back any time I need him. So while we might have to let him go to waste this time, after dinner… Watch out."

Katie shuddered from the promise of pleasure she heard in his voice. Now that she knew what to expect, how was she supposed to get through dinner without every thought focused on what would happen when they got home?

CHAPTER 23

Shane retied Katie's top, his hands brushing against her back as he worked. "There. All decent again."

"There's a lot to be said for indecency."

"Yes, there is. We'll discuss that topic further later."

"Is it later yet?"

Laughing, he said, "I wish."

They walked out of the water holding hands. When they reached the sheet he'd spread over the sand, he grabbed her towel and wrapped it around her shoulders.

"Thank you," she said.

"For?"

"For taking me swimming and making it so fun that I forgot to be scared."

"You're welcome. Nothing to be scared of. Think about how many times you swam here without incident. What happened the other day was scary for both of us, but we can't let it ruin something we love to do."

"You're right, but thank you just the same."

"It was fun for me, too."

He piggybacked her to the stairs, where he put her down and then let her go ahead of him. "What a view," he whispered from behind her.

"Stop."

"You stop."

"What am I doing?" Katie asked, genuinely baffled.

"You're being hot and sexy when we have somewhere to be."

"How am I being hot and sexy, as you put it?"

"Um, you're breathing?"

Katie was still laughing at his ridiculous statement when she reached the porch, where Laura was nursing a glass of ice water while Adele enjoyed a glass of wine at a table overlooking the beach. Katie wondered how much they'd seen and was doubly glad now that she'd put an end to the naked touching.

Laura smiled at them. "Hey, kids. Have a nice swim?"

"Yeah," Shane said. "It was great."

"Looked like fun from here," Adele said with a wink.

"I told you people were watching," Katie said to laughter from the two women.

Shane took hold of her hand. "We'd love to stay and chat, but we've got somewhere to be."

"I'll see you there," Laura said. "We were invited, too."

"Great," Shane said, leading Katie inside.

"That was mortifying," Katie muttered when they were in the kitchen, which bustled now as Stephanie's staff prepared for the dinner rush.

"I bet if you asked them both, they'd say they're delighted to see us together. I know Laura is, because she told me so."

"My grandmother is, too."

"So there you have it."

"Just because they're happy to see us together doesn't mean they want to watch us frolicking in the surf."

"Is that what we did? Frolic?"

"You know what I mean."

Laughing, he said, "They saw us having *fun*, Katie. No need to be embarrassed."

"So you're into PDA, then?"

"At times. Depends on the circumstances. What about you?"

"As that was my first instance of PDA, the jury is still out."

"Keep me posted. I have a vested interest."

"Ha-ha. Very funny."

"I'm serious." He left her with a kiss at her door. "Hurry up. I don't want to be late to your mother's. Got to make a good impression."

"As if. She's already in love with you."

"As nice as that is, she's not the one I'm trying to impress."

He was gone to his room before his words registered. Katie fumbled with her key and stepped into her dark room, standing there for a full minute, thinking about what he had said. Anticipation made her skin prickle and her nipples tighten. In a few minutes, she'd get to be with him again, and she was more than ready.

In the shower, she spent extra time with her razor until every inch of her was smooth. She towel-dried her hair and combed it out, applied lip gloss and mascara, chose underwear with special care and put on a red halter dress. As she tied the dress behind her neck, she had a vision of Shane untying it later.

Whatever her mother had planned for dinner, Katie hoped it didn't take too long to eat.

*

Shane rushed through his shower but took the time to shave. As much as Katie had liked the feel of his whiskers against her face earlier, he planned to kiss her all over later and didn't want to give her whisker burn.

As he relived the pleasure of kissing Katie, he realized Courtney hadn't crossed his mind all day. Apparently he'd found that off-switch he'd been looking for, and her name was Katie. All his thoughts were of her since the amazing night they'd spent together. In many ways, she was Courtney's total opposite.

Whereas Courtney was confident and ballsy, Katie was tentative and cautious. Shane had once been attracted to confident and ballsy, but now he found himself drawn to tentative and cautious. What he liked about Katie was that she knew herself. She made no excuses for how she'd chosen to live her life or why she'd made the choices she had. She owned them, and he respected that.

Her innate sweetness was also a huge draw. While Courtney had been a nice person with lots of friends and a healthy social life, sweet wasn't a word anyone would've used to describe her. Funny and loud and quick to laugh, Courtney had been fun to be around, but she'd also had a hair-trigger temper. He knew now that had been because of the drugs, but at the time, he'd worked overtime to keep the peace.

Hindsight was a bitch, he decided as he ran a towel over his face. When he'd still been in love with her, he would've said there was no one else in the world for him. But now that sweet Katie had come into his life, he had reason to question those beliefs.

Did he want to fall in love again? Did he dare risk his hard-won sanity by handing over his heart, and with it the power to hurt him, to another woman? What was the alternative? Being alone for the rest of his life? Never having children of his own? What about what she wanted? She'd waited so long to even date. Would she decide she wanted to play the field before she settled on one guy for the rest of her life?

No matter the answers to those questions, hard as he tried, he couldn't picture Katie hurting him the way Courtney had. She was softer and kinder than Courtney, for one thing. If she had to let him down, he was fairly confident she'd let him down easily. It was strange to think that before the ordeal with Courtney, he wouldn't have been quite so attracted to Katie's sweetness. Now he craved it.

He'd had more than enough of the drama that had been such a big part of his relationship with Courtney. When he'd still been dazzled with her, he'd found the drama exciting. With the wisdom that came from age and experience, he could see there was a lot to be said for tranquility.

During the darkness that'd followed his split with Courtney, he'd also had far too much time to wonder if he'd ever feel physically attracted to another woman the way he had with her. That was another question that had been resolved to his extreme satisfaction in the last few days.

He loved kissing Katie and touching her and making love with her and wanted to do it again as soon as possible. After he'd applied a dab of cologne and dressed in shorts and a clean polo shirt he unearthed from a pile of laundry he'd yet to put away, he stopped short at the realization that he should've gotten something for Sarah. Since he'd been invited as Katie's date and not as Sarah's friend, he should bring flowers or wine or *something.*

It had been such a long time since he'd done the dinner-with-the-parents thing for the first time that he'd forgotten the rules. Courtney's parents and sister had loved him. They'd loved his father and Laura and made them a part of their family. Her parents had been as surprised as Shane to learn she was addicted to pain meds, and they'd been devastated by her decision to divorce him.

For a year or so after it all blew up, her parents had remained in close touch with him, their concern for him rivaling only his own father's. After a while, though, he'd stopped returning their calls, because it was too damned painful to be reminded of what he'd lost every time he talked to them.

Again, Shane had to ask himself why he was thinking about this shit when he had a beautiful, sweet, sexy, funny woman waiting for him to take her to dinner. It was because he was terrified of history repeating itself, and every minute he spent with Katie increased the stakes. And because he'd like to think he'd learned a few things from the nightmare he'd been through. He sat on his bed and ran his fingers through his damp hair. He was still sitting on the bed when a soft knock sounded at his door. He got up to answer it.

"Hey," he said to Katie, who looked gorgeous in a sexy red dress that left her shoulders bare.

"Did I really get ready faster than you?" Her smile faded when she took a closer look at him. "What's wrong?"

"Come in." Shane stepped aside to admit her and then closed the door. "Could we talk for a minute?" He hated that he had to do this, but what choice did he have?

"Of course. Are you all right?"

He sat on the bed and gestured for her to join him. "I'm better than all right for the first time in a really long time. And it's because of you."

"That's nice of you to say. So why do you seem upset?"

He took hold of her hand and brought it to his lips, meeting her gaze. "I like you, Katie. I really like you. I like hanging out with you and everything else."

"I like hanging out with you, too. Were you worried that I didn't?"

"I wasn't worried about that so much as…"

"Just say whatever it is. Get it off your chest."

He looked into her eyes and saw nothing but interest and compassion and that underlying layer of sweetness that made everything so much easier with her. "After what happened with my wife, I was a wreck. It was as bad as it gets. I survived it, for the most part, but I don't think I'd survive it a second time. So I guess what I'm saying is if this is just a fling, a get-the-first-time-out-of-the-way-and-move-on thing, which is perfectly all right if that's what it is for you, I'd like to know that sooner rather than later."

Katie stared at him, and for a moment he wasn't sure if she was shocked or pissed or what. Had he just screwed it all up?

"It's much more than that to me, Shane. I would never use you that way. First of all, that's not who I am, and second of all, with your sister married to my brother, there's much more at stake here than what's happening between us. I've known that from the beginning."

"I didn't mean to insult you. That's the last thing I'd ever want to do. I've learned the hard way that I have to look out for myself in these situations, and the more time I spend with you, the more time I *want* to spend with you. If you aren't on the same page, I'd rather know now. That's all I was trying to say. Sorry if I made a mess of it."

"We're on the same page. I can't promise this is it for me forever—"

"I'm not asking for that." He softened his words with a smile. "Not yet anyway."

She returned his smile. "I was excited to see you tonight. Why do you think I went downstairs to get lemonade right after five? Because you told me you'd get home around five. I was hoping to see you the second you got home."

"You were? Really?"

"Yes! Why do you seem so surprised to hear that?"

"Are you laughing at me?"

"I'm laughing *with* you."

He scowled playfully. "Except I'm not laughing."

"Shane… Look at me."

He did as she asked. "I really, *really* like you, too, or I never would've done what I did last night or what I'm going to do again tonight if you're willing."

His snort of laughter made her smile. "If I'm *willing*?"

"Well, I don't want to get cocky or anything."

He took hold of her hand and placed it over his erection, drawing a gasp of surprise from her at his bold move. "Safe to get cocky."

They shared a laugh that turned into a kiss as a huge weight lifted off his chest. It was safe to relax and let it happen with her. She knew what he'd been through and understood what he needed.

"Feel better?" she asked.

"Yeah, except now I've got a whole other problem. Seems to crop up a lot when you're around."

She glanced at the unmistakable bulge in his shorts.

"Don't look at it. That doesn't help."

She bit her lip as she glanced over his shoulder at the bedside clock. "We have half an hour before we need to be there."

"*Katie…*"

"What? I was just pointing out that we do, in fact, have some time."

"No, we don't. I have to stop and get something for your mom and we'd have to shower again and… God, what the hell am I saying? Take your clothes off. Hurry. We don't have much time."

Katie fell on the bed laughing, but she didn't take off her dress. "I didn't expect you to take me so seriously."

"If you're you and you're offering sex, I'm taking you seriously."

"I'm sure my mom has gone to a lot of trouble for tonight. I don't want to be late, and if you talk me out of my clothes, we'll be late."

"You're right about that." He leaned in to kiss her. "Do I get a rain check for later?"

"Absolutely."

Shane got up and then offered her a hand, drawing her into his arms when she was standing. "Thanks for letting me talk it out."

"Thanks for trusting me enough to tell me what's on your mind."

"I'm trusting you with a lot more than what's on my mind. I hope you know that."

"I do, Shane. And that works both ways."

"Good," he said, kissing her again. "Now, what should I get for your mom?"

CHAPTER 24

The doctor had asked them to stay close for the night in case Maddie had any complications, so they were spending another night at Uncle Frank's house. She'd done nothing but sleep since they'd arrived a couple of hours ago. They'd been told to expect her to be sore for a couple of days with spotty bleeding, but otherwise, she'd be back to normal in a week or so.

They'd also been told they could try again to conceive after she'd had two regular periods. Maddie hadn't reacted to any of this information, and other than allowing him to help her get dressed, she hadn't reacted to him either.

Now Mac was left with an entire evening to himself and only his own unpleasant thoughts to keep him company. Would Maddie bounce back from this heartbreaking loss, or would she be different now? Would she ever talk to him about it, or was he expected to get through it on his own?

His dad had left shortly after Maddie came out of surgery, with promises to check in with him later. Mac still couldn't believe his father had come from the island to sit with him while Maddie was in surgery. But of course he shouldn't have been surprised. His dad had always been there for him, in good times and bad, propping him up, steering him clear of trouble and supporting him and his siblings in any way he could.

His ringing cell phone snapped him out of his thoughts. Mac glanced at the caller ID and wasn't surprised to see the word BRAT on the screen. "Hey, brat."

"Honestly, Mac. I'm calling to check on you and Maddie, which of course you know, and you still have to call me that?" Janey asked.

"Helps to keep things normal."

"Then by all means, call me whatever you want."

"Thanks, brat."

"How is she?"

"Physically, it all went well from what we were told. Routine, if such a thing can be routine. Emotionally? I don't know. She's barely said a word to me since we got the news at the clinic."

"How about you?"

"I don't know about that either. I'm all over the place. Mostly I'm worried about her and the way she's internalizing it. It's like I'm not even here or like it wasn't my kid, too. Like I said. I don't know how I am."

"It's a fresh loss, Mac. She had to get past the medical business before she could process it. I'm sure she'll be back to normal in no time."

"I hope you're right."

"When have you ever known me not to be right?"

"Such a brat."

"That's why you love me."

"Yeah, it is."

"I love you, too, Mac, and I'm so sorry you guys are going through this."

"Thanks." He sat on the sofa and pressed his fingers to his eyes, as if that could contain his tears.

"Are you going to be all right?"

"Eventually."

"I'm here if you need me. You know that, right?"

"Yeah. Thanks, brat."

"Any time. Will you be home tomorrow?"

"That's the plan, unless she has complications."

"I'll bring dinner over."

"Sounds good. I'll see you then."

After he ended the call with Janey, Adam called, then Evan and then Grant, each of them expressing sorrow for his loss and concern for Maddie—and him. Talking to his siblings made Mac feel less alone and helped to pass the time, but it was still only eight, and he was starting to feel hungry even though the thought of eating made him sort of nauseated.

The phone rang again, this time with a Providence number he didn't recognize. Thinking it was someone from the hospital, he took the call.

"Hi, Mac, it's Mallory. I thought I'd get your voice mail."

"Oh, hey," he said to the half sister he'd only recently learned he had. "How are you?"

"I'm fine, but I just spoke to… to Big Mac, and he told me you were in town and why. I'm so sorry for your loss."

"Thank you."

"He said you were staying at his brother's house on the east side, which is where I live. I was going to leave a message to let you know I was nearby if I could do anything for you or your wife."

"That's very nice of you. Thanks."

"Do you need anything?"

Mac hesitated but only for a moment. "Do you know where I can get a pizza around here?"

"I certainly do."

"Throw in a couple of beers, and we'll be friends for life."

She laughed. "You got it. What do you like on the pizza?"

"Sausage and onion?"

"Hey, me, too!"

"Really?"

"Yep. Thin crust or thick?"

"Thin."

"We must be related."

"I heard a rumor that we are, and P.S., this is really nice of you."

"I'm happy to do it. I'll be there in thirty minutes or so."

"Did Dad give you the address?"

"He did. I'm three blocks away. Is there anything I can get for your wife?"

"She's out cold, and they said she would be for most of the night."

"All right, then. I'll see you shortly."

"Great, thanks again." Mac put down the phone, feeling oddly grateful to a woman he'd met only once before, when she'd come to the island to seek out the father who hadn't known she existed. What a strange day that had been, but because it mattered so much to the dad who mattered so much to them, they were willing to make an effort where Mallory was concerned.

Mac had been prepared to dislike her. After all, he loved being the oldest sibling in his family as well as the oldest grandchild on the McCarthy side of the family. Since Mallory was older than he was, she bumped him off his oldest-child pedestal. But there was nothing not to like about her. She'd come into his parents' home on the day his father told them about her and hadn't tried to be anything other than a potential new friend to them.

Janey, who'd just had P.J. under difficult circumstances, had chosen not to meet Mallory that day. Hopefully, they would meet this coming weekend when Mallory returned to the island to get to know her new family better.

It was nice of her to reach out to him and to bring him dinner. While he waited for her, he answered a concerned text from Luke and took calls from his mother, Maddie's mother and her sister, Tiffany, all of whom were looking for assurances that Maddie was okay. What was he supposed to say? No, she's not okay. She's traumatized and silent and nothing at all like her usual self.

But that wasn't what he said. He told them what they needed to hear—that she was resting after a tough day and they'd be home tomorrow, barring any complications.

He'd just hung up with Tiffany when the doorbell rang. As he opened the door to Mallory, her resemblance to his father's mother struck Mac all over again.

The photo of his grandmother as a young woman had been on his father's desk for as long as Mac could remember, and looking at Mallory with her curly dark hair and brown eyes was like looking at her.

"Come in." Relieving her of the bag she carried, he stepped aside to admit her, his stomach growling as the aroma of pizza made his mouth water. Mac led her to the kitchen in the back of the house, took two of the beers from the six-pack and cracked them open before stashing the rest in the empty fridge. "Thanks again for this."

"No problem at all. I hadn't eaten yet either." Mallory served up the pizza on the paper plates the restaurant had provided, and they ate in silence.

"Really good," Mac said between bites.

"My favorite."

"I can see why." He noticed her glancing at him occasionally before refocusing on her pizza. "What? Do I have sauce on my face?"

"No," she said with a laugh. "It's just... You know, first time I've ever had pizza with my brother." She shrugged. "It's kind of cool."

"For me, too."

"So you don't all hate me for showing up unexpectedly and staking my claim on your father?"

Mac paused with his beer bottle halfway to his mouth. "Did you stake a claim on him? I must've missed that part."

"He's the one who staked the claim. I would've been satisfied to meet him. He wanted more."

"We don't hate you, Mallory. It's not like you set out to intentionally upend our family or cause trouble. My dad—*our* dad—is the best guy I know, and I'm not at all surprised that he staked a claim. He wasn't going to let you walk away after learning you were his. That's not who he is."

"I'm starting to understand that. He calls me. A lot."

Mac chuckled. "Welcome to my world. Not that I mind. When I lived in Miami, I talked to him almost every day. My business partners used to make fun of me. 'Is that Daddy calling to check on his wittle boy?' they'd say. I'd just laugh it off. I liked talking to him, and I know my brothers did, too, when they lived away. He's so happy to have us all home now." Mac took another sip of his beer and put down the bottle. "He's probably not going to be satisfied until you live on the island, too."

"He's said as much! He's even told me his buddy Ned can hook me up with a great place to live. I've had to remind him more than once that I have a job and already own a house."

"He can be somewhat of a dog with a bone when he gets a big idea, so stand warned."

"The funny thing is... He's got me thinking about quitting my job, selling my house and moving, because it would mean I'd get to see him every day."

"He can be rather convincing."

"Indeed."

A sound from the stairs had Mac on his feet when Maddie appeared in the kitchen, looking far too pale for his liking. "Hey, baby. How're you feeling?"

"Kinda hungry, actually."

"That's great." He held out his hand to her and was relieved when she took it. "Come meet my sister, Mallory. Mallory, my wife, Maddie."

"So good to meet you," Mallory said, shaking Maddie's hand. "I'm sorry for the reason, though."

"Thank you. Nice to meet you. I've heard a lot about you."

"Are you up for some pizza?" Mac asked.

"That sounds good. I could smell it from upstairs."

"I hope we didn't disturb you," Mallory said.

"Not at all. I was awake."

Mac put a slice of pizza on a plate and got her a glass of ice water.

She glanced at him and smiled ever so slightly. "Thanks."

That hint of a smile unlocked the tight knot of fear that had gripped him for two long days now. She was going to be all right. It might take time for her to bounce back fully, but his Maddie, his love, was still in there.

They visited with Mallory for another hour before she took her leave, promising to catch up with them over the weekend when she came to the island. She wanted to meet their children, and Mac looked forward to introducing them to their new aunt. It was funny to think that they'd grow up knowing her as another of his siblings. They wouldn't know there was anything "different" about her compared to his other sister or brothers.

After he locked up, Mac followed Maddie upstairs, hoping the small breakthrough he'd witnessed earlier would carry forth. "Do you need anything?" he asked when she was settled in bed.

"No, thanks."

"Are you in any pain?"

As she shook her head, her golden eyes filled with tears.

"Maddie…"

"No, Mac. I can't talk about it, so please don't ask me to. Not yet."

"Could I just hold you? Please?"

"Okay."

He got into bed and reached for her.

She turned into his embrace, bringing the familiar scent of summer flowers with her.

Mac breathed her in as he held her close, relieved that she'd let him hold her. "I love you, Madeline. More than anything in this entire world. Don't ever forget that."

A soft sob was the only reply he got, but he was comforted to have her close to him. For now, for tonight, that was enough.

CHAPTER 25

Sitting next to Shane at an outdoor table at her mother's new home, Katie tried to relax and enjoy the lovely evening her mother and Charlie had put together for her, Shane, Owen, Laura and Holden, as well as Charlie's daughter, Stephanie, and her fiancé, Grant, who was also Shane's cousin.

In addition to the candles her mother had placed on the long table, Charlie had strung lights through the trees overhead, creating a magical atmosphere in their small yard.

Talk turned to Grant and Stephanie's upcoming Labor Day wedding.

"As much as I'm looking forward to the wedding, I can't believe the summer is already almost over," Grant said mournfully.

"Thank *God*," Stephanie said. "I can't take much more."

"I take that to mean the restaurant had a great season," Charlie said.

"A tremendous season. Thirty percent better than last year, which about killed me."

"Perhaps it's time to acknowledge you can't do two jobs in the summer," Charlie said with an indulgent smile for his daughter.

"I can't quit the marina," Stephanie said. "I'm marrying their son!"

Grant laughed as he took hold of her hand and kissed the back of it. "Running the restaurant is not part of the prenup, honey."

"You have a prenup?" Shane asked.

"He won't hear of it," Stephanie said, rolling her eyes at Grant.

"Nothing more romantic than planning for the end of a marriage that hasn't even started yet," Grant said.

"It's not about the romance," Stephanie argued. "It's about protecting what's yours."

"What's mine is yours," Grant said, shrugging off her concerns.

"Maybe you should get him to sign one," Charlie said. "After all, we're coming into some money, and you'll be an heiress."

"An heiress," Stephanie said. "Whatever that is."

"An heiress is you after I die and leave you millions," Charlie said.

"And where are these so-called millions coming from?" she asked, seeming amused.

"You want to tell her?" he asked Sarah.

"I'd love to. The state is compensating your dad for the years he was wrongfully imprisoned. To the tune of five hundred thousand dollars per year."

"Holy cow," Stephanie said. "Even I can do that math!"

"And a chunk of it will be going directly to you," Charlie said to Stephanie.

"Oh, I, um… wow," Stephanie said on a long exhale that made everyone laugh.

"Congratulations, Charlie," Shane said. "That's the least of what they owe you."

"They could've given me nothing, and I'd still have everything I want." This was said with his gaze firmly fixed on Sarah, who smiled even as she blushed.

Watching them, Katie was filled with yearning. What would it be like, she wondered, to know exactly who you were going to love—and who loved you—for the rest of your life? She'd never expected to be so envious of her own mother, but there it was. And all this time she'd thought she didn't want love and romance and forever with a man. How wrong she'd been.

"Everything okay?" Shane asked in a low tone intended for her ears only. When he wasn't taking a turn with Holden, his arm had been stretched behind her chair, his fingers brushing against the back of her shoulder. Each touch sent a tingle of sensation rippling through her body, reminding her of their plans for later.

"Everything is great."

"You ready to go?"

"Whenever you are."

They'd eaten a delicious dinner of grilled steak and chicken, salad and potatoes with strawberry shortcake for dessert. As they toasted Katie's new job and decision to remain on Gansett Island for the winter, the champagne had flowed as freely as the conversation. When she stood up, Katie realized she was a little tipsy.

Shane's hands on her shoulders steadied her. "Thank you for a lovely evening, Sarah and Charlie," Shane said.

"It was our pleasure." Sarah hugged and kissed them both, as well as Laura, Owen and Holden, who were also leaving. "Let's do it again soon." She walked them to the driveway and eyed Shane's motorcycle with trepidation. "You're careful with my daughter on that thing, right?"

"Always," Shane said. "She's precious cargo."

"You're darned right she is."

With only the moon to light their way, Shane navigated the twisting island roads as Katie held on tight to him. She loved being tucked up against him as the bike roared beneath them. She loved the play of his muscles under her hands and the scent of his cologne filling her senses. Knowing he was as eager to be alone with her as she was to be with him kept her on the razor's edge of arousal all the way home.

The hotel was dark and quiet when they arrived ahead of Laura and Owen. Shane stashed their helmets in the sitting room and led her upstairs to his room, slowing his pace to match hers on the stairs.

Inside his room, he kept the lights off as he pressed her against the back of the door and kissed her with what felt like desperation. His tongue sought out hers, teasing and tempting her until she was just as desperate. Breaking the kiss, he set her on fire with a series of kisses to her neck.

"Such a nice time tonight with your mom and Charlie and the others," he said as he continued to devastate her with his lips and tongue. "But the whole time I was burning up from having you sitting so close to me."

"I was, too. I kept thinking about last night..."

"What about it?"

"Everything about it. It's all I've thought about today."

"Was it everything you'd hoped it would be?"

"It was so much more," she said with a laugh. "I accused you of a lack of imagination earlier. Well, that was me before last night. I had no idea it would be like that."

"You know how to make a guy feel good, Katie Lawry." He cupped her breasts and ran his thumbs over her nipples until they tightened in response to him. Then he was reaching for the hem of her dress and lifting it up and over her head. The matching bra and panties she wore landed in a pile on the floor that soon included his shirt, shorts and boxers. Twenty-four hours ago, she'd never been naked with a man and now she couldn't get naked fast enough.

He took her hands and walked backward to the bed, pulled the covers back and stretched out on the bed, bringing her down on top of him.

Katie wasn't sure what to do with her arms or legs until he arranged her legs on either side of his hips and drew her down to him, taking her lips in another incendiary kiss. His hands seemed to be everywhere, on her back, cupping her breasts, squeezing her bottom. Katie couldn't keep up with the array of emotions and sensations that zinged through her body.

Last night he had been all about slow seduction. Tonight he was about fast and furious, or so it seemed to her. "God, Katie," he said in a gruff, sexy tone. "I want you."

"I want you, too."

"Are you still sore?"

"Not like I was."

He reached for a condom on the bedside table and rolled it on while she sat back and watched, the room illuminated by the faint beams from outdoor security lights. "You take the lead, honey. If it hurts, you stop. Okay?"

"Show me how."

With his hands on her hips, he lifted her until she was poised above his erection. He released her slowly, bringing her down on him in tiny increments.

Katie gasped from the stretch and burn of her tender flesh.

"Does it hurt?"

She shook her head. It didn't hurt badly enough to stop.

Shane didn't move until she did, accepting him deeper with the slight swivel of her hips.

His protracted groan startled her. "Don't stop," he said through gritted teeth. "Please don't stop."

Knowing he wanted her so badly was a powerful incentive. Katie forced herself to relax and accept more of him.

"So hot and so tight," he whispered. "Incredible."

"Show me how you like it."

"I'm afraid I'll lose it if you move."

"I need to move."

"Give me a second, baby." While he summoned control, his hands continued to move, making her shiver from the waves of desire that rolled through her, settling into an insistent throb between her legs.

Shane sat up and wrapped his arms around her, bringing her breasts in tight against his chest and wrapping her legs around his waist. With his hands on her bottom, he eased her up and down his hard shaft, each movement setting off new sparks of pleasure.

Katie held on tightly to him and tried to remember to breathe. Last night had been amazing, but this…

"Feel okay?" he asked.

"Yes, *yes*."

Hearing her affirmation, he picked up the pace, and Katie forgot how to breathe or think or feel anything other than the orgasm that washed over her.

"Ah Christ," he muttered as he pressed hard into her and held her there while he came, too. "*Katie...*"

She continued to hold on to him, her heart beating in time with the pulsating sensation between her legs. In that moment of utter perfection, it became clear to her that she was falling in love with him. It didn't matter that she'd known him for only a short time. When he held her this way and made such sweet love to her, she felt like she'd known him forever.

Without losing their connection, he turned them so he was on top, looking down at her with those piercing blue eyes that saw her in a way no one else ever had. "Are you okay?"

"I'm great. You?"

"Never been better."

"You don't have to say that, Shane."

"I'm not saying anything I don't mean. I've had great sex before. But that was something else altogether."

"It was? Really?"

"It really was. You've got me totally hooked on what it feels like to be inside you, Katie."

"You've got me pretty hooked, too. On the whole package."

"Good," he said with a lingering kiss. "That's how I want you. Is this moving too fast for you?"

"No, not really."

"You're not overwhelming me with your conviction."

"It's moving fast, maybe too fast, but it feels good, you know?"

He pressed his hips against hers, reminding her he was still lodged deep inside her—as if she needed the reminder. "I know."

Katie smiled at his enthusiastic reply. "This has been a truly remarkable week in more ways than one. My whole life has turned upside down, but I'm finding I like the view from down here." She flattened her hands on his chest and felt his heart beating fast under her palms. "I like that I can touch you this way any time I want to."

"You can touch me that way or any other way whenever you want to."

"I like that. I like being here and having some of my family nearby and the new job and everything. I heard something sad today that reminded me of how lucky I am, despite what I endured to get here."

"What did you hear?"

"While I was at the clinic, David got some bad news about one of his patients. A young single mother who has end-stage lung cancer. It was sad."

Shane went still above her. "Did you meet her? The mother?"

"I saw her briefly. She had dark hair and a bad cough."

"Oh my God. *No*..."

"Shane? Do you know her?"

With his hand wrapped around the condom, he withdrew from her and turned onto his back. "Yeah, I know her. I'm building a house for her and her kids. I've gotten to know them really well."

"Oh, Shane. I'm so sorry."

"Those poor kids. They're so excited about the house. Shit."

"I feel so bad for dropping that on you the way I did. I forgot this is such a small place, and of course you would know her. Not very professional of me."

"It's okay, honey. I had a feeling she was really sick, but end-stage lung cancer... She's so young."

"I know. I told David I have hospice training, so I might be able to offer some assistance to her."

"I want to help them, too. Anything I can do... Kyle and Jackson are such great kids. This will devastate them. I don't think they have any other family, at least not that they've ever mentioned."

"I hope she has a plan for them if something were to happen to her."

"I hope so, too." He got up and went into the bathroom. The toilet flushed and the water ran for a long time. When he came back, he slid into bed next to her. "I'll have to tell Mac about this when he's already got so much on his mind."

Katie turned to face him. "Do you want me to leave so you can rest?"

"What? No… I'm sorry. I didn't mean to punch out on you."

"You didn't. You're upset."

He took her hand and linked their fingers. "She's right between us in age. You never know what's going to happen. Certainly puts things into perspective, doesn't it?"

"It sure does. I'm sorry for your friend and her children."

"So am I."

"We can go to Newport another day if you need to stay here to work things out."

"Tomorrow might be the best day to go since everything will be on hold until I can speak to Mac. He's got enough going on. Another day won't hurt anything."

That he was so clearly undone by the news about his friend and her children only made Katie tumble that much quicker. He was a truly wonderful guy, inside and out, and as she fell asleep in his arms, she gave herself permission to feel anything and everything for him.

*

Despite the lingering sadness he felt over the news about Lisa, Shane devoted himself to showing Katie a good time the next day, beginning with a ride on the high-speed ferry to Newport. They stood outside, her back to his front so he could keep her from toppling over in the stiff breeze.

The ferry hauled ass and got them from Gansett to Newport in an hour, and the ride itself was as much fun as the outing promised to be. When they arrived in Newport, they got a good tour of the harbor from the ferry, and Katie marveled at the huge yachts docked at the various marinas.

It'd been years since Shane had been to Newport, one of Courtney's favorite places to spend a summer evening. But he was determined not to think about the past today, when he had a full day to spend with Katie. They walked along the waterfront, window-shopping and occasionally ducking inside a shop for a closer look at something that caught her interest before grabbing a pedicab to take them up to Bellevue Avenue.

On Memorial Boulevard, he pointed out the church where President and Mrs. Kennedy had been married. When they reached Bellevue Avenue, he took her on a tour of the International Tennis Hall of Fame before they walked farther down the avenue to tour The Breakers, one of Newport's famous mansions.

"I can't believe something like this even exists," she said of the enormous house that had served as the summer residence of the Vanderbilt family during Newport's gilded age. "Let alone that it was someone's *summer* home."

"You have to see it to believe it," Shane said. "I haven't been here since I was a kid and my dad brought me and Laura to see a couple of these places on a rainy Saturday. I expected to be bored, but I thought they were amazing."

"Do we have time for another one after this?"

"Sure we do," he said, amused by her enthusiasm. "We've got all afternoon."

They toured Marble House and Rosecliff before grabbing a late lunch on one of the wharfs near the ferry landing.

"This was so much fun," Katie said. "Thank you for bringing me here."

"My pleasure. How's the foot?"

"A little sore, but it was worth it. I can't wait to come back again when we have more time. I want to see everything."

"We didn't get to do Cliff Walk or Ocean Drive, but we'll definitely come back." That they were making plans that included each other wasn't lost on him. But after their conversation the night before, Shane felt safe making plans with her. She was sticking around and seemed to be enjoying the time they spent together as much as he did.

On the ride back to the island, they found a spot inside the cabin, out of the wind. Katie snuggled up to him, her head on his chest, and was asleep before the ferry left the harbor. That gave him an hour to himself to think about the time he'd spent with her, the day together in Newport, the last two nights in bed. She made him feel hopeful, which was a minor miracle considering the mess he'd been not that long ago.

He was falling for Katie, and he was happy about that. It felt good to be happy and optimistic. Hearing the devastating news about Lisa's illness truly brought home how lucky he was for all the blessings in his life, and it was time to focus on them rather than on the misery of the past.

Shane ran his hand up and down Katie's back, loving the way she felt and smelled and looked. He loved the way she laughed and teased him and mostly he loved that she was easy to talk to and easy to get along with.

Katie roused when the boat slowed as they reached the breakwater for South Harbor. "Did I really fall asleep?"

"You were snoring and everything."

"I was not!"

He cracked up at the indignant face she made. "Just kidding."

"That's not funny."

"Yes, it is. I've been keeping you up too late at night."

"And you're going to keep doing that, right?"

"I thought it was girls' night out?"

"It is, but it's not a sleepover as far as I know. So maybe I can come find you later?"

He kissed her sweet lips. "I wish you would."

"No more talk of snoring, though."

"I promise to never mention it again. It'll be our little secret."

She elbowed his ribs. "I do not snore."

"If you say so."

Holding hands, they walked from the ferry landing to the Sand & Surf, laughing and bickering about whether or not she really snored. She didn't, but he wasn't about to let her off the hook too easily. They were halfway up the stairs when he heard someone call his name. He looked over to the row of rocking chairs on the porch and thought he was hallucinating when he saw Courtney sitting in one of them, obviously waiting for him.

He dropped Katie's hand and stared at Courtney.

She got up and came toward him, looking thinner than she had before, but still as strikingly pretty as ever. Her dark hair was longer than he'd ever seen it.

"Um, Shane?" Katie's tentative inquiry snapped him out of the shocked state he'd slipped into at the sight of Courtney.

"Could I catch up to you in a minute?" he asked Katie.

"Sure," she said.

He wasn't so far gone that he didn't see and feel the hurt coming from her, but he couldn't process that on top of Courtney's unexpected appearance. What was she doing here? And why now? He hated himself for so badly wanting answers to those and many other questions.

Katie went inside, the screen door slamming shut behind her.

"What're you doing here, Courtney?"

"I came for you."

CHAPTER 26

Standing inside the main door to the Sand & Surf, Katie heard Shane's ex-wife say she'd come for him. Katie took off for the stairs before she could make a scene in the lobby.

"Katie," Laura called. "Wait up. How was your day in Newport? Aren't the mansions awesome? Are you crying? What happened? Where's Shane?"

"He's… um, he's outside talking to Courtney."

"He's *what*? What the *hell* is she doing here?"

"He asked her that question, and she said she's come for him."

"Over my dead body." Laura squeezed her arm. "Don't worry. I'll get rid of her."

"I think he wanted to talk to her."

"I don't care what he wanted. No way is that woman getting her claws back into him. Not while I'm around." She patted Katie's shoulder. "Go on up. I'll find you after I get rid of her."

Because she didn't know what else to do, Katie did as Laura suggested and went up to her room. When she recalled the way he'd dropped her hand as if he felt guilty for having been caught with another woman, her heart ached and so did her stomach. So this was what it felt like to have your heart broken, she thought as she stretched out on her bed. Her entire body hurt.

What would happen now? Courtney had said she'd come for him. Was he happy to hear that? Had he been killing time with her while hoping Courtney would come back to him?

In bad need of advice, she wiped up her tears and placed a call to Julia.

"Can you talk?" she asked when her sister answered.

"I'm on a break. What's up?"

Katie's throat closed, making it impossible to speak.

"Katie? What's wrong?"

"I went out with Shane."

"Finally! Yes! And was it awesome?"

"It was. All of it was awesome."

"*All*? What else happened?"

"Everything happened."

"Oh, Katie, I'm so happy for you!"

Katie broke down all over again.

"Why're you crying? He didn't *hurt* you, did he?"

"Not like you think." Hating herself for giving in to the emotional breakdown, Katie wiped her eyes. "We've been having a really great time, and I thought, you know... It was going to be something. Special."

"And it's not?"

"His ex-wife showed up. We were holding hands, and he let me go like a bad habit when he saw her."

"Oh God. I heard about his wife. Mom told me a little of it."

"She treated him like crap, Jule, and he takes one look at her and forgets all about me?"

"I'm sure he didn't forget about you. He was probably shocked."

"He was shocked. I could tell."

"So it's not like he got in touch with her, invited her over for a visit and then acted like you were a big secret when she showed up."

"No, but still..."

"Katie, listen to me. Are you listening?"

"Yeah."

"He's a good guy. I could tell that in the short amount of time I spent with him. He's got history with this woman, and he might be better off working things out with her so he can put the past where it belongs."

"He made me feel like I don't matter."

"He was shocked, Katie. Give him a chance to explain."

"I was starting to really like him."

"That happened fast."

"I know it did, but when a guy saves your life and then he turns out to be sweet and charming and sexy, he's hard to resist."

"He's apt to be telling her to get on the ferry and go back to wherever she came from."

"What if he's kissing her and dragging her up to his room so they can pick up where they left off?"

"From what I heard about their breakup, I'd be very surprised if he was doing that."

"But what if he wants to? What if he took one look at her and all he could see was how much he loved her?"

"You're going to drive yourself crazy with that kind of thinking."

"Too late. I'm already crazy—about him. This is exactly why I've avoided this stuff."

"This isn't why. You avoided it because you were afraid you'd end up with a guy like our father. Shane McCarthy is *nothing* like our father. He has a past just like you do, and the past has a way of rearing its ugly head. That might be all this is, and maybe he can get some closure."

"He said he had no idea why she divorced him the way she did."

"He'll probably get some answers, Katie. Is there something else you can do until he's able to talk to you?"

"I'm supposed to be going out with Laura and her friends tonight."

"Then that's what you're going to do."

"I'm a wreck, Julia."

"Go make yourself gorgeous and have a good time with Laura. Make it so he has to come looking for you if he wants to see you."

A soft tap on her door had Katie running to open it and trying to hide her disappointment when she saw Laura and not Shane—and Laura looked annoyed. "Hey, Jule, I've got to go. I'll call you tomorrow."

"Don't sit around crying over him, Katie."

"I won't."

"So he's talking to her in the sitting room," Laura said, her mouth straight with tension. "We're going out."

Katie had never seen Laura look so furious.

"He's actually talking to her."

"Yes. He asked me to leave them alone, so that's what I'm doing."

Katie's heart sank at that news, and Julia's words rang loudly in her mind. "Girls' night out. Still on?"

"Damn straight it is."

"Give me ten minutes to get changed."

"I'll be right back." She started to walk away but then turned back. "I promised Owen that my brother wouldn't hurt you. I'm sorry I wasn't able to keep that promise."

"It's not your fault."

"Still, I'm sorry about this. Her timing always was exquisite."

"I'll see you shortly." Katie closed the door and went to the closet to choose something to wear, determined to think about anything other than the fact that Shane was downstairs, behind closed doors with his ex-wife.

*

"I don't freaking believe it," Laura said as she stormed into the apartment.

Owen looked up from the floor, where he was playing with Holden, who began to cry. "It's okay, buddy."

Holden crawled into Owen's arms, seeming to hide from her.

"What brought that on?" Owen asked.

"My brother is an *ass*. He's downstairs right now talking to Courtney—the wife who nearly bankrupted him with her pill habit and then dumped him after he paid for rehab. *He's talking to her*!"

"She's *here*?"

"Yes! And the worst part? He was with Katie when she found him, and he left your sister twisting in the wind after he asked for 'a minute' with Courtney. I'm so mad at him, I could… Well, I don't know what I could do, but it'd be bad."

"Calm down, hon. You're scaring Holden."

"I'm sorry." Laura dropped down to the floor and reached for her son, who clung to Owen. She tickled the baby until he relented and let her hold him. "I can't stop thinking about what a mess he was when she left him and how hard he's worked to climb out of that hole. If she undoes all that progress by coming here…"

"He's a lot stronger than he was. He won't let her walk all over him."

"I don't know, O. She's crafty. I wouldn't put it past her to charm her way back into his life and then pull the rug out from under him again. And poor Katie… I could tell she'd been crying when I went to check on her."

"Crying over Shane? Has it gone that far? They haven't known each other that long."

"Um, I'm not sure how I should answer that…"

He stared at her, eyes bugging. "What are you not saying?"

"Nothing."

"Laura…"

"I've got to get ready for girls' night out."

"Is he sleeping with her?"

"I know nothing."

"Don't lie to your new husband. That's grounds for annulment."

"You can't annul when you've already consummated multiple times." She patted her round belly. "And I can prove it."

"Just tell me. I can take it, and I won't hurt him."

"Swear to God?"

"Swear to God," he said with a sigh.

"I think they're sleeping together, but I don't know if they're sleeping or you know… *not* sleeping."

Owen grimaced.

"But if I had to guess… Not sleeping."

"I don't think she's ever had so much as a date let alone a… a…"

"Lover?" Laura asked, her brow raised in amusement.

"Don't be disgusting."

Though she was upset about Shane talking to Courtney, Laura had to laugh at Owen's distress. "She is a grown woman, you know."

"She's my little sister."

"Who's sleeping—or *not* sleeping, in this case—with my little brother."

"I take back my promise not to hurt him."

"You swore to God! You can't take it back."

"She's really upset?"

"She was, but I'm taking her out, and I'm not going to let her wallow. If he screws things up with Katie… I'll hurt him for both of us."

"I can live with that."

*

Shane felt like he was being skinned alive as he paced the sitting room listening to Courtney "explain" why she'd divorced him after he'd paid for her to go to rehab. "Let me get this straight. You're trying to tell me you did it to *protect* me?"

"Yes! That's it exactly. I was given the opportunity to testify against the dealers in exchange for them dropping all charges against me." Her dark curly hair was longer, her skin clearer and her brown eyes brighter than he'd ever seen them. In all the time he'd spent with her, he'd never seen her totally sober—until now.

"What charges? You were never arrested!"

"I was going to be. After rehab. They were going to charge me with possession and intent to deliver narcotics."

"Intent to *deliver*?"

"I was dealing, Shane. Toward the end, I was desperate for money and, well… They had me totally nailed. But I wasn't the big fish, and I helped them nail the three guys who were running a huge operation in Providence. They were convicted yesterday, which means I'm now free to speak to you about this."

"You *divorced* me, Courtney. After everything we'd been through, do you know what it felt like to get those papers on the day I thought you were coming home?"

"I had no choice. It was that or face charges. I couldn't tell anyone what I was doing, and the only way I could keep you out of it was to leave you." She stood and came over to him.

When she tried to lay her hands on his chest, he stepped back, out of her reach.

Her hands fell to her waist. "Please try to understand. I was trying to clean up my mess so I could come back to you free and clear."

"*Come back to me*? You think you're going to waltz back into my life like the last two years of fucking *hell* never happened? Do you *know* what you did to me? Do you have any idea?"

"If the pain I felt at not seeing you for all this time is any indication, then, yes, I do have an idea of what you've been through."

"You can't possibly know. All this time, you were fully aware of what was going on and why, while I was left in the dark. Instead of talking to me and telling me what was happening, you pulled the plug and tossed me aside like I meant nothing to you."

"That couldn't be further from the truth. Leaving you nearly killed me."

Shane blew out a deep breath as he shook his head. "I can't listen to any more of this. I'm sorry. It's just... It's too little too late."

"Shane, please. Please take some time to think about it. I love you as much as I ever did, and I always will. Everything I did was intended to keep you—and your family—out of the nightmare my life had become. I did what I did because I love you so much."

Her words bounced around in Shane's mind like painful darts. What he would've given a year ago to hear her tell him she loved him. But as he looked at her now, the woman he'd once planned to spend the rest of his life loving, all he could see—and feel—was the pain.

"I'm here for the night. Could we talk again in the morning when you've had some time to think about everything I've said?"

"How did you find me?" he asked.

"I went to your old boss. He told me you were working out here now. I asked around when I arrived and was directed here. The girl at the desk said you were away for the day but would be back later. So I waited."

Filled with nervous energy, he rubbed at the late-day stubble on his face.

"The woman you were with... Is that serious?"

Katie... God, Katie. What she must be thinking. "It could've been, until you showed up and ruined everything."

"I never meant to do that. I never meant to ruin everything for us or for you. I hope you'll let me prove I'm not the person I once was. I've been sober for more than two years, and I'll never go back to that life. I want the life I had back. I want *you*, Shane. You're all I've thought about for two long, lonely years."

"You can't do this to me, Courtney," he said gruffly. He felt like his insides were being squeezed in a vise. "I won't allow it."

"Please... All I'm asking for is a chance to show you I'm different now. Will you sleep on it? Please, Shane. After all we've been through, can you give me one night?"

"You didn't even give me the courtesy of a phone call when you had me served with divorce papers on the day I thought I was picking you up to come home. Not even a *phone call*, Courtney." He was nearly blinded by rage—mostly at himself, because he'd been happy to hear she'd never stopped loving him. What did it matter now? "And now you want me to put my life on hold, *again*, for you. I'm not going to do it. The answer is *no*. We're *over, divorced*. You saw to that. Now go home and *leave me alone*."

He headed for the doors to the sitting room, which were never closed the way they were now. Throwing open the doors, he came face-to-face with Laura and Katie, who were on their way out."

"Shane, *please*," Courtney said, pleading as she followed him.

"Courtney was just leaving," he said to his sister as he brushed past them and went up the stairs, taking them two at a time. He couldn't bring himself to look at Katie, who'd probably forgotten by now what she'd ever liked about him.

"Go," he heard Laura say to her former sister-in-law. "And don't come back. You're not welcome here."

Shane went into his room and slammed the door, seething with the pent-up frustration of the last two hideous years of wondering why. Why, why, *why*. The answers hadn't made anything better. They had only made everything worse because now he knew she hadn't left him because she wanted to—or so she said.

For all he knew, she could've made up the whole story, hoping to win him back because single life hadn't worked out the way she'd hoped it would. With her, you never knew, and he'd had more than enough of that madness during the years he'd spent with her.

After only a few days with Katie, he already knew he could trust what she told him. He already knew her better than he'd ever known Courtney. When he thought about the way he'd let go of her hand and sent her away earlier, he felt sick. "God, what've I done?"

He had to go after her and apologize. Maybe she'd never speak to him again—and he wouldn't blame her if she didn't—but he had to tell her how sorry he was for the way he'd treated her.

Shane pulled open the door and found Owen standing there with a stormy expression on his face. "Owen… I need to go. I have to find Katie."

"Not so fast."

In the year he'd known Owen, he'd never seen him look so angry.

"Owen, please. I screwed up, but I was caught off guard. I sent Courtney away."

"For now or for good?"

"For good. I care about Katie. I want to be with her, if she'll still have me."

"For now or for good?"

"I… I don't know yet. I won't make a promise I might not be able to keep. All I know is I like who I am when I'm with her. I like who she is all the time. She's… amazing." Shane felt like he was fighting for his life or something equally dramatic. All he knew was if he let Katie slip away, he'd regret it forever.

"You don't have to tell me that."

"I'm sorry to have disappointed you—and her. I never meant to. I was broadsided when I saw my ex-wife. I handled it badly." Shane was going to lose his mind if Owen didn't get out of the way and let him go find Katie. But with his brother-in-law's broad-shouldered body filling the doorway, there was no getting out unless Owen decided to move.

"I like you, Shane, or you never would've gone out with her once, let alone done anything else with her."

Shane wanted to tell Owen he liked him, too, but he thought it wise to stay silent until Owen had his say.

"She's not like other women."

"I know that. I like that about her. She's… She's sweet and genuine and honest." And all those qualities mattered tremendously to him—more than they ever had before.

"I left you alone because Laura told me I could trust you with my sister."

"You *can* trust me. I swear you can. I'm going to fix this with her, if you'll let me out of here. When I set things straight with her, you won't have anything to worry about where she's concerned."

"What if she doesn't want to fix it?"

The thought of that made him ache fiercely, and that was when he realized that at some point during the last few incredible days, he'd fallen for Katie Lawry's particular brand of sweetness. "Please, Owen…"

Owen stared at him for a long, uncomfortable moment. "Did you know that on Gansett Island, the guys always crash girls' night?"

"They do?"

"Every time."

"Are you crashing tonight?"

"Hell yes."

"What about Holden?"

"My mom and Charlie are watching him."

"Will you take me with you?"

"You promise I won't regret it?"

"I promise you'll never regret it."

"Okay, then."

"Can we go now?"

"Later."

"How much later?"

"I'll let you know."

Shane knew defeat when it stared him in the face. He wasn't going to be able to go after Katie until Owen had made him suffer first.

CHAPTER 27

Mac and Maddie returned to the island on the five o'clock ferry, which had them driving off the boat right at six o'clock. They'd get some time with the kids and then Maddie would join girls' night out already in progress. She glanced at Mac, whose eyes were fixed on the road. Judging by the tight lock of his jaw, he was tense and worried.

She hated being the cause of his distress. He wanted to talk about it, but she couldn't. Not yet. Maybe never. But definitely not yet. How could she talk about how empty and sad she felt or how guilty? She'd told everyone what a big accident this baby had been. Thinking about that now made her cringe.

The night they'd conceived the baby, she'd gotten tipsy on champagne and had pounced on Mac. Thomas had caught them having sex, which had been the source of endless laughter among their family and friends. The whole thing had been one big laughfest, and now the joke was on her.

Adding to her guilt, she felt fine despite what she'd been through. The hardest part of the medical procedure had been the anesthesia that had left her feeling nauseated and exhausted. Other than a few aches and pains where her baby had once been and some spotty bleeding, she felt almost normal today. How was that possible?

She wiped subtly at a tear that escaped despite her determination to stop crying before she saw her children. Thomas had known about the baby. He'd have questions, and she had no idea what she would tell him. How did you tell a three-year-old that the baby brother or sister he'd been so excited about wasn't going to be born now?

"What do you plan to say to Thomas?" Mac asked, reading her mind, as he often did.

"Nothing for right now. I'll talk to him about it in a couple of days."

"He'll want to know where we've been."

"We'll tell him I had to go to the doctor on the mainland." Maddie watched the island go by outside the passenger window. Thankfully, Hailey was too young to have even known about the baby. Maddie was grateful for that small favor.

Mac took the last right onto Sweet Meadow Farm Road. As their big, beautiful home came into view, Maddie was also thankful that they hadn't yet bought anything for the new baby, so there was nothing to get rid of. They pulled up next to her stepfather's cab and her mother's small car.

The minute Mac put the truck into Park, Maddie was out the door.

"I would've come around for you," he said when she was halfway up the stairs that led to their deck.

"I want to see the kids," she said over her shoulder.

Thomas spotted her the second she opened the sliding door. He came running to her, and Maddie scooped him up, filled with overwhelming gratitude for him and his sister. "You came back!"

Maddie peppered his adorable face with kisses. "I told you I'd be back."

"Dada come back, too?"

"He sure did. He's getting our bags."

Ned got up from his post on the sofa and went to help Mac.

Francine hung back, holding Hailey, trying to give Maddie a minute with Thomas. But Hailey was straining to get to her mother.

"Here I come, baby girl." Maddie put Thomas down and went to take Hailey from her mother. Hailey snuggled into her arms the way she always did, and Maddie breathed in the sweet scent of baby shampoo.

Her mother's hand on Maddie's back conveyed a world of support and love that Maddie appreciated.

"Everything okay here?" she asked Francine.

"Everything is just fine."

"Who's ready for some bedtime stories?" Maddie asked.

"Me!" Thomas said.

"Let's go, then."

"You want me to do it, honey?" Francine asked, concern bracketing her mouth.

"I got it. Thank you, though. Appreciate the help the last few days."

"I can come back tomorrow to lend a hand if you'd like."

"No need. We're good. I'll call you tomorrow?"

Francine nodded. "Glad to see you home."

"Glad to be here. Come on, Thomas, you get to pick the first story." He picked them all, but Maddie was preparing him for the day when Hailey would get a say, too. In total, she read four stories—two more than usual because she wanted the time with them—and got them tucked into bed.

Mac came up to kiss them both good night.

"Will you be here when I wake up?" Thomas asked.

"You bet, buddy," Mac said. "We'll be right here."

"Good." He turned on his side, popped his thumb in his mouth and drifted off to sleep.

Mac left the room, but Maddie lingered for a few minutes, sitting on the bed running her fingers through Thomas's soft hair. She remembered the sheer terror of learning she was expecting him after a brief relationship with his biological father that had ended when the man left the island abruptly. She'd been so alone then and so afraid for both of them.

Thomas would never remember any of that. He wouldn't remember life without Mac McCarthy as the only father he'd ever know, and Maddie was thankful for that. Her son would know nothing but the comfort and security that came with being a McCarthy. At the same time, Maddie was determined that her children would be aware of those who were less fortunate.

She leaned in to kiss Thomas's soft cheek and left him to sleep. In the master bedroom, Mac was in the shower. Maddie slipped into her closet and changed into jeans and a tunic top, both of which were loose around her tender middle. She was slipping on a pair of cork-heeled sandals when Mac emerged from the shower.

"What're you doing?" he asked.

"Girls' night at Syd's."

"You're going *out*?"

"Yeah, why?"

"*Why*? You're asking me *why*?"

Steeling herself for a fight, she turned to face him. "Yes, I'm asking why. Why wouldn't I go when I feel fine and the kids are safe and settled in for the night? I'd like to see my friends."

"So you can talk to them instead of me about what happened?"

"I don't want to talk to anyone about that. I just want a few hours away from it. Is that all right with you?"

"By all means. Don't let me stop you."

"You're good with the kids?"

"Sure."

"Thanks." She could tell by the set of his jaw that he was pissed, but she didn't have the wherewithal to manage his pain at the same time she was trying to cope with her own. Maybe it was selfish to want to get away from it for a few hours, but that was what she needed. As she went downstairs to wait for her sister to pick her up, she hoped he'd find a way to understand.

*

With the girls due in less than an hour, Sydney Donovan was on pins and needles waiting for her husband, Luke, to get home. He'd texted a short time ago to let her know he was on his way, fully aware that the girls were taking over his house for the evening.

He had plans to meet up with the guys for dinner in town, after which they were sure to crash the girls' gathering. They always did. It was tradition now.

Sydney smiled, recalling the many times the guys had come strolling into girls' night out, acting like they hadn't known exactly where to find the women and how it was all a comic misunderstanding.

Sydney felt like she was going to explode with anticipation. It had been a very long day of waiting to see her husband, who was trapped at the marina with Mac off-island and Big Mac helping out with Mac's kids. Since he'd been by himself at the marina, he'd been unable to leave even for a few minutes.

So she'd waited. And waited. And waited some more.

Her dog, Buddy, let out a cry of delight, which meant Luke was finally home. "Go get him, Bud." Sydney opened the screen door to let Buddy out to greet Luke, which was another new tradition in her life. Buddy was crazy about Luke, which pleased Sydney to no end. After her children, Max and Malena, had been killed in a car accident, she'd thought the sweet dog might die of a broken heart mourning for Max, the boy he'd adored.

Buddy's affections had been transferred to Luke, which was fine with Syd. They came into the house together, Buddy panting with excitement and Luke looking exhausted after a long day at work. "I won't be here long," Luke assured her as he kissed her. "I know it's girls' night."

"I feel bad overtaking your house. You look wiped out."

"It's *our* house, and nothing a shower and some food won't fix."

"Before you hit the shower, could I have just one minute of your time?"

"I could spare one minute for you." He cupped her bottom and lifted her into his arms.

Sydney squealed with surprise, grasping his shoulders as he carried her into their room.

Luke laughed at her reaction.

"Didn't see that coming."

"I don't want you getting bored with your old man. Got to keep things interesting around here."

"I could never be bored with my old man," she said as she kissed him with all the love and desire and gratitude she felt for him.

"Whoa," he said after many passionate minutes had passed. At some point, he'd pressed her against the wall in the hallway. "What brought that on?"

"Very happy to see you."

"You see me every day."

"And I'm always happy to see you, but today is special."

"How so?"

"Put me down, and I'll show you."

He let her slide down the aroused front of him but kept a firm grip on her hand.

She towed him into the bathroom that adjoined their bedroom and stepped aside so he could see the objects she'd arranged on the countertop. "What's all that?"

"Take a closer look."

He leaned in, his brows furrowed adorably the way they did when he was concentrating on something. And then, as she watched, his eyes widened with surprise and pleasure. "Really?"

Sydney nodded, tears filling her eyes. "Ten tests. Ten positives."

"We're pregnant?"

"We're pregnant. It's not official until Victoria says it is, but ten tests—" She didn't get to finish the sentence, because he was kissing her. Sydney wasn't sure whether the dampness on her face was from her or him, but what did it matter?

After she'd had her tubal ligation reversed earlier in the summer, they'd been told there were no guarantees she'd ever conceive. They'd also been told it could take a year or more.

"A baby," he whispered when he finally came up for air.

"Our baby." She loved him desperately and was thrilled by his emotional reaction to her news.

"I want a little girl who looks just like you."

"I want a little boy who looks just like you."

They shared a smile and another kiss.

"How am I supposed to go out and leave you tonight after you've told me this?"

"We can celebrate later."

"I don't know if I can wait that long."

"Luke... People are coming very soon."

"Yeah," he said with a dirty grin. "You and me."

"Luke! We can't!"

"I'll be so quick you won't even know it happened." As he spoke, he was lifting her skirt and removing her panties.

"Luke... Seriously."

"I'm so serious." He lifted her against the bathroom door and was inside her before she could begin to form even the slightest protest.

As he moved in her, Sydney forgot all about the friends who were due any moment, the appetizers that might be burning in the oven for all she cared or anything other than the sublime pleasure she found in his arms. When she'd thought her life was over after the deaths of her husband and children, Luke had been there to show her otherwise. And now there would be a baby, too.

"I love you so much, Syd. You've made me so damned happy."

Surrounded and possessed by him, she could barely breathe, let alone speak. "Love you, too."

True to his word, he drove her to a quick, full-body orgasm that had him groaning and thrusting into her with ruthless abandon.

"Damn," he whispered. "I need to get you pregnant more often."

Sydney laughed through her tears, laying her lips on his.

"Are you happy?" he asked.

"So happy."

"Scared?"

"Witless." Her fears of bringing another child into the world only to possibly lose it had nearly kept Sydney from trying in the first place.

"I'll be right there with you the whole way. I promise."

"You're the only reason I was able to take this chance." She was determined not to spend the next eight months and eighteen years worrying that disaster was going to strike again. Luke had convinced her that she'd used up her lifetime share of bad luck. It was all smooth sailing ahead, or so he told her. "We can't say anything about this for a while."

"Because of Mac and Maddie."

"Yes."

"People will be asking why I'm smiling so much."

"A couple of weeks at most."

"I can do that." He kissed her again, lingering when she responded enthusiastically. Still lodged inside her, he began to harden again.

"Luke! No more. Put me down. Now."

"Syd?" A female voice called from the living room.

"Shit, Jenny's here early to help. Let me go."

"I'll never let you go." He kissed her once more before withdrawing, harder now than he'd been before. "You're really going to leave me in this condition?"

"Take a cold shower." She opened the bathroom door a crack. "Be right there, Jenny." She cleaned up quickly, pulled on her discarded panties and smoothed the wrinkles in the dress she'd taken the time to iron earlier. For all the good that had done her.

"You're a heartless woman, Sydney Donovan," Luke whispered.

"About that..."

"About what?" he asked as he pulled off the shirt he'd worn to work, putting his deep "farmer's tan" on full display. Sydney teased him about his tanned arms and neck and white torso all summer long.

"My name. I never changed my last name when I married Seth, and it was always kind of awkward when the kids were in school. I was thinking, this time, I'd like to change my name to Harris so we'll all have the same last name."

"I'd love that." He hugged her, which brought her in tight against his rekindled erection. His endless desire for her was a source of constant amazement to her. "Just when I think I can't love you any more than I already do, you blow my mind all over again."

"If you wait a couple of hours before you crash my girls' night, I'll blow something else later."

As his mouth fell open in shock at her unusually blunt language, she patted his face and left him to shower while she went to meet Jenny.

"Am I interrupting something?" Jenny Wilks asked when Sydney joined her in the kitchen.

Sydney started to deny it, but then shrugged. "We were done."

Jenny cracked up laughing. "Milking this newlywed thing for all its worth, huh?"

"Something like that." Sydney wanted to share her news with Jenny so badly she burned with it. "If I tell you something, do you promise not to tell anyone? Even Alex?"

"Well, I don't usually keep things from him, but I suppose I could make an exception since I'm now *dying* of curiosity."

"I'm pregnant," Sydney said in a soft whisper.

Jenny's eyes closed and then reopened, filled with tears. "Thank goodness." She hugged Sydney. "I'm so happy for you both. Congratulations."

"Thanks. We're not going to tell anyone else for now because of Maddie..."

"You know she'd be happier for you than anyone."

Sydney nodded. She had no doubt her old friend would be thrilled for her. "Still, my news can wait a few weeks."

"I take it Luke was happy to hear the news?"

"You can safely assume that," Syd said with a small, satisfied smile.

"Good for you. For both of you. Couldn't happen to better people."

"Thanks. I feel like I can finally breathe again. Since I had the surgery, I've been preparing myself for the possibility that it would never happen. I needed to be okay with that outcome. But this outcome is so much better."

"It certainly is."

Luke came into the kitchen, his hair wet from the shower and his face freshly shaven, making Sydney wish for one second that they were still alone. "I thought we weren't telling anyone," he said with an indulgent grin for his wife.

"Jenny doesn't count," Syd said. "I had to tell her."

"That's right," Jenny said. "And your secret is safe with me." She kissed Luke's cheek. "Congratulations, Dad."

"Dad… Wow. Thanks."

His reaction to the word "dad" filled Sydney with joy. That she would be able to give him that experience was priceless to her. Now that it had actually happened, she felt safe admitting how badly she'd wanted it.

"And now I'm off to keep the guys out of trouble for a while," Luke said.

"Alex and Paul are looking forward to it," Jenny said of her fiancé and his brother. "Things with Marion have been tough lately."

"Is the new nurse working out okay?" Sydney asked.

"Hope is amazing," Jenny said. "She's saved our lives. Dementia is a bitch, though. I wouldn't wish it on anyone."

Sydney poured her friend a tall glass of wine and handed it to her.

"I'll make sure the boys have a good time tonight." Luke kissed Sydney. "See you later."

"Much later."

"I have my orders and a few promises tucked away." He winked at her on his way out the door.

"Promises?" Jenny asked.

"A little incentive package to make sure girls' night isn't crashed too early."

"Oh, I do like how you think."

"So does he."

CHAPTER 28

Jenny and Sydney dissolved into laughter and were still giggling when Janey, Abby, Stephanie and Grace came in together. Everyone had brought appetizers and wine. Next came Laura and Owen's sister Katie, followed shortly after by Kara.

"Get Katie a glass of wine, stat," Laura said, pointing to her sister-in-law.

"Everything okay?" Syd asked.

"She's been dating Shane and having a grand time until Shane's ex-wife showed up out of nowhere today. More than two years without a freaking word, and she has the nerve… Ugh. She makes me sick."

Katie patted Laura's shoulder. "I'm worried about her blood pressure."

"The sight of that woman sends everything into the red zone," Laura said. "I mean why, after all this time, does she have to show up right when he's starting to seem like his old self again? Does she have an *ounce* of compassion in that skinny little body?"

Sydney had never seen Laura mad, let alone furious. "What did Shane do?"

"Sent her packing, thankfully. But God only knows how much damage she left behind."

A knock on the door interrupted Laura's diatribe.

"Come on in." Sydney gasped when Maddie came in, followed by her sister, Tiffany. "You're back." Sydney went right over to Maddie and gave her a hug.

"I'm back, and I'm empty-handed because I didn't have time to make anything."

"Stop," Sydney said. "You didn't have to bring anything. We're so glad to see you."

"Do me a favor," Maddie said, her eyes glistening. "Let's just have a good time tonight and not talk about the elephant in the room. Please?"

"Anything you need."

"That's what I need."

"How about a big glass of wine?"

"That would be good, too."

Sydney met Tiffany's worried gaze over Maddie's shoulder. Tiffany shrugged as if to say she was following Maddie's lead.

"Who's hungry?" Sydney asked, hoping to divert the attention away from Maddie. Everyone was worried and sad for her, but tonight they'd give her exactly what she'd asked for—a night away from it all.

*

Shane felt like a pent-up tiger waiting for Owen to tell him it was time to go. By the time Owen knocked on his door, Shane was ready to pounce. "Where are they? Do you know?"

"Yes, I know, but we're not going there."

"What do you mean? I need to see Katie."

"All in good time."

"You're enjoying this, aren't you?"

"Torturing you? Yes. Seeing my sister cry? Not so much."

"I'm really sorry about that. I can't tell you how sorry I am."

"You need to tell her."

"Which I would if you would *tell me where she is*!" In all the time they'd known each other, Shane had never had reason to yell at Owen, who stared at him now like he was seeing someone he'd never met before.

"Don't make me change my mind about helping you out tonight."

"How would you feel if Laura was upset with you, and no one would tell you where she was so you could go fix it?"

"You're comparing you and Katie to me and Laura?"

Shane refused to squirm under Owen's intense glare. "What if I am?"

"That would make things between you two awfully serious, and you only met last week."

"Okay."

Owen continued to study him with that intense glare that made Shane want to squirm. But he couldn't do that. Not with so much riding on Owen's approval and willingness to help him fix his massive screw-up. "How can you be that serious about her already?"

"How long did it take for you to know Laura was the one for you?"

"We're not talking about me."

"Answer the question."

"I knew the day I met her that she was going to change my life."

"There you have it."

"That fast?"

"Believe me, I'm still trying to get my head around it myself. All I can tell you is that Katie has been more right for me in five days than Courtney was in five years."

Owen smiled then, a big, bright smile that made his eyes crinkle at the corners. "When you see her later, make sure you tell her that. It'll matter to her."

"How much later will I see her?"

"A couple of hours."

"Owen, come on. Have a heart, will you?"

"Crashing girls' night takes finesse and strategy. We can't just stroll in there like we meant to. We have to act like we didn't know they were there. If I tell you where she is, you'll go in there like a bull in a china shop and ruin it for the rest of us. I've got to think of my brothers-in-arms."

"I used to like you, and now I kinda hate you."

Owen, that bastard, laughed hard. "You'll like me again once you fix things with Katie. *If* you fix things."

"Thanks for the vote of confidence. Much appreciated. You're all smug in your newly married bliss, but someday you'll screw up, and I promise to enjoy it twice as much as you're enjoying this."

"Don't hold your breath waiting for that to happen. Your sister is *all* about me."

"Blissful and arrogant. A deadly combination. Don't forget—I've been married, and you're a rookie. Blissful arrogance leads to rookie mistakes. Don't say I didn't warn you."

"I stand warned and unconcerned." Owen checked his watch. "Let's go. We're meeting the boys for dinner at the Beachcomber in ten minutes."

"Dinner? I don't want dinner. I want to talk to your sister."

"I have to wonder why you don't just pick up the phone and call her if you're so all-fired anxious to talk to her."

"Because. We live on the same hallway. We haven't needed to call each other. Yet."

Owen laughed again. He really was a rotten bastard when it came right down to it. "So you don't even have her phone number. Speaking of rookie mistakes."

"If I didn't need you to get me to Katie, I wouldn't be speaking to you right now."

"Good to know."

"I'm going to tell Laura how you tortured me."

"I bet she'll side with me."

"I've known her longer."

"I'm sleeping with her."

"Shut the fuck up. Will you please? Just shut the fuck up."

Owen laughed all the way to the Beachcomber, where they met up with Joe, Adam, Grant, Evan, Blaine, Alex, Paul and Dan. A short time after they arrived, Shane's other cousins Riley and Finn joined the party. Shane was forced to sit through several rounds of beers and somehow managed to choke down the burger Owen ordered for him.

"What's the matter with you tonight?" his cousin Evan asked. "You're wound tighter than a drum."

"I'm being held hostage against my will." Shane used his thumb to point at Owen. "I need to speak to his sister, who is with my sister at girls' night out, but my jackass brother-in-law won't tell me where they are."

"I know where they are," Evan said. "We all do."

"Are you going to tell me?"

"Depends. What'd you do to Katie?"

"Oh my God. Not you, too. You're my freaking *cousin*. Whose side are you on?"

"If you did something that will make all the women mad, I'm on her side. Firmly on her side."

"If being blindsided by my ex-wife while returning from a day in Newport with Katie counts as me doing something to piss them all off, then feel free to take her side."

"Dude," Evan said gravely. "Courtney was *here*?"

"Yeah."

"And?"

"And I had it out with her, but not before I released Katie's hand at the sight of her and asked her to give me a minute with Courtney. Apparently, that wasn't the right thing to do."

"Whoa… Yeah, bad move."

"I was *blindsided*. I hadn't seen or talked to Courtney in more than two years. She served me divorce papers without so much as a *conversation*, and I'm sorry, but I had a few questions for her after all that time."

Grant and Adam tuned in to their conversation, both of them listening intently.

"Did you get any answers?" Adam asked.

"Some. I guess. She says it was all done to protect me. She was in trouble, and it wasn't going away for a while, so she set me free to spare me. Yada, yada. Now she wants me back."

"Holy shit," Grant said in a hushed tone. "What'd you say to that?"

"I said no. No fucking way am I going back to her after what she put me through. And if what's his name would let me see Katie, *I'd tell her that*." This was said loudly enough for Owen to hear.

"We know where they are," Adam said, glancing at his brothers. "We can take you there."

"Would you *please*?"

"It's up to him." Adam pointed to Evan. "His turn to be the designated driver."

"I'm happy to help the cause," Evan said. "Let's go."

They stood up and tossed money on the table to cover their tab.

"Wait," Luke said. "Where're you going?"

"Time to crash," Evan said.

"Not yet. I promised Syd a couple of hours, and it's only been an hour and a half."

Shane would've sworn he'd been there for at least eight hours, or so it seemed.

"By the time we get there, it'll be almost two," Grant said. "That counts as a 'couple' of hours."

"I was made promises," Luke said. "*Good* promises. You wouldn't want to screw that up for me, would you?"

All eyes turned to Shane. Under normal circumstances, he was happy to help a brother out. These were not normal circumstances. "Sorry, Luke. I need to see Katie, and I need to see her right now."

Evan shrugged. "The man is on a mission. We're just his wingmen."

Bolstered by his cousins' support, Shane got up and started to leave with them.

"Wait a minute," Owen said.

Groaning, Shane turned to him. "Don't start again."

"All I was going to say is good luck. And please, don't do anything to hurt her. She's been hurt enough in her life." Gone was the earlier torment and swagger. All that remained was a concerned older brother. Shane extended his hand to his brother-in-law. "You have my word that I'll never again do anything to hurt her."

"Don't make promises you can't keep."

"I never do."

Owen shook his hand.

"Come on," Shane said to his cousins. "Let's go." He followed them down to the street where Evan had parked Grace's four-door sedan. The four men piled into the small car. Shane was crammed into the backseat with Adam. "This is like a clown car."

"It'll get us to Luke and Sydney's house," Evan said in defense of the car.

Shane blew out a sigh of relief at knowing where he'd find her. Now he could only hope she'd give him the chance to apologize and explain.

"Anyone heard from Mac?" Grant asked, breaking the silence.

"They came back on the five o'clock boat," Evan said. "I left him a message to call me if he wants to come out." His phone rang as soon as he finished speaking. He handed it to Grant. "Maybe that's him now."

"It is," Grant said. "Hey, it's Grant. Evan's driving. You want to come? What about the kids? Okay, sure. We'll come get you."

"Where will we put him?" Shane asked. "In the trunk?"

"We'll switch cars," Grant said. "Tiffany drove Maddie, so Maddie's SUV is at the house. We'll have to take the car seats out, though, which will piss off Maddie. We never get them back in the way she wants them."

Shane moaned at the thought of more delays. "And here I thought you guys were on my side."

"We are," Adam assured him. "But we gotta get Mac."

"Yeah," Shane said. "I know."

"Who's with the kids?" Evan asked.

"Mom came over," Grant said. "She encouraged him to go out since Maddie went with Tiffany."

After a long pause, Adam said, "Is it weird that she went out tonight after everything?"

"She was probably in bad need of a diversion," Grant said.

"True."

"I can't imagine that scenario," Evan said. "You go in for an ultrasound all excited to see your baby, and there's no heartbeat."

"It's unbearable," Grant said.

"Unimaginable," Adam added.

"You think they'll be okay?" Shane asked.

"Yeah," Evan said. "They're solid. I can't picture them any other way but solid."

They arrived at Mac's house a few minutes later and went through the motions of removing the car seats from Maddie's car so they could take the big SUV.

"Thanks for coming to get me, you guys," Mac said.

"No problem." Grant put his hand on Mac's shoulder. "I'm really sorry. We all are."

Mac released a deep sigh. "Thanks." He glanced at Shane. "How'd you end up with these characters?"

"He's a man on a mission." Evan filled his oldest brother in on what was going on with Shane.

"So Courtney actually came here?" Mac asked as they got into the backseat together. "With no warning?"

"I had no clue I was about to run into her. She told me she went to my old job and asked my boss where I was, and he told her I was out here. It didn't take much effort to figure out where she could find me here. She's just lucky that Laura didn't see her first, or she never would've gotten to talk to me."

"That must've been so shocking," Mac said, seeming eager to talk about someone else's problems rather than dwelling on his own.

Shane was happy to indulge his cousin. "It was so shocking that I totally screwed up with Katie, and now I'm desperate to fix things with her."

"You and Owen's little sister," Mac said with a chuckle. "How's he handling that?"

"He was handling it pretty well until today when I made her cry without meaning to."

"Ouch," Mac said with a wince. "I remember how annoyed I was with Joe—for the first time in our lives, I might add—when he started dating Janey. There's something about baby sisters that makes older brothers crazy."

"No," Adam said, "there's something about *you* that makes *you* crazy."

Evan and Grant joined Adam in laughing their asses off.

"Soooo true," Evan said. "We're her older brothers, too, and we weren't annoyed with Joe for dating her."

"You're not the oldest," Mac said. "Special responsibilities come with being the oldest."

"You're not the oldest anymore," Evan reminded him.

"Speaking of our older sister," Mac said, "I saw her last night. She brought me a pizza and a six-pack. We had a nice time."

"That's cool," Adam said.

"She met Maddie, too. They really liked each other."

"Dad said she's coming over this weekend to spend the week before the wedding with him and Mom," Grant said. "How do you suppose that'll go?"

"I think it'll be fine," Mac said. "There's nothing not to like about her—and believe me, I tried to find something."

"Why am I not surprised?" Grant asked dryly as the others laughed.

By the time they finally pulled into Luke and Sydney's long driveway, Shane had convinced himself that Katie would have gone from hurt to furious by now, making his task that much more challenging. The second the SUV came to a stop, he was out the door.

He'd been to a cookout here earlier in the summer, but he wasn't particularly close to Luke. However, that didn't stop him from jogging to the door on the side of the house. With one quick knock, he stepped into a room full of women, who went silent at the sight of him.

"Here they come," Abby said.

Shane zeroed in on Katie, who was sitting between Laura and Maddie. He walked over to her and extended his hand. "Could I please speak to you outside?"

She stared at his outstretched hand for what felt like an hour while the others looked on.

Shane would never know if she took his hand because she wanted to talk to him or because everyone was watching and she didn't want to say no in front of them. What did it matter? She was coming with him as he led the way through the kitchen to the deck on the back of the house, where it was dark except for a string of white lights around the rail. He took a deep breath, prepared to put it all on the line to make this right with her.

CHAPTER 29

The moment they were outside and alone, Shane turned to face her. "I'm so sorry, Katie. I've been trying to get to you for hours now so I could say that to you. I was completely shocked to see her, and I reacted badly. It kills me that I hurt you and made you cry after you put such faith in me."

After a long pause, Katie said, "Why did she come?"

"She had things she wanted to tell me."

"What things?"

"It doesn't matter. It has nothing to do with you and me."

"Is there still a you and me?"

"Yes, Katie! I sent her away. She's not the one I want."

"And I am?"

"God, yes. Every minute I spend with you makes me want more of you. For the first time in longer than I can remember, I feel hopeful and happy. Because of you."

"That's very nice to hear."

"But?"

She took a deep breath and seemed to be summoning the courage to say what was on her mind. "I'd like to know what Courtney said to you today."

"I don't want to talk about her. I sent her away. It's truly over between us."

"Hmm, see, I thought it already was—before today."

"So did I! I had no idea she was going to suddenly show up here the way she did. I hadn't seen or talked to her in more than two years."

"And when you saw her, the first thing you did was let go of me. That hurt me, Shane."

"I know." He leaned his forehead against hers and put his hands on her shoulders. "I'm so, so sorry I did that. You have no idea how badly I'd like to go back and have that minute to do over again."

"What would you have done differently?"

"I would've introduced you to her as my girlfriend. If I had done that, you'd know what you mean to me, and she'd know there was no hope of reconciliation."

"*That's* what she wanted?"

Shane wanted to shoot himself for telling her that. He was truly batting a thousand today. "It's what *she* wants. It's not what *I* want. I want *you*."

"You were with her for years, Shane. You've known me for days."

"And I've loved every minute we've spent together. I told your brother earlier that you've been more right for me in five days than she was in five years. He said I ought to tell you that."

When she sniffled, he realized she was crying.

"Katie, please… I'm so sorry. The last thing in the world I want to do is hurt you or make you cry. It's killing me to see you cry."

"You talked to Owen? About me?"

"Um, yeah, he basically tortured me by not telling me where you were and dragging me along to dinner with him and the guys. He's not too happy with me for making you cry."

"I don't blame you for what happened earlier. You had no way to know she'd be there waiting for you."

"I didn't know. I swear it."

"I believe you." She took a deep breath. "You were married to her for a long time, so it's only natural that the sight of her would make you feel guilty for holding hands with someone else."

"I don't feel guilty being with you, Katie. Not one bit. I'm single, and I have been for almost two years."

"And in all that time, you wondered why she left you. Isn't that what you told me?"

"Yes," he said, resigned to having this conversation when all he wanted was to take her home so they could be alone to work this out.

"Did you find out why?"

"She said it was because she had to testify against some big-time drug dealers to get immunity on being prosecuted herself for dealing. Or something like that. Apparently, the big guys were convicted yesterday, and she's now free and clear."

"So she divorced you to protect you?"

"That's what she said. Who knows if it's the truth?"

"Would your father know? Doesn't he have connections with the court?"

"What does it matter at this point, Katie? I don't want her back. I don't want a life of always wondering where she is, if she's lying, what she's doing, who she's doing it with. I almost lost my mind being with her. It's not what I want anymore."

"When did you decide that?"

"You want an exact date?"

"An estimate would be good."

"I don't know. Last winter, maybe? I thought about what I'd do if she sought me out. And quite some time ago, I made up my mind that when or if she came looking for me, I wasn't going to be available."

"So before you met me."

"Long before."

"And when you saw her today, how did you feel?"

"Shocked. I never actually expected her to come after the way she dumped me. Plus, I didn't think she knew where I was."

"Did you feel anything else besides shock?"

"I feel like I'm on the witness stand here. Let's cut to the chase. What do you really want to know?"

"Do you still love her?"

"No!"

"And when did you know you weren't in love with her anymore?"

"I've suspected for quite some time, but today I knew for certain."

"That's what I was afraid of."

"I do not love her. I do not want to be with her. Judging by the way I felt earlier when I had no idea where to look for you, it's quite possible that I actually love *you*, and I know for damned sure I want to be with you."

"You... You love *me*?"

Nodding, he took hold of her hand and placed it over his chest where his heart beat so hard and so fast it was a wonder he didn't pass out from the exertion. "That's what my fear of losing you is doing to me. I just found you, and I don't want to lose you."

"You have unfinished business with her."

"No, I don't. Our business was finished the day our divorce was final."

Katie shook her head.

"What're you saying?"

"You need closure."

"I need *you*."

"What if... What if a year or two from now, you wake up one day and realize you let your true love get away?"

"Will you still be with me then? If so, my true love didn't get away."

"You can't possibly know that about me in only a few days' time."

"Yes, I can." Unable to refrain from touching her, he cupped her face in his hands and kissed her. "I can know that. I *do* know that."

Her hands curled around his wrists. "Shane..."

"Courtney is my past. You're my future. I feel that strongly for you, Katie. I think I knew it the day I pulled you out of the water and blew air into your lungs. You're *mine*. Mine, Katie." Pushing the hair back from her face, he gazed into her eyes. "If you send me away right now, I wouldn't go back to her. I'm never going back to her. Why would I do that when everything I want and need is right here in my arms?"

"You have to be sure, Shane."

"I'm three thousand percent positive." He knew if they got a hundred years to spend together, Katie would never deceive him the way Courtney had. She would never use him or steal from him or make him feel like shit the way his ex-wife had. Katie simply wasn't wired that way. "Will you please accept my apology for what happened earlier and give me a chance to prove I'm worth the risk?"

"I want to. I really do. But I need a little time to think."

"How much time?"

"I don't know yet."

"Katie, please. Don't do this. Let's spend that time together working this out."

"I want you to know… I've heard everything you've said, and I appreciate that you apologized. I also respect the fact that you were caught off guard by her appearance here today. I understand all that."

"So why do you need time?"

"I need to process everything that's happened in the last few days and figure out where I go from here."

"Where you go? I don't get it. You said you understand what happened today, but you still want time?"

"I *need* time."

He put his arms around her and whispered in her ear, "I'm crazy about you. I want to be with you. I want to work this out with you so we can get back to where we were before we were so rudely interrupted."

"I want that, too."

"Then let's go."

She extricated herself from his embrace, and the resolute expression on her face gave him pause. "I care about you very much. You know I've been closer to you than I have to any other man, and I loved every minute we spent together."

Shane experienced a surge of panic that reminded him of a time he'd rather forget. "Why do I feel like you're saying good-bye to me?"

"I'm not saying good-bye. I'm saying I need a few days to myself. That's all."

He'd said everything he could to convince her that he was genuinely committed to his relationship with her, but it hadn't been enough. "Okay, then. I guess I'll see you around."

Shane felt like he was walking through wet cement as he left her, went into the house and headed straight for the door that would lead him out of there. He needed to get away from everyone and everything before he said or did something he'd regret.

Of course, Laura and Owen were right behind him as he went out the door.

Laura called out to him. "Shane, wait!" She grabbed his arm. "What happened? Where're you going?"

"Katie needs some time to think, and I'm going back to the hotel. I'll see you tomorrow."

"You shouldn't walk home in the dark," his sister said. "It's not safe."

Evan materialized out of the darkness. "I'll take him."

"Thanks, Ev," Shane said.

"Will you be all right?" Laura asked.

"I'm fine. Go back to girls' night. Apologize to Luke and Sydney for me, will you?" He kissed her cheek and left her with Owen while he went with Evan.

"Thanks again for this, Evan."

"No problem." After a long pause, Evan said, "So I take it things didn't go well with Katie."

"I'm not exactly sure. She said she understands what happened today and why, but she needs 'time.'"

"Ouch."

"Right? What the hell does that mean?"

"I wouldn't want to speculate."

"It's not good, though, is it?"

Evan rubbed his face as he thought about that. "It's not good *today*, but it might be okay in a day or two. You just have to be patient."

"It took me two years after Courtney left me to go out on a date. The first time I went out with Katie, I knew she was special. Things were going really well with us, and then Courtney shows up and it all goes to shit in one minute?"

"Maybe Katie needs a few days to make sure she's ready for a relationship."

"Yeah, maybe." Shane agreed with his cousin, but the sinking feeling inside was indicative of his true sentiments, which he kept to himself.

"You want to hear something I just found out?"

"Sure." Anything was better than thinking about his own problems.

"The resort where Grace and I booked our wedding had a water main break, and they're going to be closed for months while they fix the damage."

"So where does that leave you guys?"

"They're going to try to rebook us somewhere else, but they aren't making any guarantees."

"And you just heard this?"

Nodding, Evan said, "I made the mistake of checking my email on my phone while everyone else was drinking."

"Did you tell Grace?"

"Not yet. I figured I'd let her have a good time tonight, and we'll deal with it in the morning."

"That sucks, but I'm sure you'll find somewhere else. You've got a couple of months, right?"

Evan nodded. "Five months."

"Good luck with that."

"Thanks. We're going to need it." Evan pulled up to the hotel and turned into the parking lot. "Hang in there, buddy. It'll work out."

He shook hands with his cousin. "Hope it works out for both of us. Thanks again for the ride." Shane got out of the car, went into the hotel and straight up to his room, where the scent of Katie's perfume lingered from her earlier visit.

What had started out as a rather great day had gone to shit, and it was all Courtney's fault. Lying on his bed, staring up at the ceiling he'd helped to paint, he wondered if he'd ever be free of her.

*

From his vantage point in Luke's kitchen, Mac had a perfect view of Maddie, sitting among the women, laughing and chatting as if she hadn't a care in the world. She didn't have a word to say to him, but had no trouble talking to her friends. He was hardly ever truly angry with her, but he was right now. What were they even doing here? They should be home alone, recovering from their loss together.

Did their friends and family think them uncaring because they'd come out to socialize so soon after losing their baby? No one would ever say such a thing, but he was sure they were thinking it, because he was, too.

"Mac?" Grant offered him another beer.

"No, thanks." The one he had wasn't going down well. He had no desire for another.

Grant followed his gaze to the living room. "She seems to be doing well."

"A little too well, if you ask me."

"What do you mean?"

The moment the words left his mouth, he felt disloyal to his wife. "I shouldn't have said that." As Grant eyed him inquisitively, Mac released a deep sigh. He was unaccustomed to problems in his marriage and had no idea how to handle this situation. "She's acting like nothing happened, when I feel like I'm going to be sick."

"Perhaps that's her way of coping?"

"Maybe," Mac conceded. "She's been really, really quiet since we found out, especially around me. Last night, with Mallory, she seemed more like herself, but as soon as Mallory left, she was right back in the shell."

"It's only been a couple of days. I'm sure she'll bounce back to her old self before too long."

"I'm mad with her," Mac said softly. "I'm never mad with her."

"Don't go there. Nothing good will come of that."

"Believe me, I know. Can't help it, though."

When Stephanie came into the kitchen, Grant extended his hand to her.

She took his hand and snuggled up to him. "I just got some horrible news."

"What is it?"

"One of my best waitresses is resigning because she's really sick. She has lung cancer, of all things."

"Not Lisa Chandler," Mac said as a sense of dread overtook him.

"Yes, right, you know her, too. The house and everything."

Mac felt like he'd been gut punched. "Oh my God. This is awful. She was at the house the other day and couldn't stop coughing. She said she couldn't afford the clinic, so we asked David to check on her."

"I hate to hear that she couldn't afford the doctor," Stephanie said. "I pay my staff as much as I possibly can, but it's still not enough for some of them."

"Her poor kids," Mac said.

"I know," Stephanie said tearfully. "They're adorable." She looked up at Grant. "Do you mind if we go home? I'm not much in the mood to party after hearing this."

"Sure, hon. I'm ready to go." To Mac, he said, "I'll call you tomorrow."

"Sounds good."

"Hang in there," Grant said, "and stay calm, okay?"

"I will." He knew Grant was right. Allowing his anger to fester wouldn't help the situation. It would only make things worse. Mac pushed off the counter and went into the living room.

Maddie looked up when she saw him coming. But rather than the usual adoring look he always received from her, this time she seemed wary.

"Can we go?" he asked.

"I didn't drive. Did you?"

"No." Mac's frustration grew when he realized they were stuck there until they could get a ride.

"I'll take you," Tiffany said. "I promised Blaine I'd be home early."

"He was with us earlier but went home after dinner."

"He has to work tomorrow."

"The rest of us do, too," Mac said, thankful for the diversion that gave him something else to think about besides Maddie's unusual silence.

"Blaine is ridiculously disciplined on work nights. So much so I'll probably have to trick him into having sex with me tonight."

"I can just imagine the kind of tricks you're capable of," Maddie said dryly.

Tiffany winked at her sister. "Works every time."

Mac had little doubt that Tiffany had sensed the tension between him and Maddie and was trying to lighten the mood with her irreverence. The three of them said good night to the others and headed out the door. Mac took the backseat so Maddie and her sister could sit together.

The two of them chatted about the kids, the carpool for Thomas and Ashleigh's art camp in the morning and the possibility of a beach outing in the afternoon.

"I'll call you in the morning," Tiffany said when they arrived at Mac and Maddie's house.

"Sounds good. Thanks for helping Mom with the kids while we were gone."

"It was no problem at all. We adore them."

Maddie hugged Tiffany and got out of the car.

"Mac," Tiffany said in a low tone. "I want you to know how sorry I am. If there's anything I can do…"

"See if you can get her to talk about it. I've had no luck."

"I will. Tomorrow."

"Thanks." He followed Maddie up the stairs and into the family room, where his parents were watching TV—or he should say his mom was watching. His dad was asleep next to her but came to when they walked in.

"You're home early," Linda said.

"We're tired," Mac replied.

"I'm sure you are. We'll get out of your hair."

Maddie hugged and kissed her in-laws. "Thanks for coming over tonight."

"We're happy to do it any time, honey," Big Mac said.

Maddie gave him a grateful smile and said good night.

Watching her go up the stairs, Mac had never felt more impotent. He knew in his heart of hearts that she was suffering, but she refused to let him in, and he didn't understand why.

"Give her time, sweetheart," Linda said softly.

"It's killing me that she won't talk to me."

"She will. When she's ready. Try to be patient."

"I'm not exactly known for my patience, especially where she's concerned."

"It's what she needs right now, Mac. I know it's so hard for you, but please try."

"I will." Mac hugged both his parents and waited for them to get into his dad's truck before he turned off the outside lights and locked up. He trudged up the stairs without the enthusiasm he always felt when it was finally time to go to bed with Maddie.

Tonight he felt anxious and sad. While he knew his mother and Grant were right and he had to be patient, he wanted to scream with frustration and grief and a million other emotions that swirled through him. Instead of screaming and raging, though, he checked on the kids, then took a shower and shaved before getting into bed beside Maddie.

She shut off the bedside light and turned on her side, facing away from him.

Staring at her back in stunned disbelief, Mac began to feel truly afraid.

CHAPTER 30

After Shane left, Katie remained on the deck, trying to get her emotions under control before she rejoined the party. The conversation with him had been one of the most grueling things she'd ever been through. When she'd wanted to pull him close and hold on tight to him, she'd had no choice but to push him away. And now her heart was truly breaking, especially as she recalled the stricken expression on his face when he realized she'd meant it when she said she needed time.

The sliding door opened, and Owen and Laura came outside.

"Are you all right?" Concern caused Owen's brows to furrow the way they used to when he was dealing with their father. "We tried to give you a minute to yourself, but when you didn't come back in…"

Katie nodded. "I will be. Did you talk to Shane?"

"He said you asked for some time," Laura said as she rubbed her hand over Katie's back soothingly.

"That's right."

"Do you want to talk about it?" Owen asked.

"I told him I needed some time to think, but I'm not the one who needs the time. He does."

"How do you mean?" Laura asked, clearly perplexed.

"He found out today that Courtney still loves him, that she always has. I can't help but assume he needs to process that information before he moves on with me or anyone."

"He sent her away," Laura reminded her.

"That doesn't mean he wasn't affected by what she said to him. How could he not be after the way he suffered over her?"

Owen folded his arms and studied her intently. "So what you're saying is *you* sent *him* away because *he* needs time to think, not you?"

"That's right. I know what I want, but I need to make sure he's ready before I commit to a relationship with him."

"He said he never wants to see her again," Laura said gently.

"I know all that. But what happens if he wakes up tomorrow or the next day and feels differently? Where does that leave me?" Chilled, she rubbed her arms. "I need to be sure. *He* needs to be sure." She drew in a deep breath. "Sending him away just now was one of the hardest things I've ever done. It was the last thing I wanted to do." Her voice broke on the final words.

Owen took off his jacket, put it around her shoulders and then drew her into a hug.

"You're just like your brother," Laura said with a kind smile. "Always thinking of others before yourself."

"I care about him. I want to be with him, but only if he's truly free." Tears rolled unchecked down her face, and Owen wiped them away. She looked up at her brother. "Did I do the right thing, O?"

"You did, honey. You're right that he needs to think things through now that he's seen Courtney. And you're absolutely right to protect yourself, too."

"I'm more worried about him than I am about me. Did he leave?"

"Evan took him back to town."

"Oh, good. I was afraid he was walking in the dark."

"How about we head home, too?" Laura said. "Something tells me you're not in the mood for girls' night this time around."

"I don't want to take you away from your friends."

"I'm in a constant state of exhaustion these days." Laura patted her belly. "You'd be doing me a favor if you took me home."

"In that case," Katie said, forcing a smile, "I'd love to go home."

They made their excuses to the others and headed out just as Evan was returning from taking Shane.

"Is he okay?" Katie asked.

"He's upset and confused, but he's all right."

"I hate this," Katie whispered to her brother, who squeezed her shoulder in support. While she ached from head to toe, at least she understood why everyone made such a big deal about romantic entanglements. Nothing had ever hurt more than seeing Shane with his ex-wife or having to take a step back from him tonight out of self-preservation.

She used to think her sister was being a drama queen when she'd weep for days over a breakup. Now she got it. As Owen drove them back to the hotel, Katie sat in the backseat, brushing away tears. "Don't let me go to him when we get there," she said.

"We'll tuck you in," Laura assured her.

"Will you check on him?"

"Of course I will."

"Thanks."

True to their word, Laura and Owen walked her to her room and stayed until she was ready for bed. Katie climbed into the big comfortable bed where she and Shane had shared such magical hours together and broke down all over again.

Laura and Owen stretched out on either side of her, making her laugh through her tears.

"You guys are on your honeymoon," she said. "You don't need me in the middle."

"We don't mind staying for a while," Owen said.

"I'm all right," Katie said after several quiet minutes. "It's safe to leave. But thanks for holding me up the way you always have."

"And I always will." Owen kissed her forehead and got up.

They left, promising to check on her in the morning.

As soon as she was alone, the tears flowed freely down her face as she thought about the wonderful day she'd spent with Shane until it veered off course. She relived every minute they'd spent together, from that fateful day at the beach through to the painful conversation on Luke's deck and everything in between. The trip down memory lane only made her cry harder as she hoped they'd get the chance to make more memories together. His words ran through her mind, torturing her and threatening her resolve to keep her distance from him.

I'm three thousand percent sure.

I actually love you.

I sent her away. It's truly over between us.

You've been more right for me in five days than she was in five years.

Had she done the wrong thing? Would he want her back after she pushed him away? Was she in love with him? Was that why she hurt so badly? Questions filled her mind, but answers were elusive as she drifted off to sleep even as sobs continued to rack her body.

She woke when a crack of thunder crashed through her room, making the windows rattle. Lightning lit the darkness, sending Katie burrowing deeper into her bed, pillow over her head, which was how she nearly missed the soft knock on her door.

She flew out of bed and threw open the door to find Shane, wearing only a pair of basketball shorts.

"I thought you might be scared."

Thrilled to see him and overwhelmed by his kindness, she took his hand and all but dragged him into the room, closing the door behind her. They got into bed, and Shane reached for her.

Katie snuggled up to him as another loud boom of thunder made her whimper.

"It's okay, honey. I'm right here."

He held her close as the storm raged, reassuring her with soft words and the gentle caress of his hand on her back.

Katie fell asleep in his arms, no more certain that she belonged there than she'd been earlier, but comforted nonetheless by his tenderness.

*

Tiffany arrived home to find Blaine in bed but still awake. Her daughter, Ashleigh, was cuddled up to him, her dark hair spread out on the pillow. "Bad dream?" Tiffany asked, moved as she always was by the sight of her child in the arms of the man she loved.

"Thunder."

"Oh, right."

Tiffany smoothed the hair off her sleeping child's face. "I can take her back to bed."

"No way are you lifting her. I've got her." He picked up the little girl and carried her to her room.

Tiffany followed and helped to tuck her in.

When Blaine leaned over to kiss Ashleigh's forehead, Tiffany blinked back tears. She was an emotional basket case these days, but never more so than when she witnessed how much her husband loved her daughter.

With his hand on her back, Blaine followed Tiffany from Ashleigh's room into theirs at the other end of the hallway. "How was Maddie?"

"Good, actually. Surprisingly good. Except for one thing. She seems to be avoiding Mac."

"Why would she do that?"

"I don't know, but he's a mess over it."

"I'd be a mess, too, if that happened to us." He rested his hand on her flat belly. "Feeling okay?"

"Better than earlier."

"Did anyone notice that you didn't drink?"

She shook her head. "I used the designated-driver excuse. No one thought a thing of it."

"You'll have to tell Maddie eventually."

"I know, but not now. Not for a while."

Blaine groaned. "I really can't tell *anyone*?"

"I know it's so hard to keep it a secret, but my sister…"

"I understand, honey. I really do. And it's the right thing. It's just hard not to shout it from the rooftops. My wife is pregnant! We're having a baby!"

She smiled at his adorable enthusiasm. "You can shout it to me all you'd like. I'm always happy to hear the good news."

"Even though you feel like crap?"

"It's a small price to pay, and it won't last forever." Tiffany kissed him. "I'll be right with you."

"I'll be right here, waiting for you."

The loss of her unborn niece or nephew had hit Tiffany hard, especially in light of her own recently discovered pregnancy. She'd been so excited to be pregnant with her sister again, like they were with Thomas and Ashleigh. And then to hear that Maddie's baby was gone… She'd cried for hours while trying to be supportive of her beloved sister.

Tiffany changed into a T-shirt and brushed her teeth before joining Blaine in bed. Thank goodness for him. He'd been her rock this week while her emotions swung from elated to despondent and back to elated.

"Come here, baby—and baby."

"You are so damned cute, you know that? I love how excited you are about the baby."

"I'm so far beyond excited they haven't yet invented the word for it."

"I'm glad you're happy. Don't get me wrong. It's just… It's kind of soon still, and anything can happen."

"Just because it happened to Maddie doesn't mean it'll happen to you."

"I know that. Of course I know that, but still…"

"I hear you, and I know it's always a risk, but I have a good feeling about this baby of ours. He's going to be fine. I know it."

"*He*? You sound awfully sure."

"I need some testosterone reinforcements around here. It's got to be a boy."

"I'm picturing another frilly girly-girl who will wrap her daddy right around her little finger the way Ashleigh has."

"That kid does have me wrapped."

"Yes, she does, and I love you so much for the way you love her."

"She makes it easy. She's adorable just like her mama, only smaller and less mouthy."

"Ha-ha," Tiffany said, even though she knew it was true. Her daughter was the image of her without the saucy attitude. That would come later. She had no illusions about her daughter's teenage years.

He wrapped his strong arms around her. "You know I love your mouth and every other thing about you."

"I do know that. Thanks for propping me up this week."

"That's my job."

"And you do it so well."

"Close your eyes and get some sleep."

"You don't want to…"

"Always. Every minute of every day I want to. But my baby mama needs sleep more than she needs me groping her."

"I wouldn't mind a little groping. You wouldn't want me to feel neglected, would you?"

His bark of laughter made her smile. She loved to make him laugh. His laugh was one of her favorite things. "I'd never want that." He rolled over so he was on top of her, looking down at her with amusement and love.

Tiffany wrapped her arms and legs around him and drew him into a kiss. "I love you."

"Ah, baby," he said with a sigh. "I love you so much it hurts."

She raised her hips, encouraging him to take what she offered. "Let's see if we can make it feel better."

*

Shane was awake all night, thinking about Katie and Courtney and everything that had happened the day before. While Katie slept in his arms, he thought it through from every angle and knew what he needed to do. First, he had to make sure Courtney went back to the mainland, and then he had to get busy convincing Katie that he was ready for all the things he wanted with her.

Energized by his plan, he moved slowly to get out of bed without disturbing her. He'd already disturbed her enough. Today he would prove himself to her. Shane ducked out of her room and headed for his, thankful to avoid any wandering family members as he went.

Since it was too early to do much of anything else, he decided to go for a run and a quick swim to shake off the grogginess of the sleepless night. The hotel was quiet as he went down the stairs and out to the beach, where he ran the full length of the town beach and back again.

When he reached the front of the Sand & Surf, he bent at the waist to catch his breath. He guzzled the bottle of water he'd brought with him and kicked off his running shoes to dive into the ocean. The cool blast of the water was a shock to his overheated body, but it helped to clarify his thinking.

He floated for a long time before he returned to the beach, picked up his shoes and empty water bottle and headed for the stairs. Shane was only partially surprised to see Courtney sitting on the second to last step with a tall coffee in her hand and another on the step next to her.

She handed the other one to him and scooted over to make room for him on the step. "Cream, no sugar."

He took the cup and sat next to her. Today her long dark curls were pulled back in a ponytail, and a headband held the wispy ends away from her pretty face. That face had haunted him for years, but not anymore.

"It's funny," she said with a laugh. "When I asked your old boss where you were and he told me you were here, I thought, of course he is. He loves that island. Where else would he be?"

Though there was much he could say to that, he chose to remain silent and let her have her say. Then he'd have his.

"I'm so sorry for everything that happened, Shane. I hope you know how sorry I am. It was completely unfair of me to marry you when I did, knowing how sick I was. I never should've dragged you into the mess that was my life. But I loved you so much. Too much. I couldn't bear the thought of losing you. I'd hoped…" She took a deep breath and a sip of her coffee. "I thought I could get it under control, and you'd never have to know. But I was incredibly naïve. I had no concept of what a vicious adversary I was up against." She looked over at him with dark brown eyes that shimmered with emotion in the early morning light. "I heard everything you said yesterday, and I deserved every word of it. All I'm asking for is a chance to show you who I am *now*."

Her plea hung heavily in the humid air between them.

Shane took a drink from his coffee and tried to find the words he needed. "I was so lost for so long after you left, and even a few months ago, I might've been willing to try again."

"But now you're not."

"I've met someone else, Courtney."

"The woman you were with yesterday."

He nodded. "Her name is Katie, and she's a really amazing person."

"Have you been together long?"

"Not long at all. I met her a week ago when she came for her brother's wedding. Her brother Owen married Laura."

"What happened to Justin?" Courtney asked of Laura's longtime boyfriend and now ex-husband.

"He never quit dating after they were married."

"Oh jeez." She pushed the sand around with her foot. "So you've only just met Katie. It can't be that serious with her."

"You'd think so, right? But we had sort of a dramatic beginning." He told her about the near-drowning incident that started their relationship. "We've become very close since then, and I like how I feel when I'm with her."

"We have a lot of years invested, Shane. I can't see how a few days with her would trump all that time."

"It might not make sense to anyone else, but it makes sense to us. I want to be with her. I'm sorry if that's not what you want to hear, but there's just too much water under the bridge between us. There's no going back to who we were before."

She covered her mouth to muffle the sound of a sob that seemed to come from deep inside her. "Everything I did was to protect you."

"And I appreciate that. More than you know. But it's over, Courtney."

Bending her head, she continued to sob softly. "If you hadn't met Katie, would you give me another chance?"

He thought about that for a long moment. "No," he said. "We've been over for a long time, as far as I'm concerned. I'm sorry if hearing that hurts your feelings, but it's the truth." After another quiet minute, he said, "I think you should go home."

"I don't really have a home anymore."

"I've continued to pay the rent on the apartment. It's all yours if you want it."

She wiped the tears from her face. "You're not going back to Providence?"

"Nope. I'm staying here."

"But your stuff..."

"Everything I need is here." With those truthful words came a powerful sense of peace that finally set him free from the past. "Take the apartment, Courtney. Start over. I'll pay the rent for another year."

"You don't have to do that."

"I know I don't, but I will. Do you still have a key?"

"Yeah, I do." She glanced at him. "You were always too good for me, Shane."

"It wasn't all bad. I'm choosing to remember the good times and let the rest go."

She stood, so he did, too. "Thanks for seeing me and talking to me. I wouldn't have blamed you if you'd told me to go to hell."

"Take care of yourself."

"You, too." She surprised him with a hug that he returned reluctantly. Then she headed up the stairs and out of his life.

Feeling lighter and freer than he had in years, Shane sat on the stair to finish his coffee. A long time later, he went up the stairs and into the hotel, where Adele was working at the front desk.

"Did you get drafted?" he asked Katie's grandmother.

"I volunteered. I've still got some game."

"I have no doubt," he said with a laugh.

"Heard there was a spot of trouble yesterday between you and my girl."

"Unfortunately, you heard right."

"What're you doing about it?"

Rather than be intimidated by the gauntlet she threw down, Shane decided to recruit her to help his cause. He leaned on the counter that sat above the reception desk. "Here's what I'm thinking."

CHAPTER 31

The sun streaming through her windows woke Katie. She blinked several times as she came awake with the scent of Shane's cologne clinging to the sheets. He'd come to her during the storm, she remembered with a flutter of butterflies in her belly. Over and over she heard the words he'd said to her the night before on Luke and Sydney's deck…

Judging by the way I felt earlier when I had no idea where to look for you, it's quite possible that I actually love you, *and I know for damned sure I want to be with you.*

"I want to be with you, too," she whispered to the humid morning sea air that floated through her open windows.

As she lay in bed and tried to puzzle her way through all the emotions running around inside her, she heard a rustling sound in the hallway before an envelope appeared under her door.

Katie jumped out of bed, wincing when her sore foot connected with the floor. She bent to pick up the envelope and tore it open to find Sand & Surf stationery and distinctly masculine handwriting.

Good morning, sweet Katie,

I've never been more thankful for thunder and lightning, because it gave me an excuse to hold you while you slept. I wish it didn't scare you so much, but know that I'll always hold you when the thunder comes.

You said you need time to think, so please think about this: You're the only one I want. There's no one else but you.

Love,

Shane

With his letter in hand, Katie went to the door and threw it open, looking for him in the hallway, but no one was there. She went back for her robe, pulled it on with trembling hands and went down the hall to knock on his door.

No answer.

When she turned back toward her room, Owen was coming out of his apartment. "Morning."

"Morning."

"Everything okay?"

"I was just looking for Shane. Have you seen him this morning?"

"He stopped by to play with Holden, but he's gone to meet Mac at the house they're building. Did you hear about the woman who was supposed to get the house?"

"I did. It's so sad."

"It sure is. They've got to figure out next steps with the house and how they can help her and her kids."

Katie wasn't surprised to learn that Shane wanted to help.

"What's that?" Owen asked of the letter.

"Oh, um, just a note from Shane."

"I thought you were taking some time apart."

"We are."

"So why is he sending you notes?"

"Because he had something he needed to tell me." She folded the letter and put it in the pocket of her robe. "You said Holden is up. Is he available for playing with aunts or does he only prefer uncles?"

"He doesn't have much experience with aunts."

"Well, we need to remedy that."

While Owen took care of some errands away from the hotel, Katie went to visit with Holden and Laura, who made coffee and breakfast for Katie, despite her objections. "You're pregnant with twins," Katie said. "I should be waiting on you."

"Nonsense. I finally feel human again after months of morning sickness." She put a plate of French toast on the table. "And besides, I need to eat, too."

"Smells great."

"It's one of your grandmother's recipes."

Katie picked up Holden and put him in his high chair and laughed at the way he grabbed fistfuls of the Cheerios Laura put on his tray.

During the hour she spent with Laura and Holden, she reached repeatedly into her pocket to make sure Shane's letter was still there.

"I suppose I ought to get downstairs to relieve Adele before she quits as my chief volunteer," Laura said after they'd eaten the French toast, cleaned the kitchen and gotten Holden dressed.

"I'm sure she's loving it. She told me how much she's missed it."

"Owen and I are still stunned by their amazing wedding gift."

"The hotel is in good hands with the two of you. We all think so."

"I'm so glad to hear that. We love it here. We'd been thinking about moving to a bigger place, but I think we might knock down a wall to make room for the babies and stay put."

"You've certainly got the best view in town."

"That we do."

Katie rinsed out her coffee mug and put it on the drainer to dry. "Thanks so much for breakfast and the playtime with Holden."

"It was our pleasure. He's here any time you need a playmate."

Katie went back to her own room and found another letter on the floor inside her door. Once again, she tore open the envelope and devoured the note.

Dear sweet Katie,

More food for thought… I saw Courtney this morning. She waylaid me after my run on the beach and again tried to convince me to give her another chance. I told her I've met someone else, and I'm happy with her. (HER = YOU, of course.) She tried to convince me that five years trumps five days every time. But not this time. She's gone back to Providence to pick up the pieces of her life. I'm staying here. With you. If you'll have me.

Love,

Shane

Katie covered her mouth with her hand and reread the note over and over. He'd sent Courtney away—again. He hadn't changed his mind or decided to go back to his ex-wife. The relief she felt at that news took her breath away as she headed for the shower.

She emerged wrapped in towels to another note under her door. Since she knew he'd left for work, he must've gotten someone to deliver them for him.

Like the others, the envelope was shredded in her haste to read what he'd written.

Dear sweet Katie,

While you do your thinking, here's what I'm thinking about… I dream about your soft skin and the pleasure I've found in your arms. I dream about how it felt to lose myself in you. I was reborn with you. I can't wait to hold you and make love to you again.

Love,

Shane

Katie was on fire for him. She wanted him right now, but it was only ten o'clock. He wouldn't be home for hours. The thought of that made her moan. She was still standing there thinking about him when another letter arrived. She ran for the door and threw it open, scaring the hell out of her grandfather.

"*Poppy*! What're you doing?"

"Um, I… ah, your grandmother asked me to bring up this note that was left for you downstairs."

"Are there more?"

"A couple more."

"I'm coming down."

"In a towel?"

That's when Katie remembered she wasn't dressed, which only added to her grandfather's discomfort. "Be right there." She closed the door and tore open the envelope.

Dear sweet Katie,

Another thing I'm thinking about… I'm so glad we didn't drown that day at the beach. I would've been so sad if I'd missed the chance to know you. You make me hopeful again. I had given up on so many things, and you led me back into the light. Don't give up on me.

Love,

Shane

She was going to spontaneously combust long before five o'clock. After she threw on shorts and a tank top and added the new letter to the growing pile on her desk, she went downstairs, moving as fast as she could on her injured foot.

"Give it up, Gram," Katie said to Adele when she found her grandmother still working the reception desk.

"I have no idea what you're talking about."

"Too late. I caught your messenger outside my door. You're busted. I want the rest of them."

"I'm afraid that's not possible. I'm under strict instructions, so you'll have to wait in your room for any future deliveries."

"That's not fair!"

"What's not fair?" Sarah asked as she came in the main door.

"Gram has letters for me from Shane, and she won't give them to me."

"Mother, are you tormenting your granddaughter?"

"Not at all. I'm assisting a lovely young man who asked me to do him a favor. He was very precise in his directions."

"Sounds like you have to wait, honey," Sarah said.

"Ugh!" Katie went back upstairs to await the next note, which arrived a very long hour later, once again delivered by her grandfather. "How many more are there?"

"I don't know. Don't shoot the messenger."

"Love you, Poppy."

"Love you, too, pumpkin. For what it's worth, he seems like a nice guy."

"He is."

"Don't let me keep you. Go see what he has to say. You know you're dying to."

"I am!" With a smile for her grandfather, Katie stepped into her room, closed the door and tore open the envelope.

Dear sweet Katie,

More food for thought… Since we're both sticking around on Gansett this winter, how about we get a place together? One with a fireplace. I love fires in the winter. Do you? Are you convinced yet that I'm serious about you? Do you believe me when I tell you you're the only one I want?

Love,

Shane

"Oh God, Shane. You're killing me." Hoping to catch her grandfather making another delivery, she threw open the door and gasped when she found Shane standing there.

There was nothing left to think about when she jumped into his arms or when he lifted her into his kiss. Holding her tightly, he carried her inside and kicked the door closed behind him.

"What're you doing home? I thought I had to wait hours to see you."

"We're at a standstill with the house, so I asked Mac if I could take another day off." He kissed her again and then set her down on her feet. "I take it you got my notes?"

"Yes, oh my God, Shane. I can't believe all the things you said."

"Believe it. I mean every word."

"You really want to get a place together? We just met last week!"

"Does that matter? We're not kids anymore, Katie. If we want to be together, why can't we just go for it?" He put his arms around her and nuzzled her neck. "What if there's a thunderstorm, and I'm not there?"

Her laughter became a moan when he rolled her earlobe between his teeth, setting every nerve ending in her body on fire for him. The thought of being with him every day filled her with the kind of euphoria she'd never felt before.

"Katie… I want you so badly. I want you in every way that I can have you. When I thought I might've lost you… Tell me I haven't lost you. Put me out of my misery."

"You haven't lost me. I want you just as badly. What you wrote, the things you said…"

"I've fallen completely in love with you." He peppered her face with kisses. "Please tell me you feel the same way."

"I do."

"Why do you sound hesitant? Are you still thinking about it?"

"I'm not hesitant about you or wanting to be with you. Not anymore. Everything you said in your notes today… They were so amazing."

"Then what is it? Remember when you told me to speak my mind and get it off my chest?"

She nodded.

He continued to kiss her while his hands explored her body. "I want you to feel that you can do the same with me. Put it out there, and let's figure it out."

"I can't talk when you're doing that."

Laughing softly, he withdrew from her, dropping his hands to his sides and sighing dramatically.

Amused, Katie got on the bed and made room for him, patting the mattress next to her.

"Let me get this straight. I'm supposed to be in a bed with you and keep my hands to myself?"

"Just for a short time."

He settled on the bed next to her, folding his hands and placing them on his chest. "I suppose I can do that."

"Before we talk about us, did you hear anything more about your friend Lisa?"

"Apparently, David consulted with his colleagues in Boston, and they agree it's too far gone for treatment other than making her as comfortable as possible."

"Oh God."

"David's friend Jared and his wife, Lizzie, have donated nurses and equipment that will keep Lisa at home. Seamus and Carolina have offered to help with the kids, and there's a fundraiser next week at the Beachcomber for the family."

"The Gansett Island community doesn't fool around."

"There are good people here."

"What about the house?"

"Mac and I are going to finish it and figure out what becomes of it later. It's the least of the many concerns in this situation. It just makes me so damned sad that they aren't going to get to live there. They were so excited about it."

"You made her really happy for months by making her dream come true."

"Still… Those poor kids. They're so young."

Katie smoothed her hand over his hair. "They're not that much younger than you were when you lost your mom."

"True, but I had my dad to get me through it. Who will get them through it?"

"People will rally around them. They'll be okay."

"I hope so. They've become important to Mac and me. We wanted to go see them today, but David said there was a lot going on there. We'll go tomorrow." He turned on his side and reached for her hand. "Thanks for asking."

"If there's anything I can do, I hope you'll let me know."

"I will." Stroking her fingers, he looked into her eyes. "Are you going to talk to me about what you're thinking?"

"I'm trying to figure out how I want to say it." She fixed her gaze on their joined hands. "I want all the things you want, but I want us to spend more time together before we decide anything for certain."

"Okay."

"Really?"

"Really," he said, smiling. "I want you to come with me to a cookout this weekend that my aunt and uncle are having so we can all meet my new cousin."

"You have a new cousin?"

"Uh-huh. Big Mac found out recently that he fathered a daughter before he was married to Aunt Linda. Her name is Mallory, and she's coming out to spend the week before Grant's wedding. And then there's the wedding… I get to bring a date, if you're not doing anything."

"I'm not doing anything."

"Great, so that gets us through the next two weekends. What do you want to do after that?"

"I'm sure we'll find something to do."

"There's always something going on here."

"I really liked all of Laura's friends last night."

"It's a fun group."

"I could see that. I love how the guys always crash girls' night."

"And how they pretend they aren't crashing. That's my favorite part." He brought her hand to his mouth and nibbled on her fingers. "Are we done talking?"

"You're sure you're okay with slowing things down a little?"

"How slow are we talking?"

"No major life decisions for a little while."

"I think we need a deadline." He thought about it for a second. "How about we give it until Grant's wedding, and then we can talk about it again. Until then, we're all fun and no big decisions."

"All fun, huh?"

He scooted closer to her, sliding his leg between hers. "*Lots* of fun."

Katie released his hand so she could caress his face. "What you said before about how you feel about me…"

"About how I've fallen in love with you? That?"

"Yes," she said with a nervous laugh, "that."

"What about it?"

"This is all so new to me. I'm not sure what that feels like."

"Could I tell you what it feels like to me?"

She nodded.

"It's hard to describe in words because we're talking about a feeling, so bear with me, okay?" With his gaze fixed over her shoulder, he seemed to be choosing his words carefully, and Katie was on pins and needles waiting to hear what he would say. "Last night, when I couldn't find you and Owen wouldn't tell me where you'd gone, I was out of my mind. I felt like I was going crazy or something, knowing you were nearby and that I'd hurt you badly enough to make you cry. When I heard that, I would've given everything I have to be able to touch you and hold you and tell you how much I care about you and how badly I want to be with you. I had to wait hours—hours and hours—knowing you were upset because of me.

"And then when I walked into Luke's house and saw you there, everything that was wound up inside of me settled. Even though nothing had been resolved between us, I felt calm because you were there. I could see you and touch you and talk to you. It was like everything I needed to survive was right there in one beautiful, sweet package. That's what it feels like to me." He shifted his gaze to her face. "Why are you crying?"

"Because," she said, wiping the tears from her cheeks, "that was the most incredible thing anyone has ever said to me."

"I mean it when I say I'm crazy about you."

Katie reached for him, and their lips came together in a passionate kiss. Her mouth opened to his tongue naturally, as if she'd been kissing him for years rather than days. She couldn't get close enough to him. Under his T-shirt, she caressed the warm skin on his back and loved that he trembled from her touch.

Breaking the kiss, he reached for the back of his shirt and pulled it over his head, baring his gorgeous chest to her appreciative gaze. "Your turn." He pulled on her tank and helped her get it off. "Everything. Hurry."

They pulled at clothes that refused to cooperate, making Katie laugh at the groan of frustration that came from him. "Goddamn it." His shorts were stuck on the work boots he'd never taken off.

Katie couldn't stop laughing.

"You're definitely laughing *at* me this time."

"I can't help it. Who forgets to take off their boots?"

"It's because you've got all the blood in my entire body traveling to one central place. I'm light-headed and woozy."

Still wearing her bra and panties, Katie sat up on her knees. "Allow me to assist you." She took her time untying his boots and removing them and his socks. The boots landed with a loud thunk on the floor.

"Someone downstairs is saying 'There's Shane McCarthy's boots landing on the floor in the middle of the day.'"

"No one is saying that." Katie removed his shorts and boxers, tossing them to the floor as well. Then she took a good long look at the naked man in her bed, licking her lips in anticipation of what was to come. Before her eyes, his erection lengthened, stretching past his belly button. She ran her hands from his shins to his thighs, which quivered in reaction.

His head came up off the pillow. "Katie… Come up here so I can touch you."

"In a minute."

He flopped back down, groaning as he went.

Katie bit her lip to keep from laughing at his distress. She bent her head and began to kiss his stomach, using her tongue to outline each cut of his abdominal muscles.

He fisted handfuls of her hair, directing her to where he wanted her.

"Tell me how you like it."

"Anything you do I'll love."

She looked up at him. "Anything?"

"Anything at all."

"Like this?" She wrapped her hand around the hot, soft skin that covered his shaft and began to stroke him, slowly at first, watching him to determine what he liked.

His hips came off the bed, which she took as a good sign. Since his eyes were closed, she was able to surprise him when she took him into her mouth.

"Ahh, God, Katie… Yes, like that. Suck on me."

She did as he asked, drawing him into her mouth as far as she could while continuing to stroke him. Going on instinct alone, she added her tongue, which drew a sharp inhale from him.

"*Katie…* Baby, you have to stop, or I'll come in your mouth."

She drew back from him reluctantly, leaving him gasping for air.

The next thing she knew, he had turned them so he was on top and poised to enter her. He pulled away so abruptly, Katie cried out in dismay.

"Condom," he said through gritted teeth as he reached for his shorts on the floor and nearly fell off the bed. "Don't laugh."

"I'm trying not to."

He rolled on the condom as he returned to her. "You're laughing."

"I can't help it. You almost fell out of bed."

"It's your fault for getting me so fired up I can't function."

"I did that?"

"Don't pull that innocent act on me. You know exactly what you do to me."

"Tell me… I want to know."

Shane gathered her into his arms, his muscular body pressed against hers. "You've got me completely addicted to you. Your sweetness, your laughter, your softness." As he spoke, he began to enter her slowly, whispering into her ear, "Your tight, wet heat. I like talking to you as much as I like doing this." He gave her more, making Katie moan from the overwhelming pleasure that overtook her. "God, Katie…

"You make me wonder how I survived for so long without you. Without this."

After that, there were no more words as they moved together. It was different this time. Katie couldn't deny there was a deeper connection between them now. And as she came apart in his arms, she accepted she was lost to him. Completely and totally lost. She'd given him everything, her heart, her body and her soul.

Chapter 32

News traveled fast in a small town. Seamus heard about Lisa's grim diagnosis while waiting in line to pay for coffee at the diner. The words "lung cancer" and "too far gone for treatment" struck him like individual blows to the gut. He barely stopped his cup from crashing to the floor.

Outside the diner, he called Joe.

"Hey, what's up?" Joe asked when he answered on the fifth ring.

"I need a favor."

"Sure."

"I know it's last minute, but can you take my eleven and two o'clock runs today?" Seamus hated to ask him, because Joe had a new baby at home, but he also hated the thought of those two little boys coping with such a devastating blow without all the support they could muster.

"Is everything okay?"

"Just heard some grim news about a neighbor. You know Lisa, who lives next door to us?"

"Of course. What's wrong?"

"Late-stage lung cancer."

"Oh my God. That's horrible."

"Your mom and I have been helping out with the kids. I feel like I need to be there today in case they need anything."

"Definitely. I've got you covered. Go do what you need to do."

"Thanks, Joe. Sorry for the late notice."

"It's no problem. We weren't doing anything today. Just the usual baby gazing."

"I appreciate the help."

"Keep me posted on what's going on."

"I will." Seamus stashed the phone in his pocket and headed for the office to let his staff know he was going home and Joe was covering for him. Driving to the house, all he could think about was those two little boys and what would become of them when they lost their mother.

He'd been six when his grandmother, his father's mother, got sick and died somewhat suddenly. The loss of someone who was part of his everyday life had traumatized him, but he'd had his parents to get him through it. Jackson and Kyle had no one.

Why the thought of that hurt him so much, he couldn't say. When and how their problem had become his he also couldn't say. All he knew was that he had to do something to help them.

As Seamus approached his house, he saw David Lawrence leaving Lisa's driveway. He slowed to a stop and waited for David to pull up next to him. "I came as soon as I heard what's going on," Seamus said. "How is she?"

"Overwhelmed," David said, seeming overwhelmed himself.

"There's nothing that can be done?"

David only shook his head.

"Where're the kids?"

"At home for now. Jared and Lizzie James have pulled off a minor miracle and brought a whole team of people out here to tend to her and the kids."

"What happens to them?" Seamus asked, relieved to hear some immediate help had arrived. "After?"

"We haven't gotten that far. She's still absorbing the news."

Seamus nodded in understanding. "You'll let me know if there's anything we can do to help?"

"I will. I've got to get back to the clinic, but I'll check in later."

"See you then." Seamus pulled up to the house he shared with his lovely bride and was relieved to see Carolina's car in the driveway. He got out of the truck and went inside, where she had set up her beads on the kitchen table. Under normal circumstances, he loved to watch her create her masterpieces.

She looked up when he came in, her brows furrowed in puzzlement. "What're you doing here? You're on the eleven."

"Joe's taking my runs today."

"How come?"

He dropped into a chair and reached for her hand.

"What's wrong? You're scaring me."

"Lisa… She's in a bad way. Lung cancer."

"What? Oh no! Oh, that poor girl and those poor kids!" Tears filled her lovely eyes. "How did you hear?"

"I was at the diner, and people were talking about it. I just saw David… I asked him if there's anything that can be done. All he could do was shake his head."

"So awful."

"Those kids have no one else, love. I don't know how they came to be so alone in the world, but they are."

"It's heartbreaking."

He took a deep breath and looked her in the eye. "We could step up for them."

"How do you mean?"

"Take them in. Give them a home. After…"

"You're serious."

"Only if you're on board, too. It's a huge big deal and a lot to ask. You've already raised your son, so I'll understand if you don't have it in you to do this. I can't explain the why of it, but as soon as I heard the news, I had this feeling come over me that I had to do something for those kids."

"You are so good," she said with a loving smile. "All bluster and blarney with the softest heart there ever was."

He scowled at her even as his soft heart skipped a beat from the way she looked at him. "It's a lot to ask of you, love."

"No, it really isn't. They're wonderful boys who've been dealt an awful hand. And you're absolutely right that we could and should step up for them. But it's quite possible Lisa has made other arrangements in case something happened to her. I don't want you to get your hopes up only to have them dashed."

"I want to see them taken care of. However that happens is fine, as long as it happens."

"All we can do is offer. It'll be up to her in the end."

"Let's go over there and see what we can do right now. There'll be time for that conversation when the initial shock wears off." When she stood to join him, he took a moment to hug her. "Thank you for this. No matter what happens, I appreciate that you didn't tell me I was nuts to even suggest it."

"You *are* nuts. And you have no idea what you're getting yourself into if this should come to pass. But I love you so much for thinking of it and being willing to step up for them."

"I love you, too."

"Let's go see how we can help."

*

Since Maddie was acting like everything in their lives was perfectly normal, Mac didn't see any reason not to go to the cookout his parents were hosting to introduce Mallory to the rest of the family. If it were up to him, he'd want to stay home and spend quiet time with his wife and children. But his wife seemed to want everyone but him, so they went to the party.

The longer the weirdness with Maddie went on, the more hollow Mac felt. Of course he'd known how essential she was to him and how much he relied on her to get through every day. But until she made herself unavailable to him for several days, he hadn't known just *how* essential she really was or how dependent he was on her.

For the first time in the two years they'd been together, he had no idea what to do where she was concerned. He'd always known what to do, from the first day they met and he'd forced his way into her life, he'd known what she needed and how to give it to her. Sure, he'd fumbled a few times, but he'd always managed to right the ship and keep them on an even keel.

Until now. Until they lost their baby and he seemed to lose her at the same time. With every day that passed in this unusual state of discontent, his worries quadrupled to the point that he felt like he would explode if it went on much longer. He'd done what everyone had told him to do and had given her some space. He'd left her alone to cope in her own way while he tried—and failed—to cope on his own.

He was to the point now, after five long days of utter misery, where he wanted to shake her and force her to deal with him. But he'd never do that. He'd never lay a hand on her with anything other than love on his mind. But the anger simmered deep inside, just below the despair, making him wonder how long he could possibly contain it before it burst forth and made everything worse.

How could she do this to him? How could she make him feel like she was blaming him for what'd happened to both of them? How could she freeze him out when he needed her more than he'd ever needed her before? As he drove his family to his parents' house, those were the questions that burned through his mind, torturing him with the lack of answers.

The only thing he knew for sure was that he would lose his mind if this went on for much longer. After he parked outside the home he'd grown up in, the house the locals referred to as "The White House," Mac retrieved Hailey from her car seat while Maddie saw to Thomas, laughing and joking with the little boy like she hadn't a care in the world.

As if she knew he needed some love, Hailey snuggled into the nook between his neck and shoulder, nearly reducing Mac to tears with her sweetness. His emotions had been all over the place this week as he tried to carry on as normal. But when he was by himself, driving to the marina or in the shower or alone on his side of their big bed night after night, the tears flowed freely.

Attending a happy family get-together was the last thing he felt like doing today, but he was going through the motions because he had no good reason not to as long as Maddie was up for going. Judging from the cars parked outside, other than Janey, they were the last to arrive. They went inside to a huge crowd that included his brothers, their significant others, his Uncle Frank and Betsy, Laura, Owen, Holden, Shane, Katie, Uncle Kevin, Riley, Finn and Mallory, the guest of honor.

Mallory caught him off guard with a kiss to the cheek. "Nice to see you again."

"You, too."

"How're you doing?"

Mac shrugged. "Okay, I guess."

She eyed him skeptically but didn't pursue it. "And who is this little angel?"

Thankful to change the subject, he said, "This is Hailey. Hailey, meet your Aunt Mallory."

"May I?" Mallory asked, holding out her hands.

Mac didn't want to let go of his daughter or the comfort she had provided, but he also didn't want to be rude, so he handed her over to Mallory.

"She's adorable. Where does she get the blonde hair?"

"Her mom was blonde as a baby."

Carrying Thomas, Maddie came over to say hello to Mallory and to introduce her to Thomas.

"Your kids are beautiful," Mallory said, her expression wistful as she gazed at Thomas.

For a brief second, Mac saw a hint of sadness in Maddie's eyes that was gone as quickly as it had come.

"We adore them," Maddie said cheerfully. "Hailey likes you. She doesn't go willingly to too many people."

"I'm honored," Mallory said.

Joe, Janey and P.J. arrived a few minutes later, Janey wearing an expression of trepidation as she was introduced to Mallory.

"It's nice to meet you." Mallory took the hand that Janey offered. "I've heard so much about you."

"Nice to meet you, too. I'm sorry I wasn't here the last time."

"No worries," Mallory said. "You're here now."

"Just don't call me Brat, and we'll get along fine."

Mallory laughed. "You got it."

Mac watched the proceedings with a sense of disjointedness. Normally he'd be thrilled to spend the afternoon with his family and to see Janey taking an important step with their new sister, but it was impossible for him to enjoy anything when he was at odds with Maddie.

*

Tucked up against Shane's side, Katie felt like she had to be dreaming. He wanted her close to him all the time. If they were together, he was touching her in some way, regardless of who might be watching. Here now, in front of his entire family, he was making a very public declaration, and Katie loved it. She loved him.

She hadn't said the words to him yet, but she wouldn't be surprised if he knew how she felt.

Yes, it had happened fast, and yes, she was a bit dizzy from the whirlwind speed of their relationship. But she was also euphoric and excited and filled with anticipation of what was ahead for them. If only she hadn't insisted on waiting awhile to talk about what came next for them.

He'd asked her to move in with him, and that was all she'd thought about since she received that note. She hadn't told anyone, even Julia, that they were talking about such things out of fear that everyone would think she was crazy to go from never having had a boyfriend to living with the man who'd taken her on her first date.

But every instinct she had was telling her to go for it, to leap with both feet and let Shane catch her. If only it weren't for the lingering, nagging doubts about whether he was truly over Courtney, she'd say to hell with the deadline and tell him now that she wanted the same things he did.

He hadn't said or done anything to lead her to believe his mind was still locked in the past. She'd picked up on subtle things, such as the way he'd zone out sometimes, staring into space, his thoughts obviously somewhere far away from her. Though he was focused entirely on her except for those infrequent periods, the doubts festered despite her desperate desire to ignore them.

After they'd eaten a delicious steak dinner, Shane's Aunt Linda asked her son Evan to play for them. Sitting on his uncle's spacious deck with Shane's arms around her from behind, the sun setting over the Salt Pond and Evan's incredible voice singing "Stay With Me" by Sam Smith, Katie had never been happier or more content.

Shane whispered the words to the song in her ear, sending a shiver down her spine.

It took everything she had not to tell him right then that she'd stay with him forever if he'd have her. Later that night, while he made passionate love to her, Katie told herself she was a fool for worrying about where else his thoughts might be when he was so obviously devoted to her.

But the doubts niggled just the same, growing and multiplying in the week between the cookout and the wedding when his periods of melancholy seemed to grow more frequent. The closer they got to their self-imposed deadline, the more worried Katie became about whether it might be a huge mistake to give him everything.

While Shane was at Grant's bachelor party, Katie went downstairs to the Bistro, where the girls were celebrating Stephanie's second-to-last night as a single woman. The women were in high spirits as they drank champagne and toasted the bride, and Katie enjoyed the evening with women who were starting to feel like friends, especially her new sister-in-law.

"I miss drinking," Laura said mournfully. "I feel like I've been pregnant for years."

"Well, you kind of have been."

"A few more months, and I'll never be pregnant again."

"Is Maddie okay? She was hitting the champagne hard."

"I noticed that, too. Tiffany will get her home." Laura shifted her gaze from watching Maddie to Katie. "So things are good with Shane?"

"Very good."

"It's nice to see him happy again."

"Does he seem happy? Really?" As she asked the question, Katie realized how badly she needed an objective opinion. Was she reading more into his frequent silences than they warranted?

"Why would you ask that? Is something wrong?"

"I don't know. I hope not, but..." She lowered her voice to ensure no one would hear her. The others were so caught up in the celebration that she and Laura could speak freely. "Sometimes, he seems... remote, as if something is weighing on his mind, but he doesn't want me to know. When we're together, he's completely focused on me, but I still sense *something* is amiss. And I have absolutely no experience at this and no way to know if I'm overreacting, looking for something that isn't there or have cause to be genuinely worried."

"Have you asked him?"

"No," Katie said with a sigh. "I haven't, because I'm afraid of what he might say."

"That's a tough one. It's possible—and I only say this as speculation, not because he's said anything to me—that he might be still dealing with some fallout from Courtney's sudden reappearance. But that doesn't mean he's not totally invested in you."

"How can he be totally invested in me if he's still thinking about her?" As Katie gave voice to her greatest fear, her stomach began to ache.

"I think you should talk to him. Ask him what he's thinking about when he punches out."

"The thought of asking him that makes me feel sick. I'm also afraid he'll be mad, because he's told me how he feels and what he wants. I'm the one who's holding out, so what right do I have to question him? You know?"

"I hate Courtney for reopening that wound just when it was finally starting to heal."

"Part of me is grateful to her because he got some answers, but the other part of me wishes he didn't know that she never stopped loving him. I feel like I'm out on a huge limb in a stiff breeze in this situation, hanging on by my fingertips."

"Do you love him?"

Katie nodded. "Very much so."

"Tell him. That might make all the difference for him." Laura rested her hand on Katie's arm. "And for what it's worth, I'm thrilled that you love him. I think you're perfect for him."

"Thank you." She hugged her sister-in-law. "I know what I need to do."

CHAPTER 33

Dan Torrington threw one hell of a bachelor party. Since Grant had been unwilling to choose one of his three brothers, he'd asked Dan to be his best man. They'd gorged on prime rib, lobster, top-shelf liquor and Cuban cigars at the party Dan had thrown for Grant at the marina.

Adam had drawn the designated-driver card that night, and delivered Shane and Owen back to the hotel just after three a.m., which was far too late to bother Katie.

Beside the fact he was more than a little drunk and nauseated from the massive overindulgence, he was also out of sorts, so he went to his own room rather than hers. He flipped on the light and noticed a white Sand & Surf envelope on the floor. When he bent to pick it up, he had to reach for the wall as the room seemed to tilt.

Taking the envelope to his bed, he sat and tore it open.

Dear Shane,

I hope you had fun tonight with your cousins and friends. I had a great time with the women. I love being part of this incredible group of people. I feel as if I've known them forever when it's only been such a short time. Sort of like the way I feel about you… How can I feel so much for you when I only just met you? But I can't deny that what I feel for you is love, as pure and simple as anything I've ever felt. I want all the things you said you want. But more than anything, I want you *to be certain. I can tell something is weighing on your mind, and if you don't feel you can talk to me about it, please talk to someone.*

If the time isn't right for us, I'll be sad and disappointed, but I'll survive. I wanted you to know that. Let's enjoy this wonderful weekend, as planned, and talk after the wedding. I'm looking forward to spending more time with you and your family.

Love,

Katie

Shane moaned as he read her sweet words. She loved him, but she knew he was tormented. And here he thought he'd done such a good job of hiding it from her. He should've known she'd notice. She paid attention.

He stretched out on the bed, still holding her letter and thinking about everything she'd said and how perceptive she was. Try as he might to deny it, Courtney's visit had screwed him up, and he needed to get some help before he ruined the best thing to ever happen to him.

His sleep was tormented and plagued by disturbing dreams about both the women who were on his mind. He woke with a pounding headache, a dry mouth and a plan. After a shower, some coffee and a couple of pain pills, Shane got on the bike and rode it to Big Mac's house in North Harbor. He stepped through the gate into his aunt's rose garden and took the stairs to the porch, where he knocked on the door.

Wearing a T-shirt and shorts and carrying a mug of coffee, his Uncle Kevin came to the door. "Hey, Shane."

"Just the guy I was looking for."

Kevin pushed open the screen door. "Come in."

"Why do I feel like hell after last night, and you're all chipper?"

"Because with age comes wisdom and the ability to say no after the tenth round."

Shane laughed. "It was a good time even if I feel like hell today."

"A fantastic time, but then any time I get to spend with my brothers, sons and nephews is the best of times."

"Yes, it is." Shane accepted the mug of coffee Kevin poured for him and stirred in cream. "Where is everyone?"

"Riley and Finn are still sleeping off last night's gluttony. Mac and Linda are off making final preparations for the rehearsal dinner tonight." Kevin leaned against the counter. "What brings you out so early?"

"Could I talk to you about something in sort of a professional capacity?"

"Of course. Let's go out on the deck."

Shane followed him through the sliding door and took a seat next to his uncle. "I'm sorry to drop in on you this way when you're on vacation and away from other people's problems for a while."

"I'm always available to you. You know that. You're all our kids. Doesn't matter which one of us fathered you."

"I love that about our family."

"So do I, but I don't think you came here to talk about our family."

"No," Shane said with a sigh. "Did you hear that Courtney came looking for me this week?"

"I heard rumblings to that effect."

"Things were great, you know? I was doing so much better. The job with Mac, living near Laura and Holden, who I'm crazy about, being here with the rest of the family and then everything with Katie... I was better than I've been in a long time."

"Your dad said as much to me, and I could see it myself."

"But then she comes here and tells me everything she did was to protect me and she only divorced me to keep me out of a messy legal situation. She said she never stopped loving me."

"Ah, Christ. I didn't hear all that."

"It's fucked me up again, Kev. I don't want to think about her. I want to think about Katie. I *love* Katie. She's amazing and wonderful and kind and attentive. She's everything that Courtney wasn't. What you see is what you get with Katie, and I need that after what I went through with Courtney. So why, why, *why* can't I stop thinking about Courtney telling me she never stopped loving me?"

"Because you waited a long time for some answers, and you've only had a few days to get your head around what she told you."

"Unfortunately, those few days have been critical days with Katie."

"Which makes it that much more complicated."

"I feel like I'm losing my shit. How can I be thinking about a woman who treated me the way she did when I've got a new girlfriend telling me she loves me and wants to be with me?"

"What do *you* want, Shane?"

"I want peace. I want a family. I want Katie. I want to stop dwelling on stuff that doesn't matter anymore."

"It must still matter if you're still dwelling on it."

"*Why* does it still matter? What difference does it make if she still loves me or that she did what she did to protect me? I'm not going back to her."

"It matters because you can't hate her anymore knowing what you do now. It was easier when you could make Courtney out to be the villain in this situation. Finding out what you did this week puts you back to square one in some ways because it changes the story of how your marriage ended."

"I can't go back to square one again."

"It's not the same square one as it was when everything first happened and the wound was raw and open. It's a different square one, but it requires some contemplation nonetheless. You lived for a long time thinking you understood what motivated Courtney. Finding out that everything you thought to be true was wrong is a shock."

"More than anything, I'm afraid I'm going to mess things up with Katie. She's tuned in to the fact that something's bothering me." He put the coffee cup on the table and sat back in his chair. "What you said about Courtney being the villain makes a lot of sense."

"We all made her the villain. You weren't alone in that."

"She said she wants me to know the person she is now, but how would I ever separate who she is now from who she was then?"

"You probably can't, which is why you sent her away."

"I told her there was too much water under the bridge, too much history, too much pain."

"Maybe you need to keep telling yourself that until you believe it. You say you want the life you have now with Katie, and it sounds like she wants you, too. So what's stopping you from having that?"

"Only my fears about whether I'm being fair by getting in so deep with her while this stuff is still on my mind."

"The only way you're being unfair to Katie is if you don't tell her that seeing Courtney messed you up worse than you initially thought, and how that has nothing at all to do with what you feel for her."

"You're saying I should tell Katie about this."

"Yes. Tell her what's been weighing on you and see what she says. All you can do is be straight with her."

"I'm the first guy she's ever dated."

"Because of her dad," Kevin said with a nod of understanding.

"Yeah, she took this huge risk on me, and I promised her I'd be worth it, and then this happened."

"It's not your fault, Shane. You couldn't have known Courtney was going to come here or that she would say what she did. It seems to me like you're blaming yourself for things that were outside of your control. Of course you're going to be affected by seeing your ex-wife again after all this time. Of course you're going to be shocked to hear that she never stopped loving you and didn't really want to divorce you. How is any of that your fault?"

"It's not, I guess."

"You didn't do anything wrong. You were a great husband to her. You did everything you could to make that marriage work. You stepped up for her even after you found out she'd stolen from you to support her habit. That would've been a deal breaker for a lot of guys but not you. At what point do you give yourself a break and acknowledge that you did the best you could in a horrible situation?"

Shane took a deep breath and blew it out.

"Are you still in love with Courtney?"

"No."

"Do you want to get back together with her?"

"No."

"Do you want to be with Katie?"

"Yes."

"Do you love her?"

"Yes."

"Then you know what you need to do."

"And I'm not being unfair to Katie by committing to her when I'm still thinking about someone else?"

"You were with Courtney for a long time. You might always think about her. But you don't want to be with her. That's what really matters—and that's what'll matter to Katie." He squeezed Shane's shoulder. "But if you honestly feel you're not ready to move forward with Katie, then you owe it to her to tell her that, too. You wouldn't be doing her any favors in the long run if you stay with her out of some misguided sense of obligation."

"That's not why I'm with her. I feel like myself again with her, if that makes sense."

"It makes perfect sense, and it sounds to me like you just answered all your own questions."

"Thanks for this, Kev."

"I'm glad you came to me. When I'm not here, I'm only a phone call away. Any time."

Both men stood, and Shane gave his uncle a hug.

"Thank you."

"Take it easy on yourself, buddy. You've been through a lot. More than some people endure in a lifetime. We're all proud of how well you've been doing lately. Your dad wasn't the only one who worried about you for a long time."

"It's been great to have you here. Wish you were staying longer."

"I've got to get home after Grant's wedding and deal with a situation of my own."

"With Aunt Deb?"

Kevin nodded, his expression grim. "She's left me for a younger guy, of all things."

Shane stared at his uncle. "And you just let me go on and on about *my* problems?"

"I was happy to talk to you. It's nice to think about something else for a change."

"What're you going to do?"

"Not much I can do. She wants out of the marriage." Kevin shrugged. "What choice do I have?"

"Do Riley and Finn know?"

"They suspect something's up because she didn't come with us for the weddings, but I figure it's up to Deb to tell them what's going on when she's ready to." Kevin went inside and Shane followed him, still reeling from what his uncle had told him. "Call me if you need to talk again, okay?"

"This has been really helpful. I appreciate the time, and I'm sorry about what you're going through."

"Don't worry about me. Take care of you—and your Katie. I have a good feeling where you two are concerned."

"Thanks again, Kev."

"I'll see you tonight."

"See you then."

Shane rode off on his bike, thinking about everything his uncle had said. He took the long way around the island before returning to the hotel and heading upstairs. He desperately wanted to see Katie again but went instead to his own room. In the folder on the desk, he found a piece of Sand & Surf stationery and went to work on a new note to her.

Dear sweet Katie,

Thank you for your note this morning. I've read it a hundred times and committed every word to memory.

You were right when you said I've had something on my mind, and I want to talk to you about it after the wedding. In the meantime, I can't wait to take you to the rehearsal dinner tonight and the wedding tomorrow. Everything is more fun when you're with me. I'll pick you up at seven.

Love,

Shane

He went down the hallway, slid the letter under her door and returned to his room. Talking to Kevin had helped. Shane had a clearer picture now of why he'd been so unsettled the last couple of days. He also had a clearer picture of where he wanted to go from here and who he wanted to take with him. Once he got past his cousin's wedding, he'd get busy making that happen.

*

Wearing a dress shirt and tie with khakis and carrying a navy blazer over his shoulder, Mac went down the stairs, where David and Daisy were entertaining his children. "Thanks for doing this, you guys," he said.

"We love spending time with them," Daisy said. "It's good practice for someday."

"We'll owe you a lot of babysitting when someday comes."

Maddie came downstairs a few minutes later, wearing a black dress that clung to her sexy curves and her hair falling in waves around her pretty face. "You guys are going to be so good for Daisy and David, right?" she said to the kids.

"Don't want you to go," Thomas said, his lip out in a pout.

"We'll be back when you wake up," Mac assured him.

Maddie hugged and kissed both kids and followed Mac out of the house. He held open the passenger door to the SUV for her and waited for her to get settled.

"Thanks." She put on her seat belt without looking at him.

He shut the door and went around to the driver's side, the frustration of the last difficult ten days boiling inside him as he drove away from the house and headed for town. Suddenly, he couldn't take the silence for one more minute. He swerved off the road into a parking lot for the bluffs and cut the engine.

"What're you doing? We're going to be late."

"I don't care."

"It's your brother's rehearsal dinner."

"I know where we're going. But we're not going anywhere until we talk about what the hell is wrong."

"You know what's wrong, Mac. Do I really have to explain it to you?"

"No, you don't, but what I don't get is why there's this awful distance between us when we both lost something we loved. I can't stand it, Maddie. It's killing me." His voice broke. "I can't take feeling like you're blaming me for what happened, or worse, you're blaming yourself."

"I don't blame you."

"Please, talk to me. Please."

Tears rolled down her cheeks, each one of them like knives to his broken heart. He released his seat belt, got out of the car and went around to her side. Opening the passenger door, he reached across her to unfasten her seat belt. With his hands on her face, he forced her to look at him as he brushed her tears away with his thumbs. "Baby, please. I'm begging you. Let me in. I can't do this without you."

She broke down into sobs.

Mac put his arms around her. "Let it out, sweetheart."

"Mac…"

"I'm here. I'm right here, and I love you so much."

"So sorry."

"For what, honey? Why are you sorry?"

"The baby..."

"You have nothing to be sorry about. This awful thing, it just happened. Not because of anything you did or didn't do. It just happened." He brushed at his own tears with his sleeve. "And it happened to both of us."

Her arms encircled his waist, and Mac felt like he could breathe again for the first time in a week. "That's it. Hold on to me." He buried his face in her fragrant hair, wallowing in the familiar scent of summer flowers. Her brokenhearted sobs killed him. "It's okay, baby. It's going to be okay."

Her hold on him tightened as she continued to cry. He had no idea how long they were there before she pulled back from him. "I'll ruin your shirt."

"I don't care about the shirt. I care about you. I want you back. Please come back to me. I can't function without you."

"I... I thought you were mad at me."

"No, baby. Everyone told me to give you space, and that's what I've been trying to do. But I miss you so much. I need you."

"I'm sorry I haven't been there for you. It was all I could do to keep myself together."

"You don't have to apologize. I just want you back, Maddie."

She looked up at him, her face tearstained and her eyes rimmed with red. "I've missed you, too. I've missed us."

"Maddie," he whispered as he kissed her.

She kissed him back with all the usual enthusiasm.

Mac clung to her. Now that he had her back in his arms, he wanted to keep her there.

"We have somewhere to be," she reminded him.

"Let's skip it."

"We can't skip it."

"Yes, we can. I'll ask Adam to tell them you aren't feeling well and we'll see them tomorrow."

"It's your brother..."

"He'll understand. He knew I was upset about things between us."

"If you're sure, I wouldn't mind skipping it so we can spend some time alone together."

"Let me just send a text to Adam." Mac sent the text and asked Adam to give their regrets to Grant, Stephanie and his parents.

I'll take care of it, Adam replied. *Take care of your wife.*

Thanks. We'll see you all tomorrow.

"Put your seat belt back on for a minute," Mac said when he got back in the car.

"Where're we going?"

"A spot I remember from my former life as a teenager here." He drove down a dirt road that twisted and turned, leading to a remote ocean overlook, which he backed into. "Come on."

"Come where?"

"Meet me outside, and I'll show you."

Mac got out of the car and went to open the tailgate. He lifted Maddie into the back and then crawled in with her, making use of the beach blanket and towels she kept in the car.

"Why do I feel like you've done this before?"

"I've never done it with you."

"Do the police come out here?"

"The chief is our brother-in-law. I think we're good."

Maddie laughed. "This is true."

He traced the shape of her smile with his fingertip. "Nice to hear you laugh."

"I've felt so sad. I've never been so sad."

"Me, too, sweetheart." When he gathered her close, she laid her arm across his stomach and rested her head on his chest. "I've been thinking that maybe we should give him a name. It might help us to remember and honor him."

"I like that idea. What name should we give him?"

"We'd talked about Malcolm the third for a boy. Do you want to give him that name or do you want to save it in case we have another son?"

"Do you want to try again?"

"Only if you do."

"I'm not sure how I feel about that."

"It's nothing we have to decide now, but how about we save Malcolm just in case? We also talked about Connor."

"We never actually decided to have him." She hesitated before she said, "Connor."

"No, we didn't," Mac said with a chuckle. "And neither of us will ever forget the night he was conceived."

"Let's hope Thomas forgets it."

They shared a laugh that ended on a sob for Maddie.

"I loved that he came from that night," she said. "I loved him, and despite what I said, I *wanted* him."

Blinded by his own tears, Mac said, "I know, honey. I wanted him, too."

"Connor. His name was Connor."

"Yes, it was. And we loved him."

"Mac?"

"Yeah?"

"I love you. I never want you to think I don't. I always do. No matter what."

While he knew that, he certainly appreciated the reminder after the week they'd had. "Same to you. You're my whole world, Madeline. As long as everything is okay between us, I can get through anything."

"We needed this. Thanks for making me talk about it, and I'm sorry if I've been locked in my own grief."

"You could make it up to me by kissing me again."

Though her eyes were still damp with tears, she smiled up at him and gave him what he wanted and what he needed more than anything.

Chapter 34

For a long time, Grant McCarthy had wondered if this moment would ever come, and now that it was upon him, he was a disaster. He'd never admit to Stephanie, who was gorgeous in a sexy, bronze-colored dress, that he was still hungover from the night before. That was all Dan's fault, the best man from hell, who'd spared no expense in making sure every man in Grant's family had far too good of a time at his bachelor party. Even his dad still looked a little peaked nearly twenty-four hours later.

But Stephanie, she was amazing, flitting from table to table in the big room at the Lobster House that his parents had reserved for the evening. There'd been no rehearsal, to speak of. Their wedding would be simple and small, the way they wanted it. All he cared about was making her his wife. He would've been happy to run off and elope, but his mother would've killed him, and Stephanie deserved better.

It'd been one hell of a year since they'd gotten together during Tropical Storm Hailey. Back then, he'd been under the misguided impression that he needed to get his old girlfriend Abby back. What a difference a year made. Abby was now happily engaged to his brother Adam, who was absolutely perfect for her. They were perfect together.

With Dan's help, they'd managed to get Stephanie's stepfather, Charlie, out of prison. The day Charlie walked out of jail, Stephanie had been set free, too.

But the path to happily ever after hadn't been smooth for them. They'd worked through a lot of painful issues and were well on their way to forever when the sailboat accident happened, and derailed them again.

Nothing had been easy for them, except the love. That had always come easily. Their love for each other was the one thing neither of them had ever questioned. And as she returned to their table and slid onto his lap, Grant wrapped his arms around her and nuzzled the auburn hair she'd let grow longer for the wedding.

She moved to find a more comfortable position on his lap and discovered his predictable reaction to her nearness. Stephanie, being Stephanie, pressed her ass down on his erection, drawing a gasp from him.

"Knock it off," he growled into her ear. "I don't get to sleep with you tonight, so don't start anything you can't finish."

"All I did was sit on your lap."

"That's all it takes."

She was still laughing when Big Mac stood up and let out a whistle to get everyone's attention.

"Oh God," Evan said. "Who gave him a microphone?"

"I finally managed to wrestle it away from you," Big Mac said, making everyone laugh at Evan.

"He totally burned you," Adam said to his brother.

"I apologize for my children and their bad behavior," Big Mac said.

"We're used to it by now," Frank said to more laughter.

"Linda and I want to thank you all for joining us tonight as we prepare to officially welcome the lovely and wonderful dynamo named Stephanie to the McCarthy family tomorrow. Stephanie, from the minute Linda and I met you in Providence the winter before you joined us here, we knew you were a special young woman. In the last year, we've come to know just how special you are, and no one was more thrilled than we were to watch Grant come to the same conclusion. We love you like one of our own, and after tomorrow, we get to call you one of our own. To Stephanie."

"I'll drink to that," Grant said, kissing her as his brothers and cousins whooped and hollered.

"He made me cry," Stephanie said.

"Grant, you've always made us proud, and tonight is no different. From the time you were a little kid, you were smart, sophisticated and classy—probably too classy for the likes of us."

"No doubt," Grant said dryly, even as he absorbed the emotional wallop of his father's words.

"We thank you, son, for bringing Stephanie to our family, and we look forward to watching the two of you become a family. We love you both. To Grant and Stephanie!"

"Tomorrow," Grant whispered in her ear as the others toasted them. "I can't wait."

She dazzled him with her smile and the sheer joy he saw in her eyes. Then she kissed him and dazzled him all over again.

*

"Why am I all weepy when I just met these people two weeks ago?" Katie asked, dabbing at her eyes with a napkin.

"It's my uncle," Shane said. "He does it to all of us." He put his arm around her and kissed her temple. "How about another glass of wine?"

"I'd love one."

"Coming right up." Shane went over to the bar and ordered the wine for her and a Coke for himself. With his stomach still recovering from the bachelor party, he wasn't drinking tonight.

Ned approached the bar at the same time, looking dapper in a shirt and tie with his normally wild white hair tamed for the occasion. "Got a place for ya right down the street from the Surf if yer still interested."

"I'm definitely interested."

"Ya wanna see it in the mornin'?"

"That'd be great."

Ned gave him the address. "Meet ya there at nine, or is that too early fer ya?"

Shane raised his class of soda for Ned to see. "I can do nine."

"See ya then."

"Thanks, Ned."

"T'aint no big deal."

Shane returned to the table with their drinks and took his seat next to Katie. She was talking to Owen, who sat on the other side of her. Without interrupting her brother, Katie smiled at Shane and took the wineglass from him. That smile, those eyes… Shane couldn't get enough of the way she looked at him and smiled at him.

Since his conversation with his uncle earlier in the day, he'd felt calmer and more settled. Kevin had helped him to see his way forward, to understand why he'd been so undone by what Courtney had said to him. He was prepared to speak to Katie about it, but he would wait until after the wedding, as planned.

When the party broke up at eleven, they walked home to the hotel through town. She'd had the stitches removed the day before and had been delighted to be able to wear heels to dinner.

"How's the foot?" Shane loved the feel of her hand in his and the easy ebb and flow of their conversation.

"So much better than it was, but I'll be glad to get these shoes off."

They arrived at the hotel and went upstairs to the third floor.

"Your place or mine?" she asked.

"Either is fine with me."

"Your bed is bigger."

"Then my place it is."

"I'll meet you there." She went up on tiptoes to kiss his cheek and then went into her room.

Shane continued on to his room, where he pulled off his tie and dress shirt and tossed them aside. Tomorrow was casual. The invitation had specified—no ties. He went into the bathroom to brush his teeth and stared into the mirror at the face looking back him.

Gone were the brackets of tension that had framed his mouth and the dark circles under his eyes. He'd been through the fire and he'd survived. This week had been nothing more than a minor setback and should be treated as such.

The life he was making for himself on Gansett was the life he wanted. There was no going back to what had come before. There was only looking forward to what was ahead.

Katie's soft knock ended the introspection. He opened the door, and his mouth fell open in reaction to the vision that stood before him.

"Let me in before Owen comes home and sees me," she said with a nervous giggle.

Shane stepped back to let her pass him in a cloud of feminine fragrance and silk brushing against his heated skin. "Where did that come from, and let me have a better look."

"I went shopping at Tiffany's store." She turned in a complete circle. "You like?"

"Oh yeah." The black silk robe clung to every delicious curve. "What do you got going on under that robe?"

"Come find out."

Madly aroused, Shane went to her and tugged at the belt that held the robe together. It fell open, revealing a short black silk nightgown that molded to her breasts and ended at the tops of her thighs. "Holy shit, that's hot."

"I'm glad you like it. Tiffany assured me it would be a showstopper."

"Tiffany was right." He placed his hands on her hips, the thin fabric heating beneath his palms. "So you bought this hoping to fry my brain cells?"

"Not exactly," she said with a low, throaty laugh that made him harder, if that was possible. "But if that's the result, you won't hear me complaining."

"Me either."

She looped her arms around his neck and pressed her body against his.

"I'm digging this sexy siren version of my sweet Katie."

"Don't make too much of it. I had to work up the nerve to even put it on and then to come down the hall hoping my brother wouldn't catch me."

"We need to get out of this hotel."

"Yes, we do."

Shane wanted to tell her about the place Ned had found, but he would look at it first to make sure it suited their needs. Then he'd tell her about that and everything else. "Come to bed with me, Katie."

"Mmm, yes, please."

He let her go only long enough to remove his pants and boxers as well as her robe. From the bedside table drawer, he produced a strip of condoms and threw them on the bed.

"Not taking any chances that you'll fall out of bed again, huh?"

"That's right." He held up the covers and encouraged her to get in first and then followed her.

Katie wrapped herself around him, surrounding him in a cocoon of silky fabric and silkier skin.

"God, you feel so good, Katie."

"So do you. Could I ask you something?"

"Sure."

"Is it wrong that this is almost all I think about these days? Being in bed with you?"

His laughter shook his body and hers because she was snuggled up so tightly to him. "If it's wrong, I don't want to be right." He ran a hand up her smooth leg and encountered a supple buttock. "Oh Christ, are you wearing a thong?"

"I might be."

"I gotta see that. Turn over."

"This is kind of embarrassing."

"No, it's hot as hell. Trust me on that."

She turned onto her belly, folding her arms under her head. She watched him warily as he placed his hands on her calves and smoothed them up her legs, taking the hem of the nightgown with him as he went.

He groaned at the sight of the tiny scrap of black fabric disappearing between her cheeks. Shane bent his head and kissed her there, making her squirm under him. "I love your sexy ass, Katie."

"God," she muttered. "I'm about to expire here."

"We can't have that." He reached for a condom and rolled it on quickly before grasping her hips and bringing her up to her knees.

She looked at him over her shoulder. "What're you doing?"

"Something new. Are you game?"

"Yes."

He loved her enthusiasm almost as much as he loved her sweetness. Under the gown, he cupped her breasts and rolled her nipples between his fingers as he pressed the hard length of his erection between her legs.

Moaning, she dropped her head onto her arms.

Shane moved the thong to the side and positioned his cock at her entrance, giving her only the very tip at first while his fingers found her clit.

She cried out—loudly—and then seemed to remember the hotel's thin walls.

It was definitely time to get out of here so they could have some privacy. He wanted to hear her cries and moans and groans and every other sound she wished to make while he loved her. When he was certain she was ready, he slid in farther and watched her hands fist the sheets as her bottom pressed back against him. "Feel good?"

"So good. More, Shane. I want more."

He didn't need to be told twice. On the next stroke, he entered her fully and loved the way her back curved from the impact. Grasping her hips, he picked up the pace, driving into her repeatedly as she met him stroke for stroke with the sweet press of her bottom. She drove him wild with her effortless sexiness.

Keeping one hand on her hip, he dragged a finger from where they were joined up through the valley between her cheeks, pressing lightly on her back entrance. Katie detonated, her sharp cries and the tight squeeze of her internal muscles triggering his release. He surged into her as the powerful orgasm drained him of any remaining questions about where he belonged or who he belonged with.

Wrapping his arm around her waist, he brought her with him when he dropped down to the mattress. His other arm served as a pillow for her, his hand nestled between her breasts, which heaved from her heavy breathing. Her tight channel continued to pulse with aftershocks that had him hardening again.

"Shane… Tell me the truth. Is it always like that? Or is it special between us?"

"It's very special between us. It's most definitely not always like that."

"What you did… With your finger…"

He did it again, drawing a sharp gasp from her. "That?"

"Mmm."

"You liked that?"

"I never would've thought so, but *wow.*"

"We'll have to try that again sometime."

"Yes, please."

His low chuckle made her shiver in his arms. "So polite, even when we're talking dirty."

"Shane…"

"What, honey?"

"So much I want to say to you."

He tightened his hold on her and kissed her cheek. "Tomorrow night. We'll say everything that needs to be said."

"Yes. Yes, we will."

CHAPTER 35

Shane slipped out of bed in the morning, leaving Katie to sleep. He took a quick shower and left to meet Ned. Unlike yesterday when he'd woken hungover and confused, today he was clearheaded and resolute. He knew what he wanted and was determined to make it happen—for both of them.

The house was about three blocks from the Surf, around the corner and set back off the road. At first glance, the weathered, shingled cottage didn't seem like anything special, but Shane reserved judgment until he could see the inside. Ned pulled up in his woody station wagon a few minutes later and jumped out to greet him.

Today Ned looked much more like his usual self in a faded T-shirt, plaid shorts, beat-up boat shoes and his wild mane of untamed white hair.

"Mornin' to ya."

"Morning." Shane accepted the cup of coffee Ned handed to him. "Thanks."

"Just cream, right?"

"You got it." The man paid attention. Shane had to give him props for that.

"Come on in." Ned produced a fat wad of keys and found the one he needed.

"How'd you become the island's resident land baron anyway?"

"Land baron," Ned said with a snort of laughter. "Kinda happened by mistake. Bought a house, rented it out. Bought another, then another. There's good deals ta be had if yer payin' attention."

"And you pay attention."

"That I do, which is how I know ya got a sweet spot fer Owen's sister."

"Yes, I certainly do."

"She's a good gal. I can tell ya that with hardly knowin' her. If she's anything like her brother, ya got yerself a winner."

"I know." Shane followed Ned into a small but tidy space that boasted hardwood floors, the fireplace he wanted, creamy-white crown molding and gorgeous built-in shelves. "This place is beautiful."

"'Tis one of my favorites. A hidden gem."

The kitchen had been recently renovated with new gray stone countertops, white cabinets and black appliances. It had two bedrooms off a small hallway and a bathroom with a deep claw-foot bathtub. He could picture Katie in that tub, up to her neck in bubbles. "I'll take it."

"Thought ya might say that."

"How is this place even available?"

"The couple that was gonna take it for the year split up and broke the lease. The lady called me crying and all apologies. I gave her the money back cuz I had someone else in mind fer the place."

"That's nice of you."

Ned shrugged. "Sounded like she needed the money more than I do."

"When can I have it?"

"Whenever ya want. 'Tis empty and available. Ya gotta order furniture from the mainland, which takes a week or so."

"I'll take it tomorrow. I'll get you a check in the morning."

"Ain't no rush. I know where ya live, and I know yer good fer it."

"Thanks for this, Ned. I really appreciate it."

Ned shook his hand. "Yer dad and uncles ain't the only ones happy to see ya moving on with yer life. Ya got a good girl with Katie. The kinda girl a man makes plans with. The kinda girl a man can count on to do right by him. Ya know what I'm sayin'?"

"I do, and I appreciate you saying it."

"See ya this afternoon. Another weddin'." He shook his head with what seemed like wonder. "Another of my kids." Outside, Ned patted Shane on the shoulder. "Maybe I'll be dancin' at yer wedding before too long."

Shane laughed at that. "You never know." At the curb, they shook hands again. "Would you mind if I brought Katie over here later to show her the place?"

"I wouldn't mind a'tall. There's a key under the planter on the front porch. Make yerselves at home."

"Thanks again for this, Ned. It's just what I needed and close enough to see Holden and the new babies any time I want to."

"Glad yer happy with it. See ya after a bit." Ned drove off in the woody with a toot of the horn and a wave.

Shane took another long last look at the cottage that he hoped would be his new home, his fresh start with Katie if she liked it as much as he did. He looked forward to showing it to her.

*

Stephanie woke to the sound of giggling from the room across the hall. The low timbre of Charlie's deep voice was followed by more laughter. Listening to her adored stepfather with his new love made her heart surge with joy. And then she remembered what else would happen on this day, and her heart overflowed.

During all the long years she'd spent alone, desperately trying to get Charlie out of jail, she had lacked the imagination to picture the life she and Charlie had now. It had all begun with the fortuitous meeting with Linda and Mac McCarthy in the restaurant where she'd bartended in Providence. In the hour they'd spent together, the McCarthys had persuaded her to come to work for them running the restaurant at their marina for the summer.

Stephanie had been in bad need of a change of scenery by then, so she'd accepted their generous offer. That decision had changed her life more profoundly than any other. She could still recall the first time she'd ever laid eyes on Grant, who'd come home to visit his family and to attend his sister's wedding.

Big Mac had brought him into the restaurant, busting his buttons with pleasure as he introduced his second-oldest son, the Academy Award-winning screenwriter, to Stephanie. And, holy smokes, had she been bowled over by how gorgeous he was! Like, movie star good-looking with thick, wavy, dark hair, brilliant blue eyes, a lean, muscular frame, prominent cheekbones and soft, sensual lips that Stephanie couldn't get enough of.

She'd fallen deep into crush that day and had stayed there even after she discovered he'd come home for more than his sister's wedding. He was also out to win back his ex-girlfriend Abby, who'd been engaged then to Cal Maitland. Stephanie had been positively smitten with Grant, even though they fought like banshees almost from the beginning of their association.

Until the night of Janey's wedding, when he'd blatantly used her to try to make Abby jealous and they'd ended up in bed at Janey's house. That'd been the beginning of their relationship, which started out as a one-night stand and turned into a life together during the four memorable days that Tropical Storm Hailey had held Gansett Island hostage.

Lying in her bed in Charlie's tiny guest room, she thought about the two nights she'd spent here last summer when she'd been convinced that things between her and Grant weren't going to work out. He'd come to find her here, and proposed to her, promising the "love story of a lifetime." She would never forget that day or all the days that followed.

She would also never forget the mind-numbing fear of the day she'd spent wondering if he was dead or alive after the tragic sailboat accident in the spring. That had been the single longest day of her life, and the relief at seeing him—battered but alive—had been the greatest relief she'd ever experienced. To know she got to spend the rest of her life with him was the most amazing gift she'd ever been given.

Hoping it was safe to leave her room with the lovebirds in residence, she ducked into the bathroom and took a shower. For once, she actually put some effort into drying and styling her hair. She'd worry about makeup later. Looking in the mirror, she stuck out her tongue and eyed the stud that sat in the middle, giggling to herself when she imagined Grant's reaction to the return of the stud she'd stopped wearing several months ago. He had a particular fondness for a certain act that involved the stud, and she looked forward to surprising him with that later.

She emerged from the bathroom to Charlie and Sarah making breakfast in the kitchen, working in harmony as if they'd been together for years. Stephanie noticed the subtle touching and the blush that invaded Sarah's cheeks when he whispered something in her ear.

"Morning, kids," Stephanie said when she joined them in the kitchen.

"Morning, honey." Charlie came over to kiss her. He'd insisted she come "home" the night before her wedding, and while Stephanie could never be accused of being traditional, she'd bowed to his wishes. "How's the bride this fine day?"

"She's ready to get the show on the road. How many hours until I get to say 'I do'?"

Charlie consulted his watch. "About five."

"I'll never make it."

"We'll get you through it," Sarah assured her.

They took breakfast outside to the table, where they ate scrambled eggs, pancakes and bacon and lingered over second cups of coffee.

"You got a beautiful day for it," Sarah said, gazing up at the clear blue early September sky. "Not an ounce of humidity."

"I wouldn't have cared if it rained and stormed. That would've almost been fitting for us since we got together during a storm."

"You survived the storm," Charlie said. "I'm so proud of my little girl today."

Stephanie got up and went over to hug him, hanging on for a long moment to the one person who'd been her constant, her family, since she was eleven years old. Even during the long years of his imprisonment, he'd been her touchstone.

A beep of a horn interrupted their embrace, and Stephanie pulled back, brushing at her eyes as Charlie did the same. Good thing she hadn't bothered with makeup yet.

Two cars containing all her closest girlfriends pulled into the driveway. Out came Grace, who was her only attendant, followed by her "honorary" bridesmaids, Laura, Tiffany, Janey, Maddie and Abby. With the girls around to keep her entertained, the hours flew by, and before she knew it, they were helping her into her dress. She'd gone with a sexy ivory silk dress that hugged her small breasts and fitted tightly to the few curves she had. Grant liked when she wore clothes that showed off her trim, sexy body—his words, not hers—so she knew he'd love the dress, and that had been the only thing that mattered to her when she chose it.

"You're stunning," Sarah said as the others nodded in agreement. "That dress is perfect on you."

"The smoky eyes are incredible, too," Maddie added. "Well done, Abby."

"Why, thank you."

Stephanie never looked at the voluptuous dark-haired woman and thought of her as Grant's ex. No, when she looked at Abby Callahan, she only saw a friend and future sister-in-law.

"Are we ready?" Charlie asked when he emerged from his bedroom wearing a navy blue suit with a crisp white shirt open at the collar. He stopped short at the sight of her in the dress. Placing his hand on his heart, he shook his head as tears filled his eyes. "Breathtaking," he finally said.

Stephanie smiled at him, and it occurred to her right then that if he hadn't been available to give her away, she probably never would've gotten married. She held out her left hand to him, her diamond engagement ring sparkling in the afternoon sunshine streaming in from outside. "Let's go, Dad."

CHAPTER 36

Grant tugged at the collar of his white dress shirt, hoping he hadn't bled on it when he cut himself shaving earlier. How many years had he been shaving, and today of all days, he had to practically open a vein?

"Is there blood?" he asked Dan, who stood next to him calmly checking his phone while Grant felt like he was going to expire in the late-afternoon heat.

Dan spared him a brief glance. "No blood, but that's one hell of a gash. First day with the razor?"

"Shut the fuck up."

Dan laughed hard. "Is that any way to speak to your best man?"

"It's the only way to speak to my best man. Don't forget I can replace you rather easily. I've got three brothers waiting in the wings."

Grant expected the usual snappy comeback, but Dan surprised him with a small, sentimental smile. "It's not our way to get sappy with each other, but I have to tell you how much it meant to me that you asked me to stand up for you when you had so many other far more suitable candidates. Since you're the only brother I've got left, I'm hoping you'll return the favor next summer."

"Dan… Christ, you're going to make me bawl. Of course I will. And I'm sorry for the joke about my brothers. That was insensitive."

"No, it was funny. I love your brothers. You know I do. The four of you have helped to fill the void a little, and I want you to know I'm hugely honored to be your best man." Dan had lost his only brother in Afghanistan.

Grant hugged him. "Thank you for doing this today and for telling me last summer that I needed to go after her. Best thing I ever did."

"She's a great girl. You couldn't have done any better."

"I know, believe me."

"Looks like show time." From their vantage point on the deck behind the Surf, Dan gestured to the flurry of activity happening inside Stephanie's Bistro. Dan put his phone away, and both men buttoned the jackets of their navy blue suits.

They'd hoped to get married on the beach, but it was just windy enough that fears of blowing sand had compelled them to move the ceremony to the deck where the reception would also be held.

Grant caught the barest glimpse of the woman in white, but forced himself to look away so he wouldn't ruin anything for her. They'd invited only their closest friends and family, who began to come out to the deck in groups and couples, giving his siblings, their spouses and children and Grant's parents the front row. The plan was for them to stand around Grant and Stephanie while his Uncle Frank married them—quick and simple so they could get to the party as fast as possible.

Frank came over to join Grant and Dan, hugging them both.

"All ready?" Frank asked his nephew.

"Never been more ready."

Frank signaled Grant's brother Evan, who, along with Owen, provided guitar music as the rest of the guests found their way to the deck, separating down the middle.

Grace preceded Stephanie, wearing a gorgeous navy dress and carrying a bouquet of light blue and purple hydrangeas. She smiled at Grant as she took her place across from him, leaving a spot that would soon belong to Stephanie. This was really happening.

"You aren't going to pass out or anything, are you?" Dan muttered.

"I don't think so, but keep your eyes open."

"You got it."

A reassuring smile from his mother gave Grant something else to focus on beside the butterflies storming around in his belly. And then Charlie and Stephanie appeared, and the sight of her chased away the butterflies and ramped up the excitement. There she was, and dear God, she was beautiful in that sexy dress as she came toward him on the arm of her adored father. The two of them were smiling so brightly. Grant didn't think he'd ever seen either of them smile quite like they were now.

"Take good care of my little girl," Charlie said gruffly when he placed her hand in Grant's.

"Always."

After she hugged Charlie, Stephanie handed her bouquet of white and blue hydrangeas to Grace and joined hands with Grant, smiling up at him.

"H-O-T," he whispered.

Her smile got even wider, and was that… Oh God, she'd worn the stud. It took every ounce of self-control he possessed not to get a hard-on in front of everyone he knew when he thought about why she might've worn the stud today of all days.

Frank led them through the ceremony and the reciting of traditional vows. They'd gone traditional because Stephanie said she would never be able to match her Academy Award-winning screenwriter fiancé in the vows department, and she wasn't about to try.

It was just as well, Grant decided, since he could barely remember his own name looking at her in that sexy dress. Grant never took his eyes off her as he said the words, listened to her do the same, pushed the ring on her finger and held out his hand for her to place his ring, the platinum band reminding him of his never-ending commitment to her. As if he'd need the reminder.

Then Frank was pronouncing them husband and wife, and Grant was kissing his wife and the love of his life. She wrapped her arms around his neck and slipped him the tongue, letting the stud rub up against his tongue, and there was no stopping his reaction to that maneuver.

Of course she knew what she'd done to him and laughed at his befuddled reaction. He lifted her into his arms and held her close until he had calmed enough to face their friends and family as husband and wife without embarrassing himself.

"Ladies and gentlemen," Frank said, "I give you Grant and Stephanie McCarthy."

Stephanie McCarthy… She was finally his to keep forever, and nothing had ever made him happier.

*

Hours later, the wedding was winding down and people had begun to leave, but Shane continued to dance with Katie, loving the feel of her in his arms and reluctant to let her go even though he was excited to show her the house. He'd had a few uneasy moments, wondering if she'd resent him making such a big decision for both of them without her input.

But then again, she hadn't yet agreed to move in with him, and he did need a more permanent place to live. Hell, if she didn't like it, Ned would find them something else. Whatever she wanted was fine with him as long as he got to keep her in his life.

Evan had taken a break to dance with Grace while Owen sang a sultry version of "Adore You."

"Is this that Miley Cyrus song?" Katie asked as she watched her brother sing the song to his new wife, who sat nearby with Holden on her lap.

"Only *so* much better coming from Owen." Shane sang the refrain in her ear and then used the lyrics to his advantage. "I need you more."

"No, I need you more," Katie said, playing along.

"No way. Not possible." He nuzzled her cheek when he really wanted to devour her mouth. "Let's get out of here."

"Where're we going?"

"Come with me, and I'll show you." Shane never released her hand as they said their good-byes to family and friends as well as the euphoric bride and groom.

Katie hugged and kissed her mother, who then turned to Shane and gave him the same loving farewell. It had been a long time since Shane had been mothered, and Sarah's affection went a long way toward soothing that particular wound on his soul.

"I love your mom," he said to Katie as they walked through the lobby toward the front doors.

"She loves you, too."

Sarah's approval made it that much easier to make his case to Katie.

"You still haven't said where you're taking me."

"No, I haven't, have I?"

"You're in a funny mood."

"Am I?"

"Stop answering everything I say with a question!"

Amused by her exasperation, he said, "Is that what I'm doing?"

"You know what you're doing." She elbowed him in the ribs. "You're driving me crazy."

He dropped her hand and put his arm around her, loving the silky feel of her shoulder under his palm. "That's how I like you."

"So where're we going?"

"Just down here and around the corner."

"At least that wasn't a question. What's down here and around the corner?

"I'll show you when we get there."

"Ugh. Are you looking to start our first fight?"

"Most definitely not. Roll with me for a minute, honey."

"Well, when you ask so nicely…"

An odd sensation trickled through him, something not easily identified. He was still chewing on what it was when they reached the cottage. "Here we are."

"What's this place?"

He didn't answer her but bent to retrieve the key that was under the planter where Ned had said it would be. Shane opened the door and held out a hand to Katie, who stood back, watching him with vexation and curiosity in her expression. "Come see."

She took his hand and followed him inside, her sharp gaze taking in every detail of the living room and kitchen in one quick glance. "It's lovely. Whose is it?"

"Ours, if we want it."

Her eyes widened, and her lips formed an adorable O. "*Ours*?"

"Only if you like it as much as I do."

She released his hand and went for a better look at the kitchen, bedrooms and bathroom.

Shane waited on pins and needles to hear what she thought of it. "You could have your own room if you're not quite ready to shack up officially."

She ran a hand over the creamy-white wall. "If I had my own room, would you visit me there?"

"As often as you wanted me to."

"Since that would be every night, it seems sort of foolish to have separate bedrooms."

His heart skipped a beat when he realized she still wanted the same things he did. "Your thinking matches mine." He took her hand again. "Come sit with me for a minute."

They sat in the corner of the empty living room. Always the lady, Katie curled her legs under her, tugging her skirt down to her knees.

"I want to tell you a few things that normally I'd prefer to keep to myself for several reasons. One, I hate talking about this stuff, and two, it really has no bearing on you or us or how I feel about you. But it's important to me that I be honest with you, so I want to tell you, okay?"

"Okay..."

He hated the trepidation he saw on her face and heard in her one-word answer, but he knew he had to come clean with her. "Earlier this week when you wrote me your adorable note, you said you'd noticed I had something on mind. You told me if I couldn't talk to you about it, you wished I would talk to someone. You were right. I did have something weighing heavily on me, and I talked to my Uncle Kevin, who's a psychiatrist."

"What was weighing so heavily on you?"

"The things that Courtney said to me... I was messed up afterward. I didn't want to be, because I've come so far from that situation, and I have so much in my life now to be grateful for. I'd started this awesome new relationship with you, and I was happy again for the first time in a very long time. So much of that happiness was because of you."

"Did Kevin help?"

"He helped a lot. We talked it through, and he said a lot of things that made so much sense, but one thing in particular really resonated with me." He took hold of Katie's hand and linked their fingers, needing to touch her while he talked about his past for what he hoped would be the last time. "He said that with this new information about what really happened, it was no longer possible for me to make Courtney the villain in our marriage. I couldn't hate her anymore, and I had to find a way to deal with the things she'd told me without derailing my new life."

"And have you? Have you dealt with it?"

"Not entirely." He gave her the honesty she deserved. "But I will. In time. The important thing for you to know is I have absolutely no desire to go back to her. I loved her very much for a long time, but I don't love her anymore. I love *you.* You're the one I want to be with. I want to live here with you or somewhere else, if this place doesn't do it for you. I want to be close to our nephew and the new babies when they're born. I want to spend time with my family and friends and your family when they come to visit."

He leaned his forehead against hers. "I want to be with your mom and Charlie, Laura and Owen and Holden, and I want to help out with my friend Lisa and her kids, who are going to need all the friends they can get. I want to be here. With you. I want a life with you. I know we haven't known each other long, but it took me no time at all to know you're special, and the more time we spend together, the more proof I get that my initial gut feeling about you was spot-on."

"Shane…" She took a deep breath and placed her free hand over her heart. "You take my breath away."

"In a good way?"

"In the best way possible."

His relief at hearing that was overwhelming.

"I love you, too," she said. "I want all the same things you do and a couple of other things that it's too soon to tell you about."

"No, it's not too soon. Tell me. I want to know so I can help you get everything you want."

"I've mentioned this once before, but when I was younger," she said tentatively, "before I understood just how screwed-up my family really was, I pictured myself with a lot of kids. I'm thirty-two, so the reality of a big family is starting to slip away."

"Then we ought to get started on this project of yours sooner rather than later."

She stared at him, seeming astounded. "You're serious."

"Completely serious. I remember you telling me before about the horde of kids you want to have. My life has been on hold for a long, lonely time. I'm ready to get busy living again, and in case you haven't noticed, I love babies. Well, I love *Holden*, but I'm sure I'll be crazy about our kids, too. I want the same thing you do, and there's no time like the present to get busy living."

"Is this really happening?"

"It's really happening, and it's amazing, and it's only going to get better." He leaned in to kiss her softly, just the touch of his lips on hers. All the turmoil and upheaval of the last week settled and calmed, leaving him in a state of peacefulness he'd rarely experienced since Courtney left him. And then he realized what he'd felt earlier, walking into the house he hoped would be theirs: pure, unmitigated joy. "About the house… Yes, no, maybe?"

"Definitely yes. I love it as much as you do. But we share a bedroom or no deal."

"Done," he said, smiling at her. "We're going to need the extra bedroom for the kids we're going to have together." He kissed her again, lingering when her sweet softness filled his senses and his heart. "So when you tell these kids of ours how we met, what will you say?"

"I'll tell them the truth." She caressed his face and slid her thumb over his bottom lip. "I'll tell them you saved my life."

"And I'll tell them that after I saved yours, you saved mine."

***

Thank you for reading Shane and Katie's story! Find the Kisses After Dark Reader Group at Facebook.com/groups/KissesAfterDark. Join the McCarthy Reader Group at Facebook.com/groups/McCarthySeries. Join Marie's mailing list at marieforce.com to be kept informed of new books, and remember to leave a review on the retail site of your choice and/or Goodreads to help other readers discover the McCarthy Series. Thanks again for your support of the McCarthys!

Much more to come from Gansett Island, so make sure you're on the mailing list at marieforce.com and never miss a book!

OTHER TITLES BY MARIE FORCE

Contemporary Romances Available from Marie Force

The Treading Water Series

Book 1: Treading Water

Book 2: Marking Time

Book 3: Starting Over

Book 4: Coming Home

The Green Mountain Series

Book 1: All You Need Is Love

Book 2: I Want to Hold Your Hand

Book 3: I Saw Her Standing There (November 2014)

Single Titles

The Singles Titles Boxed Set

Georgia on My Mind

True North

The Fall

Everyone Loves a Hero

Love at First Flight

Line of Scrimmage

Romantic Suspense Novels Available from Marie Force

The Fatal Series

Book 1: Fatal Affair

Book 2: Fatal Justice

Book 3: Fatal Consequences

Book 3.5: Fatal Destiny, *the Wedding Novella*

Book 4: Fatal Flaw

Book 5: Fatal Deception

Book 6: Fatal Mistake

Book 7: Fatal Jeopardy

Book 8: Fatal Scandal (January 2015)

Single Title

The Wreck

Printed in Great Britain
by Amazon.co.uk, Ltd.,
Marston Gate.